Blameless

Blameless

Non luogo a procedere

CLAUDIO MAGRIS

TRANSLATED FROM THE ITALIAN

BY ANNE MILANO APPEL

YALE UNIVERSITY PRESS ▪ NEW HAVEN & LONDON

A MARGELLOS
WORLD REPUBLIC OF LETTERS BOOK

The Margellos World Republic of Letters is dedicated to making literary works from around the globe available in English through translation. It brings to the English-speaking world the work of leading poets, novelists, essayists, philosophers, and playwrights from Europe, Latin America, Africa, Asia, and the Middle East to stimulate international discourse and creative exchange.

Yale University Press books may be purchased in quantity for educational, business, or promotional use. For information, please e-mail sales.press@yale.edu (U.S. office) or sales@yaleup.co.uk (U.K. office).

Set in Electra and Nobel type by Tseng Information Systems, Inc.
Printed in the United States of America.

Library of Congress Control Number: 2016952989
ISBN 978-0-300-21848-0 (hardcover : alk. paper)

A catalogue record for this book is available from the British Library.

This paper meets the requirements of ANSI/NISO z39.48–1992 (Permanence of Paper).

10 9 8 7 6 5 4 3 2 1

To Francesco and Paolo

CONTENTS

TRANSLATOR'S NOTE

Like the unnamed protagonist in *Blameless* (*Non luogo a procedere*, Garzanti, 2015), Claudio Magris is a collector. And like his protagonist, he is after the truth.

The maniacal collector who devotes his life to creating a Comprehensive War Museum for the Advent of Peace and the Disarming of History collects everything he can get his hands on: swords, cannons, cartridges, submarines, tanks, guns, weapons of all kinds, but also refuse and debris, old scrap iron, litter, discarded slips of paper containing scribbles, obscene sketches or graffiti copied from walls. Magris, on the other hand, collects stories, which are then woven into the fabric of his narrative: the story of Luisa de Navarrete, the Black Pearl of the Caribbean; of the improvident but well-intentioned Maximilian and his Carlota, and their doomed Mexican Empire; of the ethnologist, anthropologist and botanist Albert Vojtěch Frič, obliged to give lectures to make ends meet; of Cherwuish, the Chamacoco Indian from Paraguay whom Frič brought to Prague, and so on.

Collections of various types are found throughout the novel. In addition to weapons and stories, the Museum itself is a metaphoric manifestation of collecting. Other collections that figure in the narrative include the protagonist's controversial notebooks, some of them mysteriously missing; the incriminating list of names copied from the Risiera's walls; the toy soldiers that only play at war; the famous cactuses that made Frič a well-known authority throughout Europe and that he had been forced to give away, along with the crates of plants, animal skins and trophies that he had brought back from Paraguay.

Even the chapters form collections of a sort: there is a set of numbered chapters and there are those labeled "Luisa's Story," whose contents constitute a story within a story.

At some point the obsessive Museum collector, like Saul thrown by his horse, sees the light: "A flame is lit in him and for him, his obsessions disappear." He starts going after the truth, after evidence, meticulously and compulsively copying the implicating inscriptions left by inmates on the walls of the Risiera Prison. He's still a collector, but now he collects names, the names of those about to die, of those who came to visit, of those who'd died, of their informers and executioners. "He was searching for the truth, the sorrow, the infamy." Like the fictional Museum collector, Magris too is looking for the truth, for evidence of culpability and complicity.

In many respects *Blameless* continues a dialogue, a testimony, begun in *Blindly* (*Alla cieca*, Garzanti, 2005), the novel that preceded it. Indeed, it might be more accurate to say a conversation that began well before *Blindly*, since there is a conflation of themes in Magris's work, where the author-as-witness wrestles with the past and its countless instances of victimization and abuse, determined to shine a light on skeletons hitherto kept concealed in closets. Both *Blindly* and *Blameless* tell a story of wrongs endured and inflicted. Of victims and oppressors, hunter and prey, "*dannati contro dannati.*" Of prisoners and their warders, of slaves and their masters, of the betrayed and their betrayers everywhere. And over it all the pall of silence, of shrouding the truth. By those unwilling to attest to it: another form of the *occhio bendato*, of turning a blind eye, disinclined to see.

In *Blameless*, Magris's eye, far from being blindfolded, is firmly and unsparingly fixed on the specific embodiment of evil represented by the Risiera—the old rice factory in Trieste used during World War II by the Nazis to detain and execute political prisoners and to hold Jews later deported to Auschwitz—as well as on the carefully guarded secrets of the shameless, sadistic oppressors who flourished in the aftermath of the war: "The dead pass on, the living make merry." The antidote to apathy and unconcern is the inexorable process of exhuming the past, of not allowing its atrocities to remain whitewashed, as the walls of the Risiera were.

Since the past might pose a threat, no one wanted to remember; memory was excised: "Neurosurgery has made astonishing progress. In Trieste it was on the cutting edge. A huge brain, the city. . . . They managed to remove a nice piece of that brain's hippocampus, the part that contained the Risiera. Excellent scalpel job, meticulous work. . . . The seahorse extracted with such skill is sitting in a glass case at the Museum of Natural History. The memory of the atrocities is well-guarded and isolated inside the armor of osseous cutaneous shields, no one dreams of going to see what's behind the integument." Once the memory is erased, the thing never happened: "The smoke from the Risiera's chimney drifts out, recycled and blameless."

The novel's tone is often ironic, with a strong undercurrent of bitterness. Sometimes the irony is directed at those who prosper and fare well in the postwar ambience of cordial conviviality: "We're all anti-Nazi; at least after '45." And: "Who thinks about that anymore, water under the bridge, we're all friends now, together again, allies." Or those who embellish or twist the facts, exaggerating their own role or blurring their allegiances: "The Resistance is a complex business and those who resisted multiply all the more as the years go by; even those who died at that time, the dead on all sides, multiply and reproduce. Underground or in the ashes they must fuck like crazy, their number is growing and everyone is pleased about it because they can accuse their enemies of greater butchery than the one they themselves are responsible for."

At other times the biting sarcasm is directed at the Nazi way of thinking:

Not everyone suffers equally, not everyone has the same sensibility. The Aktion T4 program for euthanasia is very humane; it eliminates the disabled, the handicapped, people who don't have the proper credentials to suffer like others. It's the superior races that know pain, the pain of creating and destroying, of destroying to create. Blacks, for instance, suffer less than whites. Jews, less than the Germans. That's why they often seem so brave, when they enter the gas chamber. Sensitive people would suffer more. It's not about fear, we have more courage than anyone, but sensitivity. Even to dirt, for example. The Germans are clean, they would not be able to stand the stench and filth of the camps like the Jews.

Along the way, the novel offers some interesting insights about translation and Magris's views on it. At one point the unnamed protagonist tells Luisa, the woman assigned the task of planning the Museum: "Dr. Brooks, when you write about me, please write 'I' or 'he,' it makes no difference, write what you want, however you want, even when copying my words, because the hand that writes is the real author." A sentiment which mirrors the observation often expressed by Magris, that the translator is a coauthor.

In the novel's final image, men are dumped into the sea like garbage: "Throwing garbage into the sea is a crime and so is throwing men in, but the judge declares there is no cause to indict" — "*Im Sinne der Anklage, unschuldig,* innocent for the purposes of the prosecution." Ultimately, like *Alla cieca,* this book represents an act of faith and commitment, the author's determination to rip off the blindfold and reveal the senselessness of wars, cruelty and oppression. To abolish indifference — "absolution before trial, the decision not to prosecute" — and to attest to truth. Yet the unsettling questions planted by the narrative remain like the afterimage of a flashbulb, lingering in the eye well after we look away, forcing us to confront the horrors of the world and also the darkness within ourselves. As Galileo Galilei said, "*Non basta guardare, occorre guardare con occhi che vogliono vedere.*" It is not enough to look, one must look with eyes that want to see.

Blameless

"Used submarines — bought and sold." The ad in the *Piccolo banditore* was dated October 26, 1963. Overwhelmed by debt, tempted by million-dollar promises made by various administrations and ministries, strangled by moneylenders, persecuted by the owners of the properties where he had situated his aircraft and bombed military bridges, he had evidently felt forced to try to sell some relic of particular tonnage, though, at the very moment when he was preparing to sell, he was immediately seized by his Furies once again and had also tried to buy — who knows with what money, but anyway to buy — submarines, Panzers or minesweeping equipment.

It could be the opener in the lobby of the Museum, as soon as you walked in. On the wall facing those entering, a large black screen, rippled by an indistinct flickering, the sound of water in the background; his face appears in the darkness, a photograph from the early 1970s. Head emerging from the black waters, eyes feverish, cunning; beads of sweat, droplets of water sliding down the Pannonian cheekbones. In the middle of the room, the submarine, a U-Boat of the Imperial Royal Navy of World War I, purchased or acquired by some means. Used submarines — bought and sold. The voice pompous, insinuating. Reconstructed, with a skillful processing of various audio recordings at Radio Trieste. An innocuous commercial notice that, thanks to the reconstruction of the voice — reassembled, that is, genuine, absolute, not the random, mutable one at the moment when one speaks — becomes an enticement, the proposition of a pimp in the shadows. Entering the Museum the way you enter night, neon-lit promises; it could be a good idea, Luisa thought. Even though

3

the highlight, the most sought-after, talked-about attraction, those famous notebooks, were missing. An initiatory rite that lacks the *dulcis in fundo*, the ear of corn that ordains the initiate.

The family had been clear about it, in the letter sent to the editor of the *Corriere Adriatico* and published with a certain prominence. "You will allow us, as his heirs, to express our surprise and disappointment over the article published in your newspaper on March 12. We do not understand by what right and by what authority you can announce that his diaries—thousands of pages contained in numbered notebooks, with various cross-references and annotations—will also be placed, along with the extensive collection of martial material, in the Museum dedicated to the documentation of war for the promotion of peace, a Museum that, with one of his fanciful but always rational images, he had decided to call 'Ares for Irene,' the god of war who becomes an apostle of peace. We are the first to applaud the fact that the Foundation created by the province and the municipality has decided to set up the Museum, the dream to which he had devoted his life, renovating the buildings, stables, garages and grassy area—surrounded by the track and suitably covered—of the old Hippodrome. It is our hope that this time the project will at last be successfully accomplished; it's been talked about forever, with plans and promises made, a typical shaggy dog story. But as far as those journals are concerned, they are and will remain our exclusive property, as heirs, despite the fact that captious and to us incomprehensible bureaucratic and legal holdups have in effect temporarily seized some of them from us, though it is still our right to dispose of them in the way we see fit, always of course not in our own interest, but in that of the citizenry, the community, humanity, following his example, the example of a man who sacrificed everything—his career, his property, his health, the well-being of his family and finally his very life—to his mission, to his ideal, to his grand scheme.

"We are prepared, once again, to bequeath it all, to hand it all over—since the moral patrimony of the Museum belongs to everyone—to make available to the world those cannons, submarines, tanks and weapons of all kinds that he collected for decades in order to document the horrors of war and the need for peace. It is disgraceful that for years no public institution has taken steps to find a suitable location in which to house the Museum. Regarding the diaries in general, however, and in particular those that have strangely disappeared, so rich in priceless but also heated material, as has been noted many times in the *Corriere Adriatico* itself, we are certain, esteemed Editor, that your newspaper, aware of the importance and sensitivity of the material, will not . . ."

Rather than in the letters-to-the-editor section, the newspaper had published it on page three, turning it into a conspicuous feature, with clearly prominent headings and subheadings. It wasn't surprising that they would once again want to talk the issue up a little. The matter always struck a chord, especially after the trial, which, as often happens with trials, had left things more uncertain than before. Luisa set aside the newspaper, which she had laid over the stack of notebooks, pads, sheets of paper, cards, CDs and DVDs on which she'd been working, trying to organize and if necessary incorporate the notes scribbled in his own hand; the latter were intended to describe each piece in the Museum, explaining its function, its history and that of its inventor, of the factory that had produced it, of the engineers and others who had worked there, of the military unit to which it had been assigned, of the battle in which it had been demolished, of the person who had driven it or aimed it or loaded it or who had died in its wreckage. For example, she thought of displaying the equipment for undersea mine dredging next to the mercury-vapor rectifier; she felt they went well together, underwater death and death caused by mercury exhalations, death procured, avoided or deferred, depending, but death all the same. Death is fitting for Museums. All of them, not just a War Museum. Every exhibit—paintings, sculptures, objects, machinery—is a still-life and the people who flock to the halls, filling and emptying them like apparitions, are practicing for a future permanent visit to the great Museum of humanity, of the world, in which each of us is a still life. Faces like fruit picked from a tree and placed on a plate. Although he on the other hand, on this very point . . .

Luisa got back to work at the computer in the office assigned to her when the Foundation had given her the job of planning the Museum. No more than one room, though sizable, formerly one of the stables. She liked it, that room surrounded by so many vast vacant spaces. From one of the windows she could see several pieces already temporarily situated in the big adjacent room. Oblong, faintly cylindrical and greenish, the mine-dredging machine resembled a manatee, a sea creature moving gracelessly but silently to seize its prey. Outside, in the dusk, the wind-driven branches of an oak reached toward her window like talons, claw-like tentacles leaped out of the darkness into the light cast by the street lamp and retreated, swaying, into the shadows, their prey eluding them, who knows for how much longer. Luisa shivered; for a moment she seemed to feel the years like a wall of dark water pounding at her temples, a migraine that absurdly made her think about love — or maybe about its ending, since for her it had almost always been the same thing.

That furrow near her mouth, which overall was pleasing, wasn't exactly a wrinkle, though every now and then it felt to her like a scar. A kiss, a bite — I'm becoming just like him; as a result of reading his papers, of identifying with him and dealing with his machine guns and swords, now that I've gotten into the habit of taking some of those papers and photographs home in the evening so I can ponder how to display them until I fall asleep, I'll end up believing, like him, that everything is war and every mark a scar. She ran a finger lightly over the blade of a sword temporarily hung on the wall; the line it left on her skin, though distinct, quickly vanished.

He, despite his horrific end, was probably unaware of the scars that everything leaves on the heart; perhaps he didn't hear life snarling in the dark, and didn't see the dark, absorbed as he was by looking down at the ground, hunting, searching and collecting those senseless objects, single-masted vessels, shrapnel, dented mess-tins, bugles, crushed cartridge cases, explosive fuses. His flashlight, at night, illuminated only land that had been plowed, uneven ruts, shallow sinkholes, a rusted helmet gleaming in the grass.

That's how he'd spend his nights, exhausted but immune,

thrilled about those cold, dead things that he dug up or was given by retreating armies or scrapyards being dismantled, unaware of life swirling around him as it does around everyone, threatening death and destruction — not the good, already-dead death that doesn't hurt you, but the living, continuous dying of body and heart, the light growing dimmer in the soul, a coldness in the bones, more deadly than the flames that would engulf him in his final hour, in that long, comfortable coffin that he had chosen to sleep in, in that hangar with his tanks, missile launchers and *yataghans* piled in a jumble, the scrap iron from all the wars that were the milestones of his existence, the tank he got in 1945, the dinghy from 1947, the fragments and structures of the demolished swing-bridge, the Ponte Verde, artificial boundary between the canal and the sea. And there he was, alone with his coffin in that warehouse chock-full of weapons awaiting the Museum, alone when the fire broke out. His realm; his because it was uninhabited, emptied of all the living who obstruct peace because they require war in order to live, even at home, within the family, even in bed — sometimes, Luisa thought, taking notes for the mine-removal machine, when you wake up a little early and the faint light of dawn can barely be glimpsed behind the shutters, you look from one pillow to the other and catch sight of your sleeping companion, as if from across a trench. There won't be any attack, but you are on the alert, in the vague expectation of gunfire. When she'd had to study the Thirty Years' War at school, she had immediately thought about the family. Not about hers, no . . . but in general. As for her, she still hadn't figured out whether not having one of her own was a good or a bad thing, and why thinking about it left her heart feeling empty for a moment.

He would go to sleep in his coffin, not yet dead but composed and serene as if he already were, as he is now, when I'm rummaging through his papers as if they were his ashes, cinders of scorched flesh that only the investigators had been able to distinguish that night — or rather, the morning after, when, after several hours, the firemen had put out the blaze — from the ashes of the wooden coffin burned along with him. Maybe he'd been afraid of dying, but certainly not of death; among those jeeps, bayonets, swords and bandoliers he felt as safe as he would have among the statues and tombstones of a cemetery, where a sword, wielded by a marble knight standing guard over a grave, is never lowered violently to strike. They said he'd even written to the president of the United States, asking him for the Norden bombsight that had unleashed the bomb on Hiroshima.

2

"Ares for Irene or Arcana Belli. A Comprehensive Museum of War for the Advent of Peace and the Deactivation of History." That baroque titling of the Museum, repeated numerous times in the notebooks and journals—to modify the past, he wrote, to reverse time, reduce it to a one-way street—Luisa thought of projecting it on the inner walls of the Museum itself. Assuming that one day the Museum would be completed. For now it was all still just a hypothetical plan, a project that had been assigned to her by the Foundation and the Municipal Department of Culture, which she was attempting to develop by coming up with a possible design for housing the copious, heterogeneous material in the various rooms and spaces of the old Hippodrome complex, envisioning the sequence of the pieces, the use of icons on the monitors, the guiding theme through the program, the objects and the stories that spring from them like genies from Aladdin's lamp.

How to organize that insane Museum, excessive even after the funeral pyre had destroyed a large part of the collection, in addition to its even more excessive creator? That grandiloquent title, for example: he didn't want to have it placed at the entrance but rather projected in the inner rooms with intermittent beams of light tracing the letters and the words in various colors, as they blinked on and off continually. For him everything was a sign, a message, that the closer he came to his end, the more it heralded happiness. Nothing could surprise much less frighten someone like him, who claimed to have "a prophetic rapport with the unexpected." The discovery of any object, he wrote—a cartridge-pouch, a holster—"is an infinitely good omen and everything is related to the coming era of infinite good, when evil will be abolished and all that will remain of weapons is that part of cosmic energy that is associated with their beauty and their functionality . . ."

Where, how and in what sequence of rooms to display those notes . . . enlarge them with spotlights, frame them, record them on devices concealed in the walls to be activated at the right moment, develop a course, a progression more mental than material, so that the visitor, by pressing one or another symbol shown on the monitor next to the different objects in the various rooms might be led to other screens, come upon other stories connected with that gun or that sword, access one or another object or text at will? The Museum as a mutable hypertext in which everything streams by or vanishes and is nullified, which likely happened in his head?

However, perhaps he was right, infinite good exists, it always has. It surrounds us—yes, maybe even me, sitting in the midst of this disorder—a velvety indigo blue cloud that catches a balloon that has slipped out of a child's hand. It is happiness, though the two-dimensional creatures shuffling along on the sphere of the balloon are unable to raise their heads and realize that another dimension, the cloud that envelops them, exists and they go on shuffling along, hopelessly. She, too, so beautiful and slender, was a snail's trail; tossed by the wind, her beautiful, still dark hair—that too a legacy of two exiles, centuries-old, who had merged in her after crossing the desert and the great sea—did not know the wind existed. Luisa felt it soft against the back of her neck as she sat in the shadows cast on the wall by the table lamp buried under the notebooks. He however must somehow have managed to raise his head, to feel the wind of spaces, of unimaginable depths for those who only know width and height; he had breathed deeply of that air unknown to humans, an exhilarating laughing gas that brought joy. What's more, he claimed to have found a scientific system that enabled him to live solely on air, by means of a new breathing technique that metabolized microscopic creatures living in every little breeze and hitherto unknown nutrients contained in gases. And not because I'm hard up and let my wife support me, he added—she, from a very old, aristocratic Hungarian family, forced by me to work as a domestic, as has been maliciously insinuated numerous times—but so that I might feel light, free, happy.

The obscurity of the night of the fire—obscure to the court, for him a regal luminaria, the bonfire of a sovereign who flaunts his magnificence by throwing all his possessions and even his life into the flames—had been a divine pyre, the final red sunset of the cosmic Aeon of evil, of war, of killing. He may not even have suffered, in that coffin he used to sleep in with a German iron helmet on his head and a samurai mask over his face, it's likely the smoke suffocated him in his sleep before the flames could sting him.

In the terminology of his planned global reform of the dictionary—rigorously described and classified in his unfinished D.U.D., Definitive Universal Dictionary—he, on the night of the fire, had entered the "inverter," the accurate term that would replace the current but approximate one of "death." His new lexicon was a hodgepodge of words, interrupted by a page torn out at the letter M, that is, at the entry "malvaceous," which lacked a definition as well as everything that should have followed below. Luisa, when she had assumed the job of planning the Museum, had thought of arranging the dictionary's material, up to that word, in running lists that for an instant would associate the old, slapdash words with the new compulsory terms of hermetic precision, and then obliterate them immediately afterward, extinguishing their brightly lit letters, their old, confusing meanings swallowed up by the dark. LA MORTE, Death, projected in very large letters, in red, on the wall in front of those entering the third room, had to be revealed as a prosaic typo, quickly corrected, for Love: "L'AMOR-T-E" (p. 27 of the manuscript and incomplete dictionary).

Death does not exist, he explained; it is merely an inverter, a machine that simply reverses life like a glove, but all you have to do is let time flow backward and everything is reclaimed. Time regained, the triumph of love. Amor-t-e. Who? You, you, everyone.

In the intentions of their tireless collector, those fire-breathing objects in the Museum, tanks and cannons and the rest, were to prove to be fleeting, illusory images in the end, nightmares of a troubled, dispelled dream, a film projected backward, beginning with death and destruction and ending with people — first blown up, mangled or stabbed — ultimately happy and smiling, to make it clear that death, every death, comes before life, not after. My dear Dr. Brooks, he had once told her, Moses wrote the Pentateuch, the first five books of the Bible, and in the fifth he recounted his death on Mount Nebo, in the region of Moab. So the time of his death comes before the time when he recounted it. There is no before or after, my dear doctor, time is like space, you go west, you keep going west and you arrive east of the place you started from. East of Eden . . .

He had told her that at their first meeting, after the Foundation had decided to finance the Museum design — only its planning, for now, then they would see; meanwhile that entire Babel of objects remained piled up in a couple of large hangars and in a vast empty space of the Hippodrome itself. Rather than assisting him, they had suggested that she restrain him and keep him under control at work. Which, however, was soon interrupted by his death and resumed only years later, when interest in the eccentric man and his grandiose design — and in particular those mysteriously lost notebooks of his — had been revived in the city following several aggressive articles in the local newspaper, and as a result new funds had been found. But even well before his death their contact had suddenly become less frequent; though earlier he had been so intrusive and dependent, he'd hardly showed up anymore, as if he had suddenly been inspired by something else. It was strange, his sudden absence, though it made her work easier and less compulsive.

Those weapons boasted, trumpeted, thought that they could annihilate everything that came within range, reduce it to zero, yet despite their efforts all they did was send the soldier, blown up by a mine, flying across the screen, where everything began again and the soldier regained the life he'd seemed to have lost, yesterday's hangover with his buddies, the evening before on an inexpressibly violet sea, a mouth kissed so many years ago, the distorted words of a child starting to speak. Poor foolish men who delude themselves that they are killing and destroying; as if by turning off the light a person thought he could make all the things suddenly unseen in the dark disappear forever. For example, he wrote in one of his notebooks, one could first project the image of the large room with all its objects, then show the image of a huge fire that destroys everything and leaves the room empty until the lights are turned back on and the room reappears with all its contents, intact, resurrected, never having died. It could be an idea.

In any case, he had certainly not feared the flames, a butterfly that does not fear the light into which it rushes, burning up, and that is perhaps truly born at that moment, rather than at the time when, from a caterpillar, it had turned into a butterfly. On one of the first occasions when Luisa had met him, he, perhaps to show off his culture, had grandiosely declaimed those verses of blissful nostalgia to her in German: *"keine Ferne macht dich schwierig, kommst geflogen und gebannt,"* "distance does not make you falter, / now, arriving in magic, flying, / and finally, insane for the light, / you are the butterfly and you are gone," a burst of flame.

3.

Perhaps a mere conjecture, of course, those scribblings that so agitated his heirs—though they weren't the only ones—and which strangely enough had been the only notebooks of his to have disappeared, had ended up being burned in the funeral pyre in his warehouse, well hidden somewhere though to no avail; those pages in which it was said that he had recorded the writings jotted on the walls and in the toilets of their prison by inmates about to die, also by fire, in the Nazi cremation oven at the Risiera, the only crematorium in Italy, right there in Trieste. Later, in tranquil times of peace, a coat of lime had been applied to those walls and to the names presumed to have been written on those walls. After war comes peace, which even has the white color of a sepulcher and of the whited sepulchers in the heart.

It seems, however, that he had seen and copied those writings before that, at least some of them; even the names, it was whispered, the vile names of collaborators in high places or good friends of the executioner at any rate, scratched on the walls of filthy latrines by victims on the brink of death, later erased by lime—quicklime, white, innocent and caustic to the flesh—and later still perhaps erased again by the fire in his warehouse, a destructive fire that cleansed all filth and restored a false innocence to the most sordid, abominable infamy, to wretches protected forever by the disappearance of their names dissolved in lime and reduced to ash, illegible to human judges, like the magistrate who'd had to conclude the investigation of the Risiera's crimes with what amounted to no conclusion; illegible maybe even to higher judges, they too robbed of any material evidence, and certainly illegible to the children of those perverse murderers, unaware that at one time those names had been corroded by lime or crumpled by flames; on the contrary, proud to bear the respectable names of their fathers who had borne them when the victims—whom they had propelled or maybe only observed going to a horrific death and whose fate in any case had not perturbed their indifference—had written them on the walls. Names erased and therefore honored forever.

However, Luisa thought, it was actually a good thing that some people—judging by the letter to the newspaper as well as statements by the vice president of the Foundation, Dr. Pezzl—believed or feared that some of those dangerous papers might still be around. Just as well, *timor Domini initium sapientiae*. To the discomfiture of many, people were finally beginning to speak about that infamy, the old rice factory in Trieste where the Nazis had slaughtered, or sent to slaughter, several thousands of individuals in a general silence that went on even after the end of the war. And it was partly thanks to the persistence of that singular man and his maniacal searching, which in his case was illuminated by the fury of a prophet angry with his infamous people and zealous in his desire to expose the infamy. Dr. Pezzl, replying to one of the many letters in the *Corriere Adriatico*, had written, for example, that "there is perhaps no need to announce these journals before they, or what may ultimately remain of them, have been cataloged and classified and before having considered the possible timeliness of declassifying several passages of a delicate nature, that it might still be too early . . ."

Too early for whom? If anything it was too late; at least for him, having now passed on to a better life—which wasn't difficult, given how he had lived, though maybe for him, however . . . —too late in any case for those others, who in all those years had had time to wash their hands of the blood or filth of those other hands, even more bloodstained than theirs, which they had so cordially shaken countless times during the Nazi occupation. Too late, moreover, because after so many years they too, along with their names whitewashed on the walls of the Risiera or burned that night in the warehouse, had gone to the other world, at least many of them had; they must not have been children even then, in the final months of the war, so by now they'd probably already been given the death penalty, whether they were guilty or innocent. Justice, at least capital punishment, is the same for everyone.

4

To begin with, they could erect a wall in the Museum, starting perhaps with the stables of the old Hippodrome, a wall entirely plastered with blank sheets of paper, at least to show that there was something missing, in fact, that the most important thing was missing . . . and then, right after that, to accentuate the contrast and emphasize the disturbing absence of those notebooks even more, display all the papers and countless objects, even the insignificant ones, that he had begun to collect and save at the age of eight, pages torn from notebooks, paper napkins, used envelopes—one addressed to his father, empty, with only the sender's name printed on the back, Tergeste Import-Export. Even a sheet of paper on which was scrawled: "Today I asked my father: 'Papa, who is I?' 'You're you,' he replied. I was disappointed."

Luisa wondered if they could start with that exhibit, perhaps because she remembered that after having declaimed Goethe's lines to her that time, about the butterfly rushing into the flame, he had added: "The only thing I don't like in this admirable lyric—learn it by heart, Doctor, poems, true ones, must be learned by heart; those which you can't manage learning by heart are not true poems—the only thing I don't like about it is the familiar 'you,' the *du*, by which he addresses the butterfly and then, at the end, even the reader. How dare he, who does he think he is? As far as I'm concerned, I'm not even on close enough terms with myself to use the familiar 'you.' Much less say 'I.' Have you ever heard me say that word? Truly disgraceful. With a lady, besides . . . 'He,' on the other hand, is fine. 'He' has nothing to do with what we do, 'he' is any ordinary person, for example he might be the newspaper man at the kiosk on the avenue; he sells papers, nothing to worry about, he hardly concerns us. But war especially, which is a serious matter, must have as little as possible to do with 'I,' with that presumptuous draft dodger and deserter on the battlefield. The masters of the art of war never say 'I,' beginning with the earliest, and greatest, Sun Tzu, who is perhaps Sun Wu or some others, namely no one, an unspecified grand Master voice of many Masters, who in fact always begins his chapters 'Master Sun said . . .'

"So let's always use 'He' even when talking among ourselves, please. After all, it's almost like using the formal 'You,' as everyone does . . . The informal 'you' will come when people realize that death has been abolished, *la morte* transformed into love, *l'amore*, Amor-t-e."

5.

Luisa had not yet decided what to do with the various documents — letters, his or those of his relatives or acquaintances, scattered notes, journals dating back to adolescence or to the final months, sometimes loose sheets with only a few words scribbled on them in an illegible handwriting that she was just beginning to decipher and which would have to be recopied to make them accessible to visitors, some displayed in glass showcases, others viewed on a digital screen. It was easier with objects — cannons, tanks, javelins — their mere grim, rusty presence was eloquent testimony to the existence (and most often the end of the existence) of those who had handled, used that flamethrower or that machine gun, slept in the passenger compartment of the armored vehicle or stuck his head out of its turret, often his last act. Reminders, chroniclers of the lives and deaths — though he would not have used the word death — associated with the plane shot down in flight, with the rifle fired or dropped. It was perhaps the easiest aspect of her job; choosing the piece or pieces for each gallery, deciding which to display materially and which — since, given their number, there was not enough space for all of them physically — to project on monitors with a single click. Easy, just press a key, but design a world in which that key is a good Aladdin's lamp . . . then write captions, reconstruct the events of the man who had flown the plane or pointed the gun.

But how to organize those documents, the disconnected notes, the letters or fragments of letters . . . for example, the letter personally addressed to her by a relative of his, a cousin Ines, living in Udine. "He always recorded everything, all he did was take notes; it's the only thing he did in his whole life . . . The last time I saw him, four days before he died, he came to see me in Udine. At lunch, every so often he would pull a big bundle of loose pages and some notebooks out of his satchel, as if to make sure he still had them, then put everything back in the bag. Half an hour after he'd left to go back to Trieste, he reappeared, agitated, and began searching all over the place, under the table, on the nightstand beside the bed where he had taken a little nap. He had forgotten the satchel, he couldn't rest until he'd found it; by constantly opening and closing it so fretfully, he had moved it here and there and it had ended up under the couch. It's important, he said, it's very important . . . of course, everything is important, the smallest detail . . . the details, the particulars, the . . . He was almost talking to himself and left in a hurry . . . Afterward I never saw him again because four days later . . ."

6.

Could the notebooks have burned that night as well? Could those notebooks in particular have burned, could the fire have been set specifically to burn those disorganized notebooks and what was written in them . . . ? If a hidalgo once bought a castle, as the story goes, only because his lady wanted a rose that was blooming on the windowsill of that castle, then someone could have set fire to a place just to destroy a stack of papers, and if the man who carried them with him then perished, well, too bad, collateral damage. But what if those papers were still around somewhere, gnawed and disintegrating, after all those years . . . ? Maybe, who knows, they might still be able to be read.

Luisa, irritated, drove the fantasy away. She was there to work, not to indulge in imaginary suppositions, smoke rings that trace no figure. She lit a cigarette, turning back to the computer. The smoke, rising through the lamp's cone of light, cast a shadow on the wall, a profuse head of hair softened airily in the tawny light, a brief summer on the ocher wall. Those summers at the sea as a little girl, she and her father, just the two of them; soon afterward she understood why her mother had never wanted to go to the shore with them. Summers of sun and sea, fish have forever devoured other fish and it hadn't been so long since the fetid smoke of burning flesh coming from the city had pitched and dissolved in the Triestine sea, but the little girl doesn't know that, nobody knows, those dazzling, joyful reflections on the sea are a veil of Maya concealing the blood, the smoke and any pain.

7

Yes, it could work. A biographical profile in a display case to the left, just past the entrance to the second gallery, along with a brief video, a collage of his statements—on the radio, a couple of times even on TV—and résumés he himself had drafted for funding requests to various public and private institutions. From an Austro-Hispano Bohemian family, he would say emphatically from the screen, a bit of saliva oozing out of the corners of his mouth and mixing with the beads of his constant cold sweat, and then he would lose himself in explanations of the meaning of Bohemian, which doesn't mean Czech, he clarified, or at least not necessarily, not always; it can also mean German, a German from Bohemia. *Deutschböhme, Wir Deutschen aus Böhmen*, We Germans of Bohemia. "This is the Empire," he explained, "the world, the Tout-Monde, AEIOU, *Austriae est imperare orbi universo, Austria erit in orbe ultima*, the imperial sun never sets; it always rises somewhere. For centuries we have been, I have been, in the service of the empire, the Habsburgs of Spain and Austria and Bohemia, the Spanish galleons plying the oceans and the horse-based post delivery system of Thurn and Taxis, the lords of Duino, carrying a letter from Vienna to Madrid in three days. An entire galleon is missing, sunk with the Invincible Armada; the Museum will have it, must have it, a nautical fortress on the bottom of the sea—costly and useless like all fortresses, like the flying fortresses of World War II, sent off to drop bombs that exploded over the cities and to explode like bombs when struck . . ."

Born in Gradisca—the Princely County of Gorizia and Gradisca, one of the thirty-six official titles of Franz Joseph—in a rundown, though still noble, late fifteenth-century building acquired by his grandfather Egon, the admiral. Actually the grandfather retired with that title, though he'd distinguished himself at a young age as a midshipman in the Battle of Lissa, where, as stated in the eulogy of Admiral Tegetthoff—Tegetthoff had been the one to notice his boldness in those Dalmatian waters and recommend him for a small decoration—iron heads in command of wooden ships prevailed over ironclad ships commanded by wooden heads, that is, the *Kaiserliche Kriegsmarine*, the Imperial Navy, still composed almost entirely of sailing vessels, destroyed the Italian fleet, already fully armored motor ships. Family scuffles, given that the iron heads were Italian sailors from Venice or Lussino and the wooden heads were Italian sailors from Genoa or Ancona. At home, he writes, when he was little, they used to let the children play at the naval Battle of Lissa and he, who went at it tirelessly all day, claimed that those games—the small boats sunk in the pond in the garden, the cardboard toy soldiers that ended up sodden in the water—had opened his eyes to the need to eliminate war.

8.

Don't give too much weight or too much space to the author's biographical profile, said the note in his own handwriting given to her personally by him at the time. I should dutifully and articulately — the note went on — write your profile, indeed perhaps theirs. Whoever helps to organize the Museum and these papers will have to rearrange them, rewrite them in part to make them clearer, I realize that, and therefore the papers that explain and celebrate my work will also be, or rather will especially be, his or hers. The art of war has authors, not a single author. Although, without wishing to be presumptuous, I think that — but it doesn't matter. I continue to use these conventional forms of grammar and these meaningless tenses, the present that as soon as it is, no longer is, and therefore doesn't exist and the future that never exists; I apologize, but I don't want to put anyone on the spot, least of all you, Dr. Brooks, you who seem to have understood what it means to work for the Museum.

When you are in the inverter, grammatical tenses no longer exist, they are at most verbal tics, fillers and utterances just to catch your breath when you don't know what to say. In the beginning was the Word, but here there is no beginning and therefore no Word either. These notes about childhood, for example, let's put them — we put them, we will put them, you may put them, dear Dr. Brooks — scattered about here and there. Partly because they are of little importance. What must count in the Museum are things, objects, helicopters, quivers, machine guns, they too unaware of verb tenses; he — that is, I — realize that it might arouse support and indeed I am pleased by that, but it's not I who count.

In fact, Dr. Brooks, I've had second thoughts. Please, when it is really necessary to specify a verbal person, given that you are not yet in the inverter, always use the first person singular without hesitation. I know it's inconvenient, I've already said so, but in some cases—at least for now, later it will be different—it can't be helped. When I say that as a child I continue shooting with the small wooden gun, go ahead and transcribe my words to the letter, without worrying that someone might not be able to figure out who it was or who is shooting. All children say "I" when they talk about their games, indeed they all say "I" when they talk. I is everyone, it's the most generic and impersonal pronoun, it's not used to designate anyone. For this reason you may use it shamelessly. Moreover—given the revisions, scrawls and erasures that, I know, make my papers almost illegible—I imagine that you will recopy them, transcribe them, in short, write them, and therefore it will be, it is, you who write them, they are yours.

9

As a child I loved shooting my small wooden gun. Fine battles at the pond in the park. It's great to hit someone, make him drop, even better make him fall into the water. Ships and men sink to the bottom, vanish; you don't see a thing anymore, only the enthralling waters, they too a vast coffin, one more shot, then we'll go home, it will be the last battle, the last war, then that's it, but let's end this one. Of course, war, the joy of destroying, must be severed at the root; the hand brandishing the sword or firing the gun must be cut off, then we'll collect it and place it in a glass case in the Museum. There is already one, the skeleton of the hand of an *uhlan* gripping the regulation saber of the officers of the 3rd Regiment, a lovely withered hand, a beautiful autumn leaf. Even Leonardo — the note went on — whose bust adorned the courtyard of the palace in Gradisca, why hadn't he stuck to painting the mountains turned blue by hazy distance, instead of building those contraptions, right there, in Gradisca, to defend the city from the Turks? Intricate cages of iron and wood camouflaged underwater on the bottom of the Isonzo, so that when the Turkish infantrymen and horsemen crossed the river, those gigantic traps would spring and imprison them, men and horses pawing the ground amid the blades and snares, the huge box emerges from the current like a pillory, a gigantic toy that contains live prey, animals hurling themselves against the bars. The Isonzo is the most beautiful color in the world, aquamarine reddened by blood streaming from the cage and by even more blood so many years later; meanwhile, from the city, it's easy to shoot those entangled bodies.

Bravo, Leonardo, the smile of the Mona Lisa at the service of death, the ineffable serenity of killing and wanting to kill. I, too, do the same when I go fishing, Luisa thought as she transcribed and sorted out that page, whether in the river or the nearby sea, the sky lit by the sun and the water's reflections is a light of joy, a big smile. The fish takes the bait, the hook rips into its throat, the fisherman smiles contentedly. He was right after all, life is war, the notes speak for themselves. "All you can do is transport everything into a Museum, where there is no more war because there is no more life. Already a scientist at age five and an inventor at nine, at sixteen I conceived and actually designed fantastic, terrible weapons, but I decided that I would make those models known when there were no more wars in the world and those weapons would be harmless and useless. We must make life—all life, all things—useless, unusable. The price of usage is always, in some way, the price of killing. Blunt the spears, rust the rifles, dull the blade edge, until life, always so razor sharp, no longer cuts."

10.

It would be better not to display the biographical profile immediately, in its entirety, but break it up into successive sections in the various galleries of the Museum, childhood adolescence war postwar and death. Even though he didn't believe in the last and considered it a logico-linguistics error, as shown by his D.U.D. Or else jump right in, in medias res, as befits an epic poem, in which, if all goes well, the beginning is known about halfway through, when the end is approaching. As in life, for that matter, and not just when you learn by accident, many years later, for instance, what your husband was up to. This might also not happen if, for example, he wasn't up to anything, or told you about it immediately, almost in real time, which may be even worse.

But it's the things about you that come to be known after the fact; what you were like as a child, at a time you can't remember, how your parents met, how the ghetto was demolished before your grandparents, and maybe even your great-grandparents, were born. The Museum too should be a hodgepodge of before and after, like the objects it displays and describes. Still, it would be nice to be able to start at the beginning, like the Torah. In the beginning, God created Heaven and Earth. In the beginning, or nearly so at least, because it seems Tohu and Bohu, Chaos and Desolation, which are never absent and keep you from actually starting anything and beginning any story, already existed. But with him, for example, one could begin, albeit against his will, if not with his birth — or, strictly speaking, nine months earlier, when his story properly begins — at least with his childhood, with adolescence, which his notebooks describe, though hurriedly and breathlessly.

11

It was the toy soldiers that made me realize that we must abolish war and that the only way to do that is to play at war. Play so as not to fight; toy soldiers versus real soldiers. The nicest ones were sold by Sior Popel, once we'd already moved to Trieste. A platoon of black Prussian hussars, with frogging; magnificent work, perfect, gilded buckles on black coats, Cossack fur hats and sabers strictly conforming to the actual ones. Perhaps it was Sior Popel himself who had given them to me, one time when we'd gone into his shop, I forget. My mother gave my father lots of gifts, but only a few to me. Sior Popel instead gave everyone presents. "Who do you think I am — Popel?" people in Trieste would say when someone asked for something extravagant. *La Rena xe iluminada / sior Popel / sior Popel passava / e i muli, i muli zigava: / no gavemo, sior Popel, paiòn;* the Old Town is illuminated, Sior Popel goes by and the kids call out to him saying they haven't got a cent.

Sior Popel gave all he could to everyone. When he passed by Rena, that is, the Old Town, with his long white beard, he would give us kids fruits and sweets. Toys as well, in his shop, where his wife, a hat always on her head, also sold embroidery yarn. His shop was on the *corso*, but he came to the Old Town mainly to bring something to the children who were being treated at Pia Casa dei Poveri, the hospital for the poor, and to provide a meal to the hungry in the dining hall on Via del Trionfo. Once he gave me a bow: "It belonged to the Indians," he told me, "the ones who live in the Amazonian jungles, where the heat and mist and humidity make it always seem like evening."

Why wasn't he my father, or at least my grandfather? "Eat well and see that others eat well," he would say. *"Mal no far, paura no gavèr.*" "Do no evil, have no fear." His shop—a theater, a world. Toy soldiers, stuffed elephants, smiling or sober dolls, air guns, belts, wooden or rubber swords, cannons that fired cloth balls as big as an egg without doing any harm. There the weapons were good, polished, smooth. Playing war so as not to wage war . . . but then—even that doll . . . The eyes, I remember the eyes. Not the usual watery blue eyes with lowered pink eyelids. Yellow-green glass eyes, like those of a stuffed owl. Cat eyes. They lit up when a light struck them and gleamed in the dark, enigmatic and cruel. My mother had given it to me, she always gave me toys for girls, she'd also left my hair long; there's a photo in which you can't tell which one is me and which one is my girl cousin.

I liked to dangle her in front of a light, that doll; the eyes, looking up, glittered like gold coins in a fire, and when I lowered her head they disappeared in the dark, opaque. I liked to arrange the doll in the center with the black hussars around her. To protect, to revere, to obey her. She so much bigger than them, a mother who can pick you up, rifle and all, or keep you in her belly and pull you out whenever she wants, or maybe give you a spanking. But the doll never did that, despite those big, plump hands. She was good, the green-gold eyes good and kind, and I liked to obey her along with the little hussars. Soldiers like to obey, it's their job. Every so often I'd take the commander, a major, you could tell by the stripes on his epaulettes, and put him under her rosy-colored foot, which was also somewhat black and grimy since I made her walk barefoot on the moist soil in the little park, and he would kiss the sole of her foot, who knows if his mustache itched or tickled her, maybe she liked it, and I liked it too. The commander was really me, that hussar was only my stand-in. I felt so happy, sitting on the ground with her; I even liked her disdainful indifference. When I tried to bend and turn her head toward me, she averted her gaze, the eyes snapped to look the other way. But that was all right.

Then, for some reason, things changed. I had to kick those oblivious hussars, who weren't even aware of the glory and joy of serving her, to make them march, and even with her something broke. She didn't pay any attention to me anymore when I picked her up or placed her among the soldiers. She was always looking the other way; if only she'd been cruel, to me a bite from that permanently half-open mouth would have been better than a kiss. She simply ignored me and so I sent the hussars off to war, where their proper place is, and no more thinking about any doll. But how come they were so good at first, them and her too? Maybe it was thanks to Sior Popel, to that shop, where everything was imbued with kindness and tenderness.

If I'd had that shop, I wouldn't need my Museum. You could go in there, touch things, even shoot a cloth bullet at the snout of a stuffed bear and he wouldn't get upset, Popel liked to let children play. His place had everything under the sun; at Christmas time, fir trees decorated with Nuremberg glass globes that reflected the lights and shadows and, under the tree, a large nativity scene, with lots of shepherds and several Magi—three are too few, he'd say, and he'd add a couple of Moorish Caspars mounted on their camels. Then he'd get the black hussars, we'll put them in too, that way they'll learn to be good and see that war is a game, otherwise it's idiocy.

When he tinkered with the Christmas tree his thick white beard got tangled in the branches, like snow, a nice, soft, inviting snow—I'd like to lie beneath a snow like that. He had everything and was able to repair any toy that broke; he'd reattach a head, glue a leg back on . . . Had it been possible to fix up that doll when she broke—screw the pink arm back on after it had fallen off, firmly reseat the two glass buttons in their sockets—Sior Popel would certainly have been capable of it, he was a magician. But without him . . . "What do you think, that we're Popel?" It was always Christmas at that kindly German's. *Stille Nacht, heilige Nacht*—even Poldo, my dog, would leap up in my arms, licking my face and closing his eyes, blissful, and Sior Popel would give him a slice of prosciutto that he kept on a shelf. I'd study the doll and the black hussars, while they were still there. They would have been better off staying there; Sior Popel watched me, he too a little bemused, like me at times . . .

It's so strange that he's gone, I thought he would be there forever, like a tree, like the forest of boats that bobbed on the sea not far away.

Oh Rena Vecia, / i camini no fuma più! / Xe morto sior Popel, / paneti no'l porta più!; Sior Popel is dead, no more smoke from the chimneys, no more panettone. Even the two glass buttons on the doll's face had become dull and opaque, in the dim shadows of the house. Sometimes they seemed vacant, like those of the cat mummy later on in Old Town's underground sewers. So I no longer lined up the hussars for a nice, peaceful parade; instead I put them in a small boat in the pond, or someplace else, I pushed them to shoot at one another and fall into the water and even though it was me who hit them it was all the same, like in war for that matter. But I wasn't sad.

12

After the family moved to Trieste, he enrolled at the Nautical Institute — "despite hating the sea." As a student he apparently didn't amount to much; an essay on trade at the port of Trieste had been deemed well-written — a fine Italian, Professor Venassi had said — but off topic, since it focused almost exclusively on maritime transports of military equipment, transports that were almost nonexistent. It's clear that the conversation between his mother and the teacher must have resulted in consequences for him at home, though he himself approved them, an advocate even then, in a school setting, of "sound authoritarian principles."

He hated the sea . . . nothing strange about that, Luisa thought; phobias, obsessions and manias are fearful of the sea's great liberation that dissolves and washes away nightmares. With his mess-tin, the prisoner empties the water that enters his cell, he knows that the powerful surge has come to sweep away his bars, but he's afraid of the immense ocean waters — of that ever tempestuous ocean that is the world. He grabs hold of the bars; the gills of freedom have atrophied, if he yields to the current he'll drown. And so the prisoner constructs barricades against the terrifying liberator; dams made of paper, notes, objects, hunks of wall, carcasses, wreckage. Fill all the cracks through which the great liberation might enter; sea and wind, the ocean's Roaring Forties, too strong for poor musty lungs. Yet as a child he loved that boat so much . . . Who knows if he too suffered from migraines like my mother, Luisa wondered as she leafed through those papers. My mother had really loved the sea and when she no longer loved it, when she was no longer able to love it, after what had happened, after the devastating discovery, she'd begun to suffer from migraines; I remember how they would attack her suddenly, seeming to grip her temples in a vise, a small gentle terrified rabbit between the teeth of a stone marten.

In the sea, in one that's deep and black—blue-black, the most enchanting hair on a woman is that which is so black as to appear blue, like yours, Doctor, which in our area is very rarely seen—in the sea, as I was saying, you can descend only within the ironclad walls of a submarine, which keep out the immense dark waters. In the sea you are all right only when you are not in the sea, underwater but not in the water; maybe in the belly of a big fish, like Jonah or Pinocchio. At least until a hook rips into the fish's throat and the submarine, hit by a torpedo, explodes; blown apart, the whale, along with everything in its belly, becomes prey to swarms of minnows and other small fish that hurl themselves on it and encircle it in a shimmering cloud.

13.

(*At the center of the atrium, on the back wall, a screen with his portrait, while at intervals the voice repeats: "Used submarines. Bought and sold."*)

U-Boot 20, Austro-Hungarian Navy, World War I (evidently he had managed to buy it or have it given to him; in used condition, however, as indicated by the puncture torn in its side), hit off the coast of Venice, in shallow water, not far from the Grado lagoon.

Elongated, an elegant armor-plated dugout. Two diesel engines and two electric motors, one 88-mm cannon, a 14-mm submachine gun and two torpedo-tubes on the front. The machinery of death is often long, extended, pointy. Spears, swords, mounted bayonets; rifle and gun barrels—rounded, of course, but lengthened—missiles. Bombs, it's true, tend to be pot-bellied. Like death, which is by no means gaunt but is fat instead, and it's not surprising, given how voracious it is. The torpedo is perhaps the ideal form, rectilinear and at the same time rounded.

A gash on its side, a sperm whale caught between the enormous claws of a Kraken. It's nice to go underwater in a submarine. Strictly speaking a submersible, suitable for navigating in the depths as well, but in particular on the surface, while the submarine, a more evolved model—the age of the evolution of species is over, now it's time for the evolution of machines—is essentially made to navigate in the depths.

A video comes on, you descend in an aquarium, from the belly of the submarine the waters in which it sinks seem calm—aside from the torpedoes and mines, but that's life, which is always a surprise.

Sometimes even an unpleasant surprise. You descend; out there, in the water, as midshipman Ivo Saganić, assigned to U-Boot 20 *Kaiser Joseph*, once saw while diving in a wetsuit, the colors are toned down; increasingly subtle streaks, the blue softens before turning violet. Too bad submarines, the military ones, don't have portholes. Languid uncertain jellyfish drift in front of the diving suit's transparent window, the eye watches, enthralled, illusory flies streak past the crystalline lens fooled by some defect in the vitreous organ. The eye sees what the brain tells it to see, even if it isn't there. Many have seen the Kraken, the giant crab of the deep, which does not exist. You descend, little by little the different colored rays of light darken, first the reds, then the oranges, the yellows, the greens, and finally the purples and ultra-violets. At ten meters deep it is already evening.

You descend into the ever darker crypt of a cathedral, the vault above is still blue, a stained-glass canopy flecked with flashes of light, gradually dimmer, more opaque. Time, there below, slows down, compresses. Minutes of sleep, years. How long did you sleep, how long did you dream of sleeping? In that blue in which you descend that is soon no longer blue, everything seems to happen with centuries-old lethargy. The fisherman Urashima—Ivo clearly remembers the little book he was given by Saint Nicholas, a German edition of fairytales, the black gothic characters of the title above the white-crested waves shown on the cover—dives off the boat into the arms of the sea princess, heart sinking to the bottom; non-time of happiness and death. Ulysses doesn't realize that he's spent seven years in the cave with Calypso, Urashima doesn't realize that he's spent four hundred years in the arms of the sea goddess. But who's counting? Years are made of days and for there to be a day the sun must rise and set, but when there was no sun that could rise and set in the great primordial dark cloud and no earth that could rotate around it, and when there is no yesterday and no tomorrow in a kiss, the days no longer exist and cannot be counted. I am down here to wage war, midshipman, but down here it seems impossible to think about war, about its gathering speed, about the torpedo that rushes out, swiftly boring into the sea, a wall of time.

Struck off the coast of Venice, the submarine managed to re-ascend, slowly and obliquely, and emerged, resting on a sandbar; an Austrian corvette picked up the crew, including four killed in the attack, and returned to Pola. Midshipman Ivo Saganić is more fortunate than the others, because, unlike the sailors and officers who come from small towns and remote villages, he lives in Promontore, right on the sea, that sea from which he has surfaced and returned, and where his wife, Mila, her hair as long as a mermaid's, is waiting for him. Urashima is homesick, he misses his father his mother his brothers and sisters and asks the sea goddess to let him go, he will come back soon. Midshipman Ivo Saganić is sorry about the four sailors who died and about the submarine, which by then had become his boat, maybe more so than the one that awaits him moored almost in front of his house, still he is happy to return, however briefly; when the gods send a message you leave or return without asking any questions. As the submarine ascends—slowly, because it is moving sideways, the angle separating its emerging course from a horizontal line is very shallow—he thinks about the depths receding and vanishing, about all the plants and fish they're passing through, about the *sguazeto*, the thick stew, that awaits him at home or at the Trita Trita tavern, where maybe they'll go to celebrate, he and Mila.

To tell the truth, he would rather go straight home, but his shipmates may want to spend at least an hour getting drunk, and he, one of the few who is married, doesn't want to act standoffish or seem like a *Simandl*, a henpecked husband, as the Austrians say—he is and feels Austrian, like all of them, a subject of the emperor, but definitely not German, he's Istrian and Italian—so they will probably end up at the Trita Trita, with its black wine *the cemetery of youth* and its white wine *the graveyard of youth*, but he'll quickly leave them. For one thing because later he will have to go back to the sea, under the sea. Urashima will very soon rejoin the goddess at the bottom of the sea, who didn't say anything when he left but only gave him a small chest warning him never to open it.

There are many ways to wait for a husband who lives for a long time at the bottom of the sea—who perhaps is dead—and when

37

midshipman Ivo Saganić saw that his wife, the lovely Mila, more beautiful than the loveliest queen of the sea, had not waited for him alone, nor with only their son, little Tonko, he almost didn't recognize the house, the boat bobbing at anchor in front of the calm sea, the courtyard and the staircase leading up to the door, where Mila stood straight and silent, more distant than when he was at the bottom of the sea, the few steps and few meters between them were years and decades. Urashima, when he returns to his village, doesn't find anything left except the mountains; his house is no longer there, nor any of the houses he knew, no one remembers a family with his name, in the cemetery there are other tombstones, the eroded, almost illegible names don't tell him anything either; four hundred years have passed, he learns, since a typhoon destroyed a village that once stood in that place, and so he goes to the seacoast all alone, opens the chest, maybe there's a message from the goddess in there that will explain it all to him, a magic spell that will save him, but there is only dust immediately scattered by the wind. He looks at himself in the limpid, gentle waves at his feet, they show him a face etched by furrows, like the tombstones of those old graves, and long hair white as snow.

Urashima's knees give way and he slumps on the sand, midshipman Ivo Saganić on the other hand stared at Mila for a long time as she stood in the doorway, then he turned, went to the shore and for a long time stared at the sea, it seems no one saw him again after he set out on the road to Medulin. The records of the Imperial Marina would certainly show something, given that a few days later the crew of U-Boot 20 was called back to the sea on another vessel, but the sudden reversal of Austria, at the end of the war, meant that those records were lost.

14

And what about all those notes on the mulberry tree, in notebook number 36? Black Mulberry, he writes, *Morus nigra L.* An excellent defense, like White Mulberry, capable of combating respiratory illnesses (coughs, bronchitis, asthma, colds, sore throats); reducing fevers. Deworming. Depurative, sedative, effective against insomnia and headache, bactericidal; it vanquishes faintness, cachexia, hyperglycemia, hypertension, edema, dropsy, aphthous fever, lesions, snake and insect bites, mycosis, oral ulceration, gastric ulcers, depression. Emollient, diaphoretic, hypoglycemic properties. It enriches the blood, cures neurasthenia, hypertension, diabetes, vertigo, tinnitus, anemia and arthritis. The council of the city of Vicenza, on November 30, 1478, sanctions the loss of an eye for anyone who steals a mulberry tree plant. The false fruit of the mulberry tree is called a sorosis; a thin epicarp, brittle endocarp, and fleshy, succulent mesocarp.

The mulberry is a monoecious plant, that is, there are inflorescences of both sexes in the same specimen. The fruit, the sorosis, is just that, a false fruit, only an infructescence . . . Each fruit is false, a living lie. Two pretend to be one and fabricate a false one; pistils and stamens are also engaged to put on a burlesque *Tristan and Isolde*. False fruit, false parents, false love, disguised war. War of the sexes. If there were only one—only one sex, one man, *homo*, not *vir*—what a shame that some languages don't have the neuter. Well, only one thing, neutral, nobody to fight against . . . In German there's the neuter. Great people, the Germans. Even when they exaggerate. Put aphrodisiacs in the Museum as well; even the member that enters the vulva, the first time, and sometimes not just the first, causes bloodshed.

Mulberries fall from the mulberry tree. They fall, squashed on the ground, tinging the soil with stains of dark blood from the great, venerable, multi-branched mulberry tree in the center of the piazza in Crno Selo, the village—sometimes boastfully called city—clinging to a slope on the side of the Velebit, overlooking the Adriatic once sailed by the Uskoks. A few houses (one, an old building in Habsburgian government office style, not without a shabby nobility) clinging to a precipitous slope leading to a booming, frothy sea from which dirt paths rather than actual streets branch off. A natural well, the coolness of water in broiling summer on the white, dazzling rocks of the Dalmatian Coast. My father, he writes, once took us to Dalmatia, before the war—he loved those white rocks, I loved the mulberries that melted in my mouth, ran down my chin, stained my shirt. My mother . . . I don't know what my mother loved. She scolded me when I got dirty. It's difficult to wash away those purplish stains, the innocent blood of fruits, animals, women on their impure days, it's hard to remove the stains. Only those of brother shed by brother fade quickly, a coat of whitewash and it's done, like afterward, on the walls of the Risiera and its environs.

The few inhabitants of Crno Selo are called Di Giovanni, perhaps grandchildren of a grandfather Ivančić; etymologies of blood—the blood of reclaimed forebears, of brothers who, having grown up seeing mutual friends and former friends savage one another while shouting Mare Nostrum or Jadransko More, had decided, each turning against the other, to be Slavs or Italians and had spilled blood they felt was baseless and illegitimate to remove it from their veins, crushing their various happy childhoods like grapes in a vat or olives in a press. Hands bloodied by juicy mulberries and by their own wounds and those of others, at the moment it's not always clear; whether in the heated breath of summer or that of battle makes little difference in the end. A red-white-green arm of the sea rather than red-white-blue or vice versa makes that much more blood flow, Black Shirts burn villages, foibe, sinkholes, in the Karst hide corpses.

Crush the grapes, red and black. There are vats and there are vats, presses and presses; the ones at home that crush a couple of flasks and those in large wineries, dozens, hundreds of presses operated by men who don't even see them, pushing a button that sets them in motion, surging, swollen reddish rivers. Man is a karstic doline, a sinkhole; the underground river roils, swells, vomits the wine, choking the drinker and it's not immediately clear which is wine and which is blood. In Crno Selo the harvest was modest compared to the immense yield of the presses and vats used at the Risiera, itself a modest subsidiary of the large corporation "Adolf Hitler & Co.," bankrupt and auctioned off before it could become "Adolf Hitler & Successors."

The old mulberry tree is there, gnarled and knobby, scores of years have marked it with protuberances and bulges; brazen, juicy mulberries, more numerous than the hands of inhabitants who should have picked them, drop from that woody heritage and mix with soil, mud and a puddle or two in a dense vinaceous residue, History's cancerous menstrual.

Men and empires fall, mulberries brimming with juice plop from branches onto visitors' heads; the dark red splatters and stains everything. Clothes ruined, people jumping back. When bombs fall, people are terrified and there's a lot more red. And those silkworms besides, aren't they ghastly eating the leaves of the mulberry, which is there only to be ravaged, eaten? Eaten so that someone may have silk, beautiful silk, light as air, caressing the hand that strokes it, a diaphanous veil over shoulders or face, a silken cord with which the sultan strangled those who fell out of favor. No matter where we start, he concluded, it always comes down to weapons.

15

Among the spears and howitzers, six crates with 20,000 books on the subject of war. Among them, 428 from the Deutsche Bücherei Triest and the Hitler-Jugend Bibliothek, probably having come from the Italian-German Association — formerly the Italian-German Cultural Association (evidently at the end of the war culture was no longer considered so essential), the former Kulturverein Friedrich Schiller, though at a time when Germans in Trieste, and not only in Trieste, were gentlemen, perhaps the most gentlemanly. Nevertheless, books are books, even when they are stupid; they always make good weapons, and not just because of their heavy sharp spines that can be used to break heads. Books must always be respected and protected. Even the ones we don't like.

It's true, fortunately I saved those books in the early days of May '45, during clashes among Germans, Yugoslavs, Fascists, Italian Democratic partisans, communists, national guards who were somewhat Fascist, somewhat resistant, when, dodging stray bullets fired by everyone against everyone, I passed through Yugoslav positions as well as German lines and parleyed with one and the other, acting as an interpreter but also sometimes as a messenger, the bearer of proposals and counter-proposals of surrender to which often, as I moved along, hugging the walls to avoid the bullets, I would add something of my own or delete passages that might inflame tempers even more. Yes, gentlemen, a plenipotentiary of peace; it was I who persuaded them, it's as though I'd been the one to officially proclaim peace, after so many grueling talks, especially with myself. I knew I represented them all and so I listened to them all, especially in my mind.

The head, at times of general confusion, often becomes a crowded, tumultuous piazza.

Among those books, even a small collection on sex, not much less bellicose — "Make love, not war, no, don't make love because love is war." Those books, according to one of his notes, obviously had to be included in the Museum's library, darkly and ominously towering over a globe at their feet, held in the mouth of a large papier-mâché praying mantis — the male's head mangled and devoured after short-lived coitus, the world demolished by Eros, the Amazons, the armed virgin Camilla, Tamiri Queen of Scythia, who plunges the Persian king's head in blood, the little hooker who sucks you off and leaves you empty, a flaccid condom; the saints too, Joan of Arc, who slaughters people, it serves her right that they burned her, the stupid girl who, for some reason, thought she should love the French more than the English or God knows who. The toothed vagina that gives life and death to the Chamacoco of Paraguay, as Cherwuish, the Chamacoco brought to Prague in Kafka's time, would not stop talking about in the brew pubs of Malá Strana. The shelves — there's a photo, a bit blurry but you can make them out — were adorned with pictures of various animals dancing or strutting about in order to mate, entire maps filled with butterflies or army ants, insects that penetrate and pierce.

In other boxes, all the documentation — trial proceedings, attorneys' statements, photocopies of judgments — of an age-old, bitter suit between two of his cousins over the inheritance of an apartment in Gorizia.

"Civil law, the most ferocious field of battle." Nothing like criminal law, laughable by contrast. Yes, of course, murders, crimes, but with passion at least — love, jealousy, revenge. In civil court, on the other hand, you have children who fleece their parents, a brother who lets another brother starve to death over a miserable piece of bread, spouses who deprive one another and send the other to an insane asylum over a three-room flat, relatives who despise and torment each other like those two cousins of mine. Shades of Balzac, *Colonel Chabert*. Worse yet when wills, legacies and appropriations or misappropriations concern the remains of poets contended by those who boast that they are the sole true heir, spiritual heir in particular, the sole interpreter. The posthumous papers of poets, grabbed by those who tug at them from either side. Spouses and family members claim legitimate possession of them, friends and lovers oppose the rhetoric of legitimacy with a rhetoric of improper passions and intimate testimonies, widows or widowers quarrel with old rivals, women acting as Sybils safeguard words and anecdotes as though they were fragments of a gospel, men who set themselves up as exegetes establish an alleged definitive truth, and foundations and authorities claim them for the public good and societal edification.

The remains of poets, he went on, give off a bad odor, like damp, sweaty banknotes that have passed from hand to hand; too many hands snatching them, holding them, crumpling them. Spiritual avarice, more ferocious and aggressive than that of the flesh and of money. Not that animals are any better, as they say. But at least they don't have lawyers, judges, codicils; they don't invent procedural errors or touching, righteous sentimental mush, and above all, when they hunt and devour their prey, they don't claim to be in the right.

16.

Room no. 5 (we'll see about no. 4, it all depends on whether we manage to get those two jeeps, German and American)—AB41, Autoblinda, an armored car of the Italian Army used in World War II, also used by the Wehrmacht particularly in the Balkans and in Northern Italy. Armed with a 20-mm Breda gun and an 8-mm coaxial machine gun located in a turret in addition to another 8-mm machine gun aimed toward the rear. Steering wheel connected to four wheels, at times the cause of mishaps. Spare wheels fixed to the sides, free to rotate in order to help the vehicle advance over rough terrain and allow it to overcome tall obstacles. The vehicle may be equipped with wheels able to run on railway tracks; in some cases with checkrails to clear objects from the tracks as well. Six forward gears and four reverse gears, a driver's seat in front and another in back, requiring two crew members as drivers. Weight 7,510 tons, length 5.21 meters, width 1.93 meters, height 2.48 meters. A four-person crew (two drivers, a gunner, the commander). FIAT 6-cylinder petrol engine; speed 78 kmh, 400-km operational range. Used especially by anti-partisan units in Yugoslavia.

At the bottom left, on the side wheel of the armored car, the photograph of a burning house and people watching, more astounded than despairing.

At San Pietro del Carso the Germans, together with a couple of Italian platoons, swept up a good many Slavs affiliated with the Osvobodilna Fronta, the Slovene Liberation Front; I acted as interpreter and stamped many cards attesting that these Slavs were good people, not connected with politics, and so a fair number of individuals owe the fact that they escaped to me. In exchange I had them give me a canteen, a belt, a few boxes of cartridges, also a couple of "potato mashers," Model 24 German grenades, which Tito's people had seized. The partisans blocked the train and freed the prisoners who ran off into the woods, I even did a nice sketch of the train and the ambush; so, for me, though not for the colonel, it's not true that I did that drawing to help him figure out where those partisans' secret hideaways might be; actually he didn't know what was happening. When the Germans arrived, people ran away wearing their best clothes in order to salvage them, there was one man who wore three jackets, one for holidays.

The Germans set fire to the houses; really only one house, not a great many as they later said; there was only one old man and his wife, old like him, the others remained a little distance away, fearful, under the aim of the armored car; they watched the house burn down and wept. The Italian soldiers, seeing those two old people, also wept, more so than for the two women killed weeks before by Fascist squads that had come from Trieste. In Kočevje as well, when some members of the Tomsič battalion were shot, caught as a result of a tip-off, I recorded everything and collected what I could. To each his job, they killed and I collected and organized the belts and boots of the corpses. I love order and therefore peace. I even prefer flowers when they are asexual, even better when they're dried. My wife understood this immediately, well soon enough, it's fortunate to have found an understanding woman (from notebook no. 26).

17.

They all end up finding an understanding woman, Luisa said to herself as she returned home after locking up—it was already late, there was no one left. It's the opposite that's difficult. She, too, for example, by trying to be understanding . . . She was tired, those papers had left her dazed. A compulsive rant from which something that had eluded her would occasionally come to light. All that paper, proliferating, jumbled—blotting paper, like the kind at school, that absorbs ink blots and the heart. Paper makes you thirsty, sweaty, an acidic sweat. It gave her a sense of confusion and the perception of an indefinable malaise, like a migraine.

Yes, she understood more and more why that man had hated the sea, sucked dry as he was by all the paper, withdrawn into that cave-dweller's inner life with its viscid walls, its corners and closets where tenacious phobias and obsessions coalesced, vestiges of every fixation. The sea dissolves them, the paper with its jumbled figments curls up in a boat that vanishes over the horizon amid foamy-crested waves. When she left the office after hours spent on those papers, however, the pages stuck to her like clammy underwear.

The sea—letting go, undressing, making love, losing oneself. She could not imagine him undressed, naked, much less lulled by the waves. And her? She wondered as she undressed and got into bed. Although as usual she was almost naked under the covers, only a light petticoat, she did not feel liberated from her clothes as she did when she took them off at the beach or on the reef at Barcola. Nakedness is a way of being, and women, even when eagerly authorized or even incited, nearly forced to undress, could never be really naked, never

47

only themselves. This is what being an understanding woman means: knowing what dress you should wear to meet the man's needs, knowing what he wants you to be and becoming so, not ever changing. Forgetting what you had once wanted to be, and helping other women to forget as well. Especially—if you are a mother—your daughter, your daughters.

Così fan tutte, women are all like that. Or at least they used to be at one time. Maybe not actually all of them. Luisa sometimes had the impression that her mother had wanted to keep her in swaddling clothes forever, as if to protect her from who knows what. Maybe from becoming an understanding woman. Maybe for her mother there were too many awful things to understand—better not to understand them, not even try to, curl up within yourself, stay wrapped in swaddling clothes, not allowing anyone to slip a hand inside and touch your heart. Sometimes those swaddling strips are constricting, they hurt. Tight shoes also hurt. Who knows what tightness caused the migraine to come.

Love and migraine . . . The first could sometimes be difficult to tell in her mother, withdrawn and aloof as she was. The migraine was certainly more visible. It spread over her mother's face and gripped it like prey, stretching back the skin of her forehead. Frequently. For example, it had happened when Luisa, with the petulance of a child, began asking her to tell her about her grandmother Deborah, who— she'd heard—had risked everything to hide Sara. It was the last year of the war, when the Nazis, now in control in Trieste, were raging ever more furiously in the city that was once extremely loyal to the Habsburgs and quintessentially Italian, which had become the Adriatisches Küstenland, the Adriatic Littoral. Her uncle Giorgio, great-uncle to be exact, had told her about it once when they were alone; strangely uncomfortable, though with an apparent bitter desire to talk about it, he had started recounting how her grandmother Deborah— her grandfather Daniele had died many years earlier, even before the racial laws—had passed through the German lines with her young daughter (Sara was then fourteen), even boldly asking to take cover from the rain in a barrack of Wehrmacht soldiers guarding the road, thereby managing to reach the countryside of Salvore, at the tip of Istria, and the family that had taken in and hidden the little girl. The family of old Anna, who had been the maid in their home—it was she, only she could manage to make you eat and sleep when you were little, Luisa's grandmother Deborah had told Sara. There are born mothers, Uncle Giorgio had added, just as some are born poets. Your grandmother saved your mother, he said, therefore you owe your life

49

to her as well, don't forget it. Don't forget it, he'd repeated with a strange, sorrowful obstinacy.

In old Anna's house in the midst of meadows and seaside woods, not far from Salvore, on the other side of the Gulf of Trieste, Sara—they'd told her that from then on her name would no longer be Sara, but Laura—had cried when her mother went away. Gone forever, but at the time she couldn't know that. But afterward I was happy. Her mother had allowed herself to say it only much later, Luisa recalled, years later; it was the only time they spoke about it, and Sara had quickly stopped herself, as her face, after those brief words, tightened and lost its light, a stone rosy from the sun whose rays retreat like lizards. Happy as long as she'd remained there, because later, when she returned to Trieste at the end of the war, it was a different person who had gone on living, a different person with whom she had almost nothing in common. Happy for how long? Surrounded by that sea and that sky it was difficult, impossible, to keep track of time; there was always only one day, one hour of summer. Yes, happy. Happy and unaware.

Unaware of what? Not only of the war—as she would later realize, not only of death in the air, of the world's brutal vise. The sea is blue, a dazzling light; when it reverberates in the fierce noonday heat its brilliance is blinding, a darkness in which you cannot see anything, like at night. Three apostles follow Jesus to the mountain—old Anna had served for years in a Jewish home, but this had not caused her to set aside her Catholic peasant's faith, ineradicable as a gnarled root, and every Sunday, except when bombs and gunfire were too close, she had taken Sara, no, Laura, to Mass, to pray and listen to the sermons and readings—the apostles follow Jesus to the mountain that shines like the sun, a radiant cloud so bright and luminous that they can barely see anything. In the shimmering of the sea, Sara doesn't see anything either. She doesn't see events, doesn't see death maturing in that dazzle like a ripe, bloody fig; in that brilliance, for a moment—for a very long moment—everything is perfect and happy. The girl runs on the beach, alone or with other children, startled seagulls rise in flight from the water and vanish in that light in which everything dissolves, waves break white-crested on the rocks and all you can see is the whiteness of their crashing—a great happy smile from everything, even from the fish that twitches, ripped open by another bigger fish.

Elsewhere, behind or above the light and water that have merged into a single glimmer, there is fighting, shooting, killing; people are dying, people are being burned in the city beyond the gulf; they are alone in an immense fear, children at night awed by thunder and lightning, but on that sea you don't know any of this, you don't hear it, it doesn't exist. There is only the happiness of bare feet splashing near the shore, the receding tide leaving white seashells on the sand, wonderful empty tombs; a small crab scuttles toward the sea in hasty retreat, a lost soldier left behind chasing his regiment as they flee, mowed down as he runs. Even playing callously with the little crab, crushing it, is all happiness and delight; Sara was even able to crack open live sea urchins without hurting herself on their spines and suck the juicy pulp, so flavorful in the mouth, even if it sometimes mingled with a little blood from her lips when they bit into a spine that had remained hidden.

No, the abrupt end of childhood, unaware of war and life, that is, of death, when Aunt Nora and Uncle Giorgio had come to pick her up and bring her back to Trieste once the war had ended, had not been the only thing that put an end to it all. There had to be something else that etched her mother's face with the migraine's sudden piercing pain and sculpted it into that bleak, lost look, which made her seem a stranger to Luisa; the spasm that drove back the skin on her mother's forehead disturbed her face, like a stone disturbs a face reflected in the water.

It had been the end of another unawareness which, in her mother's heart, had put an end to the vast blue of the bay where she had lived unable to imagine that there were other things in the world besides that blue, the smell of salt and pines, that happiness. When her aunt and uncle had come to pick her up—a few months after the end of the war, when the establishment of the Allied Military Government in Trieste and the withdrawal of the Yugoslav troops meant that the situation in the city, always tense and sometimes even violent, had become at least relatively normalized—Sara had realized that she would no longer be happy, ever again; she sensed it but there was no sadness, like when you acknowledge a law, which might well be hurtful, but had to be accepted, like when Ciuki, old Anna's dog, had died, though he had not disappeared and his presence went beyond his remains buried beneath the grass in the yard, near the low wall. I'm going away, but the bay and the lighthouse and those rocks that emerge like sea creatures are here; they *are*, forever, and so it's all right, maybe I'm not even leaving the bay as I think I am, I'm only going to another part of the bay, everything is the bay and everything is in the bay.

Old Anna had cried even more than Sara, who, as she hugged the woman, had felt all the more part of the bay even though she was leaving. Perhaps even mama—she barely remembered her father—is somewhere in the bay, Sara had thought, when she was brought home to Trieste by Uncle Giorgio and Aunt Nora; it doesn't matter if I can't see her, it's like when we play hide and seek and Giovanni and Marco—now Ivan and Marko—can't see me either, just as I don't see them now; they are gone, yet they are here. She knew that her mother Deborah had died, though only vaguely; she was told that she had died at the end of the war, she didn't yet know about the people who became thin trails of smoke. Naturally they hadn't told her right away so as not to shock her, but they were wrong. She would have known and felt all the same that her mother was in the air, that she was the air around her, just as she had once been the water, the sea in which she swam. It was only later, when she'd asked for information, for some details, that those maternal waters had begun to dry up and the headache had started. Which later also became mine, Luisa thought.

At Aunt Nora and Uncle Giorgio's house they hardly ever spoke about Deborah. Just a word every now and then, when Sara insisted on asking and it couldn't be avoided. The girl had asked for a photograph to place on the bedside table or on the credenza, and after some searching, and hemming and hawing, they had given her one; not a portrait but a group photo in the mountains, Deborah with three or four girlfriends, a small snapshot that you had to study carefully to distinguish one face from another and recognize it. Maybe they're right not to talk about it, thought the girl, now almost a young woman, right not to want to talk about death, about the smoke that now and then rises from the smokestack of the Risiera, which she'd heard something about, because if you don't stop talking about it you go on breathing it, you end up breathing that smoke and dying, at least inwardly, like the person you sometimes read about who died by inhaling gas fumes from a stove.

Luisa too thought she could occasionally smell the odor that had haunted her mother, a whiff, she didn't know where it came from — maybe from the blast furnace of the Ferriera, the ironworks, the old coruscating steelworks facing the sea, toward Muggia, which manufactured cast iron; from the smoke occasioned by the combustion of carbon coke in contact with iron oxides, which, the newspapers said every so often, had caused the death of more than one worker. The Ferriera was not far from the Risiera. Of course, unlike the latter, those deaths had been a collateral albeit inevitable effect, as was later explained, for the employment and well-being of the city. At times the quickly dispelled stench seemed to come from within herself, a halitosis of the heart. But she had to think about her work. One of the next pieces to be placed was a Chamacoco ax, a small thing compared to an antitank gun or a flamethrower, but when it splits open a head . . .

18.

Room no. 15—A bow and arrow, a catapult for launching sun-dried mud balls, and a battle-ax, all used by the Chamacoco, an Indian tribe living (had lived, extinct?) in the Gran Chaco, between Paraguay and Bolivia, more Paraguay than Bolivia, as determined by some war; every border is the child of war. The bow varies in length from 1.55 meters to a maximum of 2 meters; the string—a single string, stretched from one end to the other—is entirely of fiber from Ybira, the arrows (of wood) measure an average 1.20 meters in length. Two-thirds of the arrow is made up of a light, rounded wooden shaft, with feathers for wings at the base, arranged in a helix. The tip of the arrow is a very hard, heavy, toothed wooden point, affixed to the shaft. The catapult, used to launch small, very hard balls of mud, is semicircular, flat on the inside—except for a rounded center, seven to eight centimeters—suitable for grasping with the hand. The ends of the cord, double strand, are kept open by two small wooden rods. The green stone ax adorned with feathers, with a handle of Naza-reth (Bignonia) wood, probably comes from the Tumanà, another Indian tribe.

A CHAMACOCO IN PRAGUE

Bows and ax belonging to Cherwuish Pioshad Mendoza, the Chamacoco Indian that the famous explorer, ethnologist, anthropologist and botanist Albert Vojtěch Frič (1882–1944) brings to Prague from Paraguay in 1908, to cure him of an unknown illness that was decimating his clan, the Ishira clan, in the region near the fortress of Bahía Negra, where Frič was conducting his research. *Ancyclostoma duodenale*, the doctors in Prague had discovered, all the fault of that hitherto unknown nematode worm (worms in the ass, he had noted hastily recording the story in notebook no. 67). Slithering through the rain forest of the human body, slinking unseen into the muddy channels of the duodenum, serpents of the night that we carry within us, Oleix Deič, the great aquatic four-headed snake-goddess of the Chamacoco that swims at the bottom of the Pilcomayo. Along the river females mate with animals (*äku*, they say in Chamacoco) — with the jaguar, with Bosiřibo the bird, son of the rain that brings storms from the east. Our zoo, Dr. Wedlin had told Frič, when the anthropologist brought Cherwuish to him at the Vlatch hospital, is more extensive and rich . . . Even the most rudimentary microscope reveals the dark jungle that proliferates within us; all you have to do is place the object, a clot of blood or bloody stools, at a distance between the focal length and twice that length and arrange the eyepiece so that the image framed by the lens falls between it and its focus and the virtual image emerges, inverted and magnified. The nematode expands, uncoils, the snake-goddess swims in the blind river of entrails, and mates, she isn't picky and pays no attention to sex or gender. Everything penetrates everything, the mosquito slips into the cloaca of the caiman, nocturnal gods with many heads and arms sleep in the body's darkness like Cherwuish's worm and when they wake they break through the tunnel walls, the banks of the river. In there, under there, everything gives way; microscopic star wars, worlds crumble, a universe, a man, they disintegrate explode and die.

Deep murkiness beneath the skin—white, terracotta or painted *uruciú* red, like Cherwuish in his forest. The obscurity of bones nerves and mucous membranes under the colorless outer layer, appropriate for a passport photo. In that darkness worms corrupt, penetrate; poisoned blowgun arrows pierce the pancreas, devour, are exterminated by faithful legions of antibodies, the guards die but do not surrender. If the regular troops stationed in remote outposts of the colon or the appendix aren't enough, special forces step in and bomb—pills burst and are released like torpedoes in the dark waters, blowing up dams, a cathartic flood overflows the levees, the last stopper bursts out and the sticky, yellowish-brown sludge spews out, a million spurts of poison, slaughtered bacilli float unseen in that violent estuary. Calomel and santonin like napalm and Cherwuish is out of danger, cured.

The ax atop the Nazareth wood handle has a sharp bulge in the middle—like the spike on the Prussian helmet in room no. 35, Prussians of the Amazon? He had obtained the ax—one of his notes reads—from a Bohemian relative of his mother, Dr. Hulácek, who had bought it for next to nothing in one of those periodic clearance sales, where Frič, always short of money and embroiled in projects that inevitably failed—his uncle Anton Jan, the eminent zoologist, had urged against giving him a cent, inept as he was—had been forced to give away his collections, including the famous cactuses that had made him a celebrated authority throughout Europe, and the crates of plants, animal skins and trophies that he had brought with him from Paraguay. The ax had been left to him in Prague by Cherwuish when he returned to Bahía Negra, where he died a couple of years later, having perhaps perished in the bloody war between Bolivia and Paraguay, in which the Chamacoco, uncertain of and above all indifferent to being Bolivians or Paraguayans, ended up being massacred in greater numbers than Bolivians and Paraguayans.

The head crudely carved on the handle of the ax, squint-eyed and lecherous, was sucking a kind of obscene papaya. A sailor in the Royal Navy had whittled it so he could sell it to someone, bamboozling him with those touches, and Cherwuish might have gotten it from him as he went up the Paraguay River on some boat at the time of the fish migration, maybe hoping to pass it off on someone else for a few pesos, since he obviously must have realized right away that the head was fake. Nevertheless, "a symbolic piece for my Museum, a weapon of war for peace, that has not been used on anyone's head."

During the lectures that Frič, to earn some money, gave in Prague on the culture of the Chamacoco, Cherwuish, dancing, would demonstrate how to use the ax, without actually using it. Simulating, making-believe; playing war, so as not to wage war. Popel's toy soldiers . . . Cherwuish brandished the ax striking blows only at the air; haphazardly, it seemed, and yet it was a precise grammar, established in centuries of forests and clouds of mosquitoes on the Paraguay River, war dance rain dance or mating dance, the ax decrees the fertile downpour that dissolves the spongy clouds or death that splits open a head like a coconut. Frič, though a corresponding member of the Museum of Anthropology and Ethnography in St. Petersburg and author of several books on the Indians of South America and poisonous cactuses, as well as exotic adventure books for children, found it hard to scrape by in Prague, unlike on the Pilcomayo River, which he had been the first to travel from its source to the estuary.

But no one wanted his thirty crates full of feathers, furs, the rotted, dried exotic plants, travel journals and photographs of Mato Grosso. In short, Frič wasn't doing so well, even though at the Vikárka, more of a wine bar than a brew pub, they gave him all the beer he wanted on credit, and academies from all over Europe conferred honorary degrees on him. So he decided to earn some money by giving public lectures for the Journalists' Union in Žofín, in which he spoke about how the Chamacoco make war with the Tumraha, about how to use an ax, how to fill the peace pipe, how to perform the war dance and how to sing the death of those who go to join their ancestors, while beside him Cherwuish, the Chamacoco dressed as

57

a Chamacoco, enacted his words as though in a living nativity scene, demonstrating fighting gestures, moves dodges leaps blows, sometimes knocking over the lecturer's table with its ritual glass of water or grabbing onto the curtains in back of the room, one time causing them to collapse along with the table.

He brandished the ax with lightning thrusts, mortal blows wielded on millions of invisible microorganisms since no Tumraha enemy whose skull he might split was within range, and above all because he was a man of peace who kills only in war and only those enemies on whom war has been ceremoniously declared, the way it was done at one time, at least among them, the civilized peoples of the Old World, except—one of his notes said—in the New World, Cherwuish's very ancient one. The pipe extinguished, he flourishes the ax or draws the bow with gestures orchestrated for him by an unknown score, recorded in his members like notches carved in the bark of a tree, and executed by his movements, gestures that intersect the air sketching fleeting but regular geometric figures.

A lady or two—there are few in the audience—thinks she should be offended when the rhythmic thrust of his groin exceeds all decency, but it's much worse when Councilman Wondracek, already generally glowering and pedantic, leaves the room protesting because a mud ball, shot from the bow with unerring precision during the simulated battle, struck the back of the empty chair in front of him, a few centimeters from his eyeglasses and his mustache. "In the language of the Chamacoco, funeral prayers consist not of words, but of gestures," the speaker, that is, Albert Vojtěch Frič, is meanwhile explaining—but he is clearly out of step with Cherwuish, who is writhing his hips demonstrating the nuptial ceremony and coitus instead.

It is likely that Cherwuish, unsettled by the lights and the marmoreal bust of a Professor Belačik, archaeologist, watching him, scowling, from the back of the room, got flustered and fell out of step with the words of his benefactor and protector, who is now speaking about the language of the Chamacoco which, Ladies and Gentlemen, to express negation uses the future, which belongs to the "nonindicative" mood. To say "he does not love," Frič explains, they say "he will love." This is not intended to affirm the certainty or the probability or the hope that something may happen later on—in the example cited, that the person may fall in love tomorrow—but merely to indicate an absence, a negation. Chamacoco, like Ayoreo, which is also part of the Zamuco family of languages, is a *tenseless* language, it has only one verb tense. On the other hand there are two fourth (and fifth) persons of the personal pronoun—*eyok*: we, if the we are few; *eyok-i-lo*: we, if the we are many. Many, so to speak, when you consider that the Chamacoco number about 1,600 all told.

Eyok . . . Cherwuish's slanting, darting eyes, over-prominent cheekbones, glance around uneasily, like cornered birds. *Olak-i-lo*, you many, the seated crowd watching him. There must be at most about twenty people, but he doesn't count them, he just knows that there are many of them; when many are together it is to go hunting or off to war and though those people don't seem like either hunters or warriors, if they are clapping their hands it is to incite some prey. Indeed they crowd around his friend Frič, they grab his hands, they clutch at him. The first time it happened Cherwuish jumped into their midst and knocked two or three to the ground. Now he knows that it is a way of paying tribute to his friend, but all the same he doesn't like it, there might always be an ambush; even the Tumraha once pretended to come to celebrate, bearing gifts, and instead they pulled out their axes, in any case he's watchful. The next time he'll paint his face blue, a blue that's almost turquoise. His people paint themselves to show whether they are happy or sad or angry; he'll put on the color of peaceful serenity, so they won't be on guard. He knows how to fight, *t-a-tskir*. He will love, Frič continues meanwhile, that is, he does not love. The future is a great *not* prefixed to every word, to every thing; it is what is not, nothing.

The future of Cherwuish's people, Frič knows, is also not-being, negation. The Old World discovered the New World to destroy it. Sixty years after the Europeans' arrival in the Americas, of the 80 million Indians only ten remained. And the Indians continue to die off even now, like the Chamacoco. They were dying like flies when I was there looking for plants, and no one knew anything about it.

Maybe I can save my Cherwuish, that's why I brought him back with me. Moreover he knows that the young Dr. Wedlin, who studied in Vienna, understood what it was. Maybe when they bring him back there all the others will be dead. One out of 1,600 would be a good result, in any case, when you're fighting your old friend *Hein*, as the Germans call Death. Or the Comare Secca, the bony hag, as Boggiani would have said, the only one who may have known even more about the Chamacoco than I do, and who encountered the old crone while he was dallying—at the very marsh of the Chaco River where he would end up forever, having become himself a marsh— with another woman, much younger, plumper, rosy-skinned and less clothed; under those circumstances, you don't think that the woman may be a precursor of the Comare. They rolled around in the mud and some Indian didn't like it, so he, the great explorer and photographer, dapper even in the jungle, was hacked to pieces before finding the famous bearded Indians of the forest, who never existed but whom he would certainly have photographed. He became dirt and mud and worms. Like everyone else for that matter.

"It's not as if these Chamacoco of yours were all that strange and exotic, my dear Frič"—Anastasius Taussig, clerk of the court, applauds him at the end of the talk. "Even without bringing in the Huzuli of Galicia or the Bodoli of the Quarnero—the Bodoli even sing the *Gott erhalte*, I heard them when I brought some documents to the court of Veglia, Krk, whichever you prefer, but anyway documents having to do with the Hungarians, not our business—and they are more loyal to our *proházka*, our emperor, God save him, than the Viennese, not to mention the Tyroleans and all those Germans of Austria who are the least Austrian of the entire empire. I mean, does it seem to you that our Polacken, with their violins and hora, are that much less strange than your little worm? Than your Červiček, I mean, as that other bosom buddy of yours, Jindřich Mošna, called him, a writer himself, and how could he not be, who isn't a writer in Prague . . . Yes, my dear Frič, Červiček may pull through a little, with those pills of his, though there's no guarantee, poor little worm; the dampness rising up from the Vltava is more mephitic than that of his Pilcomayo, many more corpses have polluted it for centuries without any caimans making them quickly disappear for the benefit of everyone's wellbeing. We're used to it; indeed, the damp air of all that death is good for us, our lungs would no longer be able to breathe a dry, pure wind, they'd puff and burst like bellows. However, better the chants that Červiček intones along the streets of Malá Strana, swaying in his colorful blanket, than the *Wacht am Rhein* sung by certain students whose faces are more scarred than Červiček's. Those idiots who think they are Germans and want Germany *über Alles* are fond of slashing each other with sabers; as you see, the world is the same wherever you go, apparently a scar on your face, whether from a saber or an ax, is fine with everyone today . . ."

It seems that Cherwuish actually did raise that ax against someone, twice. Against the gendarmes, when they put their hands on him, thinking he was making fun of them by bowing to their plumed caps, which among the Chamacoco are worn only by chiefs and witch doctors. Even without the ax, which one of them had wrested from him, he had decked three of them in that steep narrow alley in Malá Strana, where it was difficult for them to jump him all together, before they were able to shackle him and take him to the station house, from which Frič had had a hard time getting him released, telling them the whole story and, while he was at it, going on at great length about the Chamacoco's customs, their religious feasts, about how the women are fierce fighters but are not allowed to eat the venison reserved for the men, that they even eat certain large river fish, putting them in their mouths sideways while still alive and breaking their spines with their teeth. He even tried to pay the fine for the brawl in kind, that is by offering a couple of books he had written about the Indians and snakes of Mato Grosso, until the commander, who was sick and tired of all those stories he didn't understand anything about, but who regarded Cherwuish kindly because at least he wasn't a gypsy, threw them both out and they sadly returned home to Via Náplavní, to sleep among the crates and stuffed puma and red wolf heads Frič had accumulated, with Cherwuish continuing to chant *Polizei tupurumba*, a word that the refined Frič always refused to translate.

With Vlado Šmolka—the guy who earned a few bucks doing silhouettes of people at the Tumovka café—the matter was a bit more serious. Ten krejcary, Vlado asked for each silhouette, but when Cherwuish came in, having come to love the bitter water, as he called Staropramen, the Šmíchov beer, queen of Prague, he didn't ask for anything, in fact he paid for his beer so that he would pose for him. Cherwuish sits down, he knows that his portrait is being done and he's proud of it; in fact Král—the famous painter Král himself, the one from the Louvre café—had done one of him a short time ago and he recognized himself in the bark-colored face, in the long mop of hair covering more of him than the colorful blanket with the symmetrical stripes, in the eyes, startled and threatening, staring at something unknown.

But when Vlado, after a few minutes, shows him the silhouette, he doesn't recognize himself in that profile, he's never seen himself in profile; that bumpy forehead, the nose that starts out aquiline and broadens into a blunt end, aren't his face. They are the mask of a demon, an underworld god Anabson rising from the waters of the Pilcomayo to take revenge on the Chamacoco. Where is his face? He wants it back; if someone appropriates another man's face he enslaves him, he can destroy him. I good model, he shouts out in Czech, he's learned a few words; then he yells in Chamacoco, rushes at Vlado, knocks him to the ground and searches him, looking for his face, the face that the waters of the Paraguay, the Pilcomayo and even the Vltava, which he can see from the Charles Bridge when he goes to look at the stone Bearded Man, never took from him or disfigured, even though they flow away, because his face is always there, in the water that he looks into, a flattened moon that looks back at him with his own eyes. The moon is a friend of the Chamacoco, not like the wicked sun that parches and withers, but now he doesn't see the moon; he can't find his moon—his face—and he raises his ax against Vlado to make him produce it.

Others jump on him amid overturned chairs, they can't take him down because he's whirling the ax, but they are able to shove him out; with a stroke of the ax he slashes the sheet with the silhouette that someone is holding, but when he's tossed out through the revolving door, for an instant he again glimpses—in the glass in front of him a moment ago and now beside him—that other sharp, cruel face gliding away confusedly. So they managed to hex him, to put another head on his neck, the one reflected in the hateful glass, the head of an evil spirit. He flies into a rage but can't break that image, which has already vanished along with the glass as the door goes on revolving like a whirlpool in a river, though more slowly; he is between two glass walls, finally those pushing the door from behind eject him out onto the street.

He stumbles to the ground but gets up, runs off quickly, a guanaco disappearing among the narrow passages of the old imperial city. Before heading for home, he runs to the river and he is happy, the flowing water reflecting his face does not carry it away from him, his real face, broad and earthy and dark, Šakuruku, a virtuous nocturnal moon. I good model. This time it is Bohumil Kafka, the sculptor who helped Frič furnish his house with chests and hammocks, who pays for the damage to the Tumovka café and mollifies Šmolka by bringing him a couple of foreigners more than happy to have their silhouette done by him.

Cherwuish, leaning against a lamppost on Chotkova Street, stares at the wall. The large open door in the facade of the old flaking building is dark, the mouth of a river emerging from the earth's murky bowels beneath trees that bend over it; a gilded angel projects from the frieze of a cornice. A streetlamp comes on in the dusk, the light reflects the branches of the dark forest. Some enter that mouth, others come out, dancers appear in the circle of light, step back into the night, passersby turn the corner. The forest is also full of traps; the trunk underfoot is a mouth that opens to reveal large fangs and a spotted shadow sinks its claws into your back, but they never leave you alone in the forest. There are always so many creatures around, eyes in the darkness, the flutter of mosquito wings on the skin. Everything is alive; it devours but it's alive. That's why there are masks, dances, magic words, to keep the claws of things good. But here everything is stony. Dead. Not death that happens, that pounces, that lives. Dead stone, uninterred body. The wall is tattooed with cracks, sneers and grimaces, the plaster flakes off like the cheek of a leper; maybe the wall too has the same ailment that gnaws his bowels.

Cherwuish looks at his arms, the skin blotchy and dry; he feels his stomach contract and crouches behind a small statue of a woman in a blue mantle, her hands joined, in a niche along the street. It's not allowed, you shouldn't, it's forbidden, he knows it but he can't hold it, besides others who are not Chamacoco occasionally do it too, he's seen them. Two or three passersby look at him, someone says something, there, the plume of a gendarme appears from around the corner. He doesn't want them to put those iron bracelets on him again, like they do when he chases the chimney sweeps on the rooftops—black, covered in black soot, like the Anabson demons—and take him to that big gloomy house which you can't get out of by jumping from the window, like he always does from the house where he lives with Frič. He starts to run, not bothering to turn around to see if anyone is behind him. He runs, he doesn't know how far. Still running, he looks up, above him there is a window; he clambers up the wall in which time and bad weather have carved out good handholds, reaches the window, breaks it, but the room is empty and closed, with no doors, at least he doesn't see any, so he turns back, jumps down, it's easy, the trees along the Pilcomayo are much taller. Down below are only some kids with something that looks like a mango peel on their heads; they're shouting laughing repeating a word he doesn't understand, something like *oyila*. Maybe they've mistaken him for a woman, for one of those slaves who have to collect water in an *olla* and who, when there's no more water, are then killed, but it can't be, he's not a woman, maybe it's his long hair that makes them think he's a woman or maybe he doesn't understand that word, *oyila*, *oyile*, *oyilen*, anyway he runs off as fast as he can.

A pack of small dogs, ferocious and playful, press around him, not too close but still dangerously so. Not jaguars, only cats and kittens, but they too scratch and he doesn't know what to do, because if they were a puma or one of those great big Tumraha chiefs with feathers on his head he'd slam them against the wall, but with cubs you can't, you mustn't, you have to protect them even if they don't deserve it and are more evil than their fathers, they scramble between his legs like mice and he, killer of pumas and caimans, is a little afraid. Golem, there he is, golem they shout, laughing, let's get the golem, kill the golem, let's take his magic word. One of them puts a hand on Cherwuish's forehead scratching at it as if to rip off something he doesn't understand—life, perhaps, that throbs in all creatures, maybe even in figures of clay or iron or cloth that appear dead. He drives them off and flees, the small voracious pack at his heels, while an old man, he too with a peel on his head and curls almost as long as Cherwuish's, says something in a language even stranger than the one that Frič speaks, though it's clear he's scolding those boys; he too repeats that word, golem, and Cherwuish senses that the word is about him, maybe in that language it means Chamacoco. Nevertheless he keeps running, turning the corner he ducks into a blind alley and hides; the kids pass him by and, running and shouting, scatter.

It must have been Karel Krejčić who fabricated the story about Cherwuish meeting Jizchak Löwy and other actors from the itinerant Yiddish theater at the Café Savoy. He—Karel—made a living writing for the *Girotondo-giramondo*, a newspaper in Brno, sketches of trips to distant countries, trips he never made, apparently he never even went to Slovakia; when he said he was leaving for Italy or Morocco, he simply didn't show up around town, he stayed home. At an aunt's house. He had never married. As it is living alone is too much, he said, let alone as a couple; after a while it's like being children of incest, only the recessive traits add up and you become idiots, spiritually goitrous hypothyroids or frenetic hyperthyroids.

And why, after all, should he have had to leave Prague, to describe the world? Here in Prague there's everything, the world and even something more, too much more. He would read about Italy or Morocco and then scribble something Neapolitanizing or Moroccanizing the clever quips of Woskovec and Werich or the Madonna of Loreto with her long mantle, Baby Jesus in her arms, who in his account became a Santa Carmela for the occasion, dwelling in a little chapel in Pozzuoli—he liked to pronounce that name, especially the second syllable, uòl, pursing and protruding his lips like a chicken's behind. The opulently ornate monstrance, the glory of Prague weighing over twelve kilograms with its 6,222 diamonds from the legacy of Ludmilla Eva Franziska von Kolowrat, had given him the idea of placing a diadem on Santa Carmela's head, no, a coronet with a couple of small diamonds, which, however, he said, were of unpolished though glittering glass, since the real diamonds, he declared, had been stolen by a painter whom the nuns called in to apply a coat of whitewash when damp patches caused by broken pipes appeared on the walls inside the church. Or else he would retouch some incident that had happened in Vinohrady, for example, the story of the pickpockets, which he set in a Café di Place Clichy instead, not far from the cemetery of Montmartre. As the years went by, he didn't even stay at his aunt's house; he went to Šmichov's and between one beer and another wrote the article about crossing the Atlantic and sent it directly to Brno, maybe after reading a few pages aloud to the others, all a bit tipsy. Who knows if Frič too, he implied . . . all those Indian stories of his, his Indian uncle and the island with the snakes . . . Who knows where he got those tales, if it was he who came up with them . . .

But that was later, after Červiček had already gone—in 1909, to be exact; it was in 1909 that Frič brought him back to his Chamacoco, healed and ready to be killed shortly afterward, and not by duodenal worms. So the story about the Café Savoy is hogwash, like the one about Buffalo Bill coming to Prague with his circus, though he never did, and the only reason the rumor keeps circulating so insistently is because, through continual denials of that cock-and-bull story, the lie spread until it became true or was believed to be true by so many people. It makes little difference, because the rumor keeps going around, in short, a legend was born.

So then Frič brings Cherwuish to the Café Savoy. He looks around, the chairs are in the dark or almost, only in back is there a lit clearing and behind the clearing an even darker forest, from which people appear every so often making a racket, sometimes only one sometimes as many as three or four, then disappear again in the depths of the dark forest. When the two of them enter, men dressed in long ankle-length coats are already in the clearing, leaping about here and there, beneath a dark firmament. There the sky is still *port nántik*, the primordial blackish sky of the Chamacoco where there were not yet stars, there was not yet the *yetït carhï*, the starry sky. The great sea that Cherwuish crossed with Frič has therefore brought him further back in time than when he lived among his people; it has taken him back to the epoch when there were no gods either—or demons, it's all the same—Anabson of the Gran Chaco.

Maybe that circular clearing, where those creatures are getting all worked up, is a portent, a sign of the yellow sky that is about to sweep over the world. That's why those people are so happy, leaping, dancing, laughing. But they're not laughing at him, he quickly realizes. It's the first time, since he crossed the great sea, that no one is laughing at him, looking at him as peculiar. On the contrary, they're not looking at him at all; they don't give a hoot about him or all the others sitting next to him in the dark, who by contrast are looking at them. Until now, in this world to which his friend brought him, only dogs, cats and river gulls haven't been taken aback by him, haven't pointed a finger at him as if he were a god or a beast, anyway not one of them. To tell the truth, children don't pay all that much attention to him either; sometimes they do, a little, but a cat or a ball soon distracts them. The jaguar who, in the forest, leaped on his friend now seated beside him wasn't surprised that he was different from the tapirs or anteaters for whom he lay in wait. He leaped on Frič to eat him, as usual; if then it didn't go well, so much the worse, it happens, not even that would surprise the jaguar. Those figures over there, with their leaping, don't pay any attention to him because they know that he is one of them, everyone is one of them, everybody is part of everybody, when it comes to loving each other, eating each other, fighting, playing, and no one is a stranger anywhere. The men with the long coats leap and dance and sing repetitive chants like those of the Chamacoco, then they laugh. Sometimes the forest where he's sitting is full of people laughing and clapping their hands. And sometimes there is almost no one, but those guys who are talking, singing, leaping and dancing don't care; it's obvious, children don't care either whether anyone is watching them or not when they're playing, they simply play, and the Chamacoco, when they dance to entreat Illa to rise up—the North Wind that aided the great Anabson Nemur—have no one to watch them in the darkness of the forest and don't feel the need for anyone to watch and approve of them.

Here everyone does everything together. The two in the long coats clap their hands and leap on the walls; once the one who seems to be the leader, and often comes to sit beside his friend Frič and drink beer after beer with him, unintentionally yanks down a big dark curtain that falls on him, then you can see that there is no dark forest behind him, just a jumbled mess of things, chairs, chests, fabrics, worse than the clutter amid his friend's hammocks, and next to him the others are watching, some try to raise the curtain that looks like the deep dark black of a forest, others jump on those who earlier were singing and dancing and throw them out of that dark space but they come back in as if nothing has happened and begin singing again or talking loudly, waving their arms, one of them pulls out a knife or something like it from his coat and plunges it into the back of another one who screams and seems to fall but doesn't fall, he's all bent backward as if he were falling but without falling, he talks and talks and talks and some close to him weep and others, a little further away, that is, here, beside him, beside him Červiček, laugh, and the man finally falls but then he gets up and disappears into the forest. He tries to do it without anyone seeing him, right away you can tell. Cherwuish knows all too well how the fox flees unnoticed, taking cover, a slight rustling of tall grasses that might be stirred by a breath of wind, that fellow too would succeed, he's sprightly and nimble as a deer even though he has a big belly, but earlier, when they put that dense forest back up, well, that fallen curtain, they made a great big slash, a nice luminous hole through which you can see everything, even the dead man sneaking away, it's not all that strange after all, the dead are never still, they roam through forests and curtains, sometimes you see them and sometimes you don't.

Now they're singing and dancing and laughing there in the middle, but not about him, Cherwuish, like the people on the street many times. They're not laughing at anyone in particular, but at everyone and everything, even themselves, so they can also laugh at him, he isn't offended, children laugh too, but well-meaningly, delightedly. Someone shouts out, they all shout, the one drinking a huge tankard of beer shouts something and his friend repeats *Hupp Cossack!* as those standing around dance even more wildly, chasing one of the men, it's a hunt, that's the way the Chamacoco hunt Piti̇́nno, the anteater bear. *Hupp Cossack! Hupp Cossack!* and then Červiček joins the fray, it's not fair, so many against one, even with animals one fights according to the rules, like his friend with the jaguar. He snatches a spear from one of them, a knife from another, he even knocks someone to the ground and ends up on the ground as well, and everyone laughs but contentedly, happily, like friends, even the bear laughs, then the big man carrying the tankard of beer around gets into it too and grabs one of the hunters by the coat, turns his pockets inside out and collects a fistful of coins, the Chamacoco don't have coins and that's why they don't swindle anyone.

The bear, exhausted, sits down and takes off his fur coat, the hunters sit down next to him, almost all of them, two or three remain in the lit clearing and now more arrive, there is also a woman, they're holding a belt, one end in her hand and the other held by a man, it must be a wedding ceremony, very similar to that of the Chamacoco. It's logical, given that marriage is the same all over and no matter where you go, you end up doing the same things that men, women, gods and even the animals in the forest like so much.

Červiček, excited, jumps back into things again; he's happy about the dust, the smell of sweaty armpits, the bare feet. Bodies have a good smell, it doesn't matter much whether you rub them with scented guaiacum powder or papyrus oil or *uruciú* red or nothing at all, skin and life and leaping around are all it takes to give off the strong, intoxicating smell of a damp forest. The woman is beautiful, two papayas spill out from a white shirt which is held closed by a button, one of those buttons that he is so good at filching from people's clothing without them noticing, but the pale face with its prominent cheekbones and pronounced lips could be the moon so propitious to the Chamacoco, a moon not quite full due to the dark hat concealing her hair. Women here are not allowed to show their hair, how ridiculous, but during the dance, at a certain point, the hat falls off and nobody cares, her long loose hair tumbles over her cheeks and down her neck, a light mist obscures part of the moon, between the veiled cheeks the prominent mouth is an ardent, eager smile, even Cherwuish grabs the belt and circles round and round.

Far from what was written by the learned professor, whom Karel sneers at proclaiming: "Dramatic encounter-clash between different cultures, the man—who? Červiček? or any Praguer who sees him on the street?—loses his identity and his place in life because elements and values which are foreign to him are introduced into his worldview." Who is foreign to whom? Each of us to each of us, of course, that's life, what can you do, it's not as if we invented it, but this also holds true for two people who were both born on Via Židovská and attended the same *cheder*, or two people who were married in the cathedral of San Vito or in Town Hall, it depends, each of us has his own witch doctor whom he prefers when he needs a benediction.

Among the people dancing, one of them—he must be the tribe's medicine man—has placed a bottle on his head, the others do the same as they go on dancing, crouching nearly to the ground and kicking out their legs. The bottles fall with a clatter, each shattering amid the applause and drawn out singing of the one who was just balancing it. Červiček feels as if he is among the Chamacoco. There is only a small commotion when he sticks his hand into the dancer's neckline and deftly undoes the button. This too is a fabrication on the part of Karel, who was well aware of Cherwuish's mania for collecting buttons, deftly removing them with a knife or with his hands. There is the famous incident with the general, in fact, from whose full dress uniform he had snatched a gold button without him even noticing, and it's true that misunderstandings sometimes arose when he went to rip the buttons off a woman's blouse or skirt. In any case not with the lady of that evening, the famous Tschissik, because she, according to Karel, had taken it off herself, giving it to Cherwuish. Regardless ...

Over there, they say, across the great sea, in the forests to which Cherwuish returned, there is war. One of many. Bolivian Junkers and Paraguayan Potez 25s wheel and drop bombs at random on who knows who, many or no one. They discharge them on the tropical araucarias the soldiers crouch among, hitting or missing, bushes and ridges in flames. Bolivia and Paraguay are battling for a piece of land, of jungle, including the jaguars the Chamacoco the Tumanà and the Caduvei condemned to die for being Bolivian or Paraguayan without knowing what it means, but beneath the jungle there is oil, the black sea of the Anabson. Everyone naked sweaty and equal under the bombs, soldiers and Indians and women who are lactating or giving birth under the rain of fire. Swarms of *osáseŕo*, the birds of rain, swoop down on the scrub, now they are a cloud, *täniyo*, dark clouds stream through the lowering sky, the cloud's darkness is ripped open and huge white teeth sink into anyone around, pulverizing them. It is always difficult to distinguish one blood from another, blood flowing out of a severed limb from that which supplies the placenta, let alone that of a Bolivian from that of a Paraguayan, that of a Chamacoco from that of a Caduveo, that of Cherwuish, if by chance he's there, from that of another, he himself doesn't know when he breaks away from an enemy who slumps to the ground and sees it running down his own body. Bombs fall, hordes of green flies swoop down on the bodies, living and dead; they enter nostrils, open wounds, cause a few drops of blood to well up even from the dead; what do the flies know about their victims, whether they are dead or alive, white or mestizo or Indian. Perhaps Cherwuish died in that rain of fire, it's impossible to know where a worm dies in the duodenum and where another worm dies in the jungle and who dies. He doesn't even know himself and maybe he didn't realize he'd died, in that deluge of fire you don't see the flame that has already consumed you.

The gun barrel is scorching in the hands of the Chamacoco who squeezes and shoots because they told him to shoot, the sharp thorns of prickly pear and *guaimipirés* jab his skin, but he doesn't feel it; who's fighting against whom, killing and dying for what?

Ragged banners flap in the wind, one with red-yellow-green stripes advances, other stripes flash in the gunfire's smoke, red-white-blue stripes. *Yakaveré* dive from the sky, sink their claws into flesh, the smell of blood or *guayacán*, blood gushing from nose and mouth, Fort Boquerón has fallen and must be recaptured, win for Paraguay die for Paraguay shouts the white *cacique*, the Paraguay is a river and the ancient *cacique* who are spoken about, like the legendary *pelota* Basebüġü, a connoisseur of ancient words, never said anything about making sacrifices for the Rio Paraguay. The red-yellow-green jackets passed over many of our dead bodies but the red-white-blue ones, which the government made us wear, often passed over our dead bodies as well, there or someplace else. The Anabson want to kill us, they are all Anabson, you can recognize them by the *di'ora*, the crooked ankles, their only vulnerable spot, though by walking and walking through the forest with your feet pointed inward to avoid the thorns and poisonous insects, everybody's ankles, those of the Chamacoco, of the Caduvei, of the Tumraha, my own, are crooked. It is the end of the Chamacoco, the end of the world; every Chamacoco becomes an Anabson before dying. Men, if they were to remain men, would be immortal, but death is clever, it convinces them that being Anabson, being demons, means more than being men, so they become demons, who pretend to be lords of death but are its slaves.

Čurbit, the great *cacique*, got together with General Belaieff to attack Fortin Bogado, the swampy wasteland that no one must cross because beyond it lies the end of everything, the swamp of death. Cïrï—the great forebear, the Father who generated all the Chamacoco by entering the womb that gave birth to him as well, the womb of Eśnuwarta, the Great Mother of the World and of all people—

announces the end, the breach of that belly in which everything was contained. Sky sun moon stars and forests burst and disintegrate along with the jaguar that mates with our women, *äku*, even the great Mother mates with the *osásefo*, the birds of rain.

Fort Boquerón falls, it has fallen. Flashes of fire, sun in the veins, Deí-ć, Sun, the enemy of the Chamacoco. If instead there were the good moon—pallid Śakuruku, cool pallor. Better yet no moon at all, at one time we were afraid and we danced and screamed when the moon vanished, swallowed up by the dark night—oh if only everything were now dark like at the beginning of the world, like when I was in there, in those dark, gentle waters and all the world was in there in the waters of Eśnuwarta. The Watirak, the initiate, paints himself with red, from the *uruciú*—I am all red, Watirak red with blood, it is time. Hot, fiery blood; it makes you thirsty, in the forest you even drink blood to quench your thirst, throat aflame, water, there is no more water.

There are no more Chamacoco there are no more Tumraha, everyone against everyone, *eyok-i-lo* against *eyok*, we many against we few, against me. Rain of Fire, Pïtínno eats the entire anthill, the Great Mother exterminates the world, *lata touxa laabo*, she calls her children, all her children, myself a child as well, enter a cavernous mouth. Big teeth a big cactus in the mouth of Tölörïtï the thorns prick his palate—he's hungry for anything, even cactus, even me. Thorns, spears in my chest and in my mouth, a great thunder in my head, so many yellow stars in my head, the stars explode. A huge fire, a big red rose bursts in the blackish sky, in that big city across the great sea they too often made many huge fires in the sky. Flowers gardens arrows spread out in the sky like the ripples of a stone in the water, then the red goes out, there is only black sky.

19

Room no. 7—A 7.5-cm PaK 40, Panzerabwehrkanone, just right for that room. Antitank gun used by the German Army during the Second World War, designed in 1939, built by Rheinmetall-Börsig, ready to confront the Soviet tank T-34 in 1940. Used as weaponry on the Jagdpanzer and Sturmgeschütz. Weight 1.5 tons, barrel length 3.7 meters (a long, obscene nose that seems to shoot forward like a bullet); weight of the bullet itself 6.8 kg, maximum range 7,680 meters, firing angle 45; steel gun carriage with a split double tail and rear trunnions, gunners protected by a small, sheet-steel shield. Good penetration capacity of the bullets even at a considerable distance (drilling 70 mm of steel at 2,000 meters), but reduced tactical mobility due to the considerable weight; good range but tight trajectory, only able to overcome low obstacles; has hit numerous tanks, but the low wheels and disadvantages of the gun carriage along with the substantial weight often caused it to get bogged down on the Eastern Front and be captured by the Red Army, which redeployed it against the German Army.

A spotlight continually projects a page from his notebook no. 15 on the wall. Calligraphy slightly leaning to the left, spiky, generally legible. The letters scroll past in red, vanish, reappear. He had a mania for recopying everything by hand, Luisa thought, even his notes, hardly ever resorting to photocopies.

"The 7.5-cm PaK 40 against the T-34, tyrannosauruses against brontosauruses, crocodiles against hippopotamuses at the mouth of the Zambezi, surging and spewing of gory mud, the Indian elephants of Antiochus of Syria lock fangs with the African elephants of

Ptolemy IV Philopator of Egypt, body against body until one gives in, moves to the side, but it's enough to expose his flank to the enemy's fangs that bore into him and run him through, pachyderms fleeing or on the ground, rolling around like boulders tumbling off a mountain. That time it was Antiochus's Asian elephants that routed Ptolemy's African ones, maybe because the gigantic ones from Kenya or the Ivory Coast did not enter the fray, probably they were too strong to submit to man, to kill and die for him. Emphasize how modern war looks more and more like those appalling prehistoric battles, flying fortresses and winged dragons, pterodactyls swooping down on allosaurs; armor-plated reptiles, ichthyosaurs in the swamps of the Upper Cretaceous, tanks in the jungle, giant bulldozers crushing buildings like dinosaurs in the movies, sea monsters in the unfathomable depths, hundreds of millions of years ago and today. Impossible, then and once again now, to sing 'Tapim tapim tapum' in the trenches as our fathers and grandfathers did.

"War has become human because it spares the individual, the foot-soldier of the Sassari Brigade, the Kaiserjäger, the marine, the partisan, the *hoplite* from being protagonists, perpetrators and therefore victims. Atomic weapons and toxic gases are not aimed at the single individual, they don't even know what that is. Just like earthquakes, volcanic eruptions, the tremors when the earth was still young; maybe still too young to give birth to man, a specific individual who believes he is destined to die. The others—the species, continents, forests, cities, glaciers—are shaken up, transformed, dispersed, relocated, monstrous, immortal mutants. An appalling heap of snakes that intertwine, mate and scatter en masse."

On a screen the image of a large jellyfish, individual organs illuminated in flashing light. Medusa *Physalia physalis* or Portuguese man o' war (Coelenterate or Cnidarian family). It looks like a single organism but is a collective of polyps, specializing in various functions: one procures food for the entire colony, another guards it, yet another provides the mechanism for its assimilation. Endowed with a gas-filled sac, regulated by the depth, and tentacles ranging from ten to fifty meters long, whose vesicles shoot prey with a barbed hook equipped with a siphon that injects a highly toxic poison. An extremely mobile underwater tank.

"Is the human 'I'—he continues, now from a screen—an individual or billions of cells recorded all together with the same name on a birth certificate? If he's no one or everyone, he cannot die. At what point do a few grains of rice scattered on the ground, a handful at a time, become a mound of rice? And when do a few million or billion cells become 'I'? The latter exists because many of its cells, so much of itself, continuously dies. Death is birth—priests say so too though they don't realize what they're saying. War therefore is the birth of humanity, the finger of God that scoops Adam out of the mud.

"Necessity, thanks to war. Just as at one time we tamed and utilized horses and elephants, in the future we will master volcanic craters and make them erupt on command, burying the enemy beneath oceans of fiery lava, or we will learn how to stir up the faults in the earth's bowels, to trigger earthquakes and tsunamis. Apocalypse within everyone's reach. This pitiable 7.5-cm PaK 40 was still clashing with a few poor devils shut up in a tank . . . And made quite a poor showing moreover against the T-34. Oh, if only I could get one, it would indeed be king of the Museum, the Tyrannosaurus rex, the progenitor of all tanks built after 1945, king of the steppes where it broke the Germans' backs. Unfortunately I have to settle for a photograph. Well, I will at least enlarge it . . ."

20

The enlarged photograph of the T-34, which shows it from the front, resembles an enormous pachyderm blocking the road to a vast plain behind it. Twenty-six tons. A 76.2-mm long gun, 40-caliber, capable of easily penetrating any armor of the German tanks on the assault in Operation Barbarossa, the invasion of the Soviet Union, and impervious to the latter's guns. A 12-cylinder diesel V engine that reduces the possibility of fire and allows for a speed of 55 kmh on the battlefield, previously unheard of for tanks. Very wide (55 cm) track belts—the mammoth legs of prehistoric giants—that make it possible to move in snow and mud without sinking. Prehistory of the future, man having become small again among mammoths built by his hands, increasingly rebellious and disobedient to the *cornac* who prods them, sitting on their head.

"Thanks to the providence of the machine that replaces man, saving him rather than destroying him as it does in countless silly tales. It is the T-34 that saves Great Mother Russia when the Nazis attack her in 1941 and find themselves facing an army with hardly any generals, shot by Stalin, an army militarily backward and confused, because the Kremlin dinosaur had banned the strategic principles brilliantly established by Marshal Tukhachevski, sending him to the firing squad for his brilliance and prohibiting the formation of the large armored tank units he'd called for, so that initially the Germans are able to slice through Russia like a blade through butter, overwhelming armies capturing cities and after each attack shooting one hundred hostages for every one of their men killed in ambush, until they come up against the solid yet mobile wall of the T-34 (53,000 models, throughout the war, fortified even further after the Battle of Kursk with 85-mm guns and tougher armor-plating). A Wall of China made of guns; huge elephants like towers of Babel on the chessboard, but swift, able to penetrate at lightning speed and cut the advancing enemy tanks off from the infantry following them, thereby isolating the German tanks, even the Tigers and Panthers, forcing them to come to a standstill and then firing and destroying the Führer's Blitzkrieg. In short, the T-34 seems to me to be the image of the great Russia, vulnerable and invincible, patient and regretful, the country in which the roads that lead to Moscow, for those who travel them to destroy her, pass through Poltava, through the Berezina, through Stalingrad . . . It's true, I often feel German, definitely more German than Slavic, especially in Trieste, but . . ."

21

Room no. 23—A shelf attached to the wall; books standing upright, leaning diagonally or horizontally, so as to display only the spine with the title. Inserted here and there among the books—clearly visible and illuminated, in some cases enlarged—cards of various colors with quotes in his handwriting, similar to the Card Soldiers in *Alice in Wonderland*.

Sun Tzu, *The Art of War*, 4th c. BC. "Be the director of your opponent's fate. Subdue him without fighting him. Troops must resemble water which falls from above and collects at the bottom—avoid what is strong and strike at what is weak." Added in his own hand: "Steel or water? When a river is swollen, dykes to contain it or conduits to channel it off?"

Flavio Vegezio, *Epitoma rei militaris* (late 4th c.). "Surprise attacks which cause severe losses to the enemy, and strike terror, but without risking the lives of one's own soldiers ..."

Raimondo Montecuccoli, *Treatise on War* (1641) and *On War in Hungary against the Turks* (1670). "The army must never fight all at once ..." A note in his own hand: "The first to understand the importance of commandos, of terrorist actions, the new Machiavelli. The 'Living Escurial,' as they called him, advisor to Napoleon but also to Norwegian partisans and to terrorists."

A shelf occupied by only two books, displayed with great prominence. Carl von Clausewitz, *On War* (1832–1837) and Mao Tse-tung, *On Guerrilla Warfare* (1936–1938). "Perhaps no one has understood, as the two of them have, that war is the totality, the closest connection between the particular and the universal; every soldier on the march and every guerrilla in the jungle waiting to open fire as organic parts of the Whole. Kultur, Tao. The Whole is the Void in life in which everything is contained. To understand war and therefore to win it you have to know everything that comes together in war, that is, everything, wages, television advertising, the statistical curve of marriages, divorces and rapes, family meals, tales told by your grandmother, the brotherhood that is formed only in war, the comrade beside you— more your brother than your father's and mother's children, for him you would do what you would never do for them, go back out under fire to drag him, wounded, back into the trench.

"Yes, death, of course—but fraternity in death, everyone equal in death and therefore all brothers." *Music begins to play in the room.* "*Cimitero di noi soldà / forse un giorno ti vengo a trovà / ta pum ta pum ta pum / ta pum ta pum ta pum . . .*"; "Cemetery of us soldiers / maybe someday I'll come visit you / pa rum pum pum pum / pa rum pum pum pum."

"Every death is a celebration of dialectics, Mao Tse-tung. Blossom that dies in the fruit, blossom that dying bears fruit. War, the fury of disappearance. Everything is eternal before the eyes of God— remember, Dr. Brooks? I'm sure you will read this page—love Him in me, for this instant . . . It is death that makes the instant a life, every instant is alive and eternal like the one that obliterates it—*ecce quam bonum et jucundum fratres laetare in Unum.* General Giáp pins down the French garrison and puts it out of action with frontal attacks that break every strategic rule, a few years later he will bring down the greatest power that ever existed . . . War is democratic, egalitarian; it fells the great cedars of Lebanon standing tall and proud and convinced that they will do so forever . . . Lord God of armies or rather of the universe, as priests nowadays prefer to say. Total war, General Ludendorff would say, but only because life is totality. The fish eats the worm, the fisherman fishes the fish, acids dissolve the fat in the stomach of the one who ate the fish, the one who eats the fish will soon be like the worm. War is Kultur, Kultur dies and bears fruit in war."

Sir Basil Liddell Hart: "The study of war, considered as a branch of scientific knowledge, requires work methods that are followed in university, as well as the mindset that is inculcated there" (*The Ghost of Napoleon*, 1935).

"Philosophy of Tank Warfare" (Francesco Jacchini Luraghi Archives).

Gregor von Rezzori, *An Ermine at Cernopol* (1958). Metamorphosis of the image of war as beautiful. From the perfect, orderly rows of parades and marches to the chaotic bedlam of battle to the once again perfect, orderly rows of graves in cemeteries.

Stefano Jacomuzzi, *Waterloo: The Impossible Epic?* Manuscript, undated. Is battle chaos or geometry? The ranks and grades in *Les Misérables* or in Joseph Roth's *The Hundred Days*, death and carnage as orderly as uniforms. Everything holds. In *The Charterhouse of Parma*, as at Little Big Horn in Black Elk's account, you come upon a cottage unawares, stop to eat as enemies pass nearby on the attack or in flight. Thackeray, *Vanity Fair*: scraps of news reach the city confusedly from the front, the most recent ones surpassed by those lost along the way that report the opposite. At El Alamein, Ottavio Missoni, sent to repair a telephone in a bunker in the midst of the fighting, returns to the Italian lines, sees a tank: "Come on come on," the soldier on the turret shouts. "What are you speaking English for, douchebag," Ottavio says, not having seen the soldier's uniform. When the guy points a machine gun at him, he puts his hands up, "*mona mi*, I'm the idiot . . ."

It was certainly an unforgivable breach of professional conduct, Luisa knew, but, seized by a sudden surge of sympathy for him and the rage that tore at him, she couldn't help but improperly add at the bottom of the page, imitating his handwriting as best she could — a real forgery — a few words of Sun Tzu which he had noted but then erased, crossing them out with a stroke of his pen: "Don't praise victory. Don't love war."

They didn't see much of Aunt Nora and Uncle Giorgio—Gershom, when the time came to call the person going to the grave by his real name—Luisa's mother, Sara, had told her. Every so often a dinner, followed by an evening of *musizieren*; their two daughters, her cousins, played the violin quite well—oh, no *yidl mitn fidl* and other ghetto stuff, her uncle explained; mocking, poignant music in the face of life and death, of course, but *Dudel-Dudel* isn't for us, we aren't gypsies and at our home we play cultured classical music, like the gracious Trieste salons of one time. Sara couldn't play, in Salvore the violin and cello weren't really common, if anything it was the accordion; but she loved the music of those evenings, in fact she said that in that music there was all of life.

Even unrequited love, like my love for music, she once said. Yes, at the beginning, when she came to stay with us, she was sad, Aunt Nora had remembered, though much later, but there was so much life in that sadness, whereas afterward . . . In that music, Sara had added, lies the most profound law of life. Maybe even of love, Uncle Giorgio, love is everything that one doesn't have, that I don't have, in fact *l'amour c'est tout ce que l'on n'a pas*, the mademoiselle who gives me French lessons had me read it in a book. Her aunt and uncle had seen to the French as well, in accordance with tradition, without however neglecting the fräulein's German lessons, of course, everyone in the family had always known German perfectly and certainly no Hitler would make them change their traditions, preferences and customs. The music that Sara would never be able to play expressed the very essence of life, or rather, it told her that life, in a future that quivered and wavered like a glimmering sea, would never really be her life and that for her living would mean having that absence echo inside her.

Nevertheless, apart from the *musizieren*, the girls, she and her cousins, also liked doing more enjoyable, fun things, going out with friends, meeting people, dancing, an activity that is possible and pleasurable even for those who can't play the music of that dance. But when Mrs. Preston—the wife of Major Preston, an American officer in the Allied Military Government, which since the end of the war administered the Free Territory of Trieste reclaimed by the Mother Country, toward which Marshal Tito reached out greedy hands that Italian newspaper cartoons depicted as feet with filthy, stubby toes—had invited them to a soiree at her villa in Scorcola, her aunt and uncle had thanked her but declined, perhaps because they had no desire to see certain other guests who had likely attended other soirees and frequented officers of other armies a few years earlier. The cousins, however, with a kind of good-natured, filial bullying, had obtained permission from their parents to accept the invitation of the charming, ebullient lady and began occasionally visiting the beautiful villas overlooking the sea, with waiters in white jackets, the pleasant hum of confused words on the terrace and the clinking of glasses carried along on the breeze, and sometimes, for the younger people, a turn on the dance floor. Not that they were anything special, those evenings, but a violet glow lit up the sea that could be seen from the terraces and a wind arose which, Sara felt, must have swept through Salvore.

There is no talk of war, on those evenings. Not about the one that was over, if one might say that. A few words about the ones in Africa or in Asia, which are distant and have nothing to do with either the Germans or the Italians or the Slavs. They have to do with the communists, who are everywhere, all over the world. A bit of politics, especially local, given that the guests are, more or less, those who count in the city; the Free Territory, Tito's claims, the wounds of the mutilated city. But there are no hotheads on that terrace. Not on the terrace of Colonel Lerch's villa either, sometime later, a beautiful villa that the colonel has rented for a few years on the Karst, because Trieste has lingered in his heart and he feels a sincere brotherhood-in-arms for those officers who are now allies, even though until recently they were enemies. All it takes is a few years, very few, and it no longer matters whether that trench was defended or captured; with valor and courage, in any case, by one side or the other. Who is this Lerch, Sara had asked her aunt and uncle, wondering too why she found the well-mannered gentleman vaguely repellent, with his ordinary face and his harsh, vile lips. An Austrian, her uncle had replied, without looking up from his newspaper, the president of the Tradesmen Association of Klagenfurt, where he also has a nice café. And he'd changed the subject.

No, Lerch hadn't been the cause of the migraines either. Not even when Sara, suddenly eager to know—she didn't yet know what, a bloodhound sniffing a scent that's confusing but irresistible and that insists on being followed—had begun asking who that man was, that president of the tradesmen, whom Major Preston along with other American and British officers called colonel. I hoped she would drop it, Uncle Giorgio would later say, but . . . Not that anyone really wanted to talk about it. On the contrary. Not even her aunt and uncle. Until Sami Goldfaden, the tailor who had escaped the Risiera with his life—and, unlike other survivors apparently, with a willing tongue and a desire to talk—had opened up. Colonel Ernst Lerch, chief of staff to Globočnik, the Höherer SS und Polizeiführer for the Adriatic Coast and topmost executioner at the Risiera, responsible for sending the Risiera's inmates to the small local gas chamber or extermination camps in Germany, or eliminating them personally. SS-Hauptsturmführer Lerch, once in charge of the slaughterhouse and now a host and hosted guest partaking in *la dolce vita* of Trieste. Nothing special, modest and inconsequential, but still a provincial *dolce vita*, in a provincial city cut off by an Iron Curtain and trying to amuse itself while waiting for the curtain to rise or not rise, fortunately one is on the right side of the theater after all, sitting on plush armchairs in front of the lowered curtain, chatting, exchanging greetings, hailing acquaintances, just like at a performance; *complimenti*, my respects, some elderly gentlemen still bow ceremoniously by way of greeting, in keeping with the Triestine custom of one time.

No, it had not been those handshakes and pleasantries between the assassin and those other decent people that at times caused the vein below Sara's temple to suddenly swell. The discovery that those beautiful, lit terraces were the other face of the Risiera—the formal parlor, the official face, for the Risiera as for all slaughterhouses—hadn't caused her to vomit; her stomach had not reacted to evil with waves of peristaltic contractions that, like facile tears, are common to souls too delicate to see and touch evil, to scour the bloody excrement that rises on all sides, if necessary even with their nails. Too easy, vomiting; however it is also easy to avert, pills to prevent motion sickness are also effective against nausea caused by sensitive consciences. She had spat when she'd learned that a sadistic, dull-witted butcher, an imbecilic bureaucrat of assassination, was a respectable person, well-accepted by decent people who wouldn't hurt a fly—let's say, to be on the safe side, that they have never hurt a fly, because it remains to be seen what they'd do if they were in a situation where it is normal to spread insecticides, and not only on flies.

She'd spat; a robust glob of spit full of saliva, which not everyone would be capable of at certain times. No forced contraction rising from a cramped, acidic stomach but a harsh, juicy, intentional and conscious spit—at that moment on the floor, on some tiles which mirrored faces belonging to the feet that were dancing on them. Good thing there was death and all those well-groomed, smiling faces would disappear as well, flesh rotting underground, no more lasting than smoke dissolving in air. Of course, it wasn't fair that victims, executioners and well-bred neutral parties should all end up as the same fertilizer, quickly amalgamated and no longer distinguishable; this utter equality was horrific, it was false, men are not equal, an individual who rips off a prisoner's genitals is not equal to the prisoner from whom they are torn, and if those who torture are also made in the image and likeness of God, I'm sorry for my ancestors, but Abraham was wrong to smash his father's nice wooden idols that weren't hurting anyone, to be in league with the Lord only because He was a more powerful, tyrannical Father.

Sara had felt strangely free, after that atrocious discovery. Wildly free, in absolute nonbelonging; she did not belong to anyone or anything, only to the glimmer of the waves on the rocks at Salvore and to that little pile of scattered ashes that, now and eternally, forever and ever, was her mother. Her roots were in that nothingness, in the nothingness of the blue of shimmering water impaled by a ray of sunshine, and a fine dust that doesn't exist, as though it had never been, in the air that changes color as the hours pass. There was certainly something painful in that giddy freedom, set apart from everything and everyone; the gash of a scream streaking the empty air, of a wing slicing through it and plummeting headlong—oh if only one could be freer still, more empty more dazzled by that fiery blue, the heart scorched and charred until it is a handful of embers soon volatized, thoughts in the cranium only mollusks in the canal of a conch, protected from predators. One would suffer less, in that empty, giddy freedom in which one is not yet anyone, only a grain of life as yet unconscious.

For Sara the pain, the real pain had come later, out of the blue— but was that the right name for the boulder that suddenly broke loose from the mountain and came crashing down on her, a meteorite fallen from the sky, boring into the earth and destroying not the poor dinosaurs, but far tougher creatures, with a bigger, heavier brain than that of the giant, bygone reptiles? The boulder that suddenly dropped on her makes her head even more disastrously heavy, a weight that throws her off balance, makes her fall this way and that.

The happiness that came from having spat when she discovered that murderers don't make decent people uncomfortable as long as they are able to behave well, like them, was brief. It had ended when Sara managed to locate Ester, a second cousin and childhood friend, whom she had not seen since she'd returned from Salvore; all she knew was that Ester's parents, Dr. Simeoni and his wife, Gabriella, along with her older brother, Ettore, had died in the Risiera, after being arrested suddenly in a house where they'd been hiding and where—as Sara had learned, though almost by accident, the tone with which her aunt and uncle had mentioned it had been particularly hasty—Sara's mother, grandmother Deborah, had also been hiding until one day, reckless and imprudent as she was, Deborah went out and was arrested in the street, apparently pointed out to the Germans by some miserable individual who had recognized her.

The house in which the Simeoni family had been hiding and where they'd been suddenly arrested was a safe house, above suspicion, the home of the attorney Radich, later Radice, an old friend of the family since the early beginnings of Fascism when they had found themselves in sympathetic accord with the regime, like many of Trieste's Jews, Freemasons and Irredentists in love with an anticlerical *Italietta* and a quintessentially Italian Trieste, like Salem, the greatest of its mayors, or rather *podestà*, always remembered fondly for keeping the city clean; fondly missed even by many of those who in '38, with the racial laws proclaimed by the Duce right there in Trieste, had had to forget him or pretend to forget him.

A safe haven, then, the home of attorney Radich-Radice, of an old Irredentist family, one hundred percent Aryan in addition to being, at the time, Fascist from the start—pro-Fascist to be exact, though sincere. Yet that night, a few days after grandmother Deborah had been rounded up, all three of the Simeoni had vanished; less than half an hour between the time the SS showed up and shoved them into a truck and tossed them into the Risiera. The attorney, too, had paid for it in the end. It's dangerous when those who are quasi-good, like so many of his colleagues and friends fairly well situated in insurance firms, shipping companies or industries, start doing good for real, as in his case. It ends badly. Ester had miraculously survived, hidden, terrified, in a cubbyhole that escaped the marauders' attention.

Sara had been surprised by the fact that Ester had put off meeting her and that, when they'd seen each other, she'd acted so strange, almost hostile, certainly uncomfortable. Maybe that was as it should be, clearly; it isn't right for those who return from the dead to start chatting with each other. Can you imagine Lazarus accidentally running into someone he knew down there, whose skin, like his, had become livid and bluish in the grave and stayed that way even after his return, can you picture the two greeting one another, telling each other how things had gone for them? No, there is no "post" Risiera; there is no one who comes out of the ark unscathed, who after the flood is cradled gently on a sea now calm again, and who disembarks in a beautiful land. No one survived the flood, no matter what they tell us, because the flood has never abated and the sea is still raging. Only the fish were saved, indifferent to the stormy waters.

Sara had therefore accepted the stark, almost aggressive silence between her and Ester as something perhaps inevitable. Only once, greeting her, moved by emotion that filled her heart, as uncontainable as a swollen river and already gushing riotously from her eyes, had Sara hugged her and sobbed something about their mothers, taken away from that house and killed a few days apart, but Ester had pushed her away violently, her face suddenly hard, fierce. Leave my mother out of it, she said, leaning forward into Sara's face, and don't name her in the same breath as yours. She wanted to say something more, but then she turned and fled. Several days or weeks later, when by chance they had run into each other on the street, Ester had turned her face away; a face that, for a moment, had seemed about to relent, eyes wide open in fright, features ordered to break ranks. And she had quickened her step, virtually fleeing.

Yes, of course, that must be it, Uncle Giorgio had replied before changing the subject, when Sara had told him that Ester must still be distraught over the death of her parents and brother, the obsessive thought of that night when she had seen them taken away, led to their deaths. I wanted to ask her about mama, Sara had continued; Ester had seen her after all, spoken to her, lived with her until the end, while I never saw her again after the day I arrived in Salvore when mama placed me in Anna's arms, hugging me so tight she nearly hurt me, then turned and went away. She vanished in the blazing late afternoon sun that blinds you and dissolves figures and things. I wish I could see her, at least imagine her in that final period of her life that I know nothing about . . . Perhaps, some time when she's calmer, maybe Ester will tell me something . . . Uncle Giorgio had gone on reading the newspaper, while Aunt Nora, without a word, had gone to the kitchen where she'd noisily started to wash a few cups and dishes. There too, in her aunt and uncle's home that was now hers, it was late afternoon, like the time in Salvore; but the warm light from the window wasn't blinding, it settled peacefully over the massive pieces of dark wood furniture, illuminating them and making them gleam with a serene sabbatical majesty. Well, we'll see, wait a while, maybe let her tell you about her when she feels up to it, Uncle Giorgio had said, concentrating on his paper; then he'd lit a cigar, but not as he usually did, with the calm, satisfied moves of someone relishing a pleasure, but with a restless hand, fingers fidgeting just to do something.

Sara hadn't wondered, at first, why no one, especially none of their relatives and Jewish acquaintances, ever mentioned her mother. Vaguely familiar names would be recalled, unknown, distant ones as well, followed by a passive past participle more or less the same, burned at Majdanek, incinerated at Treblinka . . . Those names, too, however, never came up at receptions given by the Prestons or the Müllerbrunns, generous hosts of soirees where it was clear that none of those present wanted to hear about the dreadful, sad things of the past that might spoil the party. Everything is already so difficult and the future is enough to make you anxious, there is no need to add the atrocities of the past. But when they found themselves, not at elegant soirees on the terraces of villas, but gathered in living rooms, among families of survivors, at least in part, or those who'd returned, talking quietly and diffidently, among relatives who are close but don't open up much, who talk about things dispassionately, it was as if the recitation of a Kaddish flowed, unspoken but audible, and then the names would come out, always with restraint. The horror had not been stronger than the *Kinderstube*, at least not enough to erase it.

The names came out, but not that of her mother, Sara thought, and was surprised. Until one day, that day . . . Sara had asked her uncle about Grini, the Jew who with his wife, Maria, had informed on numerous Jews who, thanks to their finger-pointing, ended up as you might imagine, though Grini and his wife had not managed to escape death by doing so, and were later shot by the Germans when everything was crumbling.

Thank God, Sara had said, knowing they died like dogs gives me more pleasure than knowing their executioners died like dogs. But were they the only ones, I mean here in Trieste, to . . . were there other despicable informers like them? Yes, some, her aunt had blurted out, but her uncle had interrupted, asking her when dinner would be ready. Me too, Ester had spoken up from the shadows where up till then she had remained silent, watching her bitterly—I too am glad that bastards like those two ended up that way, although I'm horrified by the fact that the ashes of decent people may be mixed with those of the killers' accomplices who are even greater murderers . . . "I wonder," Sara had said, almost to herself, "whether my mother, when she left the house where she was hiding with you, was also seized like that, maybe recognized by someone who had hastened to denounce her." "Shut up, at least! Your mother . . ." Ester had screamed, before running from the room crying, no, not crying, uttering a throaty muffled snarl, a dog that wants to tear you apart but holds back because he knows he shouldn't, he mustn't, he flees because he knows he wouldn't be able to restrain himself. But her mother Sara, Luisa remembered, on the rare occasions when she had spoken about that period of time, had only once mentioned Ester's sudden fury before falling silent.

22.

Room no. 22 (the largest in the Museum) — In the center, a howitzer 305/17, disassembled into four huge pieces. Total weight 33.8 tons, bullet weight 440 kg each, range 17.6 km. Gun carriage, gun, tractor for towing. Nine lost at Caporetto, five later given to Franco's troops in Spain. Also used in World War II as border and naval artillery; eliminated from weaponry in 1959. The middle section, the biggest of all, features a kind of enormous saddle, the giant saddle of a Horseman of the Apocalypse, a colossal but lumbering target of death rather than an exterminator. Four ungainly antediluvian monsters that remained cyclopean and useless when the waters receded.

23

The visitor, strolling through room no. 2, unknowingly presses a button on the floor, which activates a recording of one of his interviews with Radio Trieste, following the trial for nonpayments and the publicized seizure of several of the Museum's pieces, among them the antitank gun.

"No, of course not, I would never have given them that gun, the PaK 40, I won't give it to them, it's a disgrace, a further demonstration of the plebeian ignorance and insensitivity of this city of merchants and thieves toward those who sacrifice to do it honor, like yours truly with his Museum. Had I known they were going to take it, I would have loaded it and welcomed them with gunfire. Let them dare touch the sword of my great-great-grandfather the conquistador and I'll run them through. I'd rather they throw me in the slammer."

From a CD in the next room comes a voice singing in dialect.

"*El Coroneo xè la mia casa — e i gesuiti xè 'l mio bel giardin,*" "the Coroneo is my home — and the Jesuits my lovely garden."

On the wall, a small sign: The Jesuits or rather their school, at the entrance to the infamous Cavana district in Old Town; the school was later used as a prison, then replaced by El Coroneo penitentiary.

In prison you're okay, among decent people, *i vanzumi de galera xè quasi tuti fora,* the jailbirds are nearly all outside. Like those from the Risiera. Like certain fine high-ranking names written on the walls of the Risiera's toilets — for them hell, the gas chamber, never mind jail . . . Don't worry, I won't name names, not yet, all in good time. You go to jail just like that, for next to nothing, a little wet spot on the ground and you slip on shit. It could happen to anyone. Even if you slip more easily because you drank a little in that dive across the way . . . Red wine is good for you and also makes the blood flow, just like that, for no reason, like machine guns and antiaircraft for that matter. A glass too many, a word too many, the knife tips over the wine and jabs a belly, the bombers take off in flight and drop their bombs. The entire Museum is already contained in a knife. Down below as well, in Old Town's underground sewers, I found several knives, reddish with rust, with who knows what.

"*Tuti lo conosemo / se ciama Antonio Freno / e col coltelo al seno / girava la zità*," "everyone knows him, his name is Antonio Freno, and he roamed around the city carrying a concealed knife."

They sang it at the Sgnanfo, known for its *porzina*, the Refosco and the old songs, inane but always moving because they were from bygone days. If only I had found that knife, Dr. Brooks, he'd told her during one of their interviews, the one that ended up in the guard's belly. Two parties going at each other—two armies, two drunken *smafari*, thugs, it's all the same. And wars, every war, needs songs. Every evening under that streetlamp . . . *Siam partiti siam partiti in ventinove solo sette siam rimasti qua*, twenty-nine of us left, only seven returned . . . He sang well, almost moved, Luisa recalled. Without songs, he added, war would be a slaughterhouse and that's that. It is, of course, but . . . Why all those beautiful songs, fraternal human compassionate, that make you love life, generated by slaughter? There must be something to that slaughter, if it makes so much humanity flourish, surely tomorrow you'll feel blue, but then will come a love that's new . . . all those flowers from the manure of blood. But the one about Antonio Freno—*na guardia de patulia / de posto in Via Crosada / xè stada 'sassinada / da un nostro zitadin*, a guard stationed on patrol in Via Crosada was killed by one of our citizens—we sang down below when, with those other two, I scoured out the sewers beneath Old Town.

That's right, in the alleged Red Room that had been discovered on October 14, 1926, in which the Court of the Holy Inquisition of

Trieste, presided over by a judge in a scarlet robe, held its sessions and trials. "The tub was presumably used to submerge the accused in the icy, sludgy water, until they confessed" (from the handwritten minutes of the October 16, 1926, meeting of the Trieste Archaeological Society).

A photograph shows a kind of dark, circular cavern, a long stone seat and, on the other side, a large tub.

The famous Archaeological Society. They had founded it in 1925, he, Poldy Wiesenstein and Piero Delconte. Just the three of them—we don't want amateurs or bigmouths going around blabbing about our ventures and discoveries, especially now that bulldozers, excavators and steamrollers are attacking the Old Town, gutting it, knocking it down. To restore it, they say. The Duce wants Trieste nice and clean and bright. And the *podestà*, Enrico Paolo Salem, circumcised baptized and pre-March Fascist, is applying all his proverbial know-how as bank and city manager to destroy it, strip it and make it all new. We, from down below, sabotage the destruction when we can, we close up a hole that workers above have just opened, Poldy even managed to damage the huge tire of a truck. We, from down there, resist the world up above . . .

Right, resistance . . . That's what he said to the Purge Commission, as recorded in the minutes of May 15, 1947. "Yes, gentlemen, Resistance, it's the right word; I'm not here to justify myself, but knowing that I was deserving of merit during those years of grim dictatorship. I wore the Black Shirt, like everyone else, because it's dumb to pointlessly present yourself as a target, there are always weapons ready to shoot, look at my Museum, you just have to wait for the right moment. Camouflage yourself, guerrilla tactics. Yes, it's true, on April 30 and May 1, 1945, I was negotiating with the Germans and then, on their behalf, with the Yugoslavs and two days later with the British and the Americans, but that's how I saved the city. Then too, even the Germans were gentlemen, it was a pleasure to negotiate with them. But go ask those Slovenians of San Pietro del Carso affiliated with the Osvobodilna Fronta, I already told you about it, and they will tell you how, by acting as interpreter for the Germans who were rounding them up, I saved the lives of many of them, convincing the Nazis that they were good people who did not meddle in politics. And in the end, in Trieste, it was to me that Major General Linkenbach capitulated and surrendered on May 2, he also gave me his jacket, which I like to wear every now and then when I receive someone."

24.

I should get a medal for being a Resistance fighter, never mind the Purge Commission that had the audacity to summon me. A re-sister *ante litteram*, pre-March, when I was still in high school. Down there, in those sewers, the three of us fought back, as best we could, of course, three young men, it's not as if . . . Still, we opposed the demo-lition that the regime and its Jewish *podestà* hypocritically called "re-newal." Right, for them even getting rid of the anti-Fascists and Slavs, and later the Jews, meant renewal. Castor oil is, after all, a medicine, it purges noxious substances. I will devote a section of the Museum to forced evacuations, of peoples, of individuals, of countries. I've witnessed many of them . . . In the end, even castor oil can be a weapon, in fact it was, hence it is . . . But then the same can be said for a billy club, a letter opener, the scarf with which that American strangled all those women, certainly more than the number of bel-lies my cousin Rudy may have stabbed with his bayonet during the war—but, dear God, what could he have stabbed, really, since he'd managed to get assigned to the kitchens and had maybe only used it to cut himself a piece of meat on the sly . . . But then, if anything can be, is a weapon . . .

25

We were always down there, in those sewers and tunnels that underlay Cavana—from the inn of the Zonfo, on Via dei Cavazzeni, to the Jesuits. That's the true boulevard of the most loyal city of Trieste, the Via Regia of Cavana, the *Liston* or *corso* of pureblooded Triestines; who actually do not exist, no one was born here, much less anyone's father. All strangers, children of who knows who, *tu' mare grega*, bastards. That's why as a young man, still hardly more than a boy, I'd gone to dig and rummage around down there, in the mucky origins, the origin is mud and blood . . . Maybe it was only then that I really lived in the world. The world—the streets of Cavana above and their underground passages below.

For Giorgio Voliotis, later the first to open an X-rated movie theater, well, almost X-rated, in the city, the *Liston* began with Via dei Capitelli and the bordellos' welcoming hostesses; a little past their prime, eyes heavily made up, but beautiful. He came out of those sinful doors and went to the Greek Church of San Nicolò, nearby; *dove ghe xe putane ghe xe campane*, where there are hookers, there are church bells.

He went to pray before the blue and gold Madonnas of the iconostasis. Not for myself, he said, I'm not that brazen, but for them, for those girls, so that God may give them, too, a little good luck, like mine at cards. It's not that he actually prayed, he confided; he would stand there, somewhat uncomfortable, somewhat moved, gaze at the iconostasis, then turn to look at the sea across from the church—the church itself was an iconostasis, a barrier between the profane world where one gets by somehow and the unbearable sea, sacred and sacrilegious. And then he would go play cards in an old tavern that people still called the Tre Tre Fala Denari. At his own risk, because ever since the days of the host Bartolomeo Mengotti—who, it was rumored, even many years after his death, had fabricated playing cards and placed them on the table in front of drunken players, declaiming verses invented on the spot—every now and then, no one knows how, two aces of hearts or spades would pop up. Probably because when you fabricate an ace of hearts or spades it's just as easy to make two as well. It was Voliotis who sold me those Roman daggers; he said they belonged to soldiers who sank with the Pompey's triremes in the Quarnero and were fished out, along with a pair of amphora, by some shady dealer along the coast. It's not clear how he'd obtained them, maybe he'd won them at the Tre Tre Fala Denari.

The Via Regia of Cavana leads mainly from the taverns to the Jesuits. Via Regia and Via Crucis; when the police drag someone out of a tavern with a knife still in his hand and bring him to the Jesuits, everyone follows behind talking, reporting, laughing, a procession like at the Servola Carnival. The same thing happens when the cops pick someone off the floor and the guy begins his journey to Sant'Anna—with predictable stops at the police station, the hospital and the morgue—where he ends up in the communal cemetery, even though he had been a *smafari*, feared in the alleys of Old Town and its ghetto, *sic transit gloria mundi*.

Forgive the digression—the letter accompanying the notebooks that he had given her read—you want to know about the Archaeological Society. I'll come straight to the point, I saved the minutes from that period of time. Naturally, one can't speak of just one thing, everything is linked together, interconnected, the barrel, the trigger, the cartridge, the bullets . . .

26.

From notebook no. 78, note dated May 18, 1947—Don't throw
your pearls to swine. What can they—those people, the others, the
ones on the Purge Commission as well—understand about our lives
back then in those sewers beneath the Old Town, in that darkness—
our youth in the dark . . . It's true, I always loved the dark. Even
later, during the war, those blackouts in the city during air-raids, the
rustling in the shadows, you're aware of people scurrying like rats
through cellars to get to the bomb shelters as quickly as possible.
We ran toward the nearest one, the tunnel on Via Catullo, entering
the black mouth that was like that of a big cannon . . . I've looked
into thousands of rifle and pistol barrels, mortars, culverins, torpedo
launchers. The mystery of dark eyes, keen eyesight is trained to look
into the dark; just think of that cat down there, in those tunnels, that
we found when we explored the underground passages beneath Old
Town, under the Jesuit church.

We would make our way down there by sneaking into a barely
visible opening next to the church. It's not hard to slide through the
shaft. Right away the air is damp, dust coats the hands and face with
grime. A broken exhaust pipe, who knows when, spewed out the
sewage of a latrine; now, congealed, the feces seem like relics. Who
knows if that ancient sludge came from a reverend father or from a
thief thrown in the slammer. Piero lights the way with his flashlight,
a flicker of shadow on a wall darts away like a mouse. Maybe it really
was a mouse; he too, down there, felt safe before Piero turned on
his light.

Down there you see very little, but you do see something, and you yourself are not seen. It's nice to think that up above no one knows about us exploring the depths. We are invisible, elusive, silent larvae, moles that keep digging and might one day bring down the school, the prisons, the church with its high altar.

Poldy sits on the stone seat; he's wearing a red cap, the one he pulls on when it's snowing up there. Stretched out in the dampish tub, we confess heresies and impure thoughts. Poldy waves a bone he found on the ground; he says it's a piece of a woman's pelvis, who knows what throbbed in there. I masturbate, but I stop before the other two notice. The centuries-old debris is infused with cum. "I confess that I adore the Serpent biting its tail, joining the past to the future, I believe in the eternity of everything that exists, which weapons, guns, tanks, bombs and men delude themselves that they are destroying. *Anathema sit!*" Poldy shouts and hits me with a stick.

Eternity, a big garbage dump in which nothing is lost; the shiny foil chocolate wrapper and the leg or head of the doll that my mother bought from Popel must still be there. I like everything, any piece of whatever. In fact, I especially like pieces, things that are broken; the toy soldiers sometimes broke too, when Poldy and I against Piero or Piero and Poldy against me or Piero and I against Poldy—that's right, we'd been friends since we were children—played at the Battle of Verdun and pelted each other with them; they broke, of course, and every once in a while we would even get hit in the face with one, it's easy to make mistakes. I put the plump face back on the doll and an arm as well, I suspect it was Piero who broke them off, but I'm not sure—then she disappeared, she must have ended up in the garbage, but I'd like to find them, they must be down there, the crumpled shiny foil and that bruised, rosy-colored doll's arm . . .

Blind as moles down there. And even up above. Did I ever see what there was, or rather what there wasn't, between my parents? That dull look in my mother's eyes—I see it now, but then I didn't, I thought her eyes always looked the same, like a pair of glasses. When my father, having finished reading the newspaper—he read it at the table, taciturn and angry if one of us spoke—got up and went into the bedroom and she followed him in silence, with a different expression, and other, different eyes—but how could I have seen? I was a mole, I could see better in the dark, in those underground tunnels, than above, than at home. But it's the moles who create a revolution, as I also told the Purge Commission, so they'd see that I too read my Marx after they made such a fuss about that library of German books that I saved in '45. Almost all of them Nazi, of course, even *Mein Kampf*, what else would you expect them to have at the library of the Italian-German Association in those years where I would go to borrow books, the works of Lenin or some rabbi? Marx instead was at my uncle Giuseppe's house, it came from the Casa del Popolo, destroyed by the *squadristi*, the Fascist action squads.

Moles, as I was saying, not eagles. The latter show off high above, wings spread like banners; gonfalons and red flags, but if a sniper shoots them down with the first shot, boom boom boom, the torn kite plummets to the ground, the plane crashes, not even the black box can tell how it happened, I think it repeats the lies they put in it, like a parrot. Moles on the other hand, blind stupid dogged, keep digging, gnawing away until the paving finally gives way, the main floor of History collapses with a terrible racket, and ends up amid the detritus of the sewers and tunnels, maybe even while a nice reception is being held and the *podestà*, standing below the portraits of the Duce and the king, is recognizing a *balilla* and a *piccola italiana*, the boy and girl who performed best in the parade.

I wanted to dig right underneath the *podestà*'s chair, we had even bought some stronger pickaxes, because after the Red Room the underground passage ended and there were still several meters to go to reach the area under Town Hall; down there everything was decayed and damp and we could have made it, but Poldy said no, it was too risky, and this that and the other—the truth is that the Wiesensteins were related to the Salems, they often marry among cousins, and sitting in that chair above us was Enrico Paolo Salem, *el podestà picòn*, the "pickax mayor," the one who wanted to gut the Old Town for the greater glory of the city, Italy and the Fascist Party, not realizing how long and complicated destruction is. People think they're destroying, but it's hard work, nearly impossible; building is easy, illusory but easy.

A gentleman like few others, moreover: the *podestà* who had outshined any other in keeping Trieste clean, owner of the insurance company Vita Salem, decorated with the Croix de Guerre by the Duke of Aosta during the First World War, advisor to the Adriatic Insurance Company, vice president of the Banca Commerciale Triestina, member of the National Fascist Party since 1921, and in 1938 petitioner for recognition of not belonging to the Jewish race. The certificate of baptism that he belatedly revealed is perhaps a little dubious, but in any case he was the son of a goy, a charming singer who certainly did not don a wig like a Yiddish Mamele, given the beautiful hair she had, which, along with her extraordinary voice, had caused a stir as the tresses of the Africana or Norma. The five million crowns left by his grandfather Isach Enrico, since his father, Vittorio, had died before him, had also passed on to the future *podestà*, who introduced the racial laws in a black shirt. So Poldy didn't want us to dig that hole and pull the *podestà*'s seat out from under him, though maybe the mayor would have been happy, that way he wouldn't have had to raise his butt out of that chair in August 1938 . . .

There's a passageway, in the Old Town tunnels that we go down to, which is called, or which we called, the Cat's Tunnel, because it is practically obstructed by the mummy of a cat, a carcass that must have been there since God knows when. The eyes of the cat in the tunnel are blank. When I saw them I thought for a moment that I had torn them out and I remembered the doll, maybe she's down there too, somewhere, without eyes.

The *tapetum lucidum*, in the posterior of the cat's eye, is formed of cells that reflect and break up light, enabling keen night vision. I bet that cat could see very well down there, in the dark passage leading to the underground chamber, when the narrow slit of its pupil widened to a circle and he, master of that darkness, slinked along the passageway which we had a hard time passing through. Poldy was right, but not for the reasons he said. It was a good thing we didn't demolish the ceiling of the cavern, which was the floor of the office in Town Hall. We would have caused the cavern, with its beautiful circular space, to collapse, and the tub, the stone table and the inquisitor's seat would have been destroyed, rubble exposed to the light of day.

History blinks eyes as blind as those of bats, the condemned man removes his hood and is blinder than before, dazzled by the stupid light. There's a photograph of the gutted Old Town, beams half sunk in mud, shattered, toilets overturned, obscene whitish corpses at the morgue, an intestine reduced to pulp.

It would have been too bad if we had destroyed the tunnel, which goes up San Giusto Hill, passing beneath the Jesuits, the old prisons. The cat's tunnel. I had to squeeze close to him, to that creature, because the passageway is low and narrow. The dampness mummified him. He's lying there, front legs outstretched. He stands guard at the entrance. A useless guard, like those stationed to keep watch over the entrances to the Underworld. Now everyone descends into hell, even by elevator, and comes out again. The cat's eye is dark too, a kind of empty, black hole. I wonder what his iris was like, blue-green, yellow . . . Death stopped him cold, like the lava of a volcano. Maybe a slight underground landslide surprised him in his sleep. During REM sleep a cat moves his eyes and ears, probably dreaming. I read that if you destroy a certain area of the medulla, a cat, during REM sleep, experiences small fits of rage (we could devote a small special section of the Museum to various kinds of interventions on the brain and spinal cord, treatment and destruction). It's possible he died while hissing furiously at someone, as he slept and dreamed.

27.

Room no. 11 — Saint Etienne machine gun, mod. 1907. 8-mm cartridges.

Lightweight, barrel somewhat raised, a dog sniffing and pointing at the prey, tense and ready to spring. The elegance of war. War as hunt; a sport for aristocrats and gentlemen, more attentive to their horses than to the stable boys who lead them by the bridle to the clearing they set out from. The officers who order the machine gun to be arrayed and aimed don't have eyes either for the soldiers who load it on their shoulders, set it up, drop dead and stink in the trenches.

28.

A loose sheet of paper, inserted in notebook no. 194 and dated August 3, 1936.

Why didn't mama call me sooner? When I got there, papa could no longer speak. As he lay on the bed, his hands and feet jerked nervously and his head shook convulsively. My sister tried to stroke his cheek, I took his hand, brought it to my lips, the hand pulled back, it was an uncontrollable reflex, I know, nothing to do with me, he didn't even know I was there . . . My mother, standing, didn't say a word; she looked at him without betraying any emotion. At one point papa roused himself, raising his chest, a croaky sound from his lips, then he fell back on the pillow with a gasp, and at that moment his penis suddenly stood up under the sheet, like the roly-poly tumbler I used to play with as a child. So there! That'll show you!, you will never be capable . . . My mother looked at that swelling under the sheet, he suddenly stopped breathing, a last muffled breath, cut off, and he, once again victorious in the fierce war for mama's love, lay motionless, as his mast slowly lowered, like a flag paying tribute to a fallen soldier.

29.

Room no. 12—A photo from his honeymoon, dated October 1, 1933. In the background, a mountain fading into the shadows; his wife is leaning on a shovel, in front of a pile of loose soil; he's holding a pickax, a spade behind him stuck in the ground, and with his other hand he's pointing to a riddled helmet, all smiles, his face obviously sweaty. Further on we see a wheelbarrow, apparently used to transport the findings. "Photo taken by Ivo, the innkeeper at Doberdò who loaned us the wheelbarrow," is written on the back of the photograph. The honeymoon was devoted to excavations—still amateurish, he explains in his journal—on the Hermada, the Sabotino and other mountains involved in the war on the Karst in '15–'18. One year later Leopoldo was born, so something must have taken place, despite the wheelbarrow spade pickax and sweaty face. There's a photo (no. 414) of a slit, a fissure in the rock, an obscene horizontal gash. Vertical conveys life, horizontal suggests death; issuing from that fissure in the Karst was death, lightning bursts of chaotic fire, a whole company was mowed down to scale those few meters of altitude, six of them made it there, out of one hundred and fifty, and inside the cave, behind the slit, found only one enemy soldier; enraged, they wanted to tear him to pieces, the lieutenant had had to aim his pistol at them to stop them.

The photo of the fissure, unseemly, is in the honeymoon album.

LUISA'S STORY-III

Had it been Uncle Giorgio who told Luisa's mother? Or had Sara heard it from someone during one of those evenings, a few words barely spoken, interrupted when they had seen her approaching, maybe that time when she'd suddenly run off, turning her back on the two or three who, seeing her coming, seemed to have changed the subject? At least that's what she'd been told many years later by Mrs. Weber, the longtime widow of the late general manager of the Adriatic Insurance Company, Alfonso Weber. She'd walked out, Mrs. Weber had said, as the others were nodding a greeting, I remember it very well even though it was a long time ago. She was almost running, you could tell that she herself didn't know why. Or maybe, Luisa told herself, she knew but only for an instant—a thought, no, a clear, stabbing feeling, a flash that illuminates everything but is quickly obscured, once again drowned in a dark indistinct swell.

It was strange—Luisa remembered clearly when her mother had told her, just like that, abruptly, without warning; she had paused a moment in front of the mirror, looking at herself, dumbfounded, astonished and talking almost more to herself than to her daughter—it was strange that her mother couldn't remember the exact moment when she had known. It was as if—but since when?—she'd realized that she had always known or at least for a long time; a devastating knowledge, hushed or muffled by the passing of days and months, but woven into her being like a lump in your body, which it seems you always knew you had, even though it only suddenly begins to hurt, forcing you to notice it. A face lined with wrinkles and falling apart; which every now and then—often, almost always, always—arouses dismay when, taken aback, you see it in the mirror, though it's never the first time: you look at yourself, you're startled, appalled, yet you feel you already knew it, that that face has been there—in the mirror, in your gaze—for some time. Although, truthfully, her mother's face, even years later, as far back as Luisa could remember, was still that of a young woman with the dark eyes and beautiful mouth of the Shulamite and an imperious nose.

The thunderbolt of that revelation had sunk into Sara, a lightning flash vanishing in the ground, illuminating and igniting the darkness beneath the skin, those murky rivers of the body that you only notice when a dam or a bank collapses. A volcano erupts in the depths, deafening but silent for those who can't and in any case do not want to hear it; a seething fiery magma that you can't feel burning even though it eats away and destroys layers of basalt and igneous rocks, shifts faults, and triggers earthquakes. She knows, she doesn't know, she will know what she already knows, something occasionally jams inside her head, a sapper has sabotaged the circuits. An intense stirring inside her, a woodworm digging tunnels, that continues to advance.

Words reach her ear, images, aggressive or elusive glances, polite faces though seemingly distorted and malevolent, scattered sparks from that lightning bolt flash from one neuron to another, slither between the synapses like serpents, pass quickly through the layers of the cortex to its control center, but the Supreme Command is reluctant to acknowledge it, to let Sara know what with all her heart and mind she would not want to know and doesn't know that she doesn't want to know. The infection spreads slowly and uncontainably, at all times with the willful negligence of the Supreme Command. The enemy makes inroads everywhere; no thoughts, only nerve impulses advance; they catch the defenses by surprise but other defensive reserves surround the enemy, drive him back, attack him; the battle is grueling and, as happens when it takes place within a nation's borders, victories and defeats, advances and retreats devastate the attacked territory, which is left ravaged and looking more and more like a heap of rubble.

A real war, of which the commander is still unaware — or doesn't want to know — her head surrounded and protected by abundant hair like a villa set among impenetrable trees; Sara continues to take walks, get angry, laugh, watch evening descend over the sea, despite the frenzy and the vague undertow of fear that she persists in trying not to notice. Epic wars in the veins and arteries, along the nerve endings, in the cells. Those who love war also love illness, the real war of Gog and Magog; they say that the flu was all it took for Churchill to develop a keen interest in his doctor's bellicose reports about the clashes taking place in his body, turning it into a battlefield, his favorite terrain, where he really felt alive.

The wars that flared up in Sara — unaware and unconsciously intent on remaining so, even when increasingly clear signals came at her from all sides, ever more ineffectually blocked by an abstruse desire to ignore them — were more subtle, their indications being skin that would begin to sweat for no reason, waves of nausea that rose from stomach to mouth prompting a flood of sour saliva, temples that pounded more fiercely. Neurotransmitters in the service of malicious informants — the guests that evening whose words were interrupted as she approached, allusions that she had often caught here and there though distractedly, embarrassed silences a few times when her mother's name was mentioned — were sending the cerebral cortex messages, immediately translated into an unknown, indecipherable code, for the conscious mind, uselessly at its command post. The conscious mind or whatever you want to call it; maybe its name is Sara, or maybe that too is a code name.

The message was indistinct, but not erased. Even though Sara had quashed the words heard that evening on the terrace and on numerous other occasions. Acoustic waves, towering breakers crashing in her head — "yes, only she could have been the spy" — she'd been distraught when she heard them, crazed with fear — "maybe Deborah" — Deborah? who, why, what does she have to do with . . . The eraser harshly rubs out a word or phrase written on the page, and while it certainly can no longer be read, something remains, scratches etched on the sheet, gouges under the carbon paper. Allusions, rigid silences, something that shifts away, Ester's savage yet bewildered gaze . . . The world around Sara—in front of Sara, inside Sara, her in the world and the world in her, in the video recording of the surgery an eye watches the phacoemulsifier enter it. Outside is a desert inhabited by fierce nomads ready to strike, the words gestures expressions of the faces around her, arrows shot and lodged in her temples.

Of course, a good analgesic can silence a migraine. There are many analgesics. Motrin, Tylenol, also walking, going shopping, reading a book or newspaper, exchanging a few words with a neighbor, going to the movies. Whatever is under the skin and pounding behind the temples seems to subside a little and doesn't keep on scrutinizing what's happening in lifeless sea beds, debris lulled by underwater currents, holothurians, sea cucumbers—some call them sea turds.

Meanwhile, down below, inside, they're at work, even if the commander on the deck doesn't hear or doesn't want to hear. Saboteurs creep into the clumps of neurons, opposed by loyal troops ready to die for Sara or someone else in her stead; when necessary, neurons even commit suicide using themselves to destroy what is threatening the structure, its growth and its distinctiveness. The hand would become an amorphous palm if the kamikaze that make up its tissue didn't get out of the way, thereby allowing the formation of separate fingers.

Many of those venomous messages, having infiltrated the corridors of her mind like stowaways, also die or seem to die, happily destroyed by the pulsation of life that goes on beating, moving forward, eliminating whatever must be eliminated, amputating whatever must be amputated in order to survive. Sara doesn't know, she isn't aware of ordering the echoes of those words—hidden somewhere behind her forehead or in her heart, in her blood, in her medulla—to be silent, to vanish.

So she carries on; a little nervous, tired, anxious, but she carries on. Every patient feels well, up until the time he becomes a patient— that is, as well as one can feel in this vale of tears. Until one fine day a CAT scan—nothing alarming about ordering one, a precautionary, preventive measure that everyone should occasionally undergo—

caroms into you. The dyes, halos, fluorescences, the words, the looks, the facts speak for themselves. Osteolytic metastasis, hepatic metastasis. A metal tube with an interwoven system of multiple X-rays is like God, recognizing good and evil; evil par excellence, advancing death. Sometimes that cylindrical God benevolently decides to let his servant breathe while awaiting death and, for the moment at least, ascertains the absence of evil, so the card with the name of the potential sacrificial victim remains in the files. There is a different file for victims and those who are complicitous, but the cards can get mixed up; the informer then follows the one he denounces into the crematorium's oven.

A relentless light shone on Sara; her veins, her heart, her feelings, sails torn by the wind in an unbearable radiance, a sun that's blinding though you can't help staring directly into its fire, into the appalling atomic explosions that reverberate in the brain of whoever stares at them and continues staring at them. Unable to understand why they had immediately arrested her as soon as she left that house which no one knew about, wasn't supposed to know about, Deborah must have thought . . .

Some people think that, but it may not be true, I don't believe it's true, don't you believe it, Uncle Giorgio had said, trying to protect Sara from the fiery, muddy lava that had rained down on her and kept on raining down on her, holding the gentle umbrella of a retired professor over her, against that deluge. Don't look back, it is forbidden, even the Torah says so. It is also forbidden to rummage through the ashes, trying to separate a grain, no, not even that, a mote, one speck of ash from another . . . Besides, he added, it doesn't necessarily mean that . . . Nothing necessarily means anything, nothing is certain and excluded when men are sent up a chimney, victims of lava, they too *lapilli* ejected from the lava, smoke that pollutes the flesh . . . Nothing is excluded, not even the Shoah, the unimaginable, is excluded, in fact it occurred. Don't you . . .

Your mother, some say, may have thought that the person who betrayed her, who turned her in, was the attorney Radich himself, the only one who knew, perhaps to trade her fate for that of others whom he wanted to save more, or for some other reason, and so—but it's only a thought, a guess on the part of some people, Sara, nothing is certain, when millions of individuals are burned, the only thing certain is that they are burned—and so your mother denounced the lawyer, or is supposed to have, and the SS—there were even two Ukrainians and one Italian—stormed into the house, finding the Simeoni, except for little Ester, and took them away to their death. That's the only thing certain, you see, that your mother and the Simeoni died and that they died in that way. And it's the only thing that matters. The rest is just smoke, like the smoke that came out of those chimneys. And even if your mother, feeling betrayed—wrongly, mistakenly, though not maliciously—had lost her head at the time she was arrested to be killed, the only thing one can perhaps do at such a moment, and in the furor of rage, of revenge, of fear, disgust, and hatred for everyone and everything and for herself as well, even if perhaps in that inevitable delirium she had actually . . . It's difficult, when evil triumphs, not to do evil, but you, now, should not . . .

Sara shouldn't what? She shouldn't know that she knew, she should grope along blindly, feeling hollow, put up with the headaches? How she envied that gift that seemed given to others, to so many others, to almost everybody; the ability to forget, or at least to live as though you had forgotten. Good evening, Colonel, yes, the Ravennas were our neighbors, perhaps you knew them—but one didn't say that, all you said was, Good evening, Colonel, you didn't even think the rest. And why not? Living means surviving, everyone has had many neighbors who died, one way or another, and you don't keep constantly inquiring or remembering how. Even an informer subsequently murdered by the killers to whom she'd revealed what she shouldn't have, should be forgotten; yet though others may have forgotten—the ever fewer number who on Friday went to the synagogue so as not to fall short of a quorum—Sara could not, could not have. She tried to do it, to distract the images and words that suddenly took possession of her, assailants storming the citadel, raising opprobrious banners on the ramparts of her consciousness, writing obscene scripts on the walls of her frontal lobes, which they scaled like an army's special units.

She let the driving rain slide down the pane, until the constant din eased off; no, seemed to ease off, it was still the same clatter, but invariable as it was, it ended up being a continuous background noise which gradually ceases to be noticed. The glass fogs up, figures become blurred; sharp edges are blunted, pointy icicles thaw and don't hurt anymore, or at least not as much. Sled dogs burrow under a blanket of snow, which keeps them warm, or so it seems, compared to the sharp cold air. And you live, you have to go on living. Carry on; eat, sleep, work.

30

Room no. 21 — It isn't surprising that he loved cactuses, prickly and aggressive as they are. He'd even given a talk about wars in the plant world, illustrating the carnivorous plants, those whose roots emit toxins to destroy other roots and appropriate their territory, the alliance between acacias and a species of ants for which acacias provide shelter, proper little barracks, where they settle in and fiercely fend off another species of ant, the leafcutters, which would otherwise chew up the acacia's leaves. He spoke about thorns in particular, about their function in plant wars, but also in protecting trenches and camps, particularly during the First World War. But above all he admired cactuses, which he was familiar with thanks to the work of Frič, having come into possession of it through a Dr. Huláček, who had also given him the Chamacoco's ax. Another reason, according to Luisa, why the *Echinocactus* had to be placed so as to be quite visible and draw attention, especially to its incorrigible owner, Vojtěch Frič, a great botanist and even greater *Schlimazel* for whom everything goes wrong, but who takes no note of it.

Echinocactus grusonii. Arranged in the center, so as to receive the air and light it requires. Globular, its ribs jut out aggressively like the merlons of a castle; flowers around the crown and yellow spines, 10,800 yellow spines, radial patterns of light, octahedron skeletons, the green part woolly and spongy, gentle under the finger that crushes it like a mouth biting into a fleshy fruit, tinting the liquid that comes out with a little blood. A broken spine — it must have happened when she was setting it in place — is bent over, bloody with other people's blood, dried by now; from the window rays of the yellow lowering sun dive into a reddish sea. There are millions of spines on the *Opuntia microdasys*. The *Echinocactus grusonii* is more familiarly known as mother-in-law's cushion.

CACTUS MARCESCENS HITLER

I'd like to put plenty of them under the asses of the Germans, Frič thinks as he moves the large pot — that cactus must be about 2.5 feet tall, with a diameter of nearly 5 feet — to a corner of his big room, jammed full of crates; it's the driest location and also a spot sheltered from the midday sun, which the *Echinocactus* isn't fond of.

Thirty crates full of trophies, feathers, furs, putrefied exotic plants, travel journals, photographs from Mato Grosso that nobody wants; the only furniture in his apartment on Via Náplavní, which his friend Bohumil Kafka, with his talent as a sculptor, decorated with those crates, stretching hammocks between them for sleeping since there was no room for beds and, when Cherwuish was still there, other friends sometimes slept in that crammed jungle that was dead or maybe just dozing under the old imprints of the Royal Imperial Post still stamped on the crates. In any case, the large shriveled cactuses that stuck out here and there still pricked, stuffed, glass-eyed pumas eternally lurking, especially at night if you stepped on them getting out of the hammock half asleep. The worst was when someone who needed a crate in his absence came in through the dilapidated door and just took one, emptying its contents on the floor — guanaco horns, jaguar skins, notebooks for his dictionary of thirty-six Amerindian languages, rotted tomatoes, all scattered among large dry scarlet flowers, a pool of congealed, inert blood.

Since Cherwuish left, there is only one hammock, his, suspended in the cactus jungle; if the strings loosen, as sometimes happens, especially at night, the bristling top of a *Cereus giganteus* stabs his back or his behind. He wakes up and takes the opportunity to dangle his arm out of the hammock and search around, groping, to pick off one or two of the small red fruits, which are tasty. Sticking his head up a little he sees the *Copiapoa cinerea*, a hostile globe with its spines intertwined in a bizarre arabesque; the incisions that divide its ribs are slash wounds, it's a medusa rolled up into a ball in the waters of the night.

It's not bad to live in an aquarium, in a German-occupied Prague; if those spines were actually poisonous rather than merely causing minor inflammations, all it would take is a single *Opuntia*, with its thousands of spines, to annihilate the Third Reich. For years, since the days when Cherwuish was still there, the big room has been full of cactuses and notebooks in which Frič is writing his monumental work on the *Cactaceae* family. Some bloom by day, others at night; flowers open and close, a wave fluctuates and changes color in a breeze, the reddish-green blossoms of the *Cereus* wilt, the white of their interior is a foamy crest, the woolly crown of the *Cephalocereus senilis* sinks like the hoary head of an old sailor swallowed up by the swells. The *Echinocereus pentalophus* is a rift in the darkness from which blood gushes, suns light up and collapse, phalanxes of shields pierced by arrows, spears aimed to defend the ship run aground on the shore; stars explode, black holes swallow up corollas, fleecy clouds coil around and suddenly that nebulous fleece extracts claws that prick deeply.

War or love, the beguiling beauty of grand maneuvers, abrupt, stabbing blows to the heart. Galaxies expand and contract, micro and macro Star Wars; the donkey wants to eat the tuna of the Indian fig cactus, the *nopal nocheztil* as the Mexicans say, but slavering little worms, white outside and vermilion inside, crawl along the pads and repel the rough tongue of the donkey, who retreats, not without unintentionally crushing some other cactus trying to grow, a meteorite burns up in the night. Female ovules, hairy phallic stalks, pelvic fuzz conceal barbs like the toothed vulva of the Chamacoco, the *Euphorbia aeruginosoa* rises erect as from a nest of snakes, the *Hoodia gordonii* is a butterfly that settles on the thorns, too light to be harmed, the *Astrophytum asterias* grows to more than 4 centimeters tall and the *Cephalocereus* to nearly 15 meters. Some live years, others decades, others centuries, like the *Carnegiea gigantea*, the saguaro. The Habsburg Empire also lasted for centuries. The flowers of the Queen of the Night, the *Selenicereus grandiflorus*, last only a few nocturnal hours. How long will the Third Reich last?

Frič wasn't doing too well, in fact, things were going badly for him. He had accepted the 150 crowns received from the Náprstek Museum as an advance against vague future collaborations—more unwillingly than willingly, though he had killed a jaguar at close quarters (or nearly) and had dealt with chiefs of the largest tribes as an equal—knowing that it was in fact charity, only because he had not had the courage to say no to the energetic Mrs. Náprstkova, who perhaps thought that in a city full of stone saints and beer-bellied blasphemers one might also occasionally do a good deed. But even when the 150 crowns were about to run out, he had not stopped being defiant with everyone—with the respectable family men who had a lover in Modřany yet reproached him about his Indian wife, Lora-y, Cana Nera, and his daughter, Hermina, left on the shores of Paraguay—denouncing deceitful scientists and hack reporters who wrote about the Indies without having ever seen them, until not only the *Prager Tagblatt*, but also the *Národní listy* and the parish bulletins had stopped publishing his articles, despite the fact that academies and their assorted lot throughout Europe honored them, though they didn't shell out a penny, because academies, especially the most illustrious, have no money to dispense but are in need of money, like the beggars on the Charles Bridge who may play the violin better than the musicians of the Smetana Theater but can't even afford to buy themselves a new hat with what ends up in the one held out to passersby, especially if they are not willing to give up Staropramen beer at the Smíchov pub or *burčák* in the few weeks following the grape harvest in Moravia, when you can drink it in a tavern in Prague as well. Since he no longer even gave talks at the Journalists' Union, partly because without Cherwuish they attracted fewer people, things were even worse.

And they have the nerve to ask me why I brought Cherwuish back with me that time and left my daughter, Hermina, there? It's because she's at home there, and so is her mother, Lora-y, Cana Nera. Would you have preferred that I'd brought them to Prague, frightened like nocturnal birds by a sudden, insane sun that rises at midnight—Deí-ć, the sun, is the enemy of the Chamacoco—so that drunks could get their hands on them? Abandoned them? Saved them, on the contrary, from this forest of swastikas that is much worse than that jungle down there. More to the point, what will become of us . . .

Professor Viktor Krahulík, who lectures at Karl-Universität, the oldest German university, is writing a monumental history of Bohemia, from Libussa—well, from the Přemyslid Dynasty—to the present, impugning Boleslav I for having adjoined Bohemia to the Deutsches Reich. He's been writing it for years, he'd hoped to finish it in the first decade of the free republic but the stories are complicated, they get tangled up; the monograph was to cover the subject up to the day it would be delivered to the publisher, an idea that gave him peace of mind; once you've written all of the story everything is settled, you no longer need to struggle along to live, everything has already happened, but while he was finishing it, that morning of March 15, and decided to go and read the newspapers at the café, at 10:42 A.M. German Panzers and guns were already in formation in Wenceslas Square in front of the patron saint's monument. V Praze je Klid, Prague is peaceful, the newspapers reported; the Bar Association and the Medical Association ordered their Jewish members to choose Aryan replacements for themselves, Kde domov můj, where is my home, the Czech national anthem asks. Krahulík does not finish the history of Bohemia, it is already finished, there's no need to conclude it. Frič on the other hand does not abandon his work on the Cactaceae, O kaktech a jejich narkotických účincích, The Cacti and Their Narcotic Effects; he himself doesn't know whether they are medicinal or poisonous, there's not much difference, is the opium used to help a suffering, dying soul suffer less yet depart as soon as possible a poison or a drug? Meanwhile he keeps writing; the history of cactuses, unlike that of Bohemia, never ends.

Ktož jsú boží bojovníci, You who are the warriors of God, the crowd sings, swarming out of the church of St. Nicholas and St. Salvator, the one run by the Bohemian Brethren, and into the square, to the monument of Jan Hus, the legionnaires in civilian clothes and the girls in national costume — to each his own truth, is written under the reformer's monument. The truth is reversed: that time the German crusaders fled in disorderly retreat amid the whistling of arrows and swords and the raucous chanting of that song, but the article on the front page of the *Prager Tagblatt,* which for a couple of weeks had resisted, ends up with *Heil Hitler.* Rudolf Thomas, the editor in chief, did not stay around to see it, he and his wife found a way out with a couple of pills. Luckily Hus had already been burned at the stake, or things would be worse for him now.

At the stadium of Letná, Prague beats Borussia 2–0, the first Bohemian victory over the Germans in 519 years; Jan Zižka, the one-eyed Hussite rebel, beats Emperor Sigismund at Vítek. It's good to see the Borussian goalkeeper on the ground and the ball in the net, on the hill of Vítek they raise pikes and roll heads, the Czechs at the stadium applaud, the girls in national costume do so as well, the Germans go around in dirndl, the Czech women are more coquettish and elegant. Two to zero at Letná for Bohemia, a month before Macha's corpse was carried and lowered into the grave by Halas, Hora, Seifert and Holan, the greatest Czech poets of the century; poetry still counts, though only at funerals, it lowers coffins into the grave and sinks into the grave.

That goal, especially the second, was a masterpiece, the Borussians remained speechless, dumbfounded, mouths gaping. Meanwhile, as of January 1939, Jews are ousted from public office and from any state employment, a year earlier the German university had already expelled Jewish students and faculty, and at the Bumbrlíček restaurant and the Café Technika Czech Fascist students recount their feats against synagogues and Jewish shops. Jan Vrzalík, one of the ringleaders, hates Germans Jews Marxists Masons liberals socialists communists Catholics, in a word, everybody; but when Hitler comes to power he too will eagerly cry *Heil Hitler* and discover that he loves the Germans, though not those of Bohemia, who are all Jews, who knows how a match between the Germans and the German Jews of Prague would end up.

A label *Opuntia—Opuntia bigelovii*, to be precise—hung on an arm had fallen off some time ago, maybe a mouse gnawed it; they are bolder and more numerous, in the old apartment on Náplavní Street, since he sweeps the floor less and less often and drops crusts of bread and bits of cheese while lying in the hammock, nibbling, suspended between the crates and increasingly withered plants, which he waters only rarely. If the SS, the Gestapo, Klipo Kripo and Krupo are roving through the city killing whomever they like, why should he worry about keeping the house clean? Indeed, better to let it all turn into a huge garbage dump, if that were possible; an apocalypse of rotting refuse, tons and tons of leftover food scraps, shit that rises from the sewers, flows from the toilets fills the rooms oozes out the windows runs along the streets accumulates and surges up the steep streets of Malá Strana, a stinking lava that engulfs everything. There are no volcanoes in Prague and throughout Bohemia, but everything that people eat and expel, the dust of disintegrating objects, the peeling, crumbling walls and the rotting corpses could act as lava and bury the whole lot. The dome of St. Nicholas rises above the sea of shit like an island until it too goes under, the crosses sink and with them the exterminators and their swastikas; it's all down there, left to rot and expand the dump.

He, Vojtěch, would be ready to rot to add to that mucky deluge, perhaps the only thing that can suppress the Triumphant Beast that holds Prague and the protectorate in its claws like a jaguar with an armadillo, every so often ripping off a leg or a cheek. Waiting, lying in his hammock. For weeks now, for months, he hasn't left the house, he eats old biscuits and canned meat, something a neighbor brings him, a woman he once cured of an infection, a small incision, as so often in the forest with the Chamacoco, no big deal but she had remained grateful to him. He waits, and meanwhile his cactuses wither; even the *Opuntia*'s spines are black, it means the branches are old. The red-violet flowers are dark spots, at one time they were a bud of Venus, the corolla of Lora-y that opened tender hot and passionate, now they are patches of dried blood, a dry vulva, unwashed for years.

History is all a crust of blood, scraping it away is now impossible, but perhaps there is still life under that excrescence, flowing water, a loving heart that is not afraid of Nor Yo Rī, the monster that paralyzes solely with its gaze. The Chamacoco say it looks like a caiman and lives in the vicinity of Fortín Bogado, the place from which there is no return, the swamp of death and the unknown. Under the hammock is a purulent cactus that seems to have eyes like those of Nor Yo Rī, spongy, repulsive holes; I'll call him Hitler, there's a reason why I'm the greatest cactus classifier, the Baptist of excrescences, recognized by academies across Europe, even now that Europe is no more. That mucilaginous cactus invaded the room like the *Opuntia* invaded Australia with its seeds and spiny pads, 30 million hectares transformed into bristly, sterile thickets. The *Opuntia microdasys* has millions of spines millions of bayonets pierce Europe through and through, the blood drips away as through a sieve; soon there will be no more blood, the final solution was decided at the Wannsee Conference, largely thanks to Heydrich, our *Reichsprotektor* who espoused it with particular passion, maybe he hates Jews because they made fun of him at school, calling him Jew Süss and so, furious at having been the class scapegoat, as soon as he could he went on a rampage and decided to slaughter all Jews, all the scapegoats at one time, once and for all. Who knows why he didn't kill all the Germans, the ones who spat "Süss, süss" at him; maybe some of the same ones—handsome, blond, *stur*—who later must have been part of his bodyguard in Prague, when he got his revenge, without realizing it, in the cruelest way possible, by turning them into animals and sending them out to smear their hands with blood.

Spines prick till they draw blood, but when grapes in the vat have been utterly pressed and no more wine comes out, you feel like stomping on them. In the thousand-year-old Reich there must no longer be a drop of blood left, maybe they squeezed it all out by now; everything is dry, dry rot, humanity as desiccated as sundried cod, frozen like insects encapsulated in stone. That's why they win, because there is no more blood of theirs that can be shed to stop them; our president Hácha continues running around the table crying like that time in Berlin, and Hitler and Göring run after him with the sheet of paper, all nicely written out already, unconditional surrender, and a pen for him to sign with, and he scuttles around the table and cries and then he signs, he could have at least opened up a vein and signed with his blood, that's what you do with the devil.

But there must still be good, generous blood, ready to flow from veins if necessary to stop evil spirits; the Three Kings, for example, the *Tři králové*, have it in spades, with all those attacks they carry out on the Germans, not only in Prague but even in Berlin; they would have killed Himmler as well, they had planned things meticulously, in fact the bomb exploded at the right moment, as expected, right on the dot; it was the train carrying Himmler that arrived late, after the bomb had already detonated. Yes, you can still drink to mankind's health as long as there are still people like Václav Morávek, the one who founded the resistance group of the Three Kings; when he blows up a bridge or a cistern he even sends a postcard to Heydrich, signing it with his first and last name, letting him know it was him and sending his regards.

The Germans have actually created a special group to capture him, led by a Gestapo officer, Major Oskar Fleischer, and when Václav learned that Fleischer was at a café one evening—it must have been the Bumbrlíček or the Technika, one of those where the Fascists used to go earlier—he disguised himself, went to the café, asked Fleischer for a light, thanked him properly, then left; a few minutes later Fleischer found a note in his pocket in which the King—Caspar, Melchior or Balthazar?—greeted him and informed him that he could have killed him. The devout gunman, as Václav was called, given that he always carried the Bible and his pistol in his pocket, would certainly have dropped the major on the spot, he never missed—

I believe in God and in my gun, infallible like Him, he used to say—but there were too many German soldiers in the café who would quickly have shot him and it wasn't worth dying just to kill Fleischer. I am prepared to die, my dear major, but at the price of at least ten Germans—SS, Kripo, Krupo, makes no difference—just one is not enough, you're not worth one of the Three Kings, and so I, the King, will do you a favor and grant you your life, or better yet, I'll defer the execution, see you soon. Fleischer was about to have a stroke when he read the note, some favor that was, Václav might almost have saved himself a bullet. The major ran out ranting, arresting anyone who happened to be out on the street at that moment, kicking up the kind of ruckus we Czechs like when we raise a glass in a wine cellar and after a while the glasses start flying. Fleischer even seized a tall, distinguished-looking gentleman who turned out to be a German colonel in civvies, and the officer slapped him.

No, there is still blood in the land of Žižka, the one-eyed Hussite general for whom one eye was enough to trounce the Imperialists. It is I who no longer have any, lying here in my hammock among the cobwebs, fine-spun exsanguine white threads; even the spiders have abandoned them, I hardly see them anymore, they too weary of their coffin . . . The only thing I do, each day, is throw away some of the cactuses, the finest collection in Europe. It's not easy, because there are a lot of them; they jab me from all sides, I put a foot down from the hammock and a spine sticks in my heel, I once knew how to handle them but now they prick me, they're full of spines, I too am a cactus, I prefer not to give myself a name, I am not part of my collection and my nomenclature, I will not pass down to posterity as the *Echinocesus rigidissimus* or the *Astrophytum globoso*.

My arms are grayish, almost black, like the spines of the *Opuntia*. I no longer see glochids jutting out of the membranous yellow sheaths of the tubercles, mine hangs limp and dry between my legs, from one tubercle a spine pokes out, from another excrescence who knows what may sprout, I haven't heard anything more about Lora-y, she knew my bud in bloom, or about Hermina either, though come to think of it I don't know much more about Ivan, her, our, son, properly born in Prague and not among the agaves, *caraguatá* they're called down there, but then he too, like every man, is just a seed carried somewhere by the wind and it makes no sense to wonder which womb or corolla it comes from. I put some cactuses, furtively, on the benches of the Wallenstein Gardens, I hid them, sticking them between the laths of the seat back, so that German soldiers, when they go there with Czech girls, might maybe get pricked in the ass. To each his own Resistance. I'm not one of the Three Kings and not a *Cactoblastis cactorum* either, the lepidopteran moth that routed the invasive Australian cactus, the *Opuntia*, which had overrun millions of hectares, devastating the country. In Dalby they even built a monument to the victorious general, so they say.

Shoot them all, the youngest is fifteen years old, the oldest eighty-four, the children are sent to Chełmno to be gassed, cemeteries houses orchards destroyed, burned, leveled by bulldozers. The order to expunge Lidice from the map to avenge the killing of Heydrich is executed to the letter, the Nazis throw handfuls of salt on the scorched earth, some officer did well in his classical studies and casts the little Czech town in the role of the mighty Carthage on which the Romans spread salt. He's right, every pyre, even a small one, is equivalent to the biggest; it's the pyre, the destruction, that confers absolute greatness on the victims, whether dozens or millions, the pyres set throughout the centuries never go out, the shrouded bodies writhing in the flames are eternal.

Shoot ten thousand Czechs, Hitler tells Frank by telephone. At least here you can keep accounts, a man is only a man who can be disposed of as if he were nothing, but he's still a man, a course on the menu that is nonetheless indicated on the bill. Václav Morávek shot himself in the mouth before they seized him; his infallible gun did not fail that time either.

If you removed the boots of the Nazis who are slaughtering all the inhabitants of Lidice you would see that they have the *di'oŕa*, crooked ankles, just like Čurda, the partisan traitor. Lying in my hammock I look at my feet, they've swelled up, the ankle is a little twisted, evil enters the heart and pulsates within us like putrid blood. If I weren't so tired—my eyes only dimly distinguish things, maybe not even right from wrong anymore—perhaps I too like Čurda could go and denounce Gabčík and the other heroes who killed the hyena Heydrich, Čurda was also a good man, a Chamacoco, and he became a demon, an Anabson, as they are all becoming, no, not really all, but . . . since when have I felt so tired? Hours all the same, I fall asleep I wake up, always the same light or nearly so; only a few hours must have passed, at most a few days, but if I observe how some plants have aged or rotted and died, years must have passed.

Of course I wish Heydrich were alive, to suffer. Water, I'm thirsty, how long since I've drunk anything, cactuses need water too and are able to obtain it by shrinking their surface area to retain moisture and expanding their internal tissue to store water—if only there was even one *caraguatá* here, the little plant is small but it holds a bit of water; I don't see any, just as well, I don't want to nurture the evil cactus that is spreading throughout Europe, the *Opuntia* has overrun 30 million hectares in Australia, the armies of this cactus have arrived in Paris and reached the gates of Moscow, but they have no more water, what there was is frozen, like the gasoline in the armored tanks, and I'll take it from that smelly sponge until the last drop.

Prickly spines, the Führer's mustache—I can make him die, the cancer is spreading and has completely invaded me, I am him and I'll let myself die, and him with me. My skin burns, it must be as red as that of the Watirak, the initiate, painted with *uruciú*—everyone is a Watirak when the time comes—red blood, at one time people in the forest drank it to quench their thirst—now it's in the throat pours out of the throat burns the throat. If only I could drink my urine, but I haven't pissed for days, it must be that iron file I scratched myself with fumbling among the cactuses. *Clostridium tetani.* Permanent contraction of the voluntary muscles. I'm thirsty but the glass drops from my fingers, the hand flings it away with a convulsive spasm, it twitches all on its own. Gabčík, Kubiš and the other partisans had been overcome after eight hundred SS flooded the crypt of the church of St.

Charles Borromeo; they were about to drown when they shot themselves in the mouth so as not to be taken alive, I have no need to, I wouldn't need to even if I were a soldier like them, like Červiček, that rusty iron that put poison in my veins will see to it—a scratch, a scab like when I scraped my knees playing cops and robbers in Wallenstein Gardens, but now I can't even manage to nibble this apple—my jaw is stiff, to move it I'd have to force it with my fingers like you do with a skull. Why are you laughing like that with a clenched jaw—*risus sardonicus*, the *Clostridium tetani* is a subtle, sporulating bacillus, it must already have reached the peripheral motor nerves—the apple drops to the floor, it wasn't me, it's my hand my arm that twitches convulsively. When I sailed up or down the Pilcomayo . . .

Fertig! cried the German officer when he emerged from the trap door of the crypt, all wet. Water and blood; German blood as well. For me not yet *fertig* but soon certainly—the world's sardonic laugh, Hitler shouting, the world is spastic cyanotic my face is yellow—*yetït carhï*, the yellow sky when stars and things and men and horror materialized from the good darkness, from the good nothingness. The yellow star—the world, asphyxial, suffocates, enters the gas chamber. I would like to say something but my mouth won't open and I can't swallow. If only they would give me curare—that's what the Chamacoco use to treat tetanus but here they don't believe me, they don't know, they're ignorant. If only I could speak—but I'm unable to and even if I could it would be even worse, no one would believe me.

It's time for Tölörïtï, the demon ravenous for human flesh—even rotten, putrefied flesh, like mine, like his. The soul enters another body, perhaps a jaguar, maybe a plant, a cactus, someone is devouring my body, here, there, the hammock gives way like a cobweb falling among the cactuses. Other gods, Anerto and Tobüć-Kimte, only like living flesh, fresh, with blood flowing in the veins. Pilcomayo and Vltava make the rounds of the heart, they still have a lot of living human flesh to devour, bodies writhing about screaming, shoved into the gas chamber, tortured with electric shocks, but there is still a lot to eat, to tear apart before they die. Anerto and Mengele lick their chops, Pïtínno the anteater bear gobbles up the huge anthill, deluge and fire, the proto-mother Eśnuwarta exterminates the world, *lata touxa laabo,* the mother calls her children to her, here I am, I am already sucked in, it will all be for Tölörïtï, a huge mound of carrion on which to gorge himself, Tölörïtï isn't afraid that the spines will stick in his palate — he's gluttonous for everything, even cactuses, they prick and stink but it doesn't matter, they say the Führer smells bad, *Cactus marcescens Hitler, Sieg heil* . . .

Luisa didn't know exactly when her mother had found the job as an interpreter at the AMG, the Allied Military Government, but it must have happened shortly after the end of the war. Interpreting from Croatian. Sara owed it in part to those two, nearly three years in Salvore, though later she had studied it properly. Croatian or, as it was officially called, Serbo-Croatian. The neighboring Federal Republic of Yugoslavia, which had liberated itself from the Germans and, more recently, from Stalin's iron grip as well, even though it had failed to acquire — "liberate," they said — Trieste, *Život damo Trst ne damo*, we give our lives but we do not give Trieste — had many languages and nationalities, but wanted a single unified language, in spite of all the Tomislavs and Karageorgevićs.

Sara liked interpreting. It was others who did the talking, nothing they said could upset her because it was their words, not hers. It was never her speaking, having to think about what she said, believe what she said or not. *Čekaite, poštovana gospodo,* the Yugoslav delegation gets right down to business, *mi smo Balkan oslobodili od nacifašističkog jarma, pa stoga* — you see, gentlemen, we liberated the Balkans from the Nazi-Fascist yoke, therefore we rightly believe that some territorial concession is due us . . . The words clearly enter her ear and leave her mouth, the electric potential generated by vibrations in the air passing through the cochlear nerve reach the brain but the hypothalamus doesn't care, a lethargy like after a heavy lunch, no emotion, we'll give them that piece of Trieste where the Risiera is, but this of course isn't said, it's not even a thought, it's just a particle of gray matter that melts away like a snowflake. Give, take pieces of land and sea, high and low tide; the ground on which you walk, where you are born and die, your native land, is a sand bar that shifts between the water and the shore. You tread there when the wave retreats, then back away when the wave advances again. "Consigliere"—or Colonel, depending on whether he's the Italian delegate or an American or British commander, she says in a low voice, turning to the man beside her—"should I tone down or accentuate your response? All it takes is some small thing, you know . . ."

Some small thing and everything can blow up, or maybe not, an inconsequential thing, nothing more. She even had a desk, in an office. Pigeons alighted on the ledge that projected from the window, soiled the white marble a little, pecked at something and flew away. A flutter of wings in the emptiness that for a moment shimmers; farther out, on the sea, the wake of a steamer dissolves, is erased. The welcoming address to be translated—it will be the colonel himself who delivers it to the delegation—is brief. Friendly relations with the Federal Republic of Yugoslavia are of great importance to us, a guarantee of peace among peoples. We are well aware of our duty to protect the Slovenians residing in the territory administered by us as a result of the UN's decision. We are hopeful, however, that Italians remaining in Yugoslavia . . .

Words, dense walls of words with no cracks; nothing slips between one word and another, between one language and the other, the front and back of a sheet of paper. A cup of coffee on the table, blackish sugar caked on the bottom. On the wall, a print of Muggia Gorge, a thread of smoke rising from the stacks of a couple of steamers like a question mark. Sara looks at her shoes, the small strap that crosses the top of the foot. Far off, in some other room down the hall, a door is heard slamming. Yes, Uncle Giorgio was right. You should not. I shouldn't think or do anything. A fly lands on the edge of the coffee cup. Life is out there, what you catch sight of when the windshield wiper momentarily clears the glass obscured by rain or snow. Glass is hard, it doesn't let in sounds, words, glances, glimpsed for a moment then quickly swallowed up by the exterior mist. You weren't allowed to smoke in the office, but if Sara lights up a cigarette they turn a blind eye because she's so competent and swift at her work and also attractive and courteous. When she translates, she leaves her own head and enters that of someone else; peaceful labyrinths with no Minotaurs, where, unlike in one's own, you can't get lost and there's no need to be afraid.

You should not. I should not, I shouldn't. An excellent translation, Miss Simeoni. Since you stayed late to finish it, if you'll allow me, I'll have the sergeant take you home. The car cruises along the banks, it isn't raining, everything stays outside, figures and houses and lights retreat into the sea, a persistent streak of violet, despite the hour, fades away and dissolves, the steps of the house in front of which the car stops are by then dimly lit. Not to illuminate anything, just enough to avoid tripping and manage to put the key in the lock. Climbing those stairs was already as good and unfeeling as the sleep that awaited her. Sleep, yes, that was what her mother liked, she was always glad to go to bed. She would fall asleep immediately. Luisa on the other hand put off the hour when it was time to sleep. She would put away the papers on the table and the dishes in the kitchen, even though there was no need to; she smoked, read a book, set it aside, picked up another one. Often she even brought home pages of those notebooks of his, to decide whether and how to eventually use them in the Museum. For her mother, however, it was different — at least before you appeared on the horizon, Sara had told her. But before that, every night . . . and she'd stopped, seemingly lost in a veiled memory.

Climbing the stairs to the third floor on Via Tigor. Each night the same as any other, left behind by Sara in the narrow stairwell, the following day the cleaning lady sweeps away the dust of her days. Before that night, when she put the key in the lock, she had always opened the door mechanically, wearily, almost as if it opened by itself to mark the predictable closing acts of the day, entering the dark hall, lighting the gas under the already waiting pot, setting a plate on the table and a little later in the sink, the dry river of her bed. She slipped under the covers, the cold sands of sleep soon warmed by her body's touch, encouraging her to drift off. In Salvore, when Anna sent her to bed, falling asleep meant sinking into the same blue waters of an hour before; a little darker, maybe, even black, yet luminous, an iridescent shadowiness that embraced her, lulled her, spoke to her. Fish drifted in the water like flowers in the wind, Sara sank to the bluish bottom, the school of small minnows scattered above and below her, mingling with the petals of the oleander in front of the house, stripped off by the bora and cast into the sea. She drank that water with every pore of her skin, a filter of lotus blossoms, and dropped blissfully into the ocean of sleep, so black as to seem blue. The bed on Via Tigor, on the other hand, was a stony riverbed; falling asleep— quickly, abruptly, that at least—was not the sun setting in the sea, but a command switch.

Every sunset is different, in all the thousands of millennia no two evening's glowing embers have been identical; the switch instead wastes no time with lighting effects, it's not a huckster trying to lure mothers with glittering trinkets for their children, but always turns on the same light and turns it off to the same darkness, like someone who takes his job seriously. But one night, that night, when the dark hand—dark on the back, the palm was lighter—which had gently touched her arm helping her up the poorly lit stairs had reached to turn the handle and open the door, Sara, looking at the strong, powerful brown hand, had felt that even a small mundane gesture can reveal a man and that something can change, suddenly, in your heart.

She'd gone inside, as he stepped back to clear the way, and looked around in astonishment, but with a comfortable familiarity she'd never felt, except in Salvore, when after Anna's repeated calls in the evening, she would go back in, still damp from the sea, and the house—the kerosene lamp already lit on the hefty wooden table, the bed that could be glimpsed in the dark room—was always the beloved, welcoming house whose every corner was known to her, though ever new and mysterious as well, the silver of the milk jug a moon in the shadows, the cat appearing and disappearing silently. Returning in the evening to that third-floor apartment on Via Tigor, however, had always been different. Sara would enter almost furtively, a stranger in those rooms she knew by heart, though the way a traveling salesman knows the vestibule and waiting room of the station from which he continuously departs and returns. She was too unfeeling to be uneasy; but she felt like a squatter, an authorized occupant but still a squatter. The sergeant, however, following her in after having driven her home in the office vehicle, had stepped in respectfully but confidently, like someone entering a world that he's at home in and that he feels somewhat a part of, though that did not entitle him to any improper familiarity nor the slightest disregard of ordinary custom. He had looked around with caring, unwavering attention, the attention you have toward something you already love. And I, too, had the feeling of being home, Sara had told her daughter in a rare moment when her guard was lowered, as if I had come to find myself and had found myself, I don't know if you can understand.

It was curious — Luisa thought looking at her own lovely brown hands, maybe not as brown as those that had opened the door that night, but certainly darker, or rather, differently dark, than those of the bronzed ladies who sunbathed at the seaside in summer or under a quartz lamp in winter — it was curious that her mother, so reluctant to talk, especially about herself, had spoken to her about the night to which Luisa owed her brown skin and the graceful bearing of a gazelle. A few words, just a few hints, but not sternly, with abandon, with a look of contentment so unusual for her. Not only did Luisa owe her coloring to that night, but also her last name, of course. The first non-Jewish surname in her family — though her acquaintances often continued to call her by her mother's last name, Simeoni — Luisa Brooks; or rather, Luisa Kasika Brooks, because Kasika was the name of her father's sister, whom he had not seen for many years, since she had gone to Virginia and later, during the war, to England, in one of the first black groups to be militarized, the Army Nurse Corps, and had died before the end of the war itself. Luisa loved that strange, exotic middle name. It was strange and exotic for us too in those days, her father had told her; at that time we named everyone simply Bessie, Joe or Jenny.

I will bring you into my mother's house and into the chamber of she who conceived me — how many times had Luisa heard and murmured those words of the Shir Hashirim, when on the day of Pesach they were recited under the shadow that the menorah, the great seven-branched candlestick, cast on the wall of the synagogue. "On my bed at night, I sought him whom my soul loves," but for her the line always ended with the following words: "I sought him but I did not find him." And when the lily of the valley kept saying that she had found "him whom my soul loves; I held him and would not let him go," Luisa, captivated, stared mesmerized at the lights of the menorah.

I will bring you into my mother's house and into the chamber of she who conceived me—no, that, Shulamite, you could not say, because the two-room apartment on the third floor of Via Tigor was not the house on the Karst, first requisitioned and afterward fallen into ruin, where the endless chain of events, for some reason just at that time, at that moment, had led grandmother Deborah and grandfather Daniele to the bed in the spacious room that, beyond the woods, looked out over the distant sea, which grandmother Deborah and grandfather Daniele had perhaps gazed at with eyes half closed, lying close together, panting and satisfied after having lit another flame in the menorah of the universe, the tiny quivering flame of Sara. Nor could Sara have said, as the Shulamite did, "I am black but comely," because it was he who was black and undoubtedly comely—Luisa remembered her father clearly, the dark face glowing with youth and sculpted by a melancholy no less ancient than that of her other distant forebears who were not able to sing the songs of Zion in a strange land, ancestors who were distant and at the same time present, crowded in the shadow of the temple on Friday evenings, in the shadow that echoed with not only the songs of the living but also the voices that no king of Babylon and no pharaoh had been able to silence. That room on Via Tigor still existed, unlike the bedroom in the big house now reduced to ruins, but before that evening Sara had not really seen it, any more than she had seen the other one, when she was not yet able to walk and scurried around on all fours like a kitten among the kitchen and other rooms, unaware of the horror that was already building on the horizon, of the world's bloody miasmas. She could not remember it, that childhood home, submerged in those depths where memory becomes oblivion, an oblivion that continues to nourish the heart just as the subsoil deep beneath the surface, which no one has ever seen, nourishes the plant that is unaware of it.

What could they have said to one another, the American sergeant who had survived, indeed unscathed, the German shells that, along the Gothic Line, pounded the Buffalo Division, the 92nd Infantry Division, the first unit consisting entirely of African American soldiers, and who had later, with the 88th Division, arrived in the Adriatic city that was suspended in an historical vacuum—the TLT, Free Territory, No Man's Land, a travesty of history—and the Triestine Jewess, who at times seemed ashamed to have survived the spiked maces and the chimney of San Sabba, especially ashamed of her blissful adolescence in Salvore, of that sea and wind and the scent of sea and pines where she darted about like a seagull, while across the gulf smoke rose—maybe, Luisa sometimes wondered, if you looked hard, you might be able to see it, probably not, but—the smoke that was her grandmother Deborah and also that of those who had become smoke because of her grandmother. From the small windows on Via Tigor, facing San Vito Hill, where years later the fire would fulminate the Museum and its demiurge in the inverter, you could not see the sea. Her mother had chosen it—oh dear, it's not as if she had many options to choose from—because you could not see the sea which, since that evening on the terrace with Ester, she found upsetting to look at. Indeed, she had come to hate the sea—to hate it even more than he did, capable as he was of loving only maces and firearms, because she had loved it more than anything else, and you hate more than anything else what you have loved and what you can no longer love.

That evening I entered the history of the world from nothing, Luisa thought, putting the papers away. She could not imagine, she did not want to imagine, that night, out of the reserve of children who are disturbed by the idea of their parents as lovers and gloss over that irritating and basically implausible thought; in some respects, the story about the stork isn't all that silly. It even bothered her to wonder if they had loved each other; if they still loved each other, even though certain looks that she'd caught by accident, the way a gull catches a fish flickering in the water, made her think they did; a tender look, his almost tenderly teasing, a bare hint of a smile, not actually a smile, the instant that precedes a smile, a playfulness to mask the passion, as she looked away from his eyes and stared into the distance, stern, but a sternness that gave in, that gradually surrendered, her mouth slightly parted, a kiss on the lips, a softness—restrained, yes, but a softness otherwise unknown to that face.

Her father's face could sometimes reveal a sadness even more profound, more age-old; it too a story of slavery in Egypt and Babylonian captivity, of Galuth, of exile, dating back to ancient times and extending to areas no less far-reaching than those in which the children of Israel had scattered throughout the earth. How indistinguishable, how ordinary other faces seemed compared to her father's black face and her mother's face with its big slanting eyes, like moons—or even compared to that of her uncle (great-uncle, to be exact) Giorgio, his gaze affectionate but inscrutable beneath his bushy white eyebrows—how indistinguishable the faces of acquaintances encountered at the office or at dinner seemed, faces of actors unaware that other roles exist, in destiny, besides the parts they are playing, character actors sometimes lifeless sometimes hamming it up, stock characters in the theater of the world to which they had subscribed hoping for a place on stage.

Well, she would be curious to know what they could have said to each other at the beginning, before realizing, or not yet wanting to realize, what would happen, what was already happening. Fortunately, there are words suitable to the occasion, the pleasantries, the rules of politeness, the aseptic, innocuous language in which the heart's secret discomfort is translated, even when one is not a professional interpreter. But speaking, uttering the word that spells salvation . . . How could we sing the songs of Zion in a strange land? Extinct languages of exiles whose only commonality is what they lack, a place in the world, and who recognize one another by groping silently in the dark, like prisoners in a cell, or by their labored breathing after having wandered for so long. Dere's no hidin' place down dere, I'm burnin' too. How could we sing the songs of Zion in a strange land? There's no place to hide, I'm burning too. Yet they've been able to, we have been able to sing, Luisa thought, go down Moses tell old Pharaoh to let my people go and the people went throughout the world, often as inhospitable as a prison.

Deep river, the River Jordan is wide and deep, yet another river to cross, always yet another river to cross, the promised land always on the other side. The same songs, songs of lost tribes, ten for Israel, countless for Africa; there is no place to hide on this side or on the other side of the river and the sea, under a fierce sun that leaves prey exposed to the hunter. Run nigga' run, I'm burnin' too, crossing the desert, the armored train rushes to Treblinka, the stench of piled-up bodies and the stagnant pall of their breath is the fetid reek that they will soon smell though they will cease smelling it forever the next moment. The train of History has bad breath, even the SS are nauseated, it isn't pleasant for anyone, even if it's satisfying to see how the Jews stink. So it's true what people have always said, now that they can no longer smear themselves with ointments and other vile balms from the Orient you can see how filthy they are, even after they're shoved under those showers they're still filthy. Their breath isn't bad, that's true, because there is no more breath coming from their mouths, but the stench of all those people piled up is nauseating, fortunately the squads are at work and the oven, the purifying fire that cleanses all filth, is quickly put into action.

31

Maybe it was my great-grandfather, no, my great-great-grandfather I think, Carlo Filippo, who caused the death of the cat in the tunnel beneath the Old Town, when he went down there to hide that treasure of his—yes, because it must be close by there, I'm sure, gold and precious stones buried in the fetid soil, agates and topazes, cat's eyes—or maybe it was the cat that caused his death, he saw something gleaming in the dark, crawled over there on all fours, the sharp claws lacerated his cheek, he screamed but down there you can't hear a thing, the feline eyes glittered in the dark, two large emeralds, then they narrowed, slipped away and vanished, Carlo Filippo also slipped, falling into the Well of Souls—a giant, perfectly geometrical crystal, a strange, regular morphology; first octagonal, then square then circular then square again then circular again.

It may be that he fell into the muddy water; when the three of us went down, there was a lot of water and we drained it with pumps to see what was on the bottom—nothing, just dirt and mud, maybe that mud is all that remains of my duplicitous great-great-grandfather. Who knows, he must have had a torch, which fell out of his hand and for a moment, before sputtering out in that sludge, lit up the massive rectangular bricks, the rough marble blocks, the viscous fluting, the trickling rivulets of blackish water slithering down like blind little snakes. Sparks of color light up in the dark, cat's eyes everywhere, quickly extinguished, and he falls, crashes down, maybe he lies there a long time, wounded, left there to die. His bones mingle with those of the Jesuits of the church of Santa Maria Maggiore, some perhaps suspected of heresy, others the inquisitors of heretics. Still, better to end up down there than in the mouth of a shark in the oceans of his scams.

Who knows if he had come to hide the treasure—treasure from across the sea, from Africa, some say from the West Indies—or to look for it after having hidden it, that yellow gold that died out in the cat's eye. I pictured him rooting through underground passages even deeper than those that we three were familiar with and it wouldn't have surprised me if he had found that treasure of his—which, of course, would have solved a lot of problems for me later on and enabled me to establish my Museum without asking anyone for anything. After the failure of the Imperial Asiatic Company of Trieste in the good old days of Emperor Charles VI and Empress Maria Theresa, my great-great-grandfather spent a few weeks in prison for having sold those African goods on his own account, the tea, wood, coffee, pepper and sugar that he had managed to conceal in the hold and carry off when the *Kaiserlicher Adler*, one of the new company's ships, was seized in Cádiz by creditors alarmed at the drop in the price of tea.

Luisa wondered when he had written those pages found by chance among his notes. He had included them among the papers of the Archaeological Society, perhaps adding them later. For example, shortly after the honeymoon, after the heartbreaking photo taken in Doberdò. Or maybe he had written them a few years later, leafing sadly through the accounts of his adventures underground; perhaps with a sudden desire to escape, to play, like that purported ancestor of his, he who must never have played—even his tin soldiers or cardboard warriors convey the sadness of a barracks on Sunday . . . By contrast, the ship that runs aground in Delagoa Bay, the largest estuary of the four rivers, dark as the dark Africa through which they progress in an obscure unknown and from which they empty into the ocean in a thunderous churning, the snorting of a giant beast that emerges from the depths, water squirting from its nostrils, and shows its teeth, pointed rocks against which a vessel is shattered before being swallowed up . . . The ship had run aground on sands furiously pounded by waves spat out of the mouth of the largest of the rivers, the Espírito Santo—what can you do, *vivere non est necessarium, navigare est necessarium*—maybe because they had changed its name, *Giuseppe e Teresa* instead of *Earl of Lincoln*, and all sailors know that brings bad luck.

The photo from the honeymoon on the Hermada and on the Sabotino is on the bedside table, the first and last image getting out of bed and going to sleep, his wife's faded face amid the shovel, spade and riddled helmet . . . and suddenly the backdrop of each day is ripped away, the eternal day-to-day backdrop, the usual props for the show and its repeat performances are not backstage behind the curtains, or at least they're not the only things back there, there are crates of material to sift through, sort and arrange in the Museum. Toward the rear of the usual stage—a few meters, after all, behind the proscenium where the habitual script is being recited—an immense sea suddenly appears in a dazzling glare of lights, unknown islands for which one can set sail, leaving everything behind. A wild, distant wind from the sea. Ships, no longer just AB41 Autoblindas or PaK 40 antitank guns.

Set off, as Carl Philipp did—yes, also Carlo Filippo or Carlos Felipe, when it suited him. No, my dear Dr. Brooks, I did not invent my kinship with him. If he had at least been my grandfather, he perhaps even better than Popel . . . It's true, the family never spoke about him, they were ashamed of that ancestor, for them an unworthy stain on the genealogical tree of Admiral Egon, whereas I instead—when I found those papers of his in a drawer in the attic and read about his misadventures, well, it's probably the only time when it seemed to me that life could also be a game, joyful, full of things, smells, lights, laughter, whereas in my house everyone was always silent, irritated by everything that happened . . . Carlo Filippo, on the other hand . . .

No, his troubles with the authorities don't bother me in the least, that little bit of money from the tea and coffee that ended up in his pockets instead of in the company's, or the advances he received to set up a mercury and otter fur-trading company in Nootka, on Vancouver Island, and to outfit the required ship—which was never outfitted, it's true, but go find out how and why and as a result of whose scheming, I know something about it, having sacrificed everything I had for the Museum and getting nothing in return except ingratitude, injunctions, condemnations, confiscations, disappointments, protests . . . He at least was able to choose the right mates, like that Captain Bolts who took him with him to Delagoa Bay, never mind all those accountants, clerks, secretaries, counselors, judges who scrutinized my papers promising to help and causing trouble. He at least traveled through seas and forests, while I did nothing but go up and down the stairs of offices.

Yes, they must have really hit it off, he and that Bolts. Two cheaters are quick to recognize each other at any card table and for that very reason, unlike what usually happens between two people, they can trust one another. A god out on the oceans, that Bolts, as well as in the stock exchanges of London and Amsterdam. A Mercury in the service of Neptune, no, a Neptune in the service of Mercury, bankrupt and the founder of companies that went bankrupt on distant seas, but not before he grabbed whatever he could grab, a trader and author of books on trade with the Indies, quick to get rich and lose everything, a thoroughbred merchant very unworthy and unprofitable servant and dangerous man, *Homo perigoso*, English and Portuguese authorities agreed, those Portuguese who with the forty guns of the frigate *Santa Ana e São Joachim* had struck down the Austrian imperial flag and thrown him out of Delagoa Bay and the garrison of St. Joseph where, when he'd departed for India, he'd left a handful of men to build the fort and die of malaria, meanwhile trafficking in slaves, fabrics, baubles, alcohol, gold dust (of which there wasn't any) and ivory.

It had been Carlo Filippo who negotiated the buying of slaves from local chieftains, as part of his job but also for his own profit, and it seems he'd made an agreement with them to raise the price, a portion of which ended up in his pockets. Then he'd returned to Trieste, with the gold coins and diamonds into which he had transformed the flesh of those slaves. Finance is a chemical science, currencies are convertible and associable like molecules; a black back under the whip becomes a doubloon and a crowded, stinking hold filled with rotting black flesh becomes a credit card.

He had also brought back some fresh-faced flesh, a black gazelle, whom he claimed to have saved from the brutality of some Portuguese seamen: "Her name is Pearl," he said, and I don't think he wanted to bury her under the Old Town with the other pearls and doubloons.

How much can he have paid for Pearl? The price, in those years, ranged between twelve and sixteen pounds in any case. The slaves had to be treated well, housed in decent huts; that way they would be more willing to work, they would start a family, they would multiply. Bolts and my great-great-grandfather imagined a ring of indigenous dwellings, with vegetable gardens and orchards. Pearl must have realized early on that those proliferating huts were the walls of a fortress. When the Portuguese arrived, up in arms as later happened, to recapture the estuary, the first volleys would strike the ring of huts, excellent cushioning for the fort. So when, after firing intermittently at one another, they came to an agreement as always, the main things, or maybe the only things, left on the land would be the hardworking gardeners, corn growers, ivory transporters, those seeking gold dust to fill other people's pockets.

Pearl — my great-great-grandfather couldn't stop talking about her to everyone, even in his diaries he mentions her constantly, it must be strange to be so taken by a woman — Pearl cleaned the white elephant tusks that were brought in to be washed and stowed in the hold before transport; her eyes shone and laughed, but they looked around, they saw how many were devoured by parasites or malaria, they understood that every so often the scent of a war that would sooner or later break out was in the air, and when one of the settlers had deserted and gone to live in a village in the interior she had followed him, certainly unconcerned about not being his only woman. It seems that Carl Philipp, charged with bringing her back, had caught up with her at a bend of the Espírito Santo, not far from the sea, and had taken her to his house — to guard her, he said. After all she was valuable because she spoke Ronga and could muddle through Portuguese, in addition to making beautiful trinkets, which he bartered or hoped to barter for gold dust. Then, availing himself of the *Ferdinand*, one of two ships that plied back and forth between Africa and India, he cleared out with her before the Portuguese arrived; from India he made his way to Livorno and from there to Trieste, where he joined the new Société Impériale pour le Commerce Asiatique de Trieste e d'Anvers and trafficked, apparently for his own gain, in coffee, pepper, leather and *salmiak*.

It seems the authorities turned a blind eye on Pearl, who for a time was seen going around Trieste, not causing much of a stir; people were somewhat used to the color of her skin, well, just to some degree, of course, since a few years earlier a beautiful black woman in the service of the Countess of Bourghausen had been seen around the Teatro San Pietro, carrying baskets of fruit and hat boxes; the countess, like other fine ladies in the city, had taken a fancy to performing in the French plays chosen by Casanova, then in exile in Trieste. "I do not understand"—the ebony beauty is rumored to have said to Casanova, director and coach of those plays and especially of the actresses—"how you can be so in love with my mistress, since she is as white as a devil"; a few months later Casanova was of the same opinion.

"*Meu amor dá-me | os teus lábios | dá-me os lábios desse rio | Che delizia al corassao | xe l'amor e far cik ciuk | ma el me ga desmentegao | el mio re dei Mamaluk | ma perché sei così mesto | se per te batte il mio cuor? | Quale male sì molesto | t'avvelena riso e amor? | Rosa bianca rosa nera | rosa rossa del mio cuor | arde in me foco d'amor | che ti brucia e ti riscalda | mi son nera mi son calda | mi te strenzo mi te struco | o mio caro mamaluco | a mon bijou tanti bizous.*" "White rose black rose / red rose of my heart / love's fire blazes in me / that burns and melts you / I am black I am fiery / I clasp you to me I squeeze you / o my dear little fool / to my darling many kisses."

Smeraldina and the Love for Three Oranges. An adaptation by Cavaliere Carlo Filippo de Alcantara, of Count Carlo Gozzi's *Amore delle Tre Melarance*, with improvised dialogue. Expected to be performed in spring 1785, production financed by the aforementioned Cavaliere. He had copied the halting lines, the playbill of the Teatro

San Pietro and a draft of the contract, obviously admiring his dubious ancestor's ability to be paid—in theory at least, if numerous repeat performances and traveling shows had actually been staged in the Princely County of Gorizia and Gradisca and in Carniola.

Pearl was to have been and for one evening had been—or nearly one evening, given the chaotic interruption of the show that was never completed, as reported in the theater columns that Luisa had gone to poke around in—she was to have been Smeraldina, the black woman in the service of the evil fairy Morgana. A role that Carl Philipp thought suited her, partly because, according to Gozzi's notes, the black Smeraldina had to speak "like an Italianized Turkish woman," to make the audience howl at her gross blunders, and Pearl had soon learned a macaronic Italian filled with a few Ronga words— the African language that was spoken in Delagoa Bay—which in the script he had combined, in a hodgepodge of his own, with a Trieste dialect and some ancient Tergestino, besides the Portuguese that she knew well enough and the French he taught her in passing, thinking of some kind of future. In any case, bickering with the fruit vendors over the price of watermelons and cantaloupes, which she was crazy about—she even ate them on the street, so delightful with the red and yellow juice dribbling out of her mouth when she spat the seeds out, her teeth laughing like her eyes—Pearl had learned a dialect that was slapdash and strangled in her guttural pronunciation. Better than the *patoco*, Carlo Filippo declared, better her gleaming black skin than the face powder of those *squinzie*, those coquettes, on the stage.

In the contract, Carl Philipp had written: "She dances as if she had attended the school of Noverre, a great ballet master but not as great as the genius of Nature, which taught her Terpsichore's art on the untamed shores of Africa, indeed her dancing is in no way inferior to the *gargouillade* or the *pas seul* and *pas de deux* of Madame Dupetit Banti or Mrs. Margaretha Liskin, so rightly loved by the public. But even when she performs, even when she speaks, it's as if she were dancing, the way she moves, the way she talks are genuine music . . ."

Luisa instinctively glanced at her lovely brown hands resting on the papers, the back darker and the palm lighter, the dark and light a little more nuanced than on her father's hands, those hands that were so strong yet so tender, perhaps the thing she remembered most intensely about him, a pang of longing in her heart that was also a caress.

From the fuss the *Osservatore Triestino* was making over the fiasco of those oranges you couldn't tell if it was due to an unsuccessful adaptation, a lack of skill on the part of the motley crew of actors or an improvisation that went too far even for the Commedia dell'Arte. The story consisted of a tangled plot of clever quips and magic spells to cure Prince Tartaglia of his despondent hypochondria and restore his ability to laugh, while the evildoers enact their own spells to let him perish in his gloomy melancholy—and with him his beloved— so they can take possession of his kingdom. The Moorish girl Smeraldina was in the service of the evil fairy Morgana and, perfidious like her, was supposed to transform the prince's bride into a dove by sticking her with a pin and putting her in a pan to roast—with a side of *chifeleti* and *uérzis disfritis*, and for dessert *strucolo* and *kuguluf*. Then Pearl was to kill the prince himself with the pin, as meanwhile the roast burned.

Maybe the part didn't sit well with Pearl, the fact is that with the pin she should have used to kill the prince, she killed the evil fairy instead, who during the scene, pricked by surprise, refused to die and gave Pearl a slap, while the theater company manager shouted from backstage and Pearl, slapped by the fairy, threw an orange in her face—with all that red pulp dripping down it looked like she had killed her—and even hit her on the head with the *kuguluf* mold, having first popped a piece of the cake in her mouth. At first the audience laughed because they loved slapstick comics who beat each other up, but then they began to boo and throw rotten tomatoes, someone even jumped up on the stage and took the opportunity to get his hands on Smeraldina's backside, but he too was given a nice *s'ciafon*, slap, *ciapa su e porta a casa*, take that, Pearl half naked by now, her clothes torn here and there in the uproar.

How nice to be there in the middle of the fray, give and take a few punches, he had jotted in the margin, maybe wind up thrown off the stage, like my toy soldiers that ended up in the water. I've never come to blows with anyone, I'm incapable of using my fists; I don't know how to, it scares me. I'm not afraid of death, never have been, not even when I went around Trieste on May 1 dodging bullets. It makes me laugh, the fear of death, of something that doesn't exist . . . I'm afraid of punching, though, and kicking, how humiliating not to be able to give in return. Yet people like that probably wet their pants at just the thought of dying, though when it comes to scuffling they're quite able to fend for themselves . . . How I envy those ruffians . . .

It seems the angry theater manager, two days later, demanded back the money he had given him as an advance for the show, and that Carl Philipp had defended himself by making up a story that it had all been planned and arranged, an original adaptation of the play, adding that he was surprised that the director and impresario of such an important theater was unaware of the innovations in stage art that were triumphing throughout Europe and especially in Germany, where a famous writer, actor and comedian had caused a stir with a show that never started, just a few workers who were busy raising the curtain that did not rise until, in protest, several spectators had started pulling the curtain up themselves and the curtain had fallen on their heads, an uproar and a scuffle in which everyone had a great time. That was the new theater and even more amazing things were being done in Vienna, highly applauded plays in which the Olympian gods came down to the stage from on high to sell salami and fry sausages over a fire that rose from below the stage, the underworld of Hades, where Pluto had a liaison with Eurydice.

But in the end he'd had to give him back the money, that is the little bit of money he had left from the adequate advance. He still had, well hidden, the gold, diamonds and pearls that he had earned on other shores with the slave trade. He had also pompously announced — as the newspaper reported — a *Solomon and the Queen of Sheba*, with him as author producer and director and Pearl, of course, in the role of the queen, *roseirinha do meu jardim . . . Ši-mišweni Šidambyeni, di mattina e anche di sera, / andemo in leto a far la guera*, little rose in my garden . . . morning and evening as well, /

we'll go to bed to make war. *El ga sempre un bel morbin / col suo bel cuciarin / el frega la tecèta / più la xe nera e più el la neta,* it is always a delight / when with his spoon / he scours the little pot / the darker the cleaner. *Oh d'amor io vengo meno / cogli il fiore dell'amore / che qua semo e più no semo,* oh I swoon for love / gather the flower of love / for we are here and then we are no more.

However, nothing ever came of that rambling scenario. Perhaps Carl Philipp lacked the money, or was infatuated with Pearl, true, but not to the point of spending his own money on her, whereas with other people's money it was a different story. Nevertheless it was astonishing that—as a couple of letters preserved in the old theater's archives reveal—he would even have thought of staging a French text (French plays were the most requested, even in Habsburgian Trieste), which in Paris had ignited tempers in the controversy between advocates and opponents of the abolition of slavery. *L'esclavage des nègres* or *L'heureux naufrage* by Olympe de Gouges, *larmoyante exotique engagée et édifiante histoire* of a slave couple, two lovers who fled to a desert island, threatened with death by an evil judge who supported slavery and saved by an enlightened governor. The work had been boycotted at the second performance in Paris by the powerful slave lobby, despite the fervent support of the Société des Amis des Noirs and the antislavery writings and battles of Condorcet, Brissot, Mercier and Abbé Grégoire.

In any case he must have been a sly one, that Carl Philipp, if even before losing his head over Pearl—well, lose, up to a point—he had bothered to maintain good relations with the Société des Amis des Noirs at the time when, in Delagoa Bay, he was still trafficking in slaves on behalf of Bolts and also in his own interest. Of course, Luisa thought, putting the papers away in the drawer, every Nazi also had his Jew to protect, maybe even one he was genuinely fond of. Even in the Old South of my grandfather or my great-grandfather the aristocratic white scion loved his black Mammy more than his elegant mother who almost never took him in her arms, but that didn't mean that hatred had been conquered. Perhaps it is too late for the world to be good. *Il nous est défendu d'être innocents*, Pearl should have said in the play, playing the role of Coraline, a slave who has only a few lines but is more observant than the others.

After that things got confused or at least news of him did; Carl Philipp had probably had to take off again, or maybe he'd been put in jail, because the police chief, Baron Pittoni, had gotten wind of some other scam of his. With him gone, at least for a time, Pearl too had disappeared.

Sometime earlier, he must have hidden his treasure in one of the tunnels, more or less under the Jesuit College, the church and the castle. Apparently he had discovered those underground chambers by chance, his curiosity aroused by a neglected passage trailing off into the dark in Androna Marinella, not far from the home of the Marinellis von Merzhoffen family, which had fled from Constantinople a little before the fall and was elevated to the ranks of the nobility by Emperor Joseph I. When he had once again gotten out of jail—Pearl meanwhile had gone, and he was free to roam the streets of Trieste again, looking for someone he could talk into outfitting a ship for the mercury and otter fur trade in Nootka—he suddenly vanished one day and no one ever saw him again. He must have gone down there, now that things had simmered down a bit for him, looking for his treasure. He must have crept inside, gone below, and wandered through those underground passages that extend beneath the Castello di San Giusto and must have lost his life in some accident, a fall, an ordinary stumble. Maybe he too became a mummy, like the cat, but we didn't find him.

32

Room no. 19—Loads of uniforms, heaps of movie film, reams of military documents, and, much more fascinating, 2.8 tons of war posters and flyers. If packed tightly together, a huge, dense bale of paper, it would make a nice bomb, capable of smashing in a roof, not to mention if it fell on someone's head. In the Museum, however, posters dazibao leaflets light as a feather and cumbersome placards arranged haphazardly on the floor under a large transparent glass bell. From a vent in the room's floorboards, at regular intervals, wind machines churn out violent gusts of air in different directions, ruffling the pamphlets scattered on the floor, lifting them, causing them to spin and flutter, bump against the glass walls of the bell, rise up again like a wave.

The heavier posters, overturned, roll around on the floor as though on the deck of a ship swept by surging seas, the lighter ones lift off in flight, carnival-like streamers and shooting stars, birds flapping great wings, whooshing and dropping, stone dead, when the wind stops, then resuming their flight, first skimming then soaring, when the wind starts up again, swarms of bombers nose-diving.

The happy, smiling face of a soldier announcing "I'm going home" scrolls rapidly across the curved wall, the transparent glass lights up his smile with fleeting glints, a skeleton with a scythe in one hand and a swastika in the other rails against a cascade of tricolored butterflies. Victory Liberty Loan, the country needs your savings too, and the little family—a soldier in uniform wearing a *kepi*, smiling children in the arms of a somewhat anxious but confident wife—looks ahead, a piggy bank circling over their heads. A combatant rushes forward, tosses a hand grenade, smiles valiantly seeing the hail of machine-gun fire that is about to mow him down, the wind machine stops and suddenly he falls straight down, a portrait peeling off the wall and plummeting to the ground, where the enormous figure of an ape, red as blood and thirsty for blood, raises a hammer and sickle on a woman whose clothes he's ripped off, rolling around in the final gusts as though in the throes of death.

An aquarium of madness, of faith, of lies; colorful fish flutter by senselessly and disappear on the bottom. The bell should be large but not too large, the viewer who presses his nose to the glass sees, on the other side, faces pressed against the glass, astonished fish. A play of light intermittently reflects the image and face of those watching onto the walls of the bell, and for a moment they whirl among large airplanes painted in vivid colors. A glamorous woman glides by gracefully, a slow dance, smiles invitingly without seeming to listen to what three officers behind her are indiscreetly saying; *Keep Mum she's not so dumb*; in war *Loose lips sink ships*.

33

Pearl . . . Luisa felt as though she knew her, almost as though she knew her body; she imagined her light step, feet gliding soundlessly through life, like an animal in the forest, hardly leaving a trace, dodging entanglements and snares. A gazelle as it runs barely crushes the grass, which immediately springs back up, rustling in the wind; a moment later however the same grass is trampled under the heavy, ruthless tread of the gazelle's pursuers, hunters who eventually catch their prey, always too soon because it's always too soon to die, though always too late as well to prevent the prey, though hounded, from having at times known the joy of running in the wind and the scent of leaves and grass.

At night the hunters, wearily taking off their boots, hang the game and other rich trophies of their plundering on big hooks; everything that they, when they came to Pearl's forests and savannas, took from the legitimate owners of those woods, dark as their skin, dispossessed by the arrival of ships on the muddy shores. Heavy ships, much heavier than the canoes or dugouts carried by the rivers; heavy armor, rifles and guns *pour tenir en respect la canaille indienne ou arabe* and especially black, specified the funding granted by the Viennese government to Bolts for his expedition to the Indies.

The hunters who had come to hunt and pillage in Pearl's forests and villages, as they did in every jungle in the world, had returned home laden with spoils of all kinds, gold silver diamonds and emeralds by the handfuls; the men from whom they had snatched all that were also stashed away among those spoils, black ivory crammed into the hold along with tusks of white ivory. And it was the hunters who left traces on the ground that they had devastated and crushed under the weight of their armor, boots and guns, under the wheels of their wagons. Pearl's delicate footprints vanished beneath earth packed down by the conquerors' hooves and tractors, trails erased by wide roads, along which an armored column can easily pass. The men on those iron chariots had been under the illusion—with the brash confidence of conquerors, newcomers and nouveaux riches— of having erased all traces of Pearl, her people and other peoples like her, trampled under their boots; of having expunged them forever, vanished as though they'd never existed.

History is a *libro tavolare*, as land registers are called in Trieste, referring to the old term in use in Habsburgian Austria. Property and property owners are reconstructed clearly; if a piece of data is missing, there are always the archives, so we know to whom things, and their substance, belong and have belonged since the beginning, back to Adam, the first owner of the garden. Those who come to the garden by force, trying to extinguish even the memory, the traces of those who came before, don't count, because the surest way to deny a right is to deny the existence of the entitled party or parties. The conqueror parades past on his triumphant chariot dragging his vanquished enemies behind, now in chains and enslaved; his name is engraved in bronze and theirs have vanished like the cry of a bird shot in the forest. Genealogy is precise and meticulous; my ancestors date back to the time of ancient Rome, a person will tell you, the ancestors of his cook do not date back to any era, they didn't exist, they don't exist, they never existed and therefore the cook doesn't exist either. Pearl too disappeared without a trace, a few years after her one-night stage career. Maybe she ran off with that Greek trader who came to Trieste with his ship, others said he had kidnapped her and that Baron Pittoni's police had turned a blind eye or both, quite content to be rid of that little embarrassment.

Yet it's not true, Luisa thought; the footprints of those feet that fled into the forest have not disappeared, no drop of dried blood is ever truly erased. History, more than a land register, is a DNA bank, a valley of Jehoshaphat awaiting the resurrection of all the billions of beings who lived or live, since no atom of life is extinguished. An ocean of drops on the waiting list to inseminate, be inseminated and reproduce; hunters and usurpers try to defend themselves, to scrape their forefathers' blood from their knives, but that blood is alive, ready to seethe in the veins of bodies *resurrecturi* in the memory and conscience of the world, Pearl's forebears the legitimate landowners of the four dark rivers that flow roaring into the Bay of Delagoa.

Black Pearl, the rarest and most precious of pearls; for her color, the black moons of her breasts, her bare nimble feet, elusive as fish, he loved to kiss their faintly lighter sole, pale tender palm leaf. Black protects against the merciless, blistering light of life and its violence; blacks have endured, last of the last on earth and indestructible, in the fiery sun that scorched them in the savannas, on slave ships, on the plantations. Black absorbs light, conceals and holds it, makes it flicker, tender and impassioned, in the play of limbs; maybe that's why Carl Philipp said that Pearl danced even when she only spoke or smiled.

Most likely Carl Philipp hadn't even realized all this and would never have been capable of realizing it. Making a little money in the theater, as he had made and lost in so many other ventures; while enjoying those legs and those breasts of course and maybe even emulating Casanova, who had brought the demanding countess to Teatro San Pietro's stage, but not the beautiful black maid who had replaced the countess in his bed, or had at least joined her, apparently to his greater satisfaction. Maybe that's all he was interested in.

But why not think, Luisa wondered, that it was simply out of love? Why must every instance of a man challenging his fate be due solely to ambition, greed and role play in which one is snared and nabbed like a drunken sailor rounded up in a tavern by a press gang and thrown on a ship of His Britannic Majesty, as often occurred in the time of Carl Philipp? Who said that love can only be accessory to a man's choosing or not choosing, a walk-on extra like the servants in the plays performed at the Teatro San Pietro, useful for complicating or unraveling a tangled skein, but no more than that?

She rather liked the idea that that Carl Philipp, so devoted to the King of the Almighty Dollar and the art of having more than one trick up his sleeve, might have, in the stormy twists and turns of his life, really loved Pearl. Man is but the dream of a shadow. But when a glow, a divine gift, is given, a radiant splendor shines on us men and life is sweet. Even his great-grandson or great-great-grandson possessed by a less divine mania, by the mania of war, seemed to have realized, though only fleetingly, how love, when it comes over you, makes you go where you don't want to go and where you never would have imagined that you might one day want to go. There was a reason why he had recorded in his notes, included among the papers of his Archaeological Society, so many details of that old story, wiped out by the backwash of the years receding from the shore, rather than just documenting the 30 pieces of artillery and 375 crates of rifles given to Bolts for his expedition, which Carl Philipp had also joined.

Carl Philipp, *trapolèr*, a finagler, but an inspired one, apparently he had even thought of performing Rousseau's *Pygmalion*, perhaps because he liked the idea of a Galatea who, her white marble transformed into black flesh, makes her creator toe the line. Who knows if he had been Pearl's Pygmalion, or had at least tried to be, Luisa wondered with a pang of memory, sudden bruising flashes on the wasteland of the heart, thinking about the irresistible immoderation that urges those who love to become the Pygmalion of the person they love, love's original sin, which unconsciously and unintentionally makes the beloved into the image and likeness of their desire.

She too, without realizing it, had shown no mercy toward the one she had loved; she had tried to shape and sculpt the face, body and soul of the man who had slept beside her, that sleeping together that is contentment, not wondering whether altering the features beside her might harm them. Yet she should have known better, after the times when she had been the one to rebel at the adoring and adored hands that could not help but try to revise the makeup of her essence, of her way of being and living, flawed and imperfect but still hers, the only one possible for her. And so, each time, first she then he had broken the chains they'd taken turns forging one by one and fled, the chains broken but the shackles still attached to their ankles, because when you lock a chain around a heart that is loved and loves in turn you can later break it but you can no longer open it, the key is lost.

She could have read the marks and scars of those chains on her skin, graffiti in which the story of her life and of her heart was inscribed and told, just as the notches her father etched on the bedroom doorpost, when she was a little girl, marked her growth, the growth of a child who showed signs of becoming tall, more like her father in this regard than her mother. My father and mother—by what grace had they been spared those chains, the need to put them on the other and tear them off oneself, two creatures free of love's original sin? Each of the two had become himself with the other, thanks to the other, a plant that turns to the sun and absorbs it in its leaves just as its sap sucks water from the soil and is nourished by it; the water that they give each other is the lifeblood of their veins, each of them the other's soil. But then maybe happiness was not impossible, even if it was so hard to believe; maybe it's not only in fairytales that we find the lost key to the heart, which suddenly some *augellin belverde* or other enchanted bird brings back.

34.

Room no. 14—A showcase, 2 m tall × 1.5 m long × 50 cm deep. Irregular shelves hold small pedestals which display hard, jagged stones, sticks with tips painted in different colors, custom-made penholders, bottles of various inks, brushes with frayed ends, chisels, wax-covered tablets, scrolls of papyrus and parchment, sharp daggers, goose-quills, pen-nibs, brushes, fountain pens of all kinds, Parker Aurora 88 Montblanc, ballpoint pens, pens, pencils inserted in pencil holders like spears, colophons, an Olivetti Lettera 22, linotype machines, computers of various generations. A sign written in large letters is draped across the showcase: "The pen kills more than the sword."

Nearby, attached to the wall and covered with glass, one of his loose pages, torn at the bottom—she had recovered it from a wastepaper basket. "Writing, a sharp dagger that goes straight to the heart. It wounds and heals, but mostly it wounds. The pen is a *misericorde*—some fat, heavy pens even look like them—the short Spanish dagger with a sturdy blade, generally triangular, which delivers the coup de grâce. Books that inflame the world, that warm the heart but suddenly abandon it, as in so many stories of love or rather death. They spread poison, promise paradise and delude us into thinking that real life is something else, they betray secrets and intrude on privacy, act as informers. Anonymous letters, denunciations, vendettas. Duplicity and truth even more destructive than any lie. The pen's squiggles, labyrinths to ensnare, to make you lose your way and become lost. *Liaisons dangereuses*, an utter masterpiece of perfidy but mainly of irremediable unhappiness and, what's worse, of supreme poetry, as if to suggest an inexorable link between poetry, love and unhappiness.

Blow for blow. The stylus that engraves the wax tablets leaves scars on the soul and heart. Writing incising the body till it bleeds, see Kafka's "In the Penal Colony." Stabbing, wounding with a stiletto. Caesar defends himself against his conspirators with a dagger; he must surely have injured some of them."

Books . . . *Protocols of the Elders of Zion, Mein Kampf, Malleus Maleficarum,* old catapults of hatred, the more senseless the more destructive, though by now obsolete engines and antiquated bullets, good for a Museum. Death and destruction now stream on the net, faster than thought; you crush an ant, a tiny reddish dot invisible under your shoe, you press a key and you kill a man, invisible strings of millions of bits strangle his throat, his honor.

No blood; you press another key, cubic kilometers of banknotes fly who knows where, spill from savings accounts that are soon empty, wastepaper clogging the streets, starving millions throng those streets, rummage through the trash looking for some leftover that's still edible, some stumble and fall into the slimy, greasy piles, suffocating under there. The CEO is still at his desk, the captain who is last to leave the ship; he perseveres in front of the computer, but the printer relentlessly and mercilessly spits out email, paper snakes wind around a powerless Hercules, as around a child in the cradle, but they don't let him strangle them, they tighten around his neck and little by little strangle him, he rips up a lot of them but they are endless, email from banks corporations and monetary funds around the world. They suffocate him, in the end there he is, strangled toppled over in his chair. The sheets of paper go on rustling, more and more land on top of him, they cover him, swaddle him like a mummy, they slither along, hissing, toward other men in his office or at his door, a profusion of insubstantial sheets and finally a huge mass of paper. Soon the office, the offices are necropolises of paper.

It seems that among those notebooks of his that disappeared—
their absence will in any case have to be the nucleus, the core of the
Museum, Luisa thought with angry determination; their disappearance is the key, the strong point of the entire thing—there were also
some passages about odors in the Risiera, odors before and after, in
cells full and empty, of clothes in the laundry, and burned garbage.
Even the smell of the sea in Muggia Gorge that drifted faintly through
a window on the roof immediately became the smell of rotted sea-
weed. Only a few pages of his notes on smells remain, saved somehow.
Perhaps because they're innocuous, it's difficult to call a smell or a
note about a smell to the witness stand. There couldn't have been a
better smell than in the camp's rickety, puffing mobile laundry unit
that she was thinking of placing in room no. 17, the sweat of underwear that hadn't been changed for weeks in the trenches, in some
cases an implicit announcement of the death of one who after finally
putting on a fresh undershirt had fallen under fire. Stench in the
holds of slave ships as well, the compartment crammed with bodies
regressed to the level of embryos in the womb of History; many lost
along the way, carrion swallowed up by the ocean and devoured by
sharks, many make it across the great waters more dead than alive,
Jordan, ocean, deluge that in any case engulfs the earth, the belly of
the ship expels them onto the beach amid blood and filth, having
reached the other shore is their misfortune and the misfortune of
those to come.

It's tough to reach the Promised Land, the most unwelcoming
of all, to stain it with the original sin of black blood, which is spilled

by whipping those black backs bent over fields of cotton or sugar cane and which flows from the wounds of those backs as red as the blood in the veins of those cracking the whip, the original sin of the blood of black Abel spilled by Cain, perdition and curse of the Promised Land, and its redemption when that black blood will no longer be spilled to kill but, free and revitalized, will be the deliverance and salvation of the Earth, only then the Promised Land, the blood of redemption shed for all, in circumcision as well it's a drop of blood that allows entry into the alliance.

They entered the Land of Canaan in chains, those sons of Abraham, it makes no difference whether born of Sarah or Hagar, numerous as stars in the sky and grains of sand, the fathers of my father even more numerous than those of my mother, equally immortal though slaughtered by the millions. The Lord sent us out from Ur to give us land, the promised land of tomorrow, when the wolf and the lamb shall graze together; until that tomorrow, the land of blood guilt and pain, Shechemites treacherously put to the sword by the deceitful sons of Jacob, old and young slaughtered in San Domingo for the color of their skin, in this case white. Egyptian bondage and Babylonian captivity, the destruction of the Temple and scattering in all directions, pogroms in Galicia and lynchings in Alabama, the slave trade and the Holocaust. My father came here to prevent them from killing my mother, burn baby burn; ritual murders and raping of white women, the old serpent is a liar but he's the most credible witness for the prosecution and everyone believes him, the Jews kill babies at Easter and blacks rape white women, and yet we all climbed the rungs of Jacob's ladder, we are climbing Jacob's ladder, even my mother had learned that spiritual, an age-old but never extinguished hymn.

Men with black skin wrestle with God, though not just once, many times; they limp worse than Jacob, those chains for centuries on their feet cripple the joints. They wrestle with God through their singing that implores and defies him, moving like the waves of wheat swaying over their curved backs, singing that always accompanies the journey, Oh, I'm gonna sing, Gonna sing all along the way! In the slave ship's hold or in the plantation shack, the *conteur* sings songs of the ancient mother to faces dark as shadow, in the shadow, who repeat them, songs of the black mother of us all, It is crying, it is crying, Sihamba Ngenyanga, oh the splendid spears, the crowd anonymous and dark in the dark night listens to the singer's voice and his song the way a child in the womb listens to his mother singing and Luisa, remembering her father putting her to sleep lulling her with those songs in a language that came from afar—less far off than the sacred one that told how in the beginning God created the heavens and the earth—thought she too could hear it, snug and content in a protective womb, those strong black arms of her father were a warm dark sea that enveloped her like the one she swam in when she was still in her mother's womb. What must it be like to sleep together when you are in love, falling asleep while one is still inside the other, she thought, wondering why all that, that especially, had never really happened to her.

Who knows what my face was like, she thought, when I was in her womb, when I started to have a face of my own, unmistakable; those black faces in the dark were also indistinguishable, though the voice they listened to was beginning to draw them out of the shadow, into the light where each one would become himself and not a black dot in a black mass, my grandparents and ancestors for a long time all the same, submerged in darkness, as my other grandparents and ancestors were as well, my old Jewish forebears, the poet says, after so much suffering and haggling, buried there; souls and faces all alike.

Alike, so to speak. What similarity can be drawn between Rabbi Joachim Prinz—formerly a rabbi in Berlin and later in Newark—who at the Lincoln Memorial, in 1963, marching alongside Martin Luther King, spoke "as an American Jew" who felt "a sense of complete identification" with blacks, and his colleague from Atlanta who said he would never risk so much as a hair for the life of a *shwartzé*, the Jewish proprietors from the Miami Beach Hotel Owners Association who had tried to cancel a convention of the African Methodist Episcopal Church so as not to turn away their white clientele, and many young blacks in Memphis who sang offensive songs about Jews and when they said "Zionism" sounded like Ku Klux Klan members spitting out "nigger"?

The ship with which slave traders Aaron Lopez, Moses Levy and Jacob Franks transported slaves was called the *Abigail*, the wife and servant of David, who, as it is written, was ready to wash the feet of his servants. But Abigail sleeps in David's bed whereas the sailors, when they can't hold back after so many days at sea, though even before that, just for fun, go down into the hold to ravage the young and even not-so-young black women — in the dark there's not much difference between black and black — not even bothering to remove their chains. Often they go at it together, all of them on one woman, whose black breasts gleam even in the darkness, and all that's left is a clotted pool of blood sperm and sticky muck beneath the woman's thighs. When they land it will leave a stain like many others, down there there's no lack of secretions.

And yet, also alike. The marron who flees the plantation by escaping to the *morne* knows that he will be caught, in fact he scornfully leaves traces of his tracks in the thick, tall grass on the hill. Like everyone else, he knows that he will die, but that's no reason for him to give up; after him, thanks to him, there will be other marrons, other rebels, whom no extermination will exterminate. Forced onto a train that will take him to Auschwitz, Aaron Lieukant sends a note to his children, Bertha and Simon: "In summer, when you perspire, don't drink iced beverages." And those imbeciles in brown shirts and swastikas could think of destroying people like that? Considering Mr. Lieukant's note, the Risiera is a pathetic business. If I had that note, I would make a gigantic blowup of it that would tower over the Museum. Indeed, that note alone along with a chain torn from a marron would be enough, they would be the entire Museum. No more shall they in bondage toil, let my people go. Millions dead; them, that is us, me and my parents and my parents' parents, but these bones shall rise again, dese bones g'wine to rise again, not only bones but flesh and blood, bodies made for love. No wonder the poor pharaohs and their minions fear the flower of the black sex and the Jewish one.

Her mother too, Luisa thought, had been reborn in those dark arms, in that indomitable tenderness, candid as the teeth gleaming in the mouth that opened joyously in the black face; Sara too now black, like a river under towering trees of distant forests, in the joy that had flooded her dried-up body and heart. Shulamite and lily of the valley, *sum nigra sed formosa*, I am black but comely; black the warm color of life and of the humility with which she could now accept it. Humility, Uncle Giorgio said, comes from *humus*, our teacher Minzi Fano taught us that in secondary school; there's nothing left of him, his ashes dumped into the sea along with other garbage by the Risiera's cleansers. *Humus*, earth, the good brown mud of life.

Yes, they were, we were able to take our harps down from the willows where we had hung them and sing the songs of Zion in a foreign land, that is, throughout the foreign world. Her father, in fact—these were Luisa's earliest memories—quietly sang her songs in a strange, distant language, the language of a land of fairies and animals and talking flowers, the girl imagined, when he put her to bed, gently closing her protesting mouth with his hand, sometimes teasingly covering her whole face, that hand was the great, good dark night that descended on her and on the world. *Adieu madras, adieu foulards, adieu rob' soie adieu collier chou, doudou à moin, li qu'a pa'ti héla héla c'est pour toujou'*, my darling is leaving, alas, alas, it's forever. *Non, non, Mam'zell', il est trop tard / le navire est sur la bouée . . .* , alas, alas, mam'selle, it's already too late, the ship is about to cast off, alas, by now who knows where the ship is . . .

Muen enmeu, he said to her, and he said it to her mother as well, as Luisa, a few years later, running around the house, had been able to hear as she passed the closed bedroom door, but to her mother he said it in a different tone, a tone she didn't recognize, *Muen enmeu*, I love you, I adore you, the same thing but not the same, two phrases, two meanings close and far apart, impossible to tell which was more compelling, more tender, more true. When she recalled her father, his big smile white and shining in his black face, Luisa was reminded of the Christmas tree at the home of her friend Giovanna, a classmate whose father, a pupil of Don Marzari, had served in the Triestine

Catholic partisan brigade Domenico Rossetti during the Resistance. The tall dark fir touched the ceiling, at midnight its black branches were lit up, reaching out they seemed to embrace you like arms in which you could hide and disappear, safe and protected. Luisa imagined that many animals of the forest had hidden among the branches of the tree that blended with the night, no longer hunted but safe and content, and not just animals of all kinds, but men and women from all parts of the world as well, Indians with feathers, soldiers with rifles that fired chocolates, even the sick and wounded who recovered in there, in the dense blackness lit by candles like the night sky by stars. There was room for everything and everyone, enough that she had even put a small menorah under the tree and no one had said anything about it; indeed Giovanna's father, showing her the baby in the manger of the crèche arranged at the foot of the fir, had said to her: "See, that's a Jewish baby who changed the history of the world." She too felt like she was hidden in the fronds of that fir tree when her father took her in his arms; his bright smile was a star in the night of that tree, the candid foamy crest of an immense, safe dark sea that enveloped her.

Then those waters had suddenly dried up, a surf that recedes and does not return, the law of the tides no longer applicable; maybe the moon has vanished, the sky is certainly empty and the shore where it was so delightful to splash about is a filthy, dried-up bog. War, or rather death, continues to rage, even when you have signed a peace accord. How to include death, every form of death, how to really include it, tangible and present like a corpse, in the Museum? Without death, the Museum, even with its instruments of death, is missing something; not just incomplete, but lacking the essential. It would be like displaying only the pebble that fells Goliath and not the bombers that in one night destroy Dresden and thousands and thousands of people.

It's true, he did not believe in death when he lived for his Museum; he wanted to show that guns bombs and tanks are harmless toys, because death is an illusion, a delirium of fear, of the mind that thinks it can kill and die. He would be horrified if he could see that his Museum is becoming and will be the triumph of death, its apotheosis or the staging of its inevitable victory. But he died, despite his inverter, and I am constructing his Museum counter to him, counter to his noble folly. The Museum will be his tomb, the urn of his ashes and of his nothingness, the void of his absence, his and that of all of us, not a monument to his glory, to his presence, vainglorious and illusory, like any presence.

My mother's body had become a sweet meadow, fresh with waters and tender moist grass, but death is an herbicide that burns and desiccates moist earth, dries it up like mud that cracks in the sun among the stones. My mother's skin a withered rind, from that banal, fatal crash at Aviano. With the end of the Free Territory and its Allied Military Government, and Trieste's return to Italy, when the Blue Devils had come to the doubly torn city, Sergeant Brooks, serving with the Trieste United States Troops (TRUST) command—something uncommon among black soldiers—namely, the brilliant, well-equipped 351st Regiment created by the 88th Infantry Division, had managed to get himself assigned to the military base in Aviano, a NATO base and headquarters of the U.S. Air Force in Europe, in order to remain close to his family, since Sara did not want to go to America. Enough Promised Lands, she said, we have had too many of them, all terrible, all battlefields; even in Israel, even now, Isaac and Ishmael are killing each other.

The herbicide of her life had come from an airplane as well, though this time not from above but from a banal accident on the runway at Aviano, joint use of which had been established by the Status of Forces Agreement between the U.S. and Italian governments. Fate, always banal and senseless, had succeeded where the Germans during the war had failed, as had some drunk in Memphis, a few years back, eager to end the evening by killing a black man. Along with Sergeant Brooks on the plane that was taking off when a civilian aircraft of Zanussi—the only company authorized to land at Aviano—had ended up on top of it, the pilot, a fellow soldier from Chicago, had also been killed, officer Pat Wright, born in 1922, the first pilot of the 99th Fighter Squadron or Tuskegee Airmen, the legendary African American unit attached to the 15th U.S. Air Force, infallible in protecting heavy bombers, sent out to strike industrial plants in northern Italy and Germany, from German fighter planes.

It seems no German pursuit plane had been able to take down one of the bombers, because the pilots of the 99th, Pat Wright included, fulminated it first, so even the colonels from Texas or Mississippi, who in their offices ranted against all those blacks promoted to protect the stars and stripes in the skies, no longer had the nerve to say anything. But that skill wasn't of much use to Pat Wright when the civilian aircraft, perhaps due to poor engine maintenance or violent wind shear, ended up plowing into them, right at their window.

Luisa remembered when her father had taken her to the military base and let her climb into the fuselage, which to her had seemed like a big fish with wings, and she had thought of Pinocchio in the belly of the whale. It must be wonderful to be eaten and end up in a big belly; maybe the mice or some bird that she was so sad to see disappear in a cat's mouth were actually fine in there, happily scampering up and down as she had in the empty fuselage. The world, out there, behind the protective armor of the thick windows, was harmless; the violent rain ran down the glass, no longer a raging storm but lost tears, trees bent over in the wind, monsters' claws, but all fears and all evil remained outside, like when she was in her mother's belly, too bad she didn't remember anything. But it was the cockpit that especially fascinated her, with all those instruments — later on she had wanted to learn their grandiose names, as magical as the nonsense rhyme of ring-around-the-rosy, altimeters speedometers gauges gyrocompasses pocketful of posies ashes ashes all fall down.

A huge flying fish. Does it go in the water too, papa? No, it's a huge bird that, when the storm comes and the sea is about to cover the earth, rises up in flight and carries its little ones to safety. Many little ones. Yes, fish too, of course. This is a good whale, Luisa thought, running around in the fuselage; if papa brings us, me and mama, inside its belly it means it must be a good whale, and if it's not moving it means it's tired but some day it will set out for wonderful places, maybe toward those distant coasts, white sand spattered with red leaves fallen from the trees, from whose shore, her father said, you can see a giant rock in the middle of the sea, a white, glittering rock, a huge diamond of the sea.

But there are also deceitful, bad whales. Once there were many black little children playing happily on the beach, until one day a huge whale appeared, came up to the beach and rested its head on the sand; it watched the children with gentle eyes, spouting jets of water from its blowholes high into the air, and the children laughed, clapping their hands and pushing each other under those sprays. The whale also sang, a song that told of a wonderful country at the bottom of the sea, and the children listened to that song, spellbound, as they watched those jets, then they went into the water, climbed on the back of the whale, which opened a great big mouth with great big teeth, the sea rushed into that cavern dragging the children into the surf, and the whale went back out and disappeared into the sea.

Down below the enticing song could no longer be heard, only a harsh, croaky panting, and they say that the whale crossed the entire sea and then vomited them onto a beach on the other side of the ocean. Many of the children were dead when they were spit out by the whale; others were no longer children, they had become men, but unsightly filthy and dazed, and they were all captured by evil ogres who punished them, made them work like beasts, whipping them mercilessly. A fairytale that Luisa had learned in school — maybe in kindergarten, she didn't remember clearly, in any case in the school or kindergarten in San Luigi, a beautiful, light, airy school on the windy hill that overlooked the sea of Trieste — also told about a bad man who played the fife so captivatingly that children went after him, following him into a large room, come inside, I'll give you a nice shower, you're all filthy, you should be ashamed, it's really true that Jews are filthy, like Negroes, worse than Negroes, even the children are already filthy. Sniff how good those showers smell, strange but good; if you feel cold, don't worry, we'll warm you up, we'll turn on the oven. The Green Fisherman throws Pinocchio into a frying pan but the oven is better, it heats well and is more reliable.

The few times when mama and papa argued — oh well maybe

not argued—it was because mama was obsessed by those scary fairy-tales, children following a piper or a whale and no one ever sees them again, ogres and monsters who fatten children up to eat them, whereas papa was bothered by them, what kind of story is that about a piper luring children to follow him, what are they thinking of, fright-ening kids with fairytales that only upset them, at least the one about the little girl and the wolf that you were reading to her the other night ends with her coming out of the wolf's belly and pulling the grandmother out too, though I don't like that story either, there are already too many real things that are frightening and it's stupid to in-vent others and still be terrified by a snake. Remember, Luisa, fear is stupid, it's untruthful, it's the stupidest thing in the world, a fraud. If you're afraid of the dark, turn on the light and you will quickly see that ghosts don't exist, and, if the light has blown out, take the oppor-tunity to have a nice little nap.

The story that he liked to tell her instead—though when she was a little older and he told it with different variations, she corrected him for even the slightest deviation; they made her angry because, like all children, she wanted every story to always be exactly the same, the same adventures the same words always at the exact same moment of the episode—was the story about another Luisa who had fearlessly and cleverly crossed the raging waters to return home contentedly. He also told her that he'd wanted her to be named Luisa like that girl.

Many times, in the evening, Luisa had made him tell her the story of that other Luisa—it's good practice to improve my Italian, he'd say, promptly indulging her, you're my teacher and you have to correct me if I make a mistake, just like your teacher at school does with you. A princess, of course. Or almost. In any case a lady-in-waiting, given that she was called Luisa de Navarrete, the name of distinguished jurists and functionaries of the king of Spain with many noble titles; modest gentry, to be sure, but when one's skin is black as ebony—especially in those days, but even afterward, long afterward, even yesterday, today, tomorrow—it is a stroke of luck that doesn't seem real.

Luisa however had elevated her to the status of princess, as is only proper in a fairytale. Princess or not, it doesn't matter, her father said; what matters is that she was free, you see? Something incredible, at that time; and besides that, married to a white man, a black woman married to a white man, do you understand what that meant? But the opposite is better, right Luisa? he said, crouching next to her little bed and pointing to her mother who was nearly finished drying the dishes. Luisa couldn't understand what was so strange about the fact that a person, man or woman, was free, even to marry whomever he or she liked, she, for example, had decided that she would marry her classmate Livio, who sat three rows in front of her, and they had actually married in the park, near the fountain, without asking anyone for permission, playing with the yellow and blue butterflies that were also getting married, fluttering about and alighting on a flower.

The only thing that made her a little angry was that the story wasn't always the same, as she would have liked. I don't do it on purpose, her father would say, there beside her bed; it's just that it's hard to know how someone lived and what he really did, not only a long time ago, but all the time. We know that something happened but only because someone told us about it and then someone else tells it differently, even much of what we do ourselves is known to us only because we are told about it, not just when we're told about a time when we were little, which we can't know or remember anything about, but even when we remember we get confused every now and then. The books that taught my mother her prayers tell us that God says one thing and man, listening to Him, hears two, which cannot be the same.

One time the other Luisa was born in Africa, was kidnapped and made a slave—in a book, her father showed her the coast of a large distant gulf in the ocean and further up a kind of squat orange-colored leaf that was called Spain, which had a great, powerful king who sent soldiers to capture the Africans. But the officials of the king realized how skillful and intelligent Luisa was, freed her and sent her to school, she became a lady-in-waiting or in any case an important attendant in the palace of a great lady and accompanied her on the long journey across the big blue sea, reaching lands until recently unknown. They stopped at one island and then another—there were many of them, beyond the sea—until they settled permanently on one called Puerto Rico.

Other times instead that other Luisa was born in Puerto Rico—big Luisa, her father would say, you're little Luisa, my little one who will become as big as the other one, I mean big in mind and heart, maybe even greater, who knows what he would say seeing that she had not become queen of the Caribbean but merely a Museum planner, yes, of course, he would be happy and proud, he would admire her as always, like when she brought home her report card. In any event, it was on that island that Luisa's most incredible adventure started, involving Carib Indians, kidnappings, sunken treasures, wars, homecomings, children here and there, terrible accusations and even more terrible dangers, but Luisa, though all grown up and a mother several times over, always managed to survive just as children in fairytales escape ogres in the woods.

35

Room no. 6 — An MP-44, hung sidelong on the wall to the right. A World War II German assault rifle, supplied to Regiment 1083 of the 544th Division of the Wehrmacht, where Otto Schimek had been assigned to the 8th Panzergrenadier Company. First prototypes in 1941, first models in 1942, companies involved in the production Haenel and Walther. Elegant elongated shape, wide, heavy stock. Thirty-shot clip, bayonet and grenade launcher mounts, Zf telescopic sight. Practical, essential, eagerly welcomed by division commanders on the eastern front, where it was employed for the first time in 1942. High production costs, for that reason initially halted by the Führer, then stepped up due to the remarkable results achieved, leading the Soviets to produce the AK-47 Kalashnikov, similar in design and cartridge though made differently, milled for the Russians and non-milled for the Germans. In the final phase, equipped with a short cartridge (7.92 Kurz) and, in limited numbers, with an infrared device for night vision (the so-called Vampir). Subsequently named the Sturmgewehr 44, an assault rifle, but mainly for propaganda purposes, when the German Army was on the defensive, on all fronts. Supplied mainly to the crack infantry of the Waffen-SS. Used by the Vopos (the Deutsche Volkspolizei or German People's Police) in the GDR and in the Czechoslovakian People's Army and that of Yugoslavia until the '80s. Models sometimes used by Islamic guerrillas in the Middle East.

PRIVATE SCHIMEK

"Otto Schimek, executed by the Wehrmacht for refusing to fire on the civilian population of Poland." A plaque in gold letters at the entrance to the cemetery of Machowa, Poland. Summer red begonias on the tomb, watched over by white birches, a graceful, soaring Honor Guard among the tombstones and crosses. War and peace, perpetual peace thanks to war. A lovely cemetery, as orderly as a museum. The deceased down below surely experienced grim times, but at least they are spared further adversity.

Yes, it's as if the two of them — Dr. Pollack and Christoph Ransmayr — had written the words on that tombstone, the reporter who'd gone to dig up that story, or nonstory, had said, at least for us Austrians, who perhaps without them, especially without Dr. Pollack and his famous first article, would not have paid much attention to that Polish mess.

Luisa had never managed to meet Dr. Pollack and Dr. Ransmayr, they were always busy or off traveling. It was their assistant or collaborator, Hascher, who received her. "What I know, he knows better," Dr. Pollack had written to her. "We did the research together, and he is informed of everything." Hascher had not objected, and Luisa had gone to see him at his home in Krumpendorf, on the banks of the Woerthersee, where the lake becomes a spongy, muddy marshland.

He'd shown her in and invited her to sit down. Polite, but seemingly uncomfortable, maybe irritated, the gray watery eyes flitting evasively among the furnishings in the room. "Oh, Schimek, I see, though after so many years . . ." He tried to appear distracted, but you could see he was a bit nervous. "And what exactly would you like to know? Oh, the rifle . . ." He looked almost absently out the window to his left. And suddenly sarcastic, almost aggressive: "Which rifle, the one with which he failed to shoot the hostages or the one the firing squad used to riddle him?" He hesitated a moment. "Or the one he tossed into the bushes, when . . . It must be the same one though, right?" He was uncertain. "Yes, I think so, it must be an MP-44, which was the one supplied to his regiment." "Of course," Luisa had said, "without your research, your investigations, that poor Otto would be one of the millions of unknown casualties, at least outside of his country, whereas now a steady stream of pilgrims visit his tomb, Poles, Germans and especially Austrians . . ." "It's understandable," he had smiled bitterly. "We too finally have a hero, an anti-Nazi martyr who refused to point his rifle at those hostages, we can't believe it. Oh, do they still come?" He toyed with a button on his jacket. "You know, you really don't feel like—when you hear talk of miracles, even if it's true that the truck driver, what was his name, oh, Grębski, I think, Roman Grębski . . . that he was paralyzed and more dead than alive, as a result of the accident he'd had, whereas after they took him to that tomb he came back spry and good as new—and maybe without us he might not . . . —oh, my help was entirely secondary, I merely assisted with the research here and there, as directed by Dr. Pollack and Dr. Ransmayr. The Poles never stopped thanking us after Dr. Pollack's first article appeared, they all but kissed our hands, but afterward, when they learned that while they were still thanking and blessing us, the second article had meantime come out—oh, the two of them wrote it, my contribution was modest, just a few details, some concrete facts—later on, as I was saying, when the second article appeared—you know, like a soap opera serial, 'The Rise of Otto Schimek,' 'The Fall of Otto Schimek' . . . after the second article they were ready to spit in our faces . . ."

He'd narrowed his eyes. His face was framed in the small window behind him, the glass streaked by snowflakes that melted as soon as they hit the pane leaving slanting trails of water, scars that lengthened into the deep creases of his face, accentuated when he squinted his eyes. God knows how things must look through those narrowed slits;

the world, seen through those lidded eyes, must be a keen, sharp-edged blade, ready to wound. "Right," he continued, "you must always take cover. Build yourself a nice wall, a high, impenetrable fortification. But what good is it if all of a sudden, just when you feel safe from everything and everyone, a crack suddenly appears in the wall, a crack that widens, grows, splits it apart? The curtain suddenly rises and you're not yet ready, you're alone on the stage, in front of an audience smiling contemptuously, cheerful and ruthless; you look behind you, to the wings, but the show is late, around you there is only the absurd coming and going of people carrying in chairs, moving them around and taking them away again.

"Poor Otto must have felt like that too, shoved onto the stage of war without understanding what was happening, what was about to hit him. A soldier with a swastika on his arm who, before going on stage, looks for his rifle, can't find it; voices are heard, shouts of reproach, it must be the assistant director incensed at someone who still isn't ready, a sergeant can be seen, his fat face furious beneath his helmet. And maybe he too, Pollack I mean, had gone a little too far; he had leaped forward, landing, surprised, in the middle of the scene, and then made an even bigger leap backward, but clumsily; a tumble, more than a leap, while the audience, taking it as a cheap gag, laughs callously and boos, some in the back rows even shouting obscenities. So it's not clear where you stand; an actor hears the applause and the boos and tries to peer into the darkness, to distinguish a face, a look, in the murky dimness of the few iridescent lights, anyone in the shadowy crowd applauding or booing him, trying to figure out who's clapping and who's booing, who they are.

"No, the abandoned rifle turned up afterward"—Hascher had raised his eyelids, thick, heavy curtains, brooding and seemingly somewhat irritated—"and we were the ones who found it. Found, so to speak; how can you expect that after so many years, so many years later, under one bush or another . . . When I went to talk to the corporal who had been in the same company with Otto, he, rather than talk about Schimek, told me about all those soldiers hanged from the trees; the Feldgendarmerie wasted no time, let alone in those days when it was clear that everything was going to hell, and if someone tried to cut and run he quickly found the noose around his neck. In those days you thought about shooting, rather than not shooting; the Russians who were advancing, the Polish partisans, anyone you came across, even yourself, because in those days putting an end to it could seem like a relief. And a soldier like Otto, wounded by a Russian grenade moreover, might feel like being a hero . . .

"'I know,' the corporal told me, 'that for you, who weren't there, it can be difficult to understand. But in the smoke of those grenades, in the mud, with bombs and gunfire exploding in your ears as if it were your head firing and feeling the recoil, with those rifles blasting in your head and shrapnel that seemed to shatter inside you, shooting from your brain, when you don't know whom you're shooting at, who is shooting, well, being a hero . . . that poor Otto, after the grenade that he had taken in his pants, wasn't even sure who he was anymore and in that state of shock . . . So I had him transported to the hospital in Tarnów and then I learned that he had disappeared, maybe ran away, I don't know, and in those days you couldn't give much thought to someone . . . even today you can't . . . those times weren't times; they weren't even war, who knows what . . . an earthquake, a house caving in on you, you wake up and debris keeps falling on your head . . . it's as if no one really existed any more, one man as good as any other, comrades and enemies — Well, a piece of bread undoubtedly tells you something, maybe he left the hospital to take a loaf of bread from a bakery gutted by bombs and then, with a loaf in your hand, dry and hard but good, solid, you don't care all that much about everything else . . . and if the patrol then seizes you with the loaf and without the rifle, which is what happened . . .'

"That, more or less, is what the corporal said. In his recollection, there is no talk of rifles; he talks only about the loaf of bread. Schimek, a soldier without a rifle. It ended up somewhere, that rifle, in a bush, or under the rubble, in any case, he didn't have it.

"Why, when it was learned — oh, well, learned . . . hypothesized — that this rifle was missing, did everybody get so angry? All we found was a gun that didn't exist, that is, we didn't find anything. But how do you find a piece, even a tiny piece, of a story like Schimek's which doesn't exist yet and therefore cannot be verified or even corrected because you don't yet know what to look for to then be able to tell about it? Only at the end is there a story—sometimes not even then, there's only a handful of unrelated, incoherent facts, a jumbled pack of cards, no longer in the deck and not yet dealt according to the game. Before the end, when it is therefore a good story though it doesn't exist, you don't know what its pieces are, in the verbosity and bustle of things and events, you don't know what may be part of it. Why, for example, should a piece of that story be a rifle found or not found in a ditch rather than an empty box of ammunition or the tire of a jeep a few meters away, how can you know?

"Nevertheless, if the gun that wasn't there had already been in the first article, there would perhaps have been fewer begonias and less flag-waving. It would have been quite a disappointment for many; for our foreign minister and Vice Chancellor Alois Mock, for instance, who had at least been able to finally lay a wreath on the tomb of an Austrian anti-Nazi martyr, and also for Austria, which was thereby able to wash its face a little. Of course it's strange that it should wash its face only when a nice, unexpected opportunity to do so occurred, before that no one felt the need to. Dirty face or not, it was proud of its nice clean face, *Austria Felix*, the first victim of Nazi infamy, invaded by fire and sword and occupied by the army of the Third Reich, well, by the threat of fire and sword, with guns that had no need to spit out that fire, but did so just the same, violent invasion and barbaric occupation. Yes, 1,953 Viennese in all of Vienna vote against the *Anschluss*, not many, but what does that mean? Maybe it means something, but the story—when Hitler entered Vienna triumphantly on March 13, 1938, Hitler triumphant but also Vienna—has just begun, so we still don't know what those 1,953 opposed and millions of favorable votes mean. We will perhaps know in the end—even though we don't really know when a story ends either—and therefore we will never know.

"It would have been better for everyone if the truth about that MP-44 had come out right away—that is, if it had not come out, just as the rifle did not come up—in that case, no grave or tombstone. Of course, those priests harassed by the communists in Poland and those brave, even more harassed Polish workers in Gdansk and elsewhere in the country would have had to find some other basis of support, which they deserved, persecuted as they were by informers from the Służba Bezpieczeństwa, which the central office of the party's Security Service had set on them like bedbugs, I say bedbugs for good reason, nasty filthy little creatures that sneak around like those others, equally hidden between the skin and one's clothing. So it is not a bad thing, except perhaps for us, that the rifle hidden in the bushes did not come up that time, that no one realized it was missing. Those imbeciles fail to understand that the young man would deserve all that just the same—gravestone tomb pilgrimages church hymns prayers of thanksgiving for favors received—even if he had tossed away his rifle and been executed for that rather than for refusing to kill women and children.

"He was a good boy, Otto Schimek, of this there is no doubt, and no story, true or false, can say otherwise. He didn't want to hurt anybody, and a person who in a war doesn't shoot, especially in a heinous war like that, in those atrocious times with all those savage brutes around—'I shoot a little here and there but *no ciapo nissuno*, I don't hit nobody, my hands won't never be bloody, but don't tell nobody, for the love of God,' he'd told his sister—a person like that deserves a monument regardless, and votive candles lit under his photograph, no matter why he didn't shoot, even if it was only because he no longer had his rifle. He had retained his decency and the clean scent of wood from when he was apprenticed in Vienna's second district to become a carpenter, as the priest from the Karmelitenkirche who had helped him had said; he didn't do well, just as he hadn't done well in elementary school, where they had placed him in a special-needs class. He hadn't even learned spelling and grammar, as shown by the gross mistakes in the letter he wrote to his brother Rudi before the execution, but only a cretin can find fault with spelling and grammar errors in a gentle, loving, serene letter written by a boy just before he is shot.

"Yes, dear lady"—Hascher had said, pacing back and forth across the room between the armchair and the window, unthinkingly shifting a paperweight resting on some documents and newspapers every time he passed a small credenza—"it's appropriate not to overlook anything, not even that letter, and it is especially important to make sure that the gun is the right one, an MP-44 is a relic after all and those flag-waving bigots said we had besmirched it. As if rifles, among other things, weren't destined to be dragged through the mud, there's a reason why they are constantly being polished and God help us if they didn't shine like dancing shoes. If it hadn't been for us—especially the two of them, I only helped out—I'd like to see if all those pilgrims who came to Machowa to sing 'Glückliches Österreich, glückliche Jugend, die ein Vorbild hat für jede Tugend,' 'Fortunate Austria and fortunate youth who have a model for every virtue,' 'Wyrwij murom zeby krat Zerwij kajdany polam bat,' 'rip open the bars knock down the walls break the chains the knout and the hatchets . . .' and President Lech Wałęsa, on August 1, 1994, in a speech to mark the fiftieth anniversary of the Warsaw Uprising: 'Auschwitz and Warsaw are on Polish soil. Otto Schimek also rests in this ground.'

"Yes, in the good old days of Solidarność Otto had become a symbol of resistance to communism, and the Polish media of the regime got angry at the Archbishop of Przemyśl, His Excellency Monsignor Ignatius Tokarczuk, who in front of 300,000 pilgrims in Częstochowa had celebrated Otto for his heroic refusal to obey inhuman orders, unacceptable for a Christian, and had urged the Poles, all Poles, to follow his example, to disobey authorities who want to impose acts contrary to the principles of the Church and of morality. Monsignor Tokarczuk might be grateful, he probably is, at least he was . . . Anyway, it is likely that the rifle was not fired or was fired aimlessly, any old how, just not to be conspicuous, though without bloodying his hands, as Otto had told his sister the last time he had gone to Vienna on leave after returning from the campaign in Yugoslavia, and before being sent with his regiment to Poland, for operations against the partisans in the area of Dębica.

"Actually"—Hascher was now staring out the window or maybe

he was staring at his cigar, aimed at the window like a gun — "actually he said these things to his mother, Maria Schimek. His sister, Elfriede, heard them from her, at least so she said. Her mother, she'd added, repeated those words to her constantly, 'My hands won't never be bloody.' She instead, Elfriede that is, remembered his departure when he'd been recalled. 'He was seventeen years old, my mother and we sisters, especially me and Mina and Rosa, had always babied him so much, he was still little more than a child . . .' Elfriede, the widow Kujal, an even more inconsolable sister than an inconsolable widow . . .

"'He died because he did not want to kill,' the article by Dr. Pollack began. 'Who will ever know who Otto Schimek is, a young Austrian nonetheless revered in Poland as a martyr? Many lament the fact that our young people have no role models or that they have the wrong models; there are some, however, though too little is known about them.' He, too, Dr. Pollack, was so touched by the story that he had written it with genuine emotion, something no longer done today. Yes, we journalists should do so every now and then, to move our readers a little more. The editor of the *Oesterreichischer Beobachter* always reminds us: the public likes to cry occasionally — not actually weep, but almost. Certainly neither Pollack nor Ransmayr were fazed by the loutish insolent abuse that was later heaped upon them by those devotees of Otto who earlier had praised them to the sky. A courageous, experienced journalist isn't fazed by that, he's well-aware that every decent act of love and truth is repaid with base affronts. The gratitude of the House of Habsburg, as they say in our country. The fact is that to us, if I may humbly include myself, Otto is more dear than he is to those sanctimonious hypocrites who later . . .

"Emphatic or not, the beginning of that article is the beginning of the story, the explosion of the affair. God decrees, *fiat*, and from nothing (or from almost nothing, from a tiny ovule) everything is born; similarly, from something overheard, from a *flatus vocis* drifting in the wind, by pure chance the story of Otto Schimek is born, solely because someone accidentally passes by, hears something, a whisper, before it's lost in the wind, and concocts something based on it, repeating it so he won't forget it, in his own words, of course"—Hascher went on, irritated—"those whispers weren't yet words, and once he gets home and closes the door, leaving the howling wind outside, the story is already born, very quickly, like the world from that exploded egg. Is it true or false? Everything that happens is a master forgery. The entire universe is a retouched copy of some other world.

"A story, too, is a world, one of several possible worlds; who knows how many such universes there are besides ours—ours . . . well . . . not mine, not Schimek's either, nor those who killed him, yet in some way . . . not ours, thank God, but . . . a world, a story, with its chapters, its parts, its settings, the Galician plain and the road that goes through Tarnów and Przemyśl, and the sun that rises and sets wanly on that torpid plain and that night, millions of millennia after the big bang and years and years after Otto's death, when Elfriede . . .

"It was 1970, I think—according to our calendar, maybe Jews would assign a different date and Muslims yet another and paleontologists, geologists, physicists and cosmologists still others—that night when Elfriede had gotten off the bus on route E22, the Galician road that runs from Kraków to Ukraine. She had gotten off at the Machowa stop, where there was only a sign with the name of the village but no village, or at least none that could be seen, and found herself among the crosses of a cemetery. 'I wandered here and there at random,' she later told me when I met her in Vienna to learn more; 'I walked back and forth from one grave to another,' she repeated pensively, pacing between the few pieces of furniture in her room, in her home in Leopoldstadt. A home that gave you a feeling of great apathy, I don't know why; life seemed to have drained out of it, an odor that seeps through the cracks and slips out of the room. That night, among the graves, Elfriede had not found anything and neither had I at her home in Vienna . . .

"But on the bleak, damp Galician plain that night in Machowa, Elfriede would later say, she had been overcome with emotion and upset enough to have become confused and a little lost, so much so that for years she forgot the house and farmyard with the poultry pen that she had seen when leaving the cemetery, the birches pale in the darkness, and the farmer who had led her to the rectory of the small wooden church, where Otto's story as well as the location of his grave had been learned, as she reported, though later, much later.

"Then there is Machowa's parish priest, Eugeniusz Szydlowski, interviewed at the time by a colleague of mine, a journalist from the *Kronen Zeitung*. There's even a photograph. A broad Slavic face, not much hair, a few wisps on his nearly bald head, a raincoat over his clergyman's cassock. 'It was moving,' the *Kronen Zeitung* reported his words, 'I will never forget it. Since that time, that young martyr has been the patron saint of all of us, one of us here in Machowa. Born in Vienna, he died in Machowa — our true homeland is not where we happen to be born, but where we die, the earthly abode that becomes the gateway to the celestial homeland. The blood of a martyr made him Polish and a Christian twice over. One of us. I will never forget that day, when his sister Elfriede came to see me and told me everything. I was ashamed that I knew almost nothing about it.'

"She's there too, in the photo, between those three priests, there she is, you look at her, in front of the monastery of the Redemptorist Fathers in Tuchów, three years after her first meeting with the parish priest. 'She told me that her brother,' the priest says, 'whom she had not heard from for many years, had been shot by the Germans because he had refused to fire on some Poles, civilians, not military, women and children, twenty I believe, taken as hostages. Oh, I assure you, I had tears in my eyes, and as a priest I'd seen it all. She told me about their family, about her widowed mother with thirteen children, eight who had died at birth or were stillborn, God has them now in His glory, the others all raised in the purest Catholic faith, and about their very humble economic situation, about how difficult it was to make a living by repairing and selling used sewing machines — nearly new, the poor woman would say — to buy one of her children a pair of shoes that would later be handed down to another. A family deeply united, devout, especially toward the Madonna. It wasn't easy being Catholic in the public housing flats in Red Vienna where they lived . . .' But a Catholic, Fascist Austrian chancellor saw to it that Red Vienna's working-class neighborhoods were bombed, that everyone was sprayed with red blood. Otto Schimek was nine years old when Austrian bombs fell on Austrian housing. *Wien, Wien nur du allein.*

"'It was in front of the statue of the Virgin,' the priest had continued, 'owing to the devoutness of our faithful parishioner Franciszek Tobías, that Otto, as he wrote to his sisters when he was in Machowa, would stop to pray. I truly hope that our archbishop will be able to quickly initiate the process of beatification. It is certainly hasty to affirm it and I will not be so presumptuous as to offer him suggestions, however, the miraculous, in a word, astounding healing of our good parishioner Roman Grębski, and he's not the only one . . .'

"In fact, a few years later the Archbishop of Tarnów, Monsignor Jerzy Ablewicz, celebrating Mass at Otto's tomb in Machowa, stated solemnly (the *Oesterreichischer Beobachter* reported his words along with those of the Pope): 'As soon as the process of beatification of Karolina Kózka is completed, we will take up the case of Otto Schimek.' And His Holiness Wojtyła, deeply moved: 'I would like to remember a dear person, beloved by our people, a soldier, an Austrian: his name was Otto Schimek and during the war, given orders to shoot and kill the civilian population, he refused to do so and was executed . . . The great distinction he has attained is the distinction of Servant of God. People of my nation constantly gather to pay tribute to this young Austrian. . . .' John Paul II.

"But he did not bless the tombstone, as he wanted to. That rabid Jesuit, Reverend Groppe, SJ, interfered—all in all, given what he thought and said about the Poles, he could have added a second S to his title. He flew into a rage, one of the refugees told me, when he heard and read that at Otto's grave they sang '*Kiedy ranne wstaja zorze Tobie ziemia, Tobie morze,*' 'when the morning dawn arises, to You the Earth, to You the sea.' 'Never mind yours or his or theirs, it's our land, German soil,' he thundered—I read his homilies—preaching to the exiles from the East on Saint Hedwig's day. In any case he was glad to see that scandalous fraud come to naught; it would indeed be very fortunate for Schimek, he proclaimed, if the Lord had forgiven him and meanwhile the Polish bishops bring him up to repeat that East Prussia is *urpolnisch* when we all know that it's *urdeutsch*. Did dear Otto therefore die for Poland? Yes, because his base act helped the Poles, and if all German soldiers were like him ... Well, it's not as if it would have ended much differently, though few German soldiers were like him ...

"A big crowd, that day, at Monsignor Ablewicz's Mass, unsurprisingly, everyone singing, the Lord is my light and my salvation, whom should I fear? Of course, especially when they began singing the hymn of Solidarność ... I was there too, that time in Machowa; processions aren't my cup of tea, but to see, among all those priests and nuns, the little Samaritans, boys and girls, in their white caps and blue capes with little red hearts ... and among them so many faces of the SB — the secret police are the most transparent thing in the world, a spy is immediately recognizable, even from a distance, like the story that circulated in Poland about the Central Committee, which, to prevent its spies from being spotted, decided to hire Negroes who had never been in Poland before and were therefore unknown to everyone. Bland faces then, those spies, but nasty and obtuse, menacingly nasty, better off with those priests dressed in black, not that they inspire joy either, but preaching is still better than the SB. Even the smell, that stale odor in the sacristy, isn't as bad as the rotten stench in the party's headquarters. The agents slipped in, scribbled things on scraps of paper, tried to strike up a conversation between one psalm and another; not that they accomplished much, but it was annoying.

"But then seeing Polish and Austrian flags flying together — nothing to fear, Austria was a neutral country, not part of NATO or the Warsaw Pact — was a pleasure, because any reason, real or bogus, is good if it makes people hug and kiss rather than slaughter each other. Right, because even we in the Eastern March, as Austria was called from the time it happily entered the Reich — true, it was the Reich that entered Austria, but in the end it's the same thing — we too were happy to lose our name, no more Austria, only March of the East, *Ostmark*, the Eastern March of the Reich, everyone in agreement, no, not everyone, only 99.73 percent of Austrians in the referendum proclaimed themselves happy to become inhabitants of the Eastern March, and keep in mind that Jews could not vote, so those

0.27 percent opposed were all pure Aryans. Blood is thicker than water. However, we too had invaded Poland by fire and sword on that September 1, 1939, we Germans and Germans of the Eastern March, among them Otto as well later on, and we beat the living daylights out of them, we destroyed 99 percent of Warsaw and if it's helpful to now sing together, all together as Germans and Austro-Poles, not Austro-Germans and Poles, I too will put on the pale blue cape with the red little hearts. 'This night our historical enemy attacked the Polish State without declaration of war. I confirm this fact and let God and History be my witness. At this historical moment I turn to all Citizens of the Polish State in the belief that the whole Nation will stand by our commander-in-chief and the armed forces in the fight for freedom, independence, honor and an appropriate response to the invader . . .'—Ignacy Moscicki, president of the Polish Republic, September 1, 1939. 'This night for the first time Polish regular soldiers fired on our territory. Since 5:45 A.M. we have been returning the fire, and from now on bombs will be met by bombs . . .'—Adolf Hitler, address before the Reichstag, September 1, 1939.

"Yes"—Hascher resumed—"the bombs of the living are met with bombs. That's why you're better off with the dead than with the living, because you don't have to drop bombs or be in danger of being bombed. 'We would have buried the unknown German, even if we ourselves had killed him,' the gravedigger Paul Koza said—actually he's a farmer who for a little money and out of Christian piety also digs graves from time to time—'it happens, especially in war and times like those when you don't know what's going on anymore, in any case it had nothing to do with Christian duty, we buried him in consecrated ground, although with those Germans you never know if they are Catholic or Protestant or godless, with a Pole at least you know he's Catholic and you know where to put him, and he got the four shovelfuls of earth that everyone is entitled to. I heard about it only afterward from my daughter, she did it all, I stayed put at home, risking my life for someone they had already killed was asking a little too much, with the Germans you didn't take chances.

"'My daughter was more courageous, she was the one, and the

good Lord even rewarded our good deed, because the day after that—one or two days, I don't remember—a German who had come with his patrol told us that the dead man was a friend of his, at least so he thought, in fact, he was almost sure of it, and he let us get away before arbitrarily shooting things up a bit and burning an old sawmill near our house, for no reason, just to show that he was doing his duty; the rain, which had continued all night and all day, quickly put the fire out and we were able to get the mill back in shape when we got back.

"'Only many years later, when even my daughter had forgotten, did we learn what had happened and who that dead boy was, and I hope he's praying for us today. All things considered, it's the least he can do after all we did for him, at our peril, not even thinking of fleeing before the Germans came, though they could have killed us too, it wouldn't have been the first or last time, and maybe our fellow Poles might have taken us for collaborators, wasting our time burying a German, not to mention any Jews among them, they could have made us pay for it, me and my daughter, the one who helped me and is now in Tarnów—the other two had already fled months before, with their mother—they could have made us pay in full plus interest. Anyway, when the parish priest, yes, Father Szydlowski, told us who the dead boy was, and that he had been a hero and a good Christian, a true martyr, he was sure of it, the dead man's sister herself, Elfriede, had told him, and now everyone knows . . .'

"Even the chance meeting on the train, Elfriede had told Father Szydlowski, had been a miracle, you could say. She had never been able to find out anything about her brother Otto and it bothered her. She had even turned to the Austrian Black Cross, the section that dealt with the graves of the war dead, but the office had replied, even in 1970, that they'd been unable to obtain any information about where he might be buried. She brooded over it, she spoke of nothing but that, even to people she didn't know. Like the time on the train, on her way to Spittal to visit a cousin, when she was talking about it with a woman from Wiener Neustadt, and a man standing at the door of the compartment, who had overheard the whole story even though his back was turned to them and he was looking out the window, said that he knew Otto, that he was an old friend of his, that they had been in the same company, and that he'd heard he must have died somewhere around Tarnów or Przemyśl.

"No, not actually in Machowa, but in short, yes, in Pilzno, in the forest near Lipiny, less than ten kilometers from the cemetery of Machowa. 'Of course I've seen the place,' Elfriede said, 'I had to see the place where my brother died, in the Lipiny forest, a very nice farmer, Czeslaw Madej is his name, took me there. I myself don't even know why I set out like that, without having any idea . . . but I thought it was heaven above that let me meet that friend of Otto and so I went to Galicia. When I saw the sign Machowa it seemed to me that, in fact, the young man had been talking about that very place as he drew a sketch on a sheet of paper—not very exact—that was supposed to indicate the route to Ukraine and a couple of places where it must have happened. I got off, not really knowing where I was, what I was doing there, but, well, I felt like I was following a voice in my heart . . . Ottile, Ottile, where are you, I'm here, your Elfriede . . .' and when the farmer whose farmhouse she had knocked at had brought her to the priest and she had showed him the sketch, he'd gone with her, in the cold, gray rain, and had led her to that small mound of earth in the forest. 'Perhaps he is here,' he'd told her. 'Every so often we hear about a German soldier buried more or less here, the only one—you know, in war even Christian piety becomes difficult and after what happened it wasn't easy to think, as we should have, that even a German soldier is our brother . . .' Especially if he's dead," Hascher had remarked, brushing off some cigar ash that had fallen on his jacket like the grayish, snowy rain that was falling outside the window, and perhaps had also been falling that night in the forest where the priest and Elfriede wandered around aimlessly. "Graves, graves . . . the whole earth is a grave, isn't it? Everywhere there is someone buried, or rather, there isn't, he has become moist soil, yes, a few bones, like leftovers on a plate, but there is really no one in a grave anymore, they should write 'here does not lie' and the same goes for everyone in the world.

"'You had already heard of this story?' the reporter from the

Kronen Zeitung had asked Machowa's parish priest. 'Yes, of course . . . well, that is . . . I knew that an unknown German soldier, whose body had been placed in a munitions chest in Pilzno, where he had died—shot to death for desertion and cowardice, some had heard, that was the rumor spread by the Nazis who were frightened by his example of courage and faith, as later became clear. That lie, the widow Kujal told me, had been told to the family in a dispatch from the war tribunal operating in Galicia, which had also let the family have the last letter written by Otto before his execution. The family did not even deign to refute the slander, what sense does it make to waste time arguing with the father of lies, with the Tempter? Just pray, Our Lord will be the One to confound him. Elfriede told me that three soldiers had brought him to the cemetery in Machowa, but that November night the ground was frozen and no grave could be dug. So they left him there, Elfriede kept saying, under a watery sleet, and they went away, planning to come back and bury him the next day. Later I learned that Matylda, the gravedigger's daughter, had buried him. Without a coffin, because they had no money to pay for one and Danek Kopalski, the carpenter who made coffins for the graves in Machowa, refused, given that they couldn't pay him, and it was understandable, you can't expect a Pole to take the bread out of his own mouth for a dead German at a time of hunger . . . And so, Matylda told me, we dragged him through the snow.'

"No, no blood trail"—Hascher added—"it would be nice for the story, but the women never mentioned it; no reddish stain in the rain in the slush in the mud and in the furrow left behind by the dragged body, which quickly filled with murky water. Maybe the cold, stiff body wasn't dripping any more blood, and at the morgue, namely the forest, that awaited him they undoubtedly did not do hematic analyses. 'But you can see how they must have loved my brother,' Elfriede went on, 'if they practically apologized for not being able to pay for a coffin for him and had to bury him like that, in the cold and rain. A thing like that, in a time of war and with enemies, you only do for someone who has saved your life; maybe some of their relatives were among the hostages that Otto refused to kill.'

"By dredging up that story"—Hascher told Luisa—"we almost felt like we were the ones who buried that poor Otto in Machowa. The pen is a spade, it exposes graves, digs and reveals skeletons and secrets, or it covers them up with shovelfuls of words heavier than earth. It bores into the dirt and, depending, lays out the remains in darkness or in broad daylight, to general applause. Like until recently. Now, however, they just about call us, all three of us, *Saujude*, maybe communists. And to think that it is also our fault, sorry, I meant also thanks to us, that Monsignor Tokarczuk, in 1982, was able to thunder against General Jaruzelski, in that sermon in Częstochowa. 'Brothers and sisters! Otto Schimek said no. He was executed and buried. A hero who paid the ultimate price in order to remain true to his conscience . . . but we too have our Polish Schimeks. The Schimeks of 1956, the Schimeks of Gdansk in 1970, the Schimeks of today, whom one day we will honor and celebrate as those who saved their honor and the honor of the nation!' And what about the honor of those who dug up that honor and were then spat in the face?"

Hascher had blurted it out, no longer uncomfortable but furious. It's good for your health, being angry; you feel confident, the world is a bunch of shit they throw at you, but you give it back tit for tat, shit for shit, only when you're pissed are you really you, you know who you are, you're that anger, a solid, well-defined "I" who knows what he's doing and knows himself. You're you, ready to return a slap in the face or even two. As long as there are dogs hounding you it means you exist, and you know who you are, principled in your fury. When he flew into a rage, she actually liked Hascher.

He wasn't upset with those flag-waving bigots who called him and the two writers Jews and communists for having sullied the image of a pure Austrian Catholic hero, a banner of liberty and faith, saying that he had run off, taking advantage of being hospitalized for a slight wound, that he had been arrested three or four weeks later in Tarnów as he was roaming the streets in civilian clothes with a big loaf of bread under his arm, and shot a few days later for desertion.

According to several witnesses, German military authorities seemed more outraged over the loaf of bread than over his going

AWOL—if in fact that's what really happened, if it's really true that he defected. A big loaf, the report of the Feldgendarmerie in Tarnów said, a dark loaf, carried under his arm the way a soldier should instead carry his rifle, fighting a war is not going to the bakery. That loaf must have also led the military court to be ill-disposed. Black bread, sour, made of rye and possibly potato. It must have been quite good, at least in those circumstances, because a bigger loaf keeps a little better, it doesn't dry out until a little later. Bread, humble and good like the man himself . . . I was hungry, Colonel, Sir. All of Germany is hungry, soldier, you are here to defend it, to prevent the enemy, incited by the Jews, from taking bread away from German children. And today the German Jews, in Machowa they say, want to take away our martyr.

No, it wasn't the abusive letters from the Otto Schimek Samaritan Group, with their flags sporting the Polish and Austrian colors, their pilgrimages and their works of mercy that troubled Hascher and his friends, the accusations of sullying a hero "of faith, truth and love," as Prothonotary Apostolic Professor Monsignor Stanislaw Grzybek had said in his sermon in Kraków. And Dr. Pollack had certainly not been bothered by reading the book written against him by Lech Niekrasz, *Spór o grenadiera Schimka* (The Dispute over Grenadier Schimek), which portrays him as a malicious, caustic intellectual, perhaps of Jewish ancestry, sardonically satisfied with his iconoclasm.

No, it's not the malice of others that wounds you; were it not for fundamental reasons of dignity, you would willingly offer the other cheek to your detractors, after all, who gives a damn. In fact, if a bastard picks on you, you feel you're in the right. But if five sisters, Smilka, Dionisja, Ambrozja, Jadwiga and Marina, make a pilgrimage to the grave of that poor Otto and thank you for what you did for that hero, not knowing at the time that you later found out and wrote that he had instead deserted . . . Well, you feel somewhat hurt. Luckily there was always some SOB who made you feel you were justified, like that bastard Father Groppe who calls Schimek a coward, or like a certain Jan Suborski—they must be Jews, I'm sure, he had written from Wrocław, they destroy besmirch defile everything, they have it in for us Poles more than they do the Germans, and besides, before Hitler came they were hand in glove with the Germans against us.

Yes, Luisa said to herself, those three — Pollack, Ransmayr and Hascher — told the truth . . . but when? The first or the second time? Like Pontius Pilate, we don't really know what truth is, and, unlike Pilate, we wouldn't know whom to ask. Maybe it's a landmine; it begins by destroying others and ends up destroying itself; it knocks the pedestal out from under an idol, and crash-bang! the idol falls, but then it smashes the plinth on which the pedestal rested and there's another collapse, until the ground all around caves in and even the truth is sent flying, swallowed up by the quicksand to which it opened the way.

Sure, those priests singing hosannas at the tomb of a soldier holding a fake rifle instead of a real loaf of bread are irritating, but the spies from the Służba Bezpieczeństwa who mingle with them and mark down their names to report to the Central Security Service and the party's higher *bonzes* turn your stomach. If someone ends up in trouble for having prayed at Schimek's grave or for maybe having shouted "Long live the Schimeks of Poznań, long live the Schimeks of Gdansk!" and then someone else comes along to snatch away the flag for which that Schimek took a beating, to tell the first one that it's not true, that in that grave lies not a hero but just a poor devil who didn't make it, and if that someone then turns out to be the same one, the one who earlier sang the litanies of the hero and saint, well, then nothing makes any sense and you feel like taking it all back, the first article, the second and all the rest, like the one in the *Tygodnik Powszechny*, the Catholic weekly of Kraków, which compares Schimek to Father Kolbe and even argues that poor Otto is holier and more heroic because Father Kolbe was a priest and a mature man, whereas Otto was a boy who didn't even know how to write properly and so it's all the more miraculous that he found the strength, the courage — the last who became first. And the *Arbeiterzeitung*, an Austrian newspaper — a government publication, true, but still socialist — said more or less the same things.

So why go rummaging, nosing around underground? History is a garbage dump—of course, if you look closely useful things are also found, some object that's still good that can be reutilized and re-cycled. Those beggars, in short, those historians who stick their hands in trash bins may sometimes even find something to eat . . . however, if they bring you stew in a restaurant, it may be best not to ask whether leftovers from the day before have been thrown back in—chewed up meat, Luisa's friend Bepo always used to say, frowning and eyeing the dish suspiciously.

That's why a waiter ducks his head when the rotten apples he's served are thrown at him; he's just trying to dodge them, it's human nature, but without protesting. Mishaps along the way, when your job is that of a bloodhound and you go home with findings in your mouth, often untrue. On the other hand when you receive letters—it still happens, Hascher said, news arrives late in Galicia and in gen-eral in the Polish provinces—letters from Tarnów or Pilzno or from some other Galician village, maybe from Machowa, thanking you for having made this martyr known, this saint, this hero, and telling you how moving it was to make a pilgrimage with the priest to the tomb, and how they sang and prayed, and how one of them, Roman Gręb-ski, was miraculously healed, and thanking you for having helped bring this blessed beautiful story to light, how do you explain that when afterward, however, it seems you have discovered that . . .

It's terrible to hear those battered good people cling to Otto as if to a piece of wood in the sea and thank you for having tossed them that piece of wood, not knowing that meanwhile you've taken him away, and you'd like to tell them, tell them that for you too Schi-mek is a very dear boy, a good, religious boy, and that, even if—but how do you talk about it, words are sour breath repeating on you . . . Maybe, after sending that letter, so grateful and touched, they've read and know about the other article and are perhaps now writing you an abusive letter . . . Maybe if you make a mistake it's best not to correct it and just keep quiet, lie low, say nothing . . . yet in any case it's right to honor that boy, who at least did not want to kill, and if everyone in the Wehrmacht had done as he had, millions of people would have been saved . . . His rifle was always jamming, a witness says. That says something.

And what if things had actually gone as you had believed the first time? Stories come and go, you find them in your pocket, who knows how, then they fall out of your pocket and you can't find them any-more, a handful of leaves lifted and blown about by the wind, one leaf indistinguishable from the other, and it's useless to stand there fussily arranging them in an herbarium. With men, with their feelings, with their lives and their deaths you can't be precise; with things you can, that's better than nothing, but it's best to forget it. Instead of photo-graphs and begonias, they should just place a nice big loaf of bread on that grave in Machowa, Hascher concluded; when it gets stale and crumbles, it can be replaced by another one, like you do with flowers that have dried and withered. He deserves it, the glory, because of that loaf. And maybe we deserve a little too, we who, searching for a rifle, found a loaf of bread. Real, tangible, something you can chew and put in your mouth or maybe even give a piece to another starving man, never mind plaques and songs and medals, bread is bread . . .

Twice a hero, that's the only thing you can say. A hero for running away, for not wanting to shoot or be shot even though he was shot pre-cisely because he did not want to shoot. A hero for that loaf of bread under his arm that rises majestically against the sludge of war, flags and graves. "My heart is calm, in the hands of God, I know that we will all see each other again in heaven," he wrote before his death to his brother Rudie. The letter is full of mistakes—spelling, grammar, syntax errors. Good thing they didn't correct those gross blunders, as some pious souls wanted to. Maybe only two things are certain in this story, those grammatical mistakes and death. Maybe there is a third as well, the rifle. It exists and was certainly fired—at someone, aim-lessly, haphazardly, in any event sooner or later it was fired. Bullets aren't the only things fired from its barrel, but also stories—stories about the person who fired, about the person who was shot, about the person who dumped his weapon. Polishing the barrel is like rubbing Aladdin's lamp, the genie appears and has many tales to tell, stories and smoke screens. And every story, when it ends, Luisa thought as she said goodbye to Hascher, converges in the great inverter where everything begins or recommences.

"War didn't interest him," is how Pollack and Ransmayr summarize Schimek's life and death. Maybe it would have been better to write the second article to begin with, then the first one. That way at least there would not have been any ill-timed thank you letters, so hard to accept; being attacked for what you did is nothing, what hurts is being praised for what you did not do or maybe being praised for one thing when you did just the opposite. It's as though someone you once loved fell in love with you when you were sick and tired of him, it's worse than the other way around.

36.

Room no. 8—A *Gulaschkanone*. A caisson that carries big rich pots for the field kitchen. Fatty, bubbling soups, a few bits of meat. The general tastes it, mindful of other goulashes in some inviting *Stube*. A story going around all the fronts tells about the soldier who, standing before the general in review, thinks he's required to say that the goulash is great and gets a talking-to, that too, like the goulash, is good for the troops.

Eating flesh, pawing flesh, butchering flesh. They don't skimp on flesh, at death's little banquets. Corruption of the flesh. After death, below ground or covered by mud in the trenches. Before dying in sin, venial or mortal, agonizing attempts to grope around for a bit of happiness before disappearing. "My loneliness is yo-o-u," the song says. Rotten flesh, not only in the pot.

37

Room no. 19—Under the big block letters BEDBUGS AND EM-
PIRES. LONG LIVE THE FÜHRER, a sword belonging to the guard of
Archduke Maximilian or Maximilian of Mexico. Alpaca-steel blade,
sheath of leather, wood and silver-plated brass. Length 95–105 cm.
Engraved on the sword are the monogram "M1," the coat of arms of
the emperor of Mexico and the inscription "B.W. Ohligs-Haussmann
k.k. Hof Waffen Fabrikant in Wien."

A note in his own hand, on a page torn from a notebook, to be
placed—under glass—alongside the sword: "I would have preferred
a sword from his guard in the Miramare Castle, when he was a great
archduke with a rich future and not an insignificant emperor about
to die. Not because the swords that saluted the archduke are more
striking than those that protected the emperor, but because at Miramare they were never drawn from their sheaths except at ceremonies.
They did not spill blood—impressive and useless, that's how weapons
should be, like those of Popel's tin soldiers—whereas in Mexico they
had to be raised and lowered to strike, to no avail, as always.

"Why didn't he listen to what people in Trieste were singing
softly, when he was offered the crown? *Massimiliano non ti fidare /
resta al Castello di Miramare. / Quella corona di Montezuma / è un
nappo gallico pieno di schiuma. / Del timeo Danaos or ti ricorda /
sotto la porpora trovi la corda . . .* Oh, Maximilian, don't trust them,
stay at Miramare Castle. That crown of Montezuma is a Gallic goblet
full of froth. Remember the Greeks bearing gifts, beneath the purple
mantle you'll find the rope . . . He could have given it to me, that
crown, I would have put that too in the Museum. If everyone gave

me their weapons, if all the world's weapons were in the Museum, the world would be disarmed, there would finally be peace. But it would take a huge Museum, as vast as the world . . ."

"We proclaim, therefore, in this hour of maximum danger, our loyalty to the Führer, Heil Hitler, Sieg Heil, Heil Hitler!" High Commissioner Friedrich Rainer, formerly Gauleiter of Carinthia and Upper Carniola, dabs his brow, wipes his sweaty hand on his pants. The Führer often makes this gesture as well, when speaking to the crowds; it's hard to say if it's a conscious imitation on Rainer's part or a spontaneous instinct. Both, probably. Indeed, one and the same. Imitation is a fundamental process of evolution; a monkey mimics another who was able to get hold of a fruit that was difficult to reach, repeats the act until the act becomes his, his nature. Thus is born, no, thus he becomes *Homo sapiens*. Or *insipiens*, it depends. Sweat is universal, but there's sweat and there's sweat. Their difference should be studied.

There is Nazi sweat; frigid, different from the Bolshevik kind with its heavy human odor of long marches without a change of underwear. Also different from the sweat of those sent to the wall — of many, not all, because not everyone sweats at that moment. Franz Jägerstätter, for example, when they beheaded him because his conscience as a Catholic would not allow him to be a soldier of the Third Reich, doesn't seem to have sweated. He was cool, calm. Irritated, of course, at having to die, angry, but not hysterical or rattled; if his wife had been there, next to him, and if he had had the chance, he probably would have made love to her as usual, not bad at all, as he had done throughout his life, to the envy of his fellow countrymen. Faith, it is written, moves mountains; it certainly moves the adrenals.

Times are grave, difficult, the high commissioner says, licking and swallowing a bead or two of sweat that runs into his mouth as it trickles down his forehead and cheeks. The sun filters through the windows of the Audience Hall in the Castle of Miramare, the most suitable venue for this grand occasion with its portraits of the great sovereigns and the coats of arms of the countries of the Habsburg

Crown on the coffered ceiling. The large chandelier from Bohemia is lit, a milky gleam, my skin white as the magnolias of Miramare, the Empress Carlota would say; the slush of time, the light turns the crystal arms rosy pink, noble blood spoiled by centuries and the fevers of a morbid sea. Pearls of champagne shimmer and twinkle in the engraved goblets, more transparent and fragile than air, which perhaps Maximilian had not had time to raise but which are now raised for the Führer's birthday, April 20, 1945.

Large sprays of violet-blue jacaranda in the painting above the door in Chapultepec Castle, the Mexican viceroy's old residence, which Maximilian, unaware that he was on his way to the firing squad in Querétaro, frescoed and restored in his desire to make it a copy of Miramare — Miravalle, he wanted to call it — unwittingly preparing a prison instead, the prison that the castle would later become — well after his death, but long before Carlota's death — for other defeated men, no less unfortunate than an emperor. The improvident, well-intentioned emperor loved the jacarandas when, lying in the gardens of Chapultepec with his beautiful *india* redolent of musk, a violet and blue cascade fell on them in the evening, soon dark. The jacaranda's flowers are violet-blue; the seeds, many many seeds, fall to the ground and presently form a thick grassy carpet, a bed to sink into. A ripple billows through the branches of the large tree, bright green fronds and dark purplish flowers flutter in the hot breeze, the crests and foam of night's breakers on the sumptuously laid table in the Audience Hall. The light from the chandelier fractures into myriad glints and reflections; glimmers of red gold among the bottles and glasses, sparkling flashes from the cutlery and frosty crystal goblets.

At Chapultepec instead the darkness of swift night was tender and inviting, like a woman's garden. Fiery night, the lava of Popocatépetl and Iztaccíhuatl — the volcanoes that are so lovely to gaze at in the dark blue distance from the imperial balcony of the castle — was already seething red and blistering, a tide of blood rising from the heart of a dark, persecuted people who want to persecute those who have come to suck them up without even realizing it, a bloody surge that will engulf the weary conquistadors who have once again come from the sea, though this time to die rather than to kill.

A few nights of love, a grand, sad *noche* but without deliverance or redemption; it will not be Montezuma who dies but the conquistador, who is too nobly deluded to crush and build empires. In Querétaro bullets await him, but above all bedbugs, that strain of bugs that live only there, *Cimex domesticus Queretari*, it's a discovery he made, being an expert and enthusiastic naturalist, passionate about insects, snails, spiders and centipedes.

Maximilian discovered and classified the *Cimex domesticus Queretari* shortly before being taken captive, during the fighting and whistling of bullets, sorry that he did not have a flacon with him to save it and take it back home, to the palace, to add it to his collection. I wonder if they were the same bedbugs that had kept him and Carlota from sleeping on their first night in the Mexican Imperial Palace. In any case, he would find them again in Querétaro, probably a moment before the execution, because bedbugs prefer the blood of the living.

A belligerent creature, the bedbug. A large black body, flat dorsal-ventralwise, an elongated oval profile. The thorax reveals two lateral expansions of the pronotum. The antennae consist of four segments, the end two being thin and extended; sharp, prehensile tentacles and the claws of an excavator that chews up and seizes the debris of what it has torn up. A black ultra-mobile tank, excellent for clashes in the moors, like the Soviet T-34, and especially on the slopes. The bedbug climbs, if necessary up to the ceiling; it pierces the skin with two needles, one for extracting the blood, the other to inject its anticoagulant saliva and anesthetic. The effect on the enemy can sometimes be delayed, which increases its potency and effectiveness because it comes as a surprise, when you don't realize you are under attack. The sting can cause anxiety, stress and insomnia, powerful weapons to defeat an enemy; yellowish skin, dry as a desert, which hardly bleeds anymore even when scratched mercilessly. The 108 families of bugs are divided into 22 genuses. Military terminology of scientific classification: Cohort-Exopterygota, Subcoorte-Neoptera, cohorts and maniples agile in the assault . . .

Bedbugs, associated with savages and wretched half-breeds, like all scruffy Mexicans, the high commissioner thinks, recalling some book he hastily read when preparing his speech. It's no coincidence that when the Führer triumphantly entered Vienna, transforming Austria, with its overstated grandeur and its promiscuous cross-breeding, into a commonplace, boring Eastern March, only Mexico protested. Some farce, speaking out from those hovels that think they're protected by the ocean. For a civilized people, it's easy to eliminate the bedbugs that plagued Maximilian so much — eradicate them like the gypsies, who unlike the Jews aren't always kicking up a fuss. Disinfestation is easy, even with those filthy peasants who let themselves be eaten alive by their bedbugs, like the august imperial couple, for that matter.

Nights at Miramare, at Chapultepec. Time was different then — even the time of advancing death and madness, the death of the emperor of Mexico, the well-intentioned and vacuous *Walzerkönig*, and the madness of his wife, who went mad because she survived his world and therefore the world. Surviving is madness, the last man on the destroyed earth will be mad, he will have only himself and therefore nothing but his own delirium. Back then time had a different smell, strong, heady, satisfying, even toxic; the smell of flesh, of the rosy pink flower that opened between the thighs of the *india* who was loved by the noble, ridiculous emperor, a noble man and ridiculous emperor.

Now, on that April 20, 1945, at Miramare, time has a different stench — of burning flesh, of prussic acid. The Führer exudes the reek of the Risiera mixed with the smell of bitter almonds, of reliable potassium cyanide that wafts through the air before entering the throat and settling accounts. They say he gave off other odors as well, the Führer who suffered from stomach and intestinal issues, but the high commissioner is neither his orderly nor his secretary and doesn't notice the unfortunate flatulence. He doesn't perceive his own smell either — sweaty, which is not at odds with general toasts to the Führer and wishing him well in the extreme, heroic battle he is fighting to save Europe from the Bolsheviks and from the Jews. A battle that he will undoubtedly win if the Allies who are approaching Berlin, which the Soviets are already much closer to, realize that to save Europe it is necessary for everyone to unite against the Bolsheviks, even perfidious Albion, even America, which is run by Jews—though those needn't be killed, just kill the Jews in Europe, Russian, Polish, Czech, Hungarian and so on, especially German Jews—that way Europe and its peoples will be free.

All peoples. In fact General Domanov also raises a glass to the Führer's health on behalf of the Cossacks, whom the Germans dragged with them when retreating from the Soviet Union, promising them a homeland to make up for the one Stalin eliminated. Drinking a toast with him are General Muschitzky, who recalls the struggle of the Serbian Chetniks against the Bolsheviks, Captain Janko Debeljak, who acclaims the German-Slovenian brotherhood of arms, and Oberstleutnant Modeschin, who attests to the Croats' love for the Führer. Vultures and hyenas of the world unite, unaware that you are carrion and carcasses instead, whose stench is already attracting necrophagous feeders.

Does the flesh of the high commissioner, whom the gallows keeps an eye on from above, a large bird that will continue looming over him even when he tries to escape eight days later, already give off a bad odor? There would be good reasons to think not, because his speech is flawless. But perhaps those outspread wings are still a little distance away, more so than for others, nonetheless, the course is already set. The high commissioner shakes hands with wounded soldiers, workers, laborers, all the employees. A National Socialist is still a socialist. Impassioned, he doesn't notice the sour smell that his sweat gives off, though it causes Baron Economo to step back—albeit imperceptibly, politely—having just finished expressing his trusting gratitude to the German authorities, on behalf of the naval operation that supplies bread to so many of his citizens and which he heads and oversees. The ones who don't particularly smell the stench of History however are the unfortunate Cossacks, Serbs, Croats and Slovenes, to whom the script, revised at the last minute, assigned the role of the Nibelungs.

In the end Commissioner Rainer speaks solely for them; for the only ones who take him seriously and believe in his words and in the freedom of a Europe threatened by big red Slavia. He also knows that Prefect Coceani doesn't even believe his own words when he raises his glass, expressing on behalf of the people of Trieste — also affected by the tragedy but confident that the two great nations, Germany and Italy, will, united, be up to the task that History has assigned them — his admiration for the German people, who though attacked from all sides, are fighting heroically, *Sieg Heil.* The high commissioner will not be around to be surprised a few days later, on April 30, when Prefect Coceani guardedly and behind closed doors supports the Fascist mayor Pagnini, ready to fire on German landing craft from Town Hall, because he will have already fled two days earlier, but he would not have been surprised even if he had stayed to heroically risk his life, because he knows whom not to trust and whom to trust, namely no one.

Some, yes, he thinks listening absent-mindedly to General Esposito, who is praising the bonds of comradeship between the armed forces of the Italian Social Republic and those of the Reich, and the party secretary, Sambo, who is actually delivering the Black Shirts' greeting in German. The only ones who believe in a Western civilization defended by the Reich against Slavic and Asian Bolshevism are those four, neither Germans nor Latins and not even French or English but only Slavs, last minute hoped for allies — as he'd said shortly before — in the fight against the barbarous Slavic East, which communist Jews hurl against Europe, the new Europe of the Führer and of all Westerners. Yes, General and Feldataman Domanov, who with his Cossacks followed Krasnov and the Wehrmacht through half of Europe to find a homeland and thinks he has found it in Carnia, believes in the Reich and in the West, and repeats the toast he's just made; the other three *s'ciavi,* Slavs, also believe, not just because they are left with nothing else, but because dying for the master is the only consolation for lowliest slaves.

It's hot, in the Audience Hall, more than one would think seeing the wind rippling the waves beyond the windows of the castle. The high commissioner thanks everyone; he thanks General Sommavilla of the Home Guard, he thanks the vice president of the Industrial Union, reading a message from the president, who unfortunately is absent. Rainer is well aware that he equally subsidizes supporters of the Italian Social Republic, partisans and even the German Command — for expenses related to works necessary for the city, of course, no shady business and no corruption, which is why the gold teeth, jewelry and other possessions of the deportees are more than enough. In any case, *pecunia non olet* and on April 20, 1945, it is understandable that those who have a little money in their pockets — ship owners, industrialists, builders — would try to ensure a future for themselves no matter what, it's no coincidence that Trieste is a city of insurance companies.

The luncheon is served. It's nice to sit at the table; eating and drinking together makes you feel more like friends. Germans, Italians, Cossacks, Serbs, Croats, Slovenes. The new Europe of peoples. All peoples. Or almost. Even though the president of the Industrial Union isn't there — but it's as if he were there, with that heartfelt message of his — no matter, there are others to represent him ably and to represent the city. A greeting, a message, a good wish; one toast leads to another, faces are shiny and damp, the chandelier casts reflections on the ceiling, splotches of light on the table like the petals of overblown white roses, gold sparkles and tremulous glimmers of the sea filter through the windows and ripple over the coats of arms of the Kronländer, the Crown Lands of the old empire. Windic March, Carinthia, Carniola, Lodomeria, Upper and Lower Lusatia, Aragon, Illyria. Photographs are taken, group shots. The flash, a loud report, a burst of white smoke, the white and yellow curtains tremble, outside the window gulls scatter in a dazzling glare of white wings, German officers sing, solemn at first then a little bawdy. The double-headed eagle is stuffed and frozen on the ceiling, its claws useless in that aviary; only the eye, fixed and rapacious, is the eye of Judgment, an embalmed judge who nonetheless has already issued an irrevocable verdict, Maximilian's Mexican Empire and Hitler's Millennial Reich lasted the one a little less and the other a little longer than the time to build the castle, Carlota's madness lasted more than four times as long as the two empires put together.

They get up from the table, take a walk, scatter through the parlors. The sun goes down but it's hot, the high commissioner unbuttons the collar of his uniform, the other officers do the same, those in civilian clothes loosen their ties. They climb the grand staircase to the upper floor, a few with some effort due to the free-flowing libations, several poke their noses into the Hall of the Rose of the Winds and sniggering stick their fingers into the holes of the green billiard table. The high commissioner enters the Throne Room that Maximilian did not have time to see (nor to sit on its throne) and looks dully at the genealogical painting of the Habsburgs and the Lorraines, the family tree painted by Ede Heinrich; those faces, those wigs, those hats say very little to him.

In the Hall of Seagulls an SS major belches, as he gazes nostalgically out the window at the small harbor and the sea. Globočnik, dear old Globus, also enters the Hall of Seagulls, there is a passage connecting the two rooms, and looks at the painting portraying the slave market in Smyrna with the air of a connoisseur. Among those tits, those fleshy thighs, those big dark languid eyes, he is in his element, almost like at the Risiera. He doesn't care so much for those seagulls depicted in the coffered ceiling, however, seagulls flying around with serpents in their beaks, no, scrolls with Latin sayings. The eyes of evil birds; looking up at them like that with his head tilted back he feels almost dizzy, it might also be the wine the champagne and the liqueurs that are making his head spin — the seagulls skim the ground, curving white wings, sharp sabers; they screech, the rostrums with the scarlet scrolls wheel around his head, the sharp beaks menacing, grazing him. *In vino veritas,* says a scroll; truth is everywhere, everyone demands and expects it, the Führer, the Jews, his lawyer friend Donnenberg whose advice he does not follow. Another gull swoops past him, *Muneribus vel dii capiuntur,* the scroll in its beak reads; couldn't agree more, everything, everyone can be bought, *co'na bela mandola se giusta tuto*, a good bribe greases the wheels, even his friend Marieto had said so, the Jews know it too, better than anyone else; some even managed to save their asses that way and that's fine with him, because his pockets also gained by it and he doesn't hate the Jews, as long as they pay. He doesn't look at them with the evil eye those seagulls are giving him; better get out of there, regardless of the tits in the painting.

Globus leaves, he goes back to the Audience Hall which is a shambles, tablecloths and plates on the floor, broken glasses. The SS major, respectfully behind him at the proper distance — in Trieste Globus is the SS's highest authority — remained in the Hall of Seagulls. The major is gazing not so much at the gulls as at the harbor and the statue of the Sphinx, with a vacant expression. He senses a return home, but isn't sure where and for whom; not for him, for instance, given that his house in East Prussia vanished in the tsunami that the war washed over it, there's no way of even knowing how those who were in it ended up, but the major feels dulled, between him and his grief for his loved ones who have remained — or have not remained, it's not known, communication is so uncertain — there is a blanket of tepid snow, a somnolence that the champagne has certainly helped, but that isn't caused by champagne; it comes from who knows where, from clogged passageways of the heart, that no longer let anything get through.

In the numerous rooms and in the park they let themselves go a little, as people do at parties and as soldiers have a right to do; flesh killed in war and flesh exposed to danger in war needs a little flesh on leave from an unbuttoned uniform, especially flesh to fondle without much concern. In the shady park designed with such great, though short-sighted, love by Maximilian — black Monterey cypresses, orange-brown arbutuses of the South, the Sphinx staring at the sphinxlike sea, an island of the blessed and the dead — one is submerged and disappears.

The ilex planted by Maximilian and Carlota is beginning to bloom, the catkins hang ungainly and limp; the female flowers are smaller, as they should be, but they produce hard acorns, while the pompous swollen males dangle. In the dense green-brown, the vanguard of evening, the sated, tipsy guests grope a likely gardener, *kommt eine süsse Taube zu dir geflogen*, someone sings "La Paloma" softly in German. A dove as white as snow; white flowers of the magnolia, Carlota's white delicate skin, the dark skin of the Indians and mulattos in Mexico must be very different—those Hungarian hussars, those Polish *uhlans* and that Austrian troop that Maximilian brought there with him were fortunate; unlike us, with the hard faces of these Slavic ladies, *s'ciavi*, the women don't love us anymore because we wear a black shirt. Cracks widen in the bark of the Sabine Pine—it too came here from Mexico, but at least it arrived alive, unlike its emperor—a distressing rift; blooming is painful, it means growing old, withering.

I wonder whether statues, deep down, also bloom somehow—that is shrivel up—marble veins gradually stiffening then perhaps turning brittle, white arms that fracture, in the end even stone ages and will one day become dust, thinks the plump Bavarian captain, who in peacetime is a teacher at the lyceum in Freising. Luckily there are copies, like the one of Aphrodite in Capua near the bar in the park, or the Medici Venus there on that column. A copy is a facelift of the original. Less interesting, of course, but fresher, more enticing, with fewer scars of time. Rubbing up against the Venus de Milo . . . Obscene, all right, the teacher-captain thinks, but if it helps to keep going even with all that death around . . .

Anyway, apart from the statues and the maids and the gardeners, there are also other men's consorts, always watched but not too closely, strolling among the dark green araucarias, *Araucaria araucana*, tall and slender. The beautiful hard mouths of the ladies around here, like the ones who came to the gathering with their influential husbands. Mouths capable of biting eagerly—it's understandable, in war there is a shortage of everything and this helps—though not of giving a real kiss, as the maternal tenderness of the park's dense shadow would suggest. The blonde hair of the lady leaning against the *Gingko biloba* tumbles over her face, a golden cascade like an autumn blaze. I won't see the autumn foliage, the captain thinks, undoing his pants in the shadows and seeking the blonde lady's mouth. The mouth opens yielding and voracious, seize the bloom quickly my love before the hurricane puts an end to me, before the wind carries me away. The hurricane is coming, it has already arrived; a tornado, a horrific wind that plucks all the flowers from the meadows and trees; it scatters them, maybe showering them over graves, there are so very many unmarked graves on which to spill them. My hand grips your bare shoulder—a brief, very brief wartime coupling, half an hour under a Gingko biloba, *ist es ein lebendig Wesen / das sich in sich selbst getrennt*, Is it one living being, / Which has separated in itself? / *sind es zwei, die sich erlesen, / daß man sie als eines kennt*, Or are these two, who chose / To be recognized as one? A very brief wartime coupling, even briefer when the war is raging on its last legs and it's over; premature ejaculation under the tree, extreme unction for the ailing who are about to die. Before long they will all be united and together forever, like prisoners and jailers in the camps being bombed; meanwhile that slender hand slips into the captain's trousers, dark red nails stroking and scratching. I wonder what her name is; for that matter I didn't tell her my name either, among those doomed to die there are no introductions, and besides all I have to do is look at our name tags, they must still be on the dining table.

Cavalier Righetti, who organizes the sorting of goods looted from the homes of those deported, puts his hand in the pants of his driver instead, a handsome young man and skillful driver, though it's hard to tell if he's enthusiastic about it or not. However, skirt or pants makes little difference, with things crumbling more and more each day. Even the sea carries the odor of putrefaction and not only in Muggia Gorge where the stream dumps the bones from the Risiera; jellyfish stranded on the beach at low tide rot, corruption of the flesh, even his own, sold to slaughter that of others, his hands try to forget the anguish of death, dealt and awaited, slipping into the skirts and trousers of whoever is around.

Who knows if it's true that it stands up nice and hard when a man is hanged or if it's a merciful legend to show that Mother Nature is also benign, Mater Dolorosa at the foot of countless crosses, a last kiss for her dying son. Last kiss, last supper for the condemned man, last cigarette; when it's available, a last sniff of cocaine. The trap door opens, the feet suddenly lose their footing, the spinal cord, traumatically stimulated, sends an extreme thrill of pleasure, a nebulous exceedingly brief instant, no, not even, an incalculable fraction in a sea of time, a flash, a fond flickering obscene image with which to plunge into darkness. A useless mercy, like the blindfold in front of the firing squad; it would be better to show the condemned man, a moment before, those risqué photos found in barbershop calendars, those he would have time to look at in the few seconds between the time the officer walks away after blindfolding him and the discharging of the rifles. A few seconds are a lot; a very long time, the film of an entire life, including that below the waist. But what about women, where does that leave the idea of a final orgasm? Do the vertebra that fracture send a signal to the clitoris as well, reawakening the larvae of memories lodged in the hairy down like crab lice? It would be only fair, but it seems that's not the case. Another injustice toward women, discriminated against even with the noose around their necks. Women sent to the gallows for their loyalty to the Reich are also entitled to that final vibrator. The Reich is not sexist, it honors women who live and die for the Führer no less than their male comrades.

Meanwhile, however, given that time is running out, the high commissioner has already prepared a car for his flight. Toward Carinthia, then we shall see. Assuming that those huge birds resembling a gallows circling over the gathering don't get there first. Globus instead has returned to the Audience Hall. Gulls swoop through the windows, brazen, no fear whatsoever now; they dive onto the table devouring the leftovers, their wings overturning candlesticks and bottles, one more toast, even alone or almost, *Prosit, Heil Hitler*. Globus is stretched out on the floor, the girl straddling him — he likes it that way and she seems to as well, as she puts the neck of the bottle in his mouth. Globus can hardly breathe; the girl covers his mouth and nose with a napkin, her thighs squeeze him suck him wring him; he's nearly suffocating and comes even more intensely that way. He never allowed the Jewish women at the Risiera to mount him from on top; too bad, it's even better this way and they wouldn't have been able to tell anyone. Everything is spinning and falling; overhead the ceiling drops, the coats of arms of the old empire pecked at by the seagulls come loose from the ceiling and fall on him. Siebenbürgen Niederlausitz Widdiner Banat rain down on his head like shingles torn from roofs by the bora, smashed to pieces on the table among the plates and goblets—the Jews' revenge, they are the ones who stone people to death. There is also the crest of Auschwitz. He likes looking at it as his seed spurts out; that Jewish girl with the grimy feet must already be in Auschwitz, maybe already gone; at the Risiera he had ordered her to go barefoot because he liked those dirty feet.

The girl climbs off the horse, sweating, he sits up somewhat dazed. All around shadows rise shift retreat uncertainly; through the window he thinks he sees Cavalier Righetti put something in his pocket and set out toward his car. He's exhausted. *Calcat jacentem vulgus*, the rabble tramples those on the ground, read one of those scrolls that the gulls on the ceiling held in their beaks; it's my turn now, those banished Jew bastards are crawling out of the cesspools to do me in, but meanwhile I'm enjoying myself and fucking as much as I want. He feels like taking a shower; in the Hitlerjugend barracks they took showers all together, all of them naked, big claps on the back, on the chest, on the rear end. Jews are sent to the showers, they'd be capable of fucking even there, with them you never know. Righetti. In any case, he should hand over what he put in his pocket to command. I wouldn't want . . .

Luisa often wondered what her mother's life had been like before she was born. Probably the way it was after the day on the runway at Aviano: a mere repetition and slow trickle of hours, actions, tasks—typing, shopping, preparing dinner. Life drips away, light rain on an open umbrella on bad days, not even really bad, just gray, damp, every so often a little downpour. Luisa felt that it must have been like that before the evening on Via Tigor, and that after her father's death her mother had returned to that empty, quiet inconsequentiality, the tolerable coexistence with things that do not happen.

She wasn't hurt by knowing that she, she alone, she Sara's daughter, had not been enough to make her mother really live, once she had reentered the cushioned, insulated room that had been her life since the day of her cousin Ester's scream. Luisa understood that only behind that clouded glass was her mother able to drift from day to day, but that did not make her love her mother any less, because love can also mean standing beside that opacity without attempting to violate it, feeling content just the same to be close to her and feel—delude oneself, maybe, but no, truly feel—loved, even in those silences, in that apathy.

What was more difficult for her to imagine was how her father could have broken that glass bell jar, how he could have pried open the shell and extracted the pearl, and not just in the fiat on that evening that she could not—and with daughterly reserve did not even want to—imagine. Let there be light and there was light, strong beautiful warm light even for her mother, how beautiful your face between your tresses, Shulamite, the wind had risen and scattered the fragrances of her garden that was once locked and enclosed. Their lives had become an open garden, a garden for running round and playing; even her mother played when her father invented all those wonderful games that not only enchanted her as a child but also her mother. She remembered her mother acting silly and even laughing and she wondered, incredulously, how it was possible for her to be like that, so joyful, so happy. Every so often Sara would toss back her head and laugh, her hair fluttering down the back of her neck and around her shoulders, her mouth half-open, lips slightly parted, impudent, let him kiss me with the kisses of his mouth, winter is over.

Luisa had never seen her like that, afterward. That face, after the day on the runway at Aviano, had closed up, as it must have done before—and so forevermore, except for those few happy years, a patch of deep blue among clouds soon obscured by a murky fog, skin drawn, mouth clamped, eyes narrowed by the migraine pounding at her temples. What Luisa would have given to see her tremulous smile again, even just once, faint but inextinguishable, like the light on certain evenings—the heavens are dusky but a gleam lingers at length before being extinguished in the darkish sky that grows ever darker, and even when it's snuffed out it's still there, a barely visible ember in the darkness, a black purple that is still purple—happiness, perhaps, nothing at all. If only her mother had again smiled like that, even after the day on the runway at Aviano when the sun had suddenly dimmed—but she did not smile again, not even once like that, when just the two of them were left.

How on earth had her father been able to make her laugh and smile that way? He must have been a magician to transform her like that, a lifeless, nearly dry river that suddenly flows, sparkling and playful. Perhaps—as a child she had truly believed it—he too was a *quimboiseur*, a magician or sorcerer from that island of flowers and fire that at one time, though long long ago, he told her, was called Madinina and whose songs he sang to her in that strange language. An island where he had been when he too was barely a child, not even a boy, and maybe he too had learned to reach into a bush in which nothing is moving and pull out his hand with a *fou-fou* on its palm; and then the tiny blue and purple hummingbird, little bigger than a butterfly, would fly up, beating its tiny wings, and land on his nose. Of course he also knew how to kill the poisonous vipers, the fers-de-lance, which at one time wreaked havoc on the island; when the *quimboiseurs*, so proficient at catching them, had become increasingly rare, they'd had to introduce lots of mongooses to the island, which were very good at destroying the fers-de-lance, but not as good as the *quimboiseurs*. Perhaps those sorcerers of the forest had managed to return to Africa where they had probably found themselves worse off, because—with their garbled stories in which tenses were confused—they too had become confused and thought they were going back in time by returning to Africa, to a time before the slave ships reached the Promised Land, still lost, whereas what they'd found in Africa was a slavery worse than that in Egypt and Babylon.

Perhaps, her father had once told her, one reason why the *quimboiseurs* had become so rare or had vanished was because black kids had begun to go to school where a sign, in the courtyard, prohibited them from speaking the language used in the home, *Il est interdit de parler créole*. They were not happy about it but their parents, only recently free of shackles around their ankles, were, and so for the *quimboiseurs* the time had come to disappear. Or maybe they hadn't gone to Africa, but had been warned by the police not to go around practicing their quackery and so they had transformed themselves into mongooses, returning to the good old days of hunting vipers.

Yes, her father knew how to put poisonous snakes out of commission, it's no coincidence that he was one of the victors against the dragon that had wanted to transform the world into a Risiera. Of course, he must occasionally have had to put up with a little bit of poison; not anything significant, nothing like Zyklon B or what he must have had to endure in Memphis and certainly in Chicago as well, nevertheless poison is poison, even a wasp sting can be harmful and it is not always easy to realize it before it enters your bloodstream. Luisa had later learned to remember, to retrieve moments—though vague, only an image floating up from the black lake in her head— times when her father seemed to be momentarily stung by an insect, an inconsequential thing but for a couple of minutes the hand swells up and the fingers move numbly. Eyes turned on her father during dinner at someone's home; some awkwardness at an encounter at the Caffè degli Specchi, an impalpable dividing wall between him and the others while her mother, vigilant and determined, stepped behind that wall as well, alongside him, lightly stroking his brown hand and toying with its lighter-colored palm, it was that lighter-colored palm in particular that seemed—though maybe it was just a feeling—to cause the hands that shook his in parting a vague discomfiture. Little things, which did not unduly get in the way of the benevolent fondness, in the city, for those blacks, oh Johnny, *te jeri un negro cussì bon / e la sera, butada sul paion / te disevo /* I love, I love you John / *mi go pianto, go pianto dal dolor / perché te jeri un negro cussì bon.* Oh Johnny, you were such a good Negro and at night, on the straw mattress, I told you I love you, I love you John, I cried and cried, so sad, because you were such a good Negro. And Luisa, with the uncompromising perception of children that is so quickly dulled, realized that her father became more careful, moved more slowly, stopped clapping his hands on the shoulders of those he met, the way he used to do; he also lowered his tone of voice and his laughter.

Little things, mere trifles in the infernal *bolgia* of the world. It did not make the walk home any less enjoyable, leaving the café after the polite farewells and crossing Piazza Unità, she in the middle with one hand in her mother's and one in his; her father's hand was once again strong and dry, he looked at the two of them and then at the sea that cleansed the shore and the heart of all litter, washing it away. Luisa walked between the two of them, sometimes letting go of their hands to chase the pigeons that flew up, their fluttering encircling her for an instant, then she would run to join them again. When she looked up, she sometimes caught them looking at one another and she knew—she wasn't sure if it was more with joy or with a slight aching pang—that the look passing between them was not for her, that for a moment she did not exist, she had no place in what their eyes and their faint, forced smiles unquestionably conveyed.

When they looked away from one another, her father's gaze fell on her, different but no less warm and adoring, while her mother stared at the buildings around the piazza, the solid, dignified facade of the old Lloyd Austrico; Sara raised her eyes to the neoclassical cornice and the two winged female figures with shield, flanked by two putti respectively celebrating work and struggles at sea, the latter adorned with a laurel wreath; battling the sea deserves a laurel whether one wins or loses, it's even glorious to perish at sea, but those impassive statues had little to do with the unfathomable sea. Innocuous sirens of a decorous cemetery, beautiful, polished forms that serve to avoid seeing the unbearable, enfolded only in the mystery of an empty banality. Maybe that's why her mother loved those noble buildings on the piazza and in the city in general, stage backdrops that concealed the void. In fact she never looked at the sea that unfolded in front of the piazza, the extreme brink of life.

Why hadn't her mother, when her father was gone, ever looked at her with that love that embraces and eliminates all fear, why only with him had she looked at her with eyes full of light, a light that was then extinguished for everyone, including her child, her daughter already nearly a young girl? That violent, sudden gust of wind on the runway at Aviano seemed to have swept away not only her father, but also any warmth, any passion from her mother's heart. The river that had frozen the day of the clash with Ester or shortly thereafter, and that had begun to flow freely and brightly again after the night Sara had entered the house, no longer alone, on the third floor of Via Tigor, was once again, after Aviano, a sheet of ice. The crash had taken everything from her.

Maybe it isn't a good thing, Luisa sometimes thought with bitter dismay, maybe it isn't good for children to have parents who love each other—who are truly hopelessly in love, or rather hopeless for anything else. Not because it can hurt to see that your mother loves your father more than she loves you, and perhaps vice versa—although for her father love was something else, a gulf that embraced everything and therefore others as well, other loved ones, a breeze wafting across the face, things warmed by the love that settled on them. Luisa felt it when he held her in his arms; see, this is love, her father had once told her giving her a *matryoshka*, a doll that contained another which in turn contained another and so on. No, it wasn't bitterness over her mother's listless absence that made her suffer. It isn't good for children to have parents act as lovers all the time, even when one of them is tending the pot on the stove and the other is setting the table; it isn't good and not because — or not only because — a child may feel excluded, hurt, given the absurd irrepressible need to be loved more than anyone else that lies in every person's tangled heart, especially that of any son or any daughter. No, the harm resulting from a father and mother's exclusive happiness is caused by something else; by flaunting an island of bliss to someone who will never land there, but who can never really do without it, showing that the Promised Land exists, it's there, it's possible to live there and yet it isn't, *you* can't. The Land of Canaan, Eden, Madinina, all true, all possible, but not for you. And in fact, when Luisa thought of what her life had been, what it was . . .

Only later on, after Sergeant Brooks, the Black American Messiah who had done his part to save the world from Auschwitz, had ended his story on the runway at Aviano, had Luisa learned and understood why her father had spoken to her about that other Luisa and why he'd sung those lullabies in that strange language. She had asked her mother, dragging out of her, of course, like pulling teeth, those wonderful things that Sara was reluctant to talk about because, after his death, she had retreated to her old lifeless silence, the few words necessary to get through the dull days and nothing more, like when she was an interpreter and, being a professional, made sure not to add any color or warmth to the words spoken by others, foreign words that she translated accurately, though no more foreign than the ones that came out of her mouth when she greeted an acquaintance, entered a shop or spoke briefly with her daughter.

The warm black sun of her life had been extinguished on the runway at Aviano. They say that if the sun went out, we would notice it after eight minutes; after eight minutes the earth would begin to cool, the air to darken, the plants to wilt. The cold gray twilight had taken a bit longer to descend inexorably over her mother's heart, because the heart and mind and the network of neurons offer a little more resistance against destruction and the end; even when the end is there, before our eyes, something in the brain resists, however briefly, the intolerable and undeniable evidence, the truth, after which there will no longer be real life. It cannot be true, life cries agonizingly, but even as the soundwaves of that cry are still radiating through the air you already know that it is indeed true, irrevocably true, and the small universe clustered like a solar system around that vanished black sun begins to collapse, feelings and thoughts recede, lost in a dark void.

Life goes on, of course. Like after the napalm bombings—the relevant office of the U.S. armed forces had been very willing to grant those specimens to the Museum—even on terrain scorched by napalm something blooms, though not much. And so Luisa too had come to know that face of her mother, dull and drained yet controlled, that she had never seen before but that others had known well, since the day Sara had learned about Grandma Deborah and the knowledge had shriveled her heart the way napalm withers a field. In any case, her mother had answered her questions; undoubtedly the bare minimum required to understand where those lullabies in the strange language came from, which had sounded so foreign in her father's mouth the first time, so different from the one he spoke when he was in uniform with other men in uniform. *Adieu madras, adieu foulards / adieu rob'soie, adieu collier chou, / doudou à moin, li qu'a pa'ti / Héla! héla! c'est pou' toujou'* . . . Farewell madras scarves, silk foulards, beaded collars, my darling is leaving, alas, alas, forever . . .

Strange, guttural at first then sweet and melodious, that language that she thought was a secret language between her and her father. Later on she'd thought it was a language only meant for children, all children, though they forgot it when they got big, and that grownups weren't supposed to understand it, and in fact she didn't understand it anymore, not even the few words that she'd understood earlier, farewell madras scarves farewell silk foulards, and it was appropriate that she didn't understand them anymore, because she'd grown up, passed over to the other side, with those who don't understand, who shouldn't understand the secret language of children. All she'd understood after the day on the runway at Aviano, was *il est trop tard | li q'a pa'ti | c'est pou' toujou'*, it's too late, he's gone forever, never to return again. She recalled that her father spoke about tall trees, tamarinds they were called, about dragonflies as red as currants, which children easily captured between two fingers, about delicious fruits and tubers with strange names, mango guava yam, about brawny sweaty black men who cut sugar cane and lived in rundown wooden shacks that held a mattress of dried leaves, a pot on the stove and a table on which stood a pitcher of water and a few pieces of sugar cane which they sucked, getting their lips sticky; a filthy wide-brimmed hat and pants hung on a nail.

Most of all he spoke about his grandmother Tati, about her face, roughened and black like the soil, and her big swollen feet, a Negro woman's face, unfathomable as the earth and as good as the earth, forever trampled trodden cracked. His grandmother, my great-grandmother Tati. I wonder whether they would have understood each other, she and my great-grandmother Rachel, who had been spared from learning about her daughter Deborah. I wonder if and how they would have understood each other, the Triestine Jewess with the prominent nose and peremptory ways, whom Luisa knew from photographs taken and printed by the renowned Wulz studio, and the Negress with the thick lips that Noah's curse had assigned along with the black skin color of the tribe of Canaan, the wicked grandson who had violated Noah's nakedness and even bore the name of the Land promised to the chosen people. Yes, perhaps they would have understood each other, because those faces so utterly different displayed the same determined, unremitting resistance to centuries of duress and persecution.

Luisa tried to imagine that face of black clay—there were no photographs of her great-grandmother Tati, unlike her great-grandmother Rachel—mud-caked by the sun despite the wide-brimmed hat, the ancient face of a Mother Earth who can offer her child only two weary breasts, generous and inexhaustible, and the *morne*, the hill over which to escape and become free. A Black Madonna pierced by seven swords, who had too many times survived the torment of having her flesh ripped from her breast, and ready to offer that breast, blessed with milk, to her oppressor's child, because every child is only a child and not the child of an oppressor or future oppressor. Not your face tomorrow, little one sucking at the withered yet still splendid breast of the Negress, inscrutable as fate; not your face tomorrow, perhaps that of a slave driver, but your face right now, in the manger of Bethlehem. Sometimes I feel like a motherless child, the old immortal spiritual of all loneliness; occasionally Luisa hummed it to herself, thinking about the day in Aviano that had left her lost and abandoned, a loss worsened by the impenetrable barren sorrow in which her mother had again withdrawn since then. When she held her silent, absent mother in her arms, Luisa wished someone would hold her that way, the warm, tender arms of the Black Madonna, the Milky Way of her smile in her eyes and mouth, deep black night bright with stars, *stille Nacht heilige Nacht*, went the song that was sung at Christmas at her friend Giovanna's home.

Her father also used to tell her fairytales, but not the scary kind her mother told her, Little Red Riding Hood, Hansel and Gretel and Snow White, the poisoned apple and, even worse, kissing a dead person—those lips that must have been icy cold disturbed her, a very different type of iciness certainly than her father's or mother's cheeks when they came home from being out in the bora, when she liked to rub their faces, reddened by the cold and wind, warm them up with her little hands. Many fairytales came from that distant island, but the best of all was the one about Hummingbird, the tiny fearless little bird that, together with his faithful drum, battles all the powerful evil ones and eventually dies, though he rises again and in fact it turns out that he was never really dead but only pretending to be, remaining very very still with his beak stuck in a tree, and that's why the Indians—but who were they, the Indians? there were so many new people and animals and flowers and stories in the world, and her father knew them all—that's why the Indians call him "the resurrected one, the risen one." Like us, Luisa would later think, resurrected not once but numerous times, after numerous destructions of the Temple and final solutions. All life is death and resurrection, few go straight to heaven like the prophet Elijah. Die and become! said the poem he liked so much. Could it somehow apply to his theory of the inverter as well? And if David was still a boy when he defeated the giant Goliath, Ti-Jean was a child when, on that distant island where there were trees that shone like a sun, with their gigantic radiating yellow leaves, he killed the great Beast with the seven heads.

Her father had seen that island's mangroves, their roots submerged in the sea, and the small yellow-legged plovers that flew into their tangled maze to catch fish and insects with their long black beaks, pointed like a spear. Before being Jò-seph—her mother had told her, accentuating first one then the other syllable—your father was Jo-sèph. His father, your grandfather, was born in Jackson, Mississippi, I think. He was a ship's cook, and when he was dropped off in Fort-de-France by an American merchant ship, fed up with cooking for those white seamen who treated him like dirt, he had remained there, in Martinique, where he had gone to work for a small yam business. Your father was born a couple of years later and spent his early years in Grand Anse, burning his feet on the scorching sand scattered with red leaves that fell from the seagrapes and learning to love the sea more than anything else. Playing in the sand and water with the other boys, that's where he learned—well, learned, a few words, then he forgot most of them—that rough, sweet language, the African French of slaves, which their French masters gladly spoke and which ex-slaves, though not completely ex-, wanted to prohibit their children from speaking in the hope that they would become a little more ex-. Creole is a French of sweaty feet scored by blisters, of hands flayed by sugar cane and pulling up weeds, but a French of childhood as well, of cunning, innocent joy that does not take life seriously, since if taken seriously it's the worst thing that can happen, *pani pwoblèm*, *dèmen sé on kouyon*, don't sweat it, the future is a bitch and it's no sin to avoid trouble, since there's enough of it for everyone and for blacks even more, *débrouya pa péché*. A language still attached to things, to life, to the beating of the heart, which is just a muscle but sometimes more than a muscle, *muen enmeu*, I love you.

Certainly that sort of French—that sort of African, others down there said, as she had heard when she had finally made the trip to his homeland, one of the many lands of his fathers—was quite different from the French that mademoiselle had taught her in Trieste and that was spoken not only in the consulate, albeit merely honorary, of France but also—after German, of course, and naturally not Slovenian—by upper-class or aristocratic families, maybe *Geldadel,* moneyed nobility, merchants shippers insurers promoted to *von-* or *zu-*something thanks to the crowns and florins that they had brought to the loyal city of which His Apostolic Majesty the Emperor of Austria and King of Hungary was the immediate Lord, *Herr von Triest,* florins crowns and liras, less and less of which had arrived later, as well as AM-liras, which at the time of the Allied Military Government her father had occasionally used in clubs where people danced the boogie woogie, and were allowed to drink good beers, but little else.

Your Aunt Kasika could sing these songs, much better than me, her father would sometimes say when he hummed them in the evening, *Adieu madras adieu foulards;* even though she was littler than me, I would listen to her and make her repeat those songs, while grandmother Tati grumbled that we had to go to sleep. She was the only one there with us, he added; papa was always out. And she never spoke about mama. Maybe—Luisa would later think—they hadn't ever talked about her to him and his idea of her must be hazy and uncomfortable; maybe she was one of those women who on that island are called *matadò,* likely to walk out and maybe be seen around with the first guy she comes across, and a second and third as well, and Luisa could easily imagine that they weren't eager to talk about her at home.

But the absence of a mother didn't seem to have made the two children sad—at least not as far as Luisa could tell, remembering her father's talks—since they grew up playing in the street among numerous black mothers of numerous kids who like the two of them weren't sure who was whose mother, maybe they thought all women were mothers, for a day a month or a lifetime; like a jacaranda flower in front of the window, it can stay there forever or you can take it and put it in the window of the house across the way, without arguing or causing hard feelings, soon another flower will appear offering to be picked. At times Luisa seemed to feel the absence of this unknown grandmother, who had simply vanished like an animal, more than her father did. Perhaps Tati was everything, grandmother, mother and entire family and Luisa longed for that warm womb—which had given her father and aunt Kasika the warmth needed to live—and thought that if she had had a Tati whose big fat solid body she could clamber over like a cat, her life would have been different, especially after her father's death.

Her father had lost his Tati when her grandfather had left Martinique in the years of crisis and unrest and had settled for a time in Puerto Rico, where roads were expanding and projects to build them drew considerable dollars, even for an insignificant junior office clerk in charge of distributing the various materials, and where little Josèph had become, albeit briefly, José, at least to the kids he played with in the street. That island too, her father told Luisa, was beautiful, he and Kasika went looking for green turtles along the coral reefs, despite the barracudas and manta rays that were just beyond those reefs, and Luisa would ask him which was more beautiful, the sea of Salvore or that of Puerto Rico.

Her grandfather had soon lost the job in Puerto Rico and had gone to the States, to Memphis, where José had become Joseph again, but with the accent on the "o." Luisa knew almost nothing about those years in Memphis, where the boy had become a man, and her mother must not have known very much either. He must have been embarrassed to talk about racial insults to someone who had endured the Holocaust; only once, Sara had reminded her, did he let slip how surprised he'd been when, soon after the war ended, he'd had to go to Germany, to Augsburg, briefly with his unit and was astonished to feel more American than ever before—though he had always loved his great country no matter what—because for the first time no one seemed to pay much attention to his skin. In bars hastily and unceremoniously reopened in a Germany razed to the ground, similar to those which in Memphis he had not been permitted to enter or the one in London where his sister, on leave from the front, had been beaten to death, he was a foreigner like all the other Americans, wearing the same uniform, scowled at by the Germans for having won and brought them to their knees and occupied them, yet also well-regarded because at least they had gotten there before those other victorious enemies, who came from the East and had white skin but were more feared than the Americans, white or black, who among other things spent lavishly, and people emerging from a lengthy period of deprivation can't afford the luxury of checking whether the hands that put money on the counter are light or dark.

So in Germany for the first time he had been an American like all the others, or almost, and that almost, compared to certain things that he must have experienced, was already quite a lot. And those genial people, who sometimes seemed to actually be charmed by his black skin, were the same ones who had burned millions of people or indifferently witnessed the pyre, and he thought that if instead of being a black American he'd been a Jewish American, they would have looked at him less kindly, not to mention if he'd been a German Jew, although, in those days, it was highly unlikely that one would see a German Jew around there.

He had not had any problems in Trieste either, where he had returned after the brief mission in Germany and was part of the American troops stationed in the Free Territory. Triestine hookers, and soldiers on leave with their pockets full of AM-liras, I love you Johnny / I love you Texas / If you want to make love with me / you give me cigarettes / I give you tits. Naturally, that Johnny, albeit statistically, was primarily white, but even if he was black they weren't too picky, you give me chocolate / I give you pussy.

You don't tread on the foreigner, but on the local, the one who is a native son of your country just as you are, but you don't think he's like you, and he feels the same about you. No one had it in for the Greeks of Trieste or the Serbs, who for a couple of centuries owned the most beautiful buildings along the channel, because that handful of Greeks and Serbs could not have made Trieste become Greek or Serbian, whereas the Slovenians could have turned the city into

Slovenia, and the Slovenians didn't have it in for the Greeks or the Serbs either, because they weren't worried that they would all become Greek or Serbian, but they were worried that they would all become Italian, as many of them had become, changing their surnames on the way down from the Karst and becoming Italian patriots, and like America could become black, given that the Lord has kept his promise to make us — us? Luisa wondered — become as numerous as the stars in the sky.

Are Jews the blacks of the world and are blacks in America the Jews in Egypt, persecuted by Pharaoh because he fears them? Maybe they are one and the same, the people chosen because they were persecuted, only persecution makes a man or a people chosen; people whose land was stolen everywhere, in Africa or in Canaan — the Promised and lost Land, where both expulsion and exile as well as the return is tragic.

The Land Promised to Abraham that bears the name of the cursed tribe, the impious son or grandson who reviles the nakedness of the patriarch, father of the new humanity that rose again after the flood, more depraved than the earlier one drowned in the waters. Cursed be Canaan, the lowliest of slaves may he be to his brothers, the slave of Shem; Canaan with the dark skin and fleshy lips, black as the black fertile land of the Nile. It is just that the blacks be slaves because they are the progeny of Ham and his dark-skinned son Canaan, condemned to be his brother Shem's slave, even many WASP pastors said so. And consequently our slave, we who came to steal his land and his life? The Promised Land is thus a land of wrongdoing, plunder and atonement; the Galuth began even before we arrived in the Land of Canaan, from which we were driven out and from which we drove out the children of our brothers, of Ishmael, who had to live in the desert like a wild ass, of Canaan forever banished and an outcast, of Ham, who forged his descendants' shackles; slaves sold to slave ships by their mothers and by their brothers who delivered them from their African wilds to their slave masters, the way we children of Abraham — we who, me who, my family who? Luisa wondered — drove out other children of Abraham.

Of course, when we were still Noah cursing his son and Shem enslaving his brother we weren't yet Jews; it is only starting with Abraham that we should feel responsible, he is the first to be circumcised, but he in fact distinguishes between Sarah and Hagar, as the *békés* do between their children's white mothers and black ones. A person happens to find herself in the vicinity of Sodom when it rains fire and becomes a pillar of red-hot salt. It can happen to anyone; to us—to us Jews and to us blacks, I mean—more so than to any others. Racists aren't to blame, nor are the Jews certainly, if there were no blacks in the Risiera, and it's not the Ku Klux Klan's fault if there were no Jews among the carcasses that were unrecognizable after the lynchings—without their genitals, lopped off with a knife, you couldn't immediately tell whether they were men or women.

I don't think there were any Klansmen in the pub in London either, though you never know, when Aunt Kasika, just back from the front in Normandy for a short leave, went in to have a drink and was driven out, knocked to the ground and kicked, there were four or five of them kicking her, more and more eager to keep on kicking her. One of the kicks in the liver was deadly, and when they took her to the hospital, a hospital that, unlike the first one they'd rushed her to, had admitted her right away, she was a different color. Black, but livid black, like some menacing evening skies; not the maternal black that cradles a baby, but a squashy viscous black that signals putrefaction, and in the hospital there was no one to hold her in his arms the way she, in her Army Nurse Corps Auxiliary uniform—the first black women to enlist in the war, albeit to assist rather than kill—had held in her arms, under the bombs, so many screaming, wounded soldiers, terrified at seeing their blood gushing from them like their lives, and she clutched them to her breast as only a woman can do. This is why women are so much greater than men, not solely for this reason but partly for this reason; she hugged them to her as if she could nurse them, give them a milk as warm and black as life—certainly an unseemly promiscuity between a white soldier and a black auxiliary, that face pressed against her breast isn't right. It's okay if it's a fuck, even better when the woman isn't asked for her permission, but apart from these more than understandable situations, it's best if bodies of a different color don't touch one another.

Many blacks think so too, convinced that Allah is black and that Jehovah is the worst kind of WASP; in fact in the streets of Memphis, her father told her, Negro boys would sing obscene songs about Jews; there are those who spend their lives making lists of all the Jewish slave dealers since time immemorial, it remains to be seen whether even the slave trade can be blamed on the Jews. Strange that it isn't mentioned in the *Protocols of the Elders of Zion*, even Martin Luther King had a hard time reasoning with many of his followers, who with the excuse of anti-Zionism were utter anti-Semites. Indeed, our father Abraham descended from Noah as did the descendants of Canaan. What if we, we blacks, Luisa mused, were a lost tribe of Israel? Difficult to imagine being more lost than that.

Canaan thus fully readmitted into the land of Canaan, no longer Shem's slave but Shem's brother? It's best to move slowly, where brothers are concerned; even though Abraham J. Heschel parades alongside Martin Luther King leading the march in Alabama, history is full of brothers who kill each other more so than they do other people. Common blood does not create good blood among people and we—we who, certainly not I, I already have both, I'm already we—we know something about it.

And there he was deluding himself, Luisa thought, that he was illustrating and exposing war by exhibiting a few tanks and some guns in his Museum, laughable, kids' toys. A true war Museum would be a huge CAT scan, many CAT scans and MRIs of a single brain, any brain, randomly chosen. One big brain, the brain of a man, the command center from which attacks are launched and at the same time a battlefield. In the future much more sophisticated instrumentation will more accurately pinpoint the central control and substations that order the assault, strike and are struck.

Attacks toward the outside world but also directed internally, it would be easy for individual sectors to mutiny and attack one another, one network of neurons against another, all convinced that their comrade is an infiltrated enemy in disguise, already a number of reserve troops, such as antibiotics, are destroying friends and enemies. There is much agitation, a lot of tension in there, in the world, in the head; it's just that there are too many of us and we end up not being able to stand each other anymore, the world is overcrowded and hideous and threatening, it must be thinned out a bit, we don't all fit. But even inside us, inside me, there are too many people, there is too much crowding, and we end up hating each other, hating myself, hating the too many in me.

A Museum of hatred? Perhaps the famous self-loathing of the Jews comes down to this, hatred of too many Jews crammed into their hovels, too many brothers in the same bed, too many slaves in the ship's hold; if the Nazis had not used Zyklon B but had merely locked them up all together in the camps, after a while they would have torn each other to pieces, like thoughts and emotions pressing against a skullcap that's too tight. History's tumor, which destroys everything around it, is also in the head, maybe even primarily in the head. History books as MRI and CAT scan results?

38.

Rooms no. 42 and 43 — On the doorpost, in large letters, the inscription April 30–May 2, 1945. A variety of unrelated objects, nearly all collected by him, pages from his diaries and large photographs hanging on the wall. Several computers to call up other images and excerpts from his journals.

Ten days following the festive gathering at Miramare . . . what can happen in ten days? Enough time to bring down the Tsarist Empire and give birth to the Soviet Union, though not to get over a bout of sciatica. The high commissioner and Globočnik fled, one on the 28th and the other on the 29th; their friend *Hein*, as the Germans call the Grim Reaper, awaits them in Samarkand, one of them quite soon, the other a little later. The Collotti Band went on torturing until the end, and Tito's IX Korpus and the 2nd New Zealand Division race to be first to reach Trieste. Soon bullets begin whizzing around, people take shelter wherever and however they can; he however goes around undeterred, unconcerned about gunfire and tanks, trying to talk to one side and the other, and noting what he sees, what is happening. Slips of paper, sometimes only scattered phrases sometimes whole pages — to be sorted and weeded, of course — rambling fragments of the tattered history through which he strolls like a *flâneur*. More than days, it's hours that count, starting at 5:30 A.M. on April 30.

An air-raid siren — Marelli electromechanical siren, 6 kw, M6, three-phase AC power, 220-volt vertical axis motor, cast-iron weatherproof housing, electric resistance heating. Two control panels, locally linked by an acoustic device through a lead-covered tripolar cable, remotely attached with five bare copper wires. To be placed to the right, just past the Museum entrance; set somewhat apart, so that those entering do not immediately notice it and are startled, frightened, when they hear the abrupt deafening wail and see a large clock suddenly light up in front of them, reading 5:30 A.M.

Five thirty on the morning of April 30, 1945. Don Marzari, released the night before from Coroneo Prison, where he had been taken after being tortured at Villa Triste by the Collotti Band, gives the signal for the anti-Nazi insurrection with two wails of the air-raid siren. Two wails and the insurrection has begun. Does the referee blow the whistle to signal the beginning (of what? of freedom, of fratricide, of peace?) or the end? Two wails, it is time for freedom and death, the port and the entire city may be blown up. Freedom is an ultrasound, it detonates inside you, it rips you to shreds, countless pieces that explode, one on top of the other, one against the other—in fact bombs go off under the Chiozza Porticoes, in the city center, fragments shooting out like sparrows diving for crumbs. The CLN's Freedom Volunteers fire as best they can, with those decrepit rifles in their hands. A helmet rolls off the sidewalk into the street, the small trail of blood is soon erased.

The torture Don Marzari endured in Villa Triste still bores into his body like an earsplitting siren; it ruptures the eardrum, penetrates the brain. The back of the rudimentary but effective electric chair is high, with thin leather padding and armrests to which the forearms are strapped; affixed to one of them is a metal armband linked to the negative pole of an adjustable, rheostat controlled conductor, while connected to the positive pole is a kind of brush with an insulated handle and metallic fringe to close the circuit.

The electric current courses through the body, one pulse after another, regular, insane, unendurable—the world explodes in the head and heart. God is a word that fireworks discharge and sketch for an instant in the night before it immediately bursts and vanishes. Dark night. The sweat of blood is a secretion; what would Jesus have done, said, cried out with an electrical cable in His mouth. The Collotti Band does its work well. Brain, heart, faith are reduced to a pulp but the man of God forsaken by God does not surrender; maybe he would like to surrender, to name names, betray, dear God, of course he would, you bet, but by now the faith of years has permeated his body, his nerves, which go crazy under those electric shocks and just want to relax, give in, stop sending those fiery piercing arrows to his brain, but by now faith is his flesh, like passion for lovers, and the flesh resists, crushed yet undaunted. He would like to descend from the cross but his flesh, his faith made flesh, says no to the shout, the plea, the demands of his brain and his afflicted heart and he says nothing. The torturer can't get a word out of that mouth scorched by lava, and so, released by a sudden coup de main, at 5:30 A.M., still staggering, confused, Don Marzari gives the order to launch the two agreed upon siren wails.

When the siren wailed to sound the air-raid alarm, fifteen seconds passed between one burst and the next; how many seconds passed between one electric shock and the other at Villa Triste? Not one, not even a nanosecond; there was only the jolt, an eternal, infinite earthquake in every cell of the body—no, there was an eternity between one shock and the other, an infinite fearful waiting. History is an electroshock; that's why we've all become crazed, even the insurgents. Everyone against everyone, the Slavic KMT, Kommando Mesta Trst, against the Nazis but also against the Italian democratic brigades of the Freedom Volunteer Corps, the Pisoni and Foschiatti Brigades, which fought against the Nazis. Foschiatti died in Dachau, "Death to Foschiatti," the Fascists shouted, "Death to the partisans of the Foschiatti Brigade," cried the Titoists. Death to death that bestows death, thinks Don Marzari; this is why he gives the order for the siren to sound the insurgency. There will be more death, he knows that, all martyrs have always known it, just as they've known that death dies if you cease to fear it, if you take away its dagger. The siren's shrill whistling lacerates, bores into his head—as a child he used to whistle while playing in the park; also in the courtyard behind the church and the priests would scold him. Soldiers going on leave came out of the nearby barracks whistling, that innocent, cheerful whistling from when he was a boy is now a swift, high-pitched whine, a fiery trajectory . . . Who is that lying there on the ground with his face covered in blood?

Click, a word that wasn't in his D.U.D. and that he would probably never have admitted to his Museum. His, my . . . Click. MRI of a glioblastoma multiforme or rather, photographs of Villa Geiringer. A malignant right frontal tumor. They look alike, those dark spots, those iridescent crevices, those corroded, crumbling walls, a gnawing and eating away and pressing from within, from outside, everywhere. Villa Geiringer—also called Castelletto, on the hill of Scorcola—is where General Linkenbach is housed—with the jacket that is still his but that he will soon give to him—that is, it's the command center of the German Army. Police Headquarters is in the courthouse, more massive than a fortress, as befits the Law, somber and substantial, even when there is no longer any law in what happens on the streets. The courthouse, a cenotaph. Naval Command instead is in San Giusto, at the castle.

But it is in Villa Geiringer that General Linkenbach resides. The engineer Eugenio Geiringer, who had it constructed, has been dead for forty years, but the Trieste-Opicina tramway—inaugurated on September 9, 1902, its electrical component built by the Österreichische Union-Elektricitäts-Gesellschaft and its mechanical elements by the Weitzer Waggon Fabrik of Graz—still stops regularly right in front of the villa where he lived when Austria was an orderly country, as he himself had suggested, before climbing—with its electric engine and sizable metal cables that tow it up the steepest stretch—to reach Opicina's height of 329 meters above sea level. In those days, in fact, *el tram de Opcina nato disgrazià* goes up and down like mad, worse than on October 10, 1902, when it had derailed *vignindo zo* from Scorcola to the city, the song goes, *bona de Dio che iera giorno de lavor e drento no ghe iera che'l povero frenador*, thank God its day was a work day and the only one in it was the poor engine driver. Now it is History that is derailing, going off track worse than the old tram and plummeting faster and faster; the acceleration grows, a planet up there or down here has spun out of its orbit, a meteorite hurtles down on the world, collides and for one thing demolishes Trieste. *Zeitraffer-phenomen*, accelerated motion effect, can be the first symptom of the malignant frontal tumor, and the fact that the name is German has never been more fitting than in this case, for years everything has been happening in German.

Everything streams past more swiftly, a progressive, unsustainable acceleration, the tram plunges down from Villa Geiringer, cars, jeeps, tanks at an insane speed; the speedometer tries to reassure the mind, its indicator seems almost normal, but the glioblastoma doesn't believe it; it races along inside the head, everything races, everyone is racing, even people on the street, passersby. The world is falling, falling to pieces, bodies strike the pavement, blood gushes out. The speedometer is mistaken, only the glioblastoma perceives the breakneck speed of everything all around. An MRI scan, a photograph of History; if you color it, the image is even quite beautiful, a stratiform, flecked crystal, a geode. It could be an agate, with those stripes, agate-blue bands of chalcedony, yellow-red carnelian, black onyx . . . The eye of the hurricane over the city, over History, is hollow — the center of the geode is also hollow, without prime matter.

There it is, History; dead, still, unmoving, a stone, a geode. Yet inside everything is teeming with life, percolating, billions of corpuscles at lunatic, useless speed. Hassles and language confusion — swearing, praying and cursing in Italian, German, Slovenian, Croatian; even in English, when in the late afternoon of May 1, General Freyberg's New Zealand 2nd Division marching toward Trieste finds Monfalcone occupied by the Yugoslavians, who try to stop them and they are about to come to blows, shit! In the city however bullets will fly, *iésus mària*, they're already flying, fuck, they'll get you, *Scheisse*, long live Italy *Trst je naš*, Trieste is ours, they say it isn't good to swear at a time when you can easily die, but before or after, *jeben ti mater*, fuck your mother, in front of God it's all the same — there's that sniper, he's hiding behind that column, *kurvi sine*, son of a bitch, you can't make out a thing, *clinz*, fuck-all, we're screwed — once the firing has ceased, they'll all think they can say they've been screwed.

General Linkenbach is unyielding and, on April 29, scornfully refuses to promise the Bishop of Trieste, Monsignor Antonio Santin, that he will spare the city, but things come to a head, accelerating at exponential speed. The *Zeitrafferphenomen* has no regard for anyone, not even for a Wehrmacht general's love of order — I can personally attest to this, he often repeated, the way he removed his jacket a couple of days later, on May 3, and handed it over to me, carefully folding it, says it all. The glioblastoma plays havoc with clocks and speedometers, time contracts and congeals; the Third Reich collapses within seconds, a captured district changes the geography and the history of Europe, Hitler falls, Stalin or his representative advances, Tito's CMT-KMT is shooting in the surrounding area and in San Giacomo, the Pisoni and Foschiatti Brigades of the Italian Freedom Volunteer Corps are firing in the city center and on the waterfront, the CMT-KMT fires on the Germans but also on the CLN, shrapnel and bullets come through the window in the curia where the bishop, lying on the floor to avoid them, tries to negotiate with the German Command by telephone but it's not clear which one — the army, navy or police.

A pair of shoes. They must belong, must have belonged to a Slovenian partisan from the Kosovelova Brigade, who had come down to the city from Opicina along with others joining up with Tito's troops of the 20th and 9th Divisions. He left them at the corner of Via Carducci and Via Battisti, on the sidewalk of the Chiozza Porticoes, to cool off his feet after the long march. Under the arcades was a nice shoe store, so they looted it, smashing the window and throwing their old shoes away. So much history in those shoes, holes worn in them during the Yugoslavian Army's trek through the woods, Tarnova Forest or Mount Nevoso, soaked in streams crossed without bridges; two hundred kilometers from Lika to Trieste, through Karlobag, Senj where the bora rises and where the Uskoks raged, Crikvenica, Susak, Fiume, the attack on Mount Lesco near Fiume defended by the 12th Artillery of the RSI, the locomotive loaded with guns driven against Italian defenses, hitting them squarely — guns and ammunition explode, some manage to jump off, the shoes get muddied with dirt and blood, but they walk, they resume marching soon afterward, right to the center of Trieste.

Abandoned there on the sidewalk at the Chiozza Porticoes they are a flag; a victor's flag, much more so than the pompous banner that the Titoists, machine guns in hand, will before long impose on the windows of Town Hall. Before putting on those new shoes taken from the ransacked store, the *druže* must have been barefoot for quite a while, to rest his feet. Harvest time; peasants' feet trample the grapes in the vats, the must is red, blood is red, sometimes it's as good or at least as intoxicating as wine. Spilling blood, crushing it underfoot, is as delicious as drinking unfermented must, especially when you have been grapes crushed by the feet of others for so long, by the arrogant masters of the city that has now been conquered.

A large photograph of the bishop's curia on Via Cavana. An area both sacred and profane, ancient, squalid brothels of the lowliest grade standing side by side in the narrow alleyways with the see of the apostles' successor, a stronghold of Italian identity and of lowlife; when the battle is almost over — a victorious ending for the Resistance and above all for them, Don Marzari, released by the Nazi-Fascists after having been tortured by them a few days earlier, hoisted the tricolor flag of a new, free and democratic Italy over Town Hall, but the troops of the IX Korpus quickly forced him to take it down, *Trst je naš*—and when the Titoists send one of their men into the Cavana district to guardedly reconnoiter, he soon finds himself surrounded in the tangle of alleys, porticoes and doorways and collapses with a knife in his belly.

In the curia, the bishop tries to negotiate with the Germans while lying on the ground, since shrapnel and bullets are flying through the windows from shooting that's taking place between the public library and the Ministry of Education. Two days earlier Dr. Hubert Herbert, head of the 5th Division of the German Supreme Commissariat, had told him, on behalf of High Commissioner Rainer, that German Command was prepared to spare the port facilities and other installations, but Rainer had fled on April 28 and Globočnik would flee the following day, while the city was still in German hands, and while efforts were made to convince the Germans to hand the city over to the authorities in charge—to the Fascist prefect Coceani and the Fascist mayor Pagnini, prepared to fire at the Germans from Town Hall if they tried to blow up the port, or to the anti-Fascist CLN, to Ercole Miani and Don Marzari, tortured by the Fascists, or to Politkomisar Franc Štoka, the great advancing red-starred Slavia?—Slavic Command enjoined "Trieste and all your other colonies" to surrender.

The German patrol moves along Via Cavana toward the bishopric and opens fire, Panzerfausts very close to the curia and two partisan tanks toward Via Università; they're shooting everywhere, they shoot and fire intermittently, the SS garrison in Piazza Oberdan is attacked by CLN partisans, communists and young members of the Home Guard established months before by the Fascist mayor, but the communist Slavs try to stop the CLN, and Colonel Antonio Fonda Savio—nom de guerre Manfredi, Svevo's son-in-law and the father of three children, two already killed in Russia and one now dying under German fire—is forced to disband the CLN and order his units to fall back to avoid clashes with the Yugoslavs, after Martin Greif and Franc Štoka of the KMT had disarmed the Italian partisans and had treated him the way an occupier treats an enemy and not the way a liberator treats the one he's come to liberate.

Allied planes bomb the German rafts moored to Le Rive, a young communist partisan, alone, on foot, at the intersection of Via Cavana goes on firing until he falls, the German patrol on Via Cavana reaches the bishopric and its commander Captain Giessen enters the bishop's curia, repeats that the Germans will not surrender, especially now that Tito's Yugoslavians are taking over the city, and threatens reprisals in the communist district of San Giacomo, the red Italian Trieste that had never yielded to Fascism.

Captain Giessen leaves the building to bring the bishop's proposals to General Linkenbach; meanwhile eleven Italians, ten men and one woman, are shot by the Nazis in retaliation. On Via Cavana the birds are so frightened by the gunfire that they screech louder than the shots themselves. Politkomisar Franc Štoka makes it known that the Germans' surrender must be made only to Tito's troops. The bishop negotiates, urges, restrains. Monsignor Antonio Santin is not cut out for lying on the ground; the son of an Istrian boat captain, he was born to boldly govern rudder and sails, the church's boat as well as that of Rovigno's fishermen. Of course, in priestly ordination, the liturgy also calls for lying on the ground and Monsignor Santin loves the humble, maternal earth that teaches love and humility. *Humilis, humus;* not unctuous and servile, but warmly embracing the clay of which the Lord made us and to which we will return — accepting this return, yes, but putting it off as long as possible, at least for those whom at that moment it was his duty to protect and save from our corporal Sister Death.

There, lying on the ground, he is a soldier, crawling so as to better confront the enemy, the wolf and wolves that are slaughtering the flock. It's difficult to protect the flock, partly because at times it isn't easy to know which is your flock to defend, hard to distinguish wolves from sheep and sheep from wolves, the pursuer from the pursued, the wounded man in need of aid from the sniper to defend against. A grenade explodes nearby, images of bloody streets burst through his head like red flashes in the sky, the bloody stripes of an agate, veins in the stone of a petrified life. He too feels frozen, crystallized in the rigid role of pastor, as heavy as a stone cross.

Titovka. A cap with the red star of the partisans of the IX Korpus. Acquired personally from the partisan on Via Rossetti, in front of the entrance to the former Vittorio Emanuele II barracks, where the man, who until then had had it on his head, had thrown it, tossing it jubilantly in the air after shooting an Italian volunteer of the CLN who was guarding the German prisoners, and who had orders not to let himself be disarmed. When he refused to surrender his weapons he was done in along with the others, amid cheerful shouting; the partisan's cap flies merrily through the air and falls next to the life-less, perhaps dying, body, in any case when I picked it up the Italian was quite dead. Cheers of exultation, shouts against Italy and some skips of a *kolo* by the soldiers wearing the *titovka*. The universality and ambiguity of caps—who is under those caps? Heroes, killers, idiots? A pity I didn't manage to get hold of the German helmet under which Mussolini had hidden. Cap-ology, Lombrosian science. The internal seams, the segments of the lining, the dome corresponding to the cranial bones, a cast of those bones. My Museum is a huge cap on the world's head. A giant condom. But I don't know if and what it will be able to prevent.

The bishop never bowed his head, not even before the Duce when he came to proclaim the racial laws, right here in Trieste, and addressed him curtly with the coarseness of a sailor. During the feverish negotiations he even orders the Yugoslavian major who is disrespectfully smoking in the sacristy of San Giusto to go outside, if he really can't do without that cigarette; not in the church, however. If he now bows his head to dodge bombs and bullets it is certainly not due to cowardice, but to the fact that it is the duty of the pilot at the helm to dodge the rocks and bring to safety those sitting in his boat or clinging to its sides. But have I always protected the flock, he wonders, the Slovenes in the Karst and the Croats of Istria from the Black Shirts, the Triestines who ended up in the Risiera? When they'd sent him to prohibit the *s'ciaveto*, the ancient Glagolitic ritual of the Mass, in some villages in Istria, he certainly hadn't wanted to humiliate those Slavs, he was simply obeying his superiors—but is it right to obey? Is a Christian obedient or rebellious? The Germans who load Jews into the trucks are also obeying.

He presses his face to the floor, some shrapnel grazed him superficially but he doesn't care; blood shed *for* someone is good, it's blood shed *against* someone that is evil. He presses his nose, his mouth against the floor; who knows what his face looks like at that moment, flattened on the ground, maybe it resembles a stone statue whose nose has been pounded by a hammer and broken—I must look like an idol, he thinks absurdly, nevertheless, he manages to call, maybe the Germans have been swayed, maybe they won't blow up the port. Then everyone will claim credit, Uo-De, CVL, Kriegsmarine, even a manager from the Hotel Savoy, who will say that he convinced and dissuaded the German engineer in charge of the destruction. Now the Germans, though still attacking here and there, are on the run, the bishop, lying on the ground, knows it and he also knows it's not yet over, that all the violence filling the sky above the city has not yet been discharged, like on those oppressive summer nights when you can hear rumbling in the mass of clouds charged with electricity, lightning ready to spark, to set the world ablaze. Clouds heavy with a bloody sunset, ready to unleash a further rain of blood, who's next?

What time is it, is it day or night? Fatigue plays funny tricks on you, something in the head seems to swell up, constricting thoughts, disrupting their associations and sequences. The bishop continues talking on the phone, but at times he doesn't know or doesn't quite remember with whom; maybe the phone is at fault, maybe a bullet hit and ruptured the cable, in any case he feels disconnected from events and from those he's speaking to, though he goes on phoning doggedly, mechanically, talking, appealing, enjoining, commanding, in a feverish and disconnected but obstinate insomnia. How nice it would be to be able to sleep, but that's impossible; sleep is gone, vanished, a bullet must have hit the sleep mechanisms in the brain, no one can sleep anymore. War is also that, the destruction of sleep. And therefore also of faith, if it's true that a man who sleeps believes in God and surrenders to Him full of trust and at peace? Yes, war destroys faith, if faith were strong there would be no war. Even the MRI scan shows a sleep pathology.

The ledge of one of the large windows of Town Hall crumbles — the Germans fire on the city, especially on the buildings in Piazza Unità, from the banks and from the landing craft in the middle of the port. The temples of civil society do not have the solidity and sturdiness of that of the Law, the massive courthouse where the Germans are still holding out, they are more easily reduced to a pulp. But the Yugoslavs and Freedom Volunteers return the fire from the banks; the 4th Yugoslavian Army, reunited with the IX Korpus, is already in control of the city, the Hotel Savoy is in flames, the German fleet is increasingly in trouble.

The shooting continues, a hail of fire that the bora's gusts drive from side to side. The Italian communists protect the Freedom Volunteers from the Titoists, other Italian communists hunt them and hand them over to the Titoists, the Financial Police and the CLN's Railwaymen Brigade defend the port infrastructures, some of the Fascist mayor's Home Guard take up machine guns against the Germans, the Fascist Prefect tries to bring together Fascists and *repubblichini* and anti-Fascist Democrats against Tito and the communists—to no avail, but it will be useful for washing his face, so to speak, when the war is over. The Fascist party secretary escapes, other camerati join the Nazis in flight, flight from death, sometimes into death.

A massive stone ledge has fallen from a window of Town Hall, struck by the Germans. Inert stone, in which billions of electrons run around crazed, circling, colliding, repelling, destroying, quashing one another; shrieks of pain and agony for every particle, for every man mangled, pulverized, petrified, but you don't see or hear a thing. The hand caresses the surface of the beautiful stone, the cover of the history book; there are so many horrors in those pages but the cover is pleasing to the touch, the pages smell nice too and it's gratifying to hear them rustling between the fingers that caress them while leafing through and turning them. Similarly, appropriately colored to best highlight what it shows, the MRI's three-dimensional reconstruction that models the image of death seems like a beautiful inert gem, an agate geode striped by thousands and thousands of millennia, veins of blood desiccated by thousands and thousands of millennia. A triumph of death; a triumph of life that has been able to harden so as not to be tortured by the primordial flames, like the partisans by the Collotti Band's electric cables and red-hot pokers.

That image—his head, mine, whose interior the glioblastoma furnishes little by little in different ways; undoubtedly original, although a little brazen and aggressive. No one can be so presumptuous as to claim that it is only his head, that the network inside there, underneath there, is only his, just as one can't believe that he's the only master of the city, whose map the bishop holds in front of his face to follow what is going on in the streets. We are certainly all in there, somewhere; hidden in that map of the city, in that mosaic of lines and squares, a pawn on the chessboard, perhaps already captured. The glioblastoma devours the network; it rips into it like a minesweeper, it sinks its teeth into the torn webbing, sucks up the dangling threads as if they were spaghetti, like the wrenched telephone wire hanging from the wall of the bombed house on the Rive.

In that image the glioblastoma is blameless, static. Beautiful. A spellbound insect, a fossil, a flower imprisoned in stone. The colors look nice, don't they? Carefully chosen, without going too far. It looks like a lovely agate geode, Cretaceous, dating back 130 million years. The human brain is younger, but it resembles it. Especially when something seethes inside it and destroys it and rebuilds it from within. History is even younger, the last to arrive; maybe that's why it's so violent and messy. Inside basalts, gas bubbles are formed creating pockets—geoidal, with circular, widening bands of microcrystals. The glioblastoma works behind the frontal lobes, it carves out cavities, fills them, causes them to collapse by filling them with increasingly numerous, ever larger proliferating cells, little snakes that multiply merge split, countless small polyps, the mass of an octopus which expands and destroys its own home. Destroys to expand, to survive, to capture more *Lebensraum*. More space, that is more emptiness. Once the world is empty—a desert, uninhabited, leveled, free . . .

Debris from a window of the courthouse—Yugoslavian light tanks roaming the city fire at the Court Building, but the walls are sturdy; Justice is blindfolded like Fortune, but she's robust. The solemn halls, the columns, the foyers, the places where violence comes neatly organized on paper become instead a battlefield; crimes, blood, killings, meticulously presented in printed characters in minutes, depositions and briefs take on substance and blood, illustrated figures that emerge from the page and come alive only to die soon afterward. A vast space in which judgments are issued; the final one, a death sentence, is for a young man who crawls across Via Nizza and throws a hand grenade in one of the ground-floor windows, though before seeing it explode he is hit by a German crouched behind a column on the steps of the lobby. It's of no use; another death sentence for the German as well, who right after that tumbles down the stairs leaving a trail of blood, like a red carpet for visiting dignitaries.

A little later the partisans flood the basement of the courthouse, bodies float face down, sucked into a drainpipe they clog the opening; I help release the waters that stream out, I arrange for the bodies to be laid out respectfully for burial, I take the cartridge belts and sodden guns.

That other fine portrait? Worthy of Picasso, the splotch a kind of brownish eye, staring and teary, its pupil the point where the little ducts containing hydrothermal fluids mix with the mineral solutions. An agate 130 million years old, not very different from the MRI image of a cerebral infarction area. The cerebral infarction of a fifty-seven-year-old man, lava that has congealed in 130 million years, there's not much difference. I imagine that when I am no longer able to read and understand what I have written, which is happening to me more and more often, my eyes will become squinty and fierce like that splotch on the agate. Captain Giessen, when he parleys with the bishop, also has a look like that, severe and vicious, the gaze of an owl. Is it possible to remember when it was still an amorphous mass, not living, fiery lava that slowly crystallizes, a spent volcano that will become brain? A longing for fire and eruption, for life that annihilates and is annihilated; this is what war craves, the ancient yearning to rape stone and lichens. The primordial slime has slowly solidified and built up in the brain as well, whereas it takes very little to turn the glioblastoma back to sludge, though German Command hasn't yet realized it, it doesn't know that at its headquarters everything is now consumed.

At German Command reality is viewed with the fixed, dilated eye of the agate even more millenary than the millenarian Reich and everything rages around it at supersonic speed, the eye whose rear-guard is surrendering is unable to follow things that are changing so chaotically and frenziedly. But it is also difficult for others to follow and categorize things, to keep up with their acceleration. Liberation lasts one second and it's already occupation, the victory is already defeat. Not only does the agate's eye find it hard to pass from the fifty-one hostages hung by the Nazis on Via Ghega to the Titoists' blasts against defenseless people on Via Imbriani. The eye hardens even more, it survives in the fossilized geode—the eye of anyone, of no one—like the totem survives, though to those who built it, not for very long. God creates man, man creates the gods and the gods decree that man's fate be death. Every living thing wants to live, the body mutilated by the bomb crawls agonizingly toward shelter to escape another bomb, the mouse flees from the cat or the hawk swooping down on him and the gazelle runs from the lion, but all mice and all gazelles want to die even though they don't know it, the lemming flees but legend has it that lemmings commit suicide en masse. Life wants to die and war comes to its aid; compassionate war mother of all things, the mother rabbit that eats her young returning them to the contentment of darkness and nothingness.

Cells are ready, at any time, to self-destruct. Some are destroyed by the enemy, others destroy themselves so as not to succumb to the enemy, just as men kill themselves in prison so they won't talk when being tortured, and therefore to save other cells. Partisans who are captured do not talk. Ercole Miani, who led the units of the Justice and Freedom Brigade and was tortured by the Fascist torturer Collotti—providentially shot on the spot shortly afterward—did not say a word. When the Italian Ministry later had the bright idea of conferring a post-mortem honor on Commissioner Collotti—an honor accorded to someone who attaches an electrical cord to the genitals of a chained man fighting for freedom, one end on the glans and the other in his mouth, then turns on the current, and for this years later gets a medal, maybe to hang between his legs like a lovely pendant if he were alive, fortunately he's been stone dead for years, God sees and provides—the tortured Miani returned his own gold medal, given that they awarded one, though maybe not gold, to his torturer. The government would restore it to him posthumously when he too was dead, a post-mortem medal, like the murderer's. With decorations *melius abundare quam deficere.*

Yes, in a torture cell men kill themselves. Die rather than talk. Suicide to defend humanity, life; to oppose the death drive that pulsates in every cell. The Resistance is resistant; better to die than obey death.

A tricolor armband—The armband of the insurgent Italian Democrats, a badge of the CLN, organized within the CVL, the Volunteer Freedom Corps, which at 5:30 A.M. on April 30, after liberating Don Marzari from Villa Triste where he had just been tortured, gave the signal for the Italian insurrection, quickly crushed by the Germans, the Fascists and the Titoists supported by the communists. While still shooting at the Germans, the Yugoslavians forced the Freedom Volunteers to remove the tricolor armband, replacing it with the red star, and ordered them under the command of the CMT-KMT. This particular armband belonged to a partisan from the Railwaymen Brigade or the Finance Guard, two units especially active in the fighting. His name is not known. If he took it off, he saved his life. Otherwise, like others, he perhaps ended up in a doline.

They're still shooting, war dies hard. German landing craft fire on Piazza Unità from offshore, when they move out to sea they are mown down by Allied planes; in the sacristy of the Cathedral of San Giusto, the Germans negotiate with the bishop and with Tito's political commissar, the cigarette smoke—in the hallway, not in the sacristy, on this point the bishop does not budge—mingles with that of gunfire and bombs.

At the Castello di San Giusto Major Riegele is negotiating surrender with the Yugoslavs, but he drags it out until the New Zealand tanks get there and he is no longer dealing with Yugoslavian political commissar Štoka but with a New Zealand officer on board the first tank, Lieutenant Durable, and then with his general, Bernard Frey-berg. The city has already surrendered to the New Zealanders, who are tossing oranges to the children from the turrets of their tanks. There isn't one Triestine, especially those who were children at the time, who won't tell you—and who isn't convinced—that he caught an orange on the fly, tossed from a New Zealand jeep. I can't claim as much, because I wasn't a child then, but I picked one up in the park; it had ended up in the grass. Shriveled, of course, moldy—how about the world, then?

Hafenkommandant Riegele cancels the surrender to the Yugo-slavs and surrenders to the New Zealanders; the Yugoslavs, incensed, want to attack the Castello, *Trst je naš, jebem ti mater,* Trieste is ours, motherfucker, and the Germans, taken prisoner by the New Zealan-ders, offer to defend it with them, *Marsch in den Arsch,* up yours. Then the Yugoslavs decide to let it go, *jebi ga,* go to hell. We won't start a third world war over Trieste, Stalin has already told Tito by telephone; the Titoists clear out of the piazza under the eyes of the vanquished and the victors, fuck off Lieutenant Durable says by way of goodbye.

One of the many drawings signed by Kollmann and Josè—In the foreground Druse Mirko's feet with splayed toes, the Triestine cari-cature of the Slovenian from the Karst. Retaliation for those Slavic shoes, abandoned under the porticoes of Chiozza, which conquered Trieste? Here the bare feet do not convey advance, pursuit, flight and attack in the forest, the silent lurking of a wild beast, bare paws creeping up on the man pointing a gun at him, but are merely the un-couth, filthy feet of someone who hasn't learned civility, good man-ners, and has no right to enter the city. At least not without being ridi-culed for his filthy feet by someone who can buy Ferragamo shoes. Those derided, humiliated feet have fought, climbing Mount Kozara in Bosnia, they have sloshed through the Neretva and Sutjeska Rivers red with blood, defeating the Nazis, the strongest army in the world; they have walked the length of Yugoslavia, being wounded and get-

ting grimy, the mud and filth are their glory, the winged shoes of freedom, which little by little put the Nazi and Fascist invader on the run.
Those feet, Via Crucis and crucifying. A kick that results in a reversal.

General Linkenbach's jacket—it's the uniform coat he gave me,
slipping it off his shoulders, at the end of the negotiations for surrender; he was the only one left, along with some units of the Wehrmacht
and the Kriegsmarine, to command the city, after Rainer and Globočnik fled and after most of the German forces retreated toward
Austria. I am the one he surrendered to, it was I who spared his life.
If I hadn't been there to act as interpreter there would have been a
disaster—one more disaster, I should say.

General Linkenbach doesn't speak English and General Frey-
berg and Colonel McDonald don't speak German, but I'm there, I
speak seven languages and I understand eleven or twelve . . . General Linkenbach wants to negotiate a surrender, I translate and laugh,
there is little to be negotiated and the Brits could simply fire a few
shots and dispose of the few remaining Germans, but it's nice to negotiate, you go from the slaughterhouse to History's salon; I translate
and blather on at length, I bring the Second World War to an end,
at least in Europe. General Linkenbach signs the surrender, he has
no saber to hand over and in the end takes off his jacket; I quickly
put it on, it's a little worn but not too badly, if I had a clothes manne-
quin I would hang it, there isn't one, that's asking too much, a tailor's
dummy in this situation. A "considerable contribution to the Allied
cause," Colonel McDonald will attest on my behalf.

I also tried to tell both General Linkenbach and the British as
well as the Yugoslavs what they wanted to hear—within limits, of
course, I couldn't risk having them become aware of the tweaks, so
to speak, that I made to everything they said—and so in the end
everyone was happy. General Linkenbach enjoyed the dignity of a
noble defeat and the camaraderie of a fellow-in-arms with General
Freyberg, the British thought they had cheated the Titoists and the
Titoists thought they had cheated the British; to avoid further bitter
conflict, I left out, as I translated, several words spoken by the CLN

representative, the part where he recalled the individuals hung on Via Ghega—fifty-one of them—and laid claim to Trieste's *italianità*, its Italian identity. All in all, I orchestrated the operation.

The jacket is mine. I gladly wear it, some evenings. I sit at my table and sign blank sheets of paper. I sign the surrender, the capitulation. All that counts in a war is the end, the surrender, with which peace begins. Sometimes I sign with my name, sometimes with that of the general. Sign, that is abdicate, capitulate. Fight and lose. Just look at the pitiful condition all these cannons, tanks, planes, machine guns, rifles were in, that I collected.

A saddle—A saddle for endurance riding, with a hollow "reservoir" section obtained by rotational molding, to distribute the rider's weight evenly and not just on certain pressure points on the horse's back where the saddle rests; in addition it allows air to flow between the saddle itself and the horse's back, which aids perspiration. There were actually two saddles, but the other was not recovered. Trotting through the streets of Trieste on those saddles are Commander Sasso and political commissar Vanni Padoan of the Garibaldi-Natisone Division, the Italian communist partisan division under Yugoslav Command, meant to fight the Germans on the Karst and liberate Trieste, but sent instead to attack the Domobranci in Kočevje and liberate Ljubljana, while the Italian partisan Fontanot Brigade, disarmed by the Yugoslavs, was sent to repair bridges and roads in Suha Krajina, three hundred kilometers away.

The commander trots along, people barely glance at him, they just move on; he is even more uncomfortable than they are, luckily the division's political commissar is there with him, not that they have anything to say to one another, but still, it's a good thing, there's always something to say looking at the world around you or even just at the clouds passing by, at times more slowly, at times more swiftly than the hours.

It is May 20th, not the 1st of May as they had hoped and thought when hotly pursuing the Germans in the Natisone Valley. The Garibaldi Brigade, Italian and communist, which liberates the eastern border from the Nazis and Fascists and slaughters the Osoppo Brigade, Italian and Democratic. *Svoboda narodu*, freedom to the people; the Garibaldi-Natisone Brigade wanted to be the ones to hand that freedom to the Italians and Slovenes of Trieste, but instead the Yugoslavs sent them to liberate Ljubljana, on May 6. It's a fine thing, almost an act of duty, given that the Duce had proclaimed Ljubljana an Italian province; now it's right and good that an Italian should arrive with weapons in hand and the blood of fallen comrades—Italian comrades who died for the freedom of Italians and Slavs. An Italian to liberate Ljubljana from Nazis, Fascists, Domobranci, Belogardists. But then they want to go to Trieste with their Slavic comrades, to liberate their Trieste, and when the Slovenian Supreme Command objects they start marching to Trieste on foot. It is there, in Trieste, that the war must end and that the new world of freedom and socialist brotherhood must begin.

They set out on foot, not on those two handsome white horses that now carry them around the city the way carriages carried tourists and children at one time. They will go to Trieste on foot and if the Yugoslavs want to stop them, so much the worse for them, for everyone; if a brother strikes a brother it doesn't much matter which brother strikes who, if Abel had killed Cain it would have been the same thing. We fought, we died for Trieste and we have the right and a duty to be there when the city is liberated, thanks in part to the blood we shed. Fortunately, the Yugoslavs, seeing how determined we were, gave in, they even gave us some trucks to get to Trieste and so we made it there—but on May 20, when it was all over, a few days after the Yugoslavs had opened fire on a pro-Italian demonstration, resulting in dead and wounded.

What is there to do, if you get there on the 20th and not the 1st of May? They give him two handsome white horses, two Lipizzaners taken from the stable in Vienna that could not be outshone, where in those days, however, there were other things to worry about besides white Lipizzaners. And so the two roam through the city on horseback, two riders who got there late. The Rive are splendid as always, white crested waves in an expanse of blue fading into the purple of distant vistas. An enchanting Viennese Ring overlooks the sea: the two riders cross Piazza Unità, above them neoclassical statues vaunt bygone imperial glories, splendid, abandoned sets for a film no longer playing. Two partisans on horseback pass beneath the statues of Emperor Charles and Emperor Leopold, go up Viale XX Settembre where it is already summer, a precocious evening concealed among the branches that soon expands and spreads like dark wine from a broken cup, draping the sky and the building facades in black. The two continue riding along, at the end of the boulevard is Villa Orientale, a modest but dependable brothel that has seen better days. Still farther up is San Giovanni, where Buffalo Bill's circus had set up its tents and real fake Indians rode around on horseback, to honor the Sachem the commander and their warriors, with feathers and the red star. The commander remembers when he played cowboys and Indians as a boy; he doesn't have a feather headdress, it's true, but he has a white horse, a gift from the Kommando Mesta Trst. For that matter there's not much difference between the Garibaldi-Natisone's tattered uniforms and the ragged hats and coats of the Apaches, as they will soon begin to be depicted in movies.

At 5:30 P.M. on May 2, the bells of San Giusto peal out resoundingly; it signals peace, even though there is still shooting around the courthouse. The tolling rings through the air, particles quiver and the skies vault over the world, a blue, sweetly sonorous dome, a single sound that ripples and spreads outward like concentric circles in the water. Seen from below, the sky's vault is an enormous celestial blue bell—who knows what color the sky's dome is viewed from above. The sound is transmitted by waves, blue waves that expand, spiral through the air; the tolling is recurrent, the strokes identical, now close now distant, they pour out and course along, crests of foam on a surging sea. Vitruvius was the first to discover an analogy between the mechanics of sound propagation and the motion of waves in specific pools of water. You don't hear the shots; they're still being fired from the barrels of machine guns and a few tanks but it's now infrasonic, no, ultrasonic, more and more muted, maybe there's no shooting anymore; the German soldier firing from a sentry box at the intersection of two streets drops his machine gun, spreads his arms and slumps, but soundlessly, a silent film, the tolling of bells that in the end he no longer seems to hear.

The vault lowers, it is a hood, an ever more confining hood, over the head; a lid over the earth and the tolling resounds deafeningly, exploding like bombs in the ears and brain. The speed of sound, the tachometer says, is about 1,225 kmh, but beneath the swelling of the frontal tumor sounds travel very fast, at lightning speed, overwhelming. The bells sway to and fro like swings in the sun; the gleaming yellow of their interior can be glimpsed, illuminated by a sunbeam, a dazzling ray of light, a golden chalice of peace, but the sound reaches the ear even before the radiant flash. *Zeitrafferphenomen*, sovereign law of the cosmos, the glioblastoma doesn't give a damn about the laws of physics, of nature; it sees everything racing around it and runs faster and faster, even though war doesn't give a damn about nature, about physical laws. The atom is indivisible but war splits it and everything explodes in an instant, the sound detonates in the head, a bomb rips through billions of cells, a million billion cellular connections for each head lying motionless and bloodied on the streets of Trieste. How many billions of billions of cells and connections does History have? "Due to the extent to which it has spread," the MRI report says, "the tumor is considered inoperable."

A Museum of hatred? It was another idea of his, there are quite a few notes about it. Actually, war has little to do with hatred, neither of the two requires the other. Bombs fall on the heads of people who aren't hated at all, so much so that when the war is over those that dropped the bombs and those who were struck on the head by them shake hands and meet again at nostalgic gatherings of comrades-in-arms, former enemies, even for those who have fallen, they discover graves, dig up the dead and exchange a handshake. Hate is more genuine, more authentic than war; it is not sentimental, it does not sing "Lili Marlene," it has no need of battlefields or weapons. All it requires is a heart or a head.

Electroencephalograms, electrocardiograms, EEGs and EKGs of hatred. Hatred and beauty, hatred and sex, hatred and money, hatred and skin color. Reading those wacky notes of his, for a moment, Luisa thought, you could almost believe he was right, then you realize that they are actually so much hot air. All that quibbling over skin color—Luisa looks at her hands—and then a man and a woman in Trieste take a walk with a baby carriage on Molo Audace, the jetty stretching into the sea; the child, slightly darker than the other children on the jetty, widens her eyes at the seagulls that swoop by and skim the water, leaving passing white trails—fleeting, isolated memories, because she'd been very little, but sharp and vivid, luminous portholes in an indistinct haze—and the child tries to imitate their raucous screeching; people walking past the carriage smile and give her a caress or two, and even later in kindergarten and in school nobody pays any attention to her color. They're much more interested in the blue ribbon tying her braid and the strange words she speaks, since no one knows what they mean. Her blond classmate doesn't understand when she calls her *chabin*, and after a while she doesn't know and doesn't remember either, and nobody knows what *an dan des stile male pes* means either, yet sometimes the children say it all together holding hands in a circle.

So is that all it takes, a small swarm of children throwing snowballs or sand, depending on the season, to put an end to all those stories about skin color, entire libraries of hatred, of noble apostolates, pedantic disquisitions, graphics illustrating skull and jaw measurements? Much ado about nothing, those dermatological metaphysics, but meanwhile, arguing about skin color, a lot of people were skinned, and very gravely. Tell that to Aunt Kasika, much ado about nothing, when they kicked her out of that bar in London; a few kicks, or maybe just one, but very violent, internal bleeding flooding her abdomen—so the doctors at Guy's Hospital had said, usually they were not very eager to admit people of color and had them wait in line for emergency treatment, but since she was a member of the Army Nurse Corps who had come to defend old England from the Nazis they had been kind—and Aunt Kasika, not yet an aunt, had passed away. What the Messerschmitts had not managed to do, a couple of drunken thugs had. Of course it had also been foolish of her to wander around the Elephant and Castle, where the Jenkins and Ginger King gangs smashed windows or heads indiscriminately, times were never so good for them as periods of war when killing and dying, for freedom for a beer or just for the sake of bashing, are a commonplace daily occurrence.

Maybe someplace else they might have given her a nasty look and not touched her, but she was tired and thirsty and when you come back from the front where all you've done is see scores of people die, young men perhaps not all that different from those in the pub, and maybe you took them in your arms and gave them a sip of water as they were dying, you don't stop and think about the fact that murderers and those who assist murderers are everywhere, and that a vomit-covered floor in a pub in a civilized country that protected the world's freedom can become the blood-covered floor of a cell in the Risiera where the SS had kicked open the head of a brown, curly-haired child, a Jew or a gypsy from the Balkans, the blood spurting onto the floor and wall. Aunt Kasika's only seeped onto the floor, her blood oozed out slowly and gently, it was internally that it surged like a thick, wine-red sea.

Her father had never spoken to Luisa about his sister's death, at least as far as she remembered. Her mother had, however, and often, as if she found bitter, painful consolation in the knowledge that there are many Risieras in the world and that any bar, not just a dive in a rough district, can become a Risiera where any Otto Stadie can raise and lower his Polizeimeister's spiked mace. If her father, growing up in the South, had also suffered humiliation and violence, no one knew anything about it, not even her mother, Luisa was certain of it. In any case, he'd done well, because you avenge the wrongs and injustices you suffer, with or without the law, it depends, but you don't talk about them. When the Fascist action squads, in the streets of Trieste, beat up those who tried to resist, force-fed them castor oil or sent them to the other world, Slovenian and communists in particular but also liberals and Republicans, perhaps decorated for having fought for Italy on the Karst, Vittorio Vidali, not yet Carlos Contreras and glorious founder of the glorious V Regiment in the Spanish war and not yet alleged inglorious Stalinist liquidator of the anarchists in Catalonia but former leader of people without regard and without fear, ordered his men never to speak of the beatings they received, but only of those they gave — few, at that time, though later the score was evened out.

She wondered if her father, who obviously hadn't been able to go to his sister's funeral or even know if there had been a funeral, at least knew where she'd been buried. Not that it mattered; the whole world is a cemetery and that goes for everyone, but even more so for us, for the children of Galuth and Slavery, however it is also true that the homeland of a Jew is the place where his loved ones are buried, and even though there is nothing and no one left beneath the earth after a brief time, it is fitting to recite the Kaddish for one who is no longer anything or anyone, but continues to live with the one who loved him and therefore loves him, because to love is an indelible present infinitive. All Luisa knew, though vaguely, was that right after the end of the war her father had briefly been to London once, with a letter of introduction from his commander, Colonel Hager, for a police station in the Elephant and Castle district. They had found that letter in a drawer, along with the one informing him of his assignment to the Department of Port Activities, where he'd worked during the last years of the Allied Military Government in Trieste.

No one ever knew what he had done or not done during those days in London. Finding a couple of drunken murderers from an evening years earlier is more difficult than finding a maroon who has vanished in the *morne*. Justice is blindfolded, it's difficult for her to see who is running to get away and who is running after him. The maroon's spoor lasts longer among the reeds, the dogs pick up the trail even after quite some time; the spoor of those who kick a woman to death, one evening in a foul-smelling pub, between one air raid or curfew and another, dissipates quickly in the overall rancid stench, sweaty skin, filthy slop, grimy debris, remnants of beer and greasy plates. In the cells of the Risiera the stink of the victims, not the perpetrators, hangs heavy. Lerch, on those lovely evenings in the Karst, did not stink; perhaps more unpleasant at the time was her mother's odor, since she would start sweating when she saw him.

Luisa thought she knew what her father had gone there to do, why he'd wanted to go to London, but she couldn't imagine whether he had done it or not. A Police Station, amid the ruined remains of a Gog and Magog war and countless struck by V2 flying bombs, doesn't have much hope of tracking down someone who dealt a deadly kick, which for the woman who was kicked was indeed a V2.

The hospital has the name of the victim who arrived, dying, not that of the nameless and faceless killers who melted away in the maze of alleyways. During those final months of the war in London, the times were probably ideal for killing; the furtive petty criminal easily blends in, and under the heaps of bodies torn apart by bombs, easily conceals the person he kills for a few shillings or even just for the sake of killing—like Thomas Jenkins or Ronald Hedley, the Elephant Boys and the other gangs eager to shatter the bar's windows and cash boxes with their axes and even more eager to split heads. But the first German bombs had already unleashed youth gangs on the bombed-out streets and Harry Dobkin had set a trend, killing his wife and burying her under the rubble of Vauxhall Baptist Chapel; not a few had followed his example, in that great glut of death. It was also easy to steal weapons from armories that had been bombed, despite the fact that juries were quick to sentence murderers who could be caught to the gallows, twenty minutes to reach a death sentence for Harry Dobkin, hanged in Wandsworth Prison. Of course, while German bombs were falling, the fact that nine hundred London detectives might investigate swindlers who pretended their house had been bombed in order to receive aid, and numerous inspectors might dig through the rubble of widespread crime and thousands of corpses to find out who had killed a Miss Evelyn Hamilton, helped to understand why old England had not buckled, not even when it stood alone and shattered against the strongest army in the world.

And even if, by some miracle, he had found them, caught them, sunk his teeth into the leg or legs that had dealt the murderous kick, what would her father have done? The mastiff grips the fugitive between his teeth and holds him steady until someone comes along—an eye for an eye, a tooth for a tooth, or let no one touch Cain? Fine words that don't solve anything when you hold in your hands the one who has destroyed you. Both are false and wrong; it's torture not knowing what to do with someone who has tortured you and who is in your power, you feel you must not act like him, not even toward a monster like him, nor can you let him go, and so you're better off not finding him, keep searching for him but don't find him. Even for her father, she thinks it was good that he went back to Trieste without the snake in his teeth, its vertebrae snapped, that he returned still panting, savoring the continually exhilarating though futile hunt—following the traces, the scents, the clues, especially when the prey is a poisonous snake that doesn't deserve mercy, even though you've been told that you should have mercy on the undeserving as well.

Luisa imagined him wandering the streets of the immense city, through the rubble and ruins, a mastiff like the ones that had hunted his fathers, but a disoriented mastiff, his nose confused by so many unknown scents. A man who walks along and before long doesn't know where to go; yes, go home, search for life, not the death of those who have dealt death. Her father's hands would not have been less gentle, less pure, less good, if the blood of those Jenkinses or Geraghtys or whatever those murderers were called were on them; some of the killers may even have died under the Nazi bombs, hopefully, bombs aren't dropped to administer justice but sometimes, no thanks to those who drop them, they fall on those who deserve them as well. But so much the better, her father had done his duty, remember what Amalek did to you, and if he had failed it was not his fault; he too, Luisa felt sure, had been glad to return empty-handed, without blame.

Who knows whether those who had killed her grandmother Deborah had been left to rot in the street as well or whether they had squeezed through some net and maybe afterward had done all right in the world. But perhaps hands that had not been stained with blood that they had understandably—justly?—wanted to spill had felt at greater liberty, some years later, to open the door on the third floor of Via Tigor; more permitted and more tender in the caresses that had roused her mother from endless emptiness and brought her into the world, into the Eden of that third-floor apartment, with no sin and no expulsion—no, there had been expulsion, but later, minus the guilt, no foolish apples eaten just because they are foolishly forbidden and no foolish fancies about knowing good and evil. After the trip to London her father must certainly have had even less of an understanding about good and evil, Luisa was sure of it; only an idiot—said a great Talmudic master, mentioned to her by her cousin Moni Rosenholz, who studied such things and in the end had gone to teach in a yeshiva in New York—could think he could become like God by eating a silly apple; that's the original sin, a foolishness that made man unworthy of living in Eden.

Her father and her mother, however, had managed to stay in

Eden, at least until the day on the runway at Aviano. Via Tigor 11, third floor left, Land of Canaan, whose name is no longer that of a shameless black voyeur and worse, but a man content with his woman, as she with him, and therefore with the world. Her father had gotten assigned to the Department of the Allied Military Government for Port Operations. A post implying a certain trust in a city full of spies and plots, a city that in those years was a fairly crucial pawn in the superpowers' grand scheme for world domination. But what her father liked most of all were the ships entering and leaving the port, the smell of the crates that were unloaded, the cranes that rose and fell like large birds of prey and would have seized even the Leviathan if the monster had dared to rage in those waters. He liked the sea, its gusts slapping his face; even the bora that filled his mouth with salt, when he was on the docks or on deck overseeing operations, and the foaming whitecaps on days when the bora churned. The sea, too, a place of slavery, like every place, but clouds in the sky dispersed, distant waves crumbled the walls of oppressive prisons; in the evening, the sky on the horizon was aflame, the whole world caught fire, a fire that melted chains and opened gates everywhere to an immense freedom.

Later, when the Americans and the British had gone home and Sergeant Brooks was shuttling between Aviano and Trieste, every so often on Saturdays and Sundays he would take Luisa on a boat ride in the gulf. They sailed along the sea walls, went as far as the Bay of Duino, where they sometimes stopped and took a dip in the dark green waters. She, still little, rested her hands lightly on her father's shoulders, until he suddenly—but gently, not wrenching away—moved off from her, and so she had learned to swim. Also to do some diving from one of the rocky projections below the ruins of the old castle of the lords of Duino; lifting her out of the water, her father stood her on one and she dove in, the water, emerald green or indigo, depending on the wind, glinted with hidden treasures, dark and gleaming. A blue deep as the night, a warm, joyous night, almost an underwater Christmas, where you felt happy.

It was always just the two of them. Her mother, Sara, never came, she didn't want to come; across the gulf, on the other side of the sea, especially on clear days when the bora blew, you could glimpse Salvore. Only later would Luisa understand how and why that view was unbearable to her mother; the waves that rushed in, breaking in the small Bay of Duino and generally along the city's limited coastline, were unbearable to her as it was, given that they came from over there, from the tip of the Istrian peninsula that jutted out in vain to close the gulf, that great opening that for Luisa, instead, would always be the image of Open, of every Open, of everything that opens the heart and hurts just because it opens it, opens a wound that can't be healed, a window on all that's lacking.

Underwater, when they swam at sunset—initially it was her father who put her head under, she had swallowed and spat out the salt that got in her mouth, but she liked seeing things down there, darker and more mysterious—the white rocks and reddish algae lit up with a muted glow, gems and precious stones in a bluish night, and when they climbed back into the motorboat, after unsuccessfully objecting to the sweater that her father made her wear in the cool evening wind, she had him tell her again, during the return, the story about grownup Luisa and the treasure.

She understood that her father, too, would have liked the other Luisa to have been born in the huge country where everyone has black skin and to have reached those islands after crossing the sea on a beautiful ship, certainly in a beautiful cabin and, in fine weather, walking on deck with her mistress. While she was enjoying the strong tradewinds blowing over her face on that deck, who knows whether— though this was something little Luisa had wondered about much later—down below in the dark, smelly hold, there were others, black like her though otherwise not like her; who knows if she sometimes heard them moaning, a single muffled howl, a kind of painful breathing. But perhaps it was other ships that transported men in chains and who knows whether she knew it or not.

Grownup Luisa had also had a bad time on that island across the sea, her father told her. They had even threatened to burn her as a witch when she escaped from the Caribs and returned home, after having been abducted and held captive for four years, fleeing from her red masters and returning to the white masters who nearly sent her to the stake, as had already happened to three black witches, suspected of having spoken, danced, or worse, with the devil. The three women had actually confessed to having lain with the devil disguised as an animal, though they'd confessed it to priests—not all priests are like Don Marzari—who were having them taunted with red-hot pincers. Big Luisa, on the other hand, hadn't confessed to anything, partly because those who questioned her hadn't seared or harmed her. They listened to her kindly, open-mouthed, who knows what she must have told them to satisfy them and make them be so kind to her; the fact is that they let her go and she went back to live with the good Luís Hernández, her white husband, father of her children, at least some of them, who knows about other children in the forest.

Grandmother Deborah instead had been burned, and so had many many others, a few even because of her; burned by brutes even more brutish than those who had burned heretics and those who had massacred the Indians, more brutish than the children of Ishmael who sold the sons of Canaan into slavery, more brutish than Samuel, who cursed Saul because he did not want to kill children who were captives, and more brutish than the sons of Jacob, who had killed all the males in the city of Shechem after having them circumcised. As bad as they were, the people before the flood were not as bad as those who came afterward; God must have drunk a little too much, like his chosen one Noah, when he drowned them all, apparently he got confused about before and after.

39.

Room no. 26—A *macuahuitl*. A wooden weapon apparently dating back to the Zapotecs (third century AD) and later used by the Aztecs and other peoples of Mesoamerica. A meter long, with a 10 × 5 cm rectangular grip, the shorter sides fitted with sharp obsidian blades. Grasped like a broadsword, but also wielded point-on to stab. Testimony from the time of the Conquistadores mentions an Aztec warrior who decapitated a horse with a single blow of a *macuahuitl*.

SO DECLARES LUISA DE NAVARRETE . . .

No, she could not have had that deadly weapon of the Kali-nagos in her hand, the Carib Indians of the forest who had kidnapped her—and who had maybe become her people—would not have allowed her to carry a club or spear or ax. Even when she accompanied them—forced to?—on their raids to neighboring islands, she was made to stay on shore and guard the canoes, in some bay or other where the Indians landed furtively to go and loot a Spanish village—like the time in Humacao, in Puerto Rico, when they had abducted her and brought her to the island of Dominica, where they had sought refuge to escape the Spanish massacres and from where they set out on their piracies. So declares Luisa de Navarrete . . .

She declares so to the judges of the Inquisition, when—four years after being abducted, four years whether of captivity or complicity with her captors wasn't clear—she had managed to escape, during one of their raids, and return home, to San Juan de Puerto Rico. She was well aware that, depending on the outcome of the interrogation, that return could either mean the stake—three black witches had been burned in Puerto Rico—or, as would happen, an honorable homecoming—as *mujer negra* and *mujer de razón*, the inquisitors must have recognized—to her city and her family, to the home of her husband, Luís Hernández, who struggled along modestly (especially when you consider how much gold was pillaged in those countries in those years) but whose white skin, among all the red and black skins, unquestionably assigned him to the breed of world masters. To her husband and her children, the children of Luís Hernández, not those she bore in the four years by her Carib *amo*, lover and master, who like those children would never have a name in the story destined to be probed, retouched and retold in the years and centuries to come.

When you read the minutes of the interrogation . . . Arabesque swirls and flourishes, often indecipherable, which at first glance, at least to a layman, resemble characters of the Koran's Suras found in mosques more so than the Latin alphabet in which the clerk had scrawled them. The humidity and attrition of centuries unacquainted with photography and microfilm had also helped to erode the script, nearly reducing the marks to the insignificance of things, drops of faded ink as watery as rain streaking a window pane.

With the help of a kind archivist—exchanging a few words with him in the Escorial silence of the library, in Seville, seemed unreal—Luisa had been able to learn something, though not much, about her old namesake from the words transcribed in the proceedings. The defendant—merely questioned and in the end no longer even under investigation—speaks, the clerk (notary was his official title) records the account, bringing order to the words and disconnected phrases that tumble out, eliminating silences, filling in the blanks when the voice breaks off, as she swallows some saliva and runs her tongue over her lips to moisten them. No one, let alone a free black woman—*libre y horía*, the record specified, using a word of Arab origin from ancient Castilian, dating back to the time when a darker color indicated the subjugators and not those subjugated by them—and perhaps former slave speaks as syntax would have it, the order of subject predicate and complement, the *consecutio temporum*.

No, not even a woman *muy ladina*, very shrewd, as the inquisitors wrote. To read someone's words without hearing her voice, without seeing the expression that those words produce on her face as she speaks them is to read words that are different from what she said. *C'est le ton qui fait la musique,* even before a merciless court. What voice, what intonation had big Luisa used, the guttural, throaty voice of a black woman who for four years had spoken only the language of cannibals—"Yes, I learned their language, so I could understand what was happening among them and what they were doing"—or a voice resonant with echoes deep as the waters of a river, brown waters beneath dense, dark trees like her *muy moreno* face? What had been lost or added in the course of passing from the voice of the interrogee, which quickly vanished in the succession of soundwaves, to the clerk's recording of it in the minutes? Perhaps it was the clerk speaking in those minutes, and once he'd emptied the words from his net onto the court's bench, like the counter of a fish market, there would be no fish, only the mesh of netting.

Perhaps the minutes said little about big Luisa, just as the marks traced by Jesus in the sand when they were about to stone the adulteress likely said nothing about the obscurity of that destiny and of that heart. Experienced in human nature, that is, in evil and failings, the inquisitors instructed the scribes to record even the interrogee's pallor and silences, no less revelatory of her crimes than the words that came out of her mouth. But those silences, those pallors, had been the first to be worn away by time's attrition, well before the words, which on their own remained mute, marks on paper more enduring though not much more eloquent than those on the sand. Is it possible to know what a person meant when he told someone "I love you" without having heard his voice, felt his breath, seen his face blush?

In any case, on Luisa's face it is difficult to imagine a pallor that rather than lightens her people's blackness, lends it a livid, sickly cast. She does not seem uncertain or bewildered or overwhelmed or paralyzed by fear, a trapped animal waiting for those who hold her in their clutches to pounce. She speaks up rather than respond, anticipating and suggesting questions before they are formulated, providing unsolicited information on topics of great interest to her judges and apparently risky for her, but that diverts them from inquiring about other even more dangerous aspects. Her grave, ominous audience, quite soon, seems almost passive; they listen not only to what they want to know, but largely to what she wants to tell them. At times the notary-clerk seems to be taking dictation, recording what Luisa says and means to say. The hunted gazelle leads the chase, imposing the direction of the course on her pursuers, who often find themselves facing an opening through which she has passed, but that is too tight for them, so they must turn back.

The road that can lead to the stake passes through accusations of idolatry, participation in underworld cults and in the cannibalistic ritual meals of the Kalinagos—the name itself implies identification of the Carib Indians with cannibals—carnal intercourse with savages if not with the devil, obscene witches' Sabbaths in the shadowy forest, and connivance with the Indians, branded as pirates, in raids against Spanish villages and ships. Cohabitation with her *amo*, the Kalinago chief, father of her other children, whose name is never heard on her lips, would by itself have been more than enough for a conviction. Luisa quickly sets her own personal story aside as secondary: "They take women captive, they have carnal knowledge of them by force and do what they will with them—here the clerk's voice can be heard—and when the Indians' women see these things happening they start shooting arrows at the captives." They do what they will with them . . . No, that namesake of hers was definitely no fool; I too, Luisa thought uneasily, know something about that. Nonetheless, an inquisition with a happy ending, a gleam of tranquil light in that sky aflame with blood: ". . . a black freedwoman named Luisa de Navarrete, born in Puerto Rico and held in high regard, who after spending four years on Dominica island was made to accompany the Indians when they returned to sack the island of Puerto Rico, where she fled from them, has told us many things about the island of Dominica as well as about its captives and the treasures to be found there."

Luisa must have realized that her inquisitors weren't all that interested in knowing who ate meat on Fridays or who had renounced the true faith. Of course, they were interested in that as well, and she does not hold back. "On the island of Dominica I saw two women and a man, our kind, who became as Carib as the Caribs, the women say they do not remember God and the man says the same thing, they eat human flesh and do everything the Caribs do, and when I asked why, as Christians, they do not remember the Mother of God, the man replied that just as the Mother of God had not remembered to get them out of that place where they'd been captive for forty years, so he didn't remember her either." But Luisa realizes that the men who bombard her with questions are mainly interested in knowing where certain ships have vanished or sunk, where the treasures carried by those ships are hidden, where and how captains and admirals who never reached port disappeared. A conscious or unconscious Scheherazade, she averts her death with tales of the many things those men are eager to know.

No, it wasn't wrong to include Luisa de Navarrete and the *macuahuitl* she never used in the Museum. War is the art of dissimulation—in his papers on the Museum, he had often repeated the famous definition of Sun Tzu, the forefather of all strategists and all military strategies—and the Luisa of half a millennium ago had dissimulated her life, threatened from the outset by everything and everyone, by submitting to fate when she was defenseless against the violence that swept over her and yielding only as much as was necessary to enable her to lessen its intensity and change the course of fate, albeit slightly, with small adjustments to the rudder, almost as imperceptible as the clerk's tweaks and omissions.

Furthermore, those seas of gold and blood were a scenario that excited the obsessed museologist almost as much as the Museum itself, given that he was just as obsessed about his alleged Hispanic origins, which he never missed an opportunity to tout. In one of his notes, he had scrawled something about a galleon shipwrecked on the rocks off Dominica Island, assailed by Indians—Kalinagos, Taino, Arawak?—and plundered, whether by the Indians or by the waves that had flooded the hold was unclear, and about the treasure it was carrying, roughly 3 million pesos in gold, diamonds, emeralds, piasters and doubloons, which ended up in a grotto barely underwater or deep beneath the sea, where his great-grandfather or great-great-grandfather, Carlo Filippo himself, during one of his voyages, which no one knew anything about, or maybe one of his untrustworthy mates acting for him, may have made off with something. Indians boarding the ship, maybe brandishing the *macuahuitl* . . .

Muy ladina, that woman perhaps abducted twice—by the Indians and earlier, according to some, by whites who had enslaved her—

to have understood that at times the only strength of the weak is to display their own weakness, to wear that weakness as a disguise, something that is unsettling to the strong and those who are masters. She tells her story using the passive past participle—though she doesn't know what those grammatical terms mean. She is captured, stripped naked, forced—"we had stayed to make something to eat (that day four years ago, when she had gone to Humacao with her husband and some neighbors) and when nearly everyone had gone horseback riding, at noon, I think, I noticed that some Caribs had furtively crept up to where the animals were kept and carried off a black man who was there, and they took me as well," they took the witness, the notary secretary writes, "she was, I was bound and stripped."

Fearful, submissive, she makes no move to defend herself. It's natural, with those predators—whom at other times she would see as hunted, battered prey—leaping out of the forest, *macuahuitl* in hand, superfluous against a woman whose clothing has been ripped off and useless against muskets. She doesn't appear to be afraid as she is taken, but it is not always easy to know when someone is afraid. The jaguar grinds his teeth when he's about to pounce on a tapir and when he backs away from a snake or a man, it's not clear whether it's fierce hunger or whether it's fear, but she had learned it in the forest, a different quiver between the vibrissae and the teeth, a different smell too—the smell especially, the smell of a body excited about stalking a raccoon or a tapir with cushioned, silent steps, the tremor of the leap already in his legs but still contained. Fear instead has a different smell. No, it's not fear of the anaconda or the caiman, the jaguar attacks them springing down on their back, the anaconda's thick neck already clamped between his jaws and teeth, hard to snap, sometimes he succeeds and sometimes he doesn't, in the end he himself may die between those coils but even then ferocity is stronger than fear. It's men the animal fears, not caimans or snakes; it's the Caribs advancing with spears, the wooden *tepoztopilli* with the wedge-shaped head bristling with obsidian blades, the atlatl and the bow, which wound from a distance. The arrow flies farther than the jaguar who flees up a tree, there are too many men to leap down on one of them so he's afraid, he reeks of fear, a pong that sticks to his fur as his eyes dilate, shifting from one warrior to another down there. Jaguar warriors, they are called, and he up in that tree knows it. Some even wear his skin and grind their teeth like him and their eyes are dilated like his but more inebriated and savage. Her *amo*, too, when he takes her in the evening, is wrapped in the skin of a jaguar, the jaguar he killed under the two great waterfalls, stalking him upwind, the wind that carried the animal's scent to him but kept the jaguar from smelling him, much less hearing his soft footfalls, covered by the roar of the waterfall.

Luisa remembers — she quickly chases the memory away before the judges notice it, a memory also leaves its mark on the face, an instantaneous tattoo that it's best to get rid of — she remembers her man with her on the mat under the dense growth of trees, the old jaguar skin around him slashed here and there by the knife with which he skinned it and by the claws of the dying jaguar who today defended himself and smeared him with blood. Blood that was still fresh, a good smell of man and animal, her black skin smells good too, she knows it, especially there under the trees with her *amo*, sometimes they copulate like men sometimes like animals but it is always fierce, good.

The Kalinagos say that at night, on a bed of leaves, the black jaguar takes off her skin, a beautiful queen of the forest, but God help her if afterward, when the man is gone, she can no longer find her skin. Luisa took off her jaguar skin when she fled, no one will find it in the swamp, the judges mustn't know anything about it, not Luís, her husband, either. Luisa yearns for the sheets and blankets covering their bed, down there even without the animal skin she is a jaguar and he too, if she remembers well; when you wrap around each other and kiss and bite there's not much difference. But above all she longs for her house, its window with a few flowers, chatting with her neighbors, who always respected her as an obedient, dutiful wife. For her children . . . some here, some there, it's so different, so difficult, so strange . . . For a moment Luisa looks off into space.

They ask, she answers, she also replies to what they don't ask but what she realizes they want to know. The island, the islands, the hidden landing places, camps in the forest, people all the same yet different. She too knows little about them, only what she's heard, what the Kalinagos she lived with had heard. Just touch the monitor and images appear on the surface of the screen—ships, cliffs, a maze of forests, the bearded faces of helmeted Conquistadores, the tattooed faces of Indians. Kalinagos, that is, Caribs, Taino, Arawak, Ignibis, Igniris, Igneri, Vien-Vien, Ciboneyes, Exbaneyes, Guanahatabeyes, Guinahacabiles, Ortiröides, Saladoïdes, Casimiroïdes, Cofachites, Mocoes, Mondongo, Apalachites, Galibis, Calibites . . . clans more numerous than the islands, islets and reefs of their sea, names of today or a thousand years ago, contrasting and synonymous, names of the Other and of the Same—centuries and millennia vanished like names on the sand erased by waves, no, not ever erased, some prints that the water did not reach or wash away, runes engraved by time on stone more durable than time. Rock writing in Montravail Forest, St. Lucia, Madinina, the island of flowers and women without men. The rocks recount the origins and deeds of Maboya, spirit of evil, and of Shémine, spirit of grace and goodness, a red-speckled black bird, a flower that flies among the flowers and sees everything, even at night, and Yali child of incest and the moon, father of all Kalinagos. Rocks inscribed by the hand of the earliest writer of these seas, by the wind and rain, tell this story in the grottoes of Dominica and other islands as well.

Graffiti from a time before time, etched onto rocks immemorial, afterward graffiti from a non-time of slavery, carved onto bent backs, stooped over to scythe, prune, harvest and transport fruits of the land or underground treasures. They come from the North, from the South, from another island to which afterward—if it still exists—they return; they slaughter one another, drive each other out. Caribs massacred by the Spaniards in the Antilles where they had massacred the Taino and Arawak after fleeing from the Arawaks' slaughter in Hispaniola. Be fruitful and multiply, so you can exterminate each other all the more. Mondongo covered with red and yellow hair, Igneris—or maybe Igniris or Ignibis—hairy, bearded and long-haired, came from the North and were driven to the mountains by the Caribs where they flayed an escaped black slave, then hung his skin from tree branches, the tree reaching out bristly black limbs red with blood, Apalachites driven out by Cofachites who perhaps became the Caribs or Kalinagos. In the woods of Hispaniola men swift as deer but unable to speak, the Vien-Vien, are called that because that is the only sound they can make, the language of the Haihoe is also a single sound emitted from the nose.

Ancient times, primeval, but everything and nothing is ancient in the forest and on rocks submerged and abandoned by shattering waves; perhaps antiquity refers to a time before man, maybe even before the opossum or puma. Centuries and centuries, the blink of an eye that leaves countless traces and none at all, from fallen, rotting logs other trunks quickly spring up, indistinguishable, which in turn fall and rot, the serpent's egg is identical to the eggs that generated thousands of generations of serpents. Nothing has happened, no time has passed since it only passes if something happens; to find time you have to go back, to when the earth separated from the sea, but now time is about to come, it has come, everything is happening everything changing.

At Capesterre Saint-Vincent the Caribs make slaves of fugitive blacks from neighboring islands or from shipwrecked slave ships— Luisa is a valuable, accurate witness of those abducted blacks—who fall into line but grow too profuse in number, they have too many children, and so the Caribs kill their firstborn infants, like the Lord did with the Egyptians, but the blacks rebel and slaughter countless Caribs. Everyone the slave of everyone else, blacks of the whites and reds, whites of the reds, reds of the whites and sometimes even of the blacks, like that Garrido, Cortés's trusted man, "the first European to plant wheat in Mexico" on his farm in Coyoacán, history books will later tell us.

Caribs, Taino, Wupuyama, Ciboneyes, many names, few men, each name one man or little more, only one of the Vien-Vien has been seen as well, in the mountains; maybe not even that one, who quickly disappeared with his cry, his entire vocabulary, or maybe he never appeared, just someone or something stirring among the enormous leaves, a big stone rolling on the sodden earth. So many names, the same name, because Igneri means man, even though it also means husband, son, fox, dog, opossum and manicou, but Kalinago also means man and so does Arawak. Man is the name of each of them, which each one denies to all the others; for the Kalinagos the Igneris are not called men and are not men and for the Igneris the Arawaks aren't. Even in San Juan Puerto Rico man means white man and not black man or red man.

The inquisitors are not interested in jaguars or stories about the history of the world. Rather in piracies, shipwrecks, treasures, the ship whose course had skirted Dominica, which the Kalinagos attacked and burned, killing three or four Spaniards—Luisa is quite accurate—and capturing ten or twelve of them, along with six women, "one was called Doña Maria, another, her sister, Doña Juana, the mother of these two women whose name was Juana Díaz, and I don't remember the names of the others."

She talks about the treasure trying not to let them see that she doesn't know where it is—she doesn't know just exactly where, she suggests, but she knows enough to be useful in searching for it. More useful than Captain Juan Lopez de Sosa and Captain Vicencio Ganello, who had searched for it scouring the coast with the galleon *San Felipe* and the almiranta *Santa Barbara* but had returned empty-handed, after having tortured a few Indians to no avail. Luisa doesn't say she saw it, but she talks about it as if she has seen it. Green emeralds rolling around in the green of algae and moss, sapphires and turquoises blue as the waters of the sea, diamonds mixed in with white shells and even whiter pebbles, topazes amid equally yellowish crabs, the sun's gold glinting off gold ducats and scudi—twenty-three- and twenty-two-carat, she doesn't know this but the judges do—silver reales and copper blancs, doubloons (seven grams of gold each, this too the inquisitors know, though it's of no use to them), red maravedis among red corals, clusters of amethyst like ailing jellyfish. Underwater everything shimmers and sways, sirens' tresses, grab them by the hair and carry them off, millions and millions of years compressed into icy glittering gems, frigid stars, agates gleaming like cat's eyes. Who knows if part of it was still there, not yet eroded by centuries of salt: the treasure that Carlo Filippo had hidden under the Old Town, after having fortuitously grabbed something, when—if it was true—he had gone to the Antilles on a Dutch ship and then returned to Trieste, with or without that fortune, unaware that all those troubles awaited him.

Neither the interrogee nor her inquisitors had actually said that, as one could readily see from the minutes and the excellent study by Ricardo E. Alegría in the *Revista del Museo de Antropología, Historia y Arte de la Universidad de Puerto Rico.* But every story, every text, every life, Luisa thought, leafing through the papers that she had brought to the Caffè San Marco—she had returned to Trieste to complete the project, by now time was running out—is a palimpsest, a page wiped clean so it can be written on again, always the same story but superimposed on a previous one, writing that covers other writings with corrections difficult to read but not erased, it too destined to be retouched and rewritten but not completely obliterated, passing from mouth to mouth and from page to page. God spoke one word, I heard two, so it is written. Not even just two, many more—though ultimately the word of God remains unattainable and one, the truth, the story of an individual, albeit distorted by mirrors and echoes.

Luisa did not therefore feel like a fraud by rewriting her distant namesake's story for the Museum and filling in the gaps. For that matter, any possible fabrications had existed for some time now, by then they were part of the story. "*Noire de peau, blanche de culture, caraïbe de destin, métisse de progéniture,*" "black by skin, white by culture, Caribbean by fate, mother of mestizos": Patrick Chamoiseau and Raphael Confiant, in their *Lettres créoles,* have no doubts. Luisa was abducted or bought by the Spanish at a very young age—perhaps on the coast of Dahomey, whose sovereign trafficked in black ivory more than white ivory—and brought to Spain, where her intelligence, soon recognized, would have enabled her to become something more than a noblewoman's slave or servant, as a result of which she would soon afterward have gone to the New World, to Puerto Rico.

Her father's voice, many years ago . . . Luisa became a lady's attendant, her long journey across the great blue sea, her arrival in those islands unknown not only to her but to the world, those islands where, in the magical tale he used to tell her nearly every night as he put her to bed, the big Luisa would sometimes actually be born, a brilliant child like a small bird of paradise.

But the numbers didn't add up. Luisa returns home at age twenty-three, having fled from the Kalinagos after four years of captivity. Yes, captivity, that's what she says, although . . . Are nineteen years—even for a life incredibly full of twists and turns and even allowing for the precocious flowering of a girl born in Africa—are they enough to allow for her birth in Dahomey, her abduction in childhood or adolescence, the transplantation to Spain and the purported special upbringing she received there (modest, but still special for a little slave), the journey to the New World, marriage and motherhood, abduction and return? Half smiling and half chagrined, Luisa realized that she was adding and subtracting the other Luisa's years the way mothers once calculated when their daughters were due to have their periods in the coming months, in order to select the wedding date. In any case, the only data that could reasonably be relied on placed her birth, more likely, in Puerto Rico. Still . . .

But certain lives, it was said, certain existences suggest, almost impose another version of their story, an ending or a beginning or at least an essential chapter of their changing phases, which never occurred but which their role calls for in the script, etched in their temperament and in their blood, a gene in their DNA, as if what really happened were instead a commonplace error to be revised during stage rehearsals for the performance, much less significant than the original text. It's as if certain men and certain women asked to have the forgeries in their lives corrected, facts that actually happened but are spurious. They ask the restorer to return the original painting, stripped of what was painted over it without authorization, which for years or centuries was the painting seen by everyone.

Luisa stared distractedly into space, not seeing her image reflected back to her in the window of the café, absorbed in the bustle of things and the flow of her thoughts. She knew that some people liked the idea that the mysterious, untouchable woman had come to the New World from Spain, a black shadow against the imperial red sky of sunset over the head of Carlo V on horseback, a victim of an abomination more abominable than that grandeur, a slave or former slave, that is, cast out from humanity but able to regain it, a black woman bearing the noble surname of distinguished jurists and scholars of the *Arcana Imperii*, an uprooted plant, its thirst quenched by the anonymous blood of conquest and slavery.

Luisa on the deck of the ship, an adolescent already a woman who offers refreshments to her lady, fruit—Moroccan dates, Andalusian oranges—on a silver tray and, if requested, sings a Mozarabic song, "Bouquela hamrela," like in a Technicolor movie with dramatic turns of event, adventures and upheavals. Kitschy, true, but enjoyable in the evening, after a dull day. Nevertheless that journey across the great sea had not been made by her, but by someone else for her, and not to serve a lady but in the stench of the hold, it too a murky, oily dark sea, filthy like the bottom of the sea on which the ship was sailing, mud and fragments of crumbled bones, the nothing that remained of bodies thrown into the water, a waterlogged illegible archive of a holocaust of holocausts, as had been said, the remains of an immense obscure life torn from the womb with the knife of a butchering history, blood spilled by a collective rape that turns the ocean red. Lives tossed into the sea, sperm that swim in the waters, driven toward a destination similar to the holds yet fated to fructify that land discovered by mistake by those seeking other lands, original sin, perdition and salvation of that land which, in part thanks to Canaan the accursed, will be able to become the Land of Canaan, the Promised Land.

The journey that was not made by that Luisa, a journey across the waters of death toward death and a distant, unimaginable resurrection. That is what must have appealed to Chamoiseau and Confiant, bards of Créolité, Caribbean and not only Caribbean, a crucible as the sole possible identity and truth. Luisa, black, the mother of red children, likely born as a result of rape as were countless others whom rape tinged all colors, the mestizo, the mulatto, the cambujo, the sanbaigo, the noteentiendo. Luisa, mother of children half-white and half-black, African Eve of the New World. But it may be that those two only got it wrong, confusing "ladina," that is, shrewd, with "latina," the term used for slaves who spoke Spanish and had lived in Spain.

If Luisa herself had not arrived in those islands, who had landed there for her, her father, her mother, her grandfather? Free, the documents say. Unlikely to have been born free; perhaps freed by a master more liberal than most or simply able to see that there was something different, something special about her compared to the others. In any case, she endures, nearly unscathed, the slave trade and the servitude that mows her people down like the crops they reap as they are being thrashed. Her birth certificate is missing—if indeed she was born a slave—and that of her second birth as well, the acquisition of freedom. Also missing is the certificate of her marriage to a white man—the black queen is able to make the right moves on the chessboard and captures the white king, who by all indications is happy to be captured, given that years later he takes back, with all the dignity of a lawful wife, a woman who for years was the Caribs' concubine, suspected of piracy and maybe, by some, even suspected of witchcraft. She must also have managed to elude the law when they were married, since the ancient *Siete partidas* of Alfonso X the Wise, king of Castile, the laws that three centuries ago allowed marriage between freemen and slaves, as well as between whites and blacks, had been abolished for some time. Not for Luisa de Navarrete, evidently, however it might have come about. Married because she was declared free or declared free because she married.

A marriage duly celebrated. Perhaps the one in the forest as well—chanting under a big, fragrant tree, a frangipani, liturgical vestments of red yellow white flowers on thick fleshy limbs. Beneath other big trees, her forefathers had delivered brides to her other forefathers across the great sea, something in her remembers without knowing she remembers, the way you unknowingly remember the sea of the womb in which you swam. Under the tree where she stands with her *amo,* hers and everyone else's, shrill chanting, oh great Maboya lord of the three universes great and lofty in the circle of the sun, oh Yali father of the Kalinagos oh Laline mother of Yali, sister who lay with her brother and now the Moon shining in the night . . . the great dog-headed serpent, who comes from the time when the earth was tender and soft, slithers in the night, enormous, its coils embrace the forest, Luisa watches the flickering of the fire in the blackness of the forest, the smell of the burning sacred herb tickles her nose stupefies her, she listens to the songs unknowingly mindful of those of the Yoruba gods sung by her forefathers behind masks of violent colors, in other forests beyond the great sea, Olorun creator of all things, Oyá goddess of wind, Shango god of thunder with his two-edged ax.

But once she escaped and returned home — or rather while waiting to return and averting other possible cruel fates — the woman had not said a word about any of this. One feast or celebration is as good as any other and the same goes for what happens between a man and a woman lying on the ground at night, invisible amid the tall grass despite the dying fire, or lying in bed in a room, a darkness just as dark outside the window, streaked with a few flares lit in the distance. However she had taken care to report, during the interrogation, that the Caribs said that, with the arrival of the pale people who had slaughtered the men, doused those remaining with water and forced them to pray to their god named Yéso-Kristou, the spirit Shémine, their protector who saw everything in the night, had become an evil spirit.

Wise strategies for reintegration, sociologist Daisy Cruz-Morales writes in the institutional language of her discipline. Having survived the abduction and what had then followed — perhaps at times, though it is impossible to know, without suffering all that much — as well as potentially chilling situations, Luisa must have known that what she had gone through was too much for what a woman — the woman she wanted to go back to being — should be, a wife and mother, submissive to her husband and respected by her neighbors. Too much and too shameful for a woman who wants to return to a dull everyday serenity — to the extent possible for a black woman in those days, of course. She could not — partly because of the color of her skin—though she probably did not even want to be one of those women who in those years of violent conquest, peril and plundering had begun to throw themselves, fearless and savage, into that world of bloody gold, *mujeres-soldado adelantadas y gobernadoras*, bosom encased in a coat of mail against Indian arrows shot from the shadows at Cortés's banquet following the capture of Tenochtitlan, Maldonada searching for food in the woods, taking refuge in a puma's cave and helping the mother puma give birth to her cubs, Catalina de Erauso, nun and swordswoman, traveling around the New World disguised as a soldier, cheating in casinos, killing men in duels and sleeping with their wives.

No, Luisa who fled from the Kalinagos wants to be a good wife, a good Christian and a respectful subject. Even though there was a governor's edict hopeful that "*algunos cristianos se casen con algunas mujeres indias y las mujeres cristianas con algunos indios*," "seeing in the formation of a racially mixed society an element of peace that would strengthen the power of the Crown," Luisa is aware that being considered *indianizada*, indianized, can be a source of trouble, and in her story, not paying too much attention to the specific questions that are asked of her, she little by little strips away the color red those four years have painted on her skin as though wiping off perspiration. Even among the Caribs she had most likely adopted the strategy of womanly submission, all the more pronounced in the hierarchies of the Indians as she must have noticed right away, inserting herself into Kalinago society with studied passivity, a captive and slave who becomes the wife of the chief but—she emphasizes firmly, to stress her condition as captive and victim—forced to sleep on the ground and, like the other captives, to eat lizards, rats, snakes and raw, semirotten fish. She doesn't complain; she tends to present every experience and every incident that pertains to her as something normal, a routine custom that can have its drawbacks but that, by the mere fact of being customary, is no cause for outrage.

When the scorching heat is unbearable and burns the grass, leaves, fruits, the throat, the Kalinagos invoke rain, but it doesn't occur to them to complain, to moan about their condition, just as we aren't affected by the suffering and death of others. Rain falls on the skin and on the ground, lightning also falls on the skin and on the ground; every so often the earth splits, a river overflows its banks, a small island vanishes beneath the sea. Things happen and there is no point in complaining. "Oh, dey whupped him up de hill, up de hill, an' he never said a mumblin' word," sang the slaves on the plantations under the whip, "oh dey nailed him to de cross, to de cross, to de cross, an' he never said a mumblin' word."

For Luisa even abductions like hers are *naturaleza*, actions that are repeated and therefore predictable and foregone. Even cannibalism is mentioned in subdued tones, a ritual practice limited to captives with special characteristics, like the story she tells—in two lines of the minutes, without any pathos—about the monk she had seen being devoured.

Submissive to her husband, to the authorities, to her inquisitors. She senses that her story is a valuable commodity for those questioning her, who though they have her life in their hands need her, the old game between torturer and victim, but in her case with no torture and no violence. She understands what interests those questioning her and almost anticipates their questions; her account is a supply that exceeds the demand. It describes coastlines, bays and mouths of Dominica's rivers; it pinpoints fertile lands and marshy ones, rich only in mud and snakes; it lists the villages and the distribution of their inhabitants; it explains the military organization of the Caribs, their alliances and wars with other tribes from the neighboring islands, shows the routes they take when moving to attack, the weak points of their defense and the times when it is easiest to catch them by surprise.

She says little about herself, as little as possible; she realizes that the most important card she holds is what she knows about García Troche Ponce de Léon, son of Juan Ponce de Léon II and great-grandson of the conquistador of the same name, who had accompanied his father on the expedition to Trinidad that ended badly and who—while his defeated father, thinking him dead, returned to Puerto Rico—had been captured by the Indians of that island who then delivered him to the Kalinagos of Dominica, where he'd been a slave for eleven years. Luisa says she saw him, talked to him, that she knows the Kalinagos want a ransom; the news creates a stir in the city, the governor and the bishop intercede with the distant king so that he may arrange for the release or ransoming of the young man, whose illustrious father, old and broken, is pining away in a Dominican convent to which he retreated. Who has time to care about what a black woman who returned home has or hasn't done or thought? The interrogee has become a valuable informant, almost a collaborator, an infiltrator. Governor Diego Menéndez de Valdés, who was personally involved in the interrogations, declares that he is very satisfied with the information they received.

Yes, each of us, Luisa thought as she was leaving the café, is often a repository, without realizing it, of things that can be decisive for others, liberating or ruinous knowledge for someone. At times we are spies, unintentionally and unknowingly, we innocently reveal things that should remain unspoken and secret, that can hurt someone . . . Luisa de Navarrete is not innocent; she knows very well that what she says can trigger reprisals and the slaughter of men who have nothing whatsoever to do with what happened to her, on the other hand, in her situation, she certainly can't worry about them. There should be a place in the Museum for the word, a powerful weapon, both offensive and defensive, exceedingly sharp . . . But isn't silence sometimes a weapon as well? Yes, but then . . .

During a war dance or a victory dance, Luisa tells the judges, the Kalinagos shout, but otherwise they are silent. Like she is, when no one is interrogating her. Yes, the Kalinagos — she replies briefly when asked more insidious questions about the purported magic cults and ritual orgies — *"llaman y hablan con el diablo,"* "they summon the devil and talk to him," especially at ceremonial banquets where they feast on human flesh, that of captives — mainly Indians, because the flesh of white men is bad, it must be poisoned. They say, in fact, that two Kalinagos who ate it died. They have the captives make wine by chewing *casabe,* a pap of cassava and mushrooms, maybe even fish. Then they get drunk on the wine and sing and dance and shout and fall to the ground; the wine is strong, especially the mushroom, it's a special mushroom. She has never tried it, actually, she spit it out on the sly when they tried to force her to eat it, but they told her that without that mushroom you can't see the woodland spirits or the vast blissful forest, a land free from evil where you will go after death.

Meanwhile they drink and drink that thick, moldy wine and speak with the devil. She had heard them, those invocations to the Lord of Evil, who however only rumbled howled growled bellowed panted in the night, and unlike the jaguar or the giant snake, did not leap on men. From the jaguar head on the body of the snake that could be glimpsed in the dark, swaying amid the foliage, dappled by the flickering light of the fire, mutable scales on its squamous skin, only raucous cries could be heard, the muttering of incomprehensible, recurrent words—impious utterances, the inquisitors immediately thought—but Luisa had not been able to hear, much less understand, a single word, even though she thought she recognized the tattooed face under the jaguar head that sometimes slid down onto the shoulders of that shadow. Only an indistinct gurgling in the night, while some Kalinagos danced, fell to the ground and sometimes fell asleep. Yes, every so often she could distinguish a voice, cavernous and shrill, like the drunk Kalinagos who were dancing. What language does the devil speak? That of the Caribs, which Luisa had learned, a diabolical language that no one can understand because it is the language of Nothing, of what is not there, of one who does not exist? The voice issuing from the abyss of the Nothing that preceded the creation of the universe—or of the three universes, as Luisa had heard in the forest—can only utter nonsense, with the emphasis of a barker, because it doesn't know anything, it hasn't seen anything, it has remained always and forever in darkness, it only knows what is not there.

Luisa is also a little tired of those strangled chants; she gets up, slips, black, into the black night, her skin gleams under the torches, she disappears, plunged into darkness, reappears between one torch and another, shadows roll around in the tall grass, raucous feverish drunken words lost in the night, even the jaguar-headed snake across the fire moans with pleasure, a woman beside him, under him, his prey but not for eternity, only for a brief moment of that night. Luisa is not afraid of demons, she has no fear of what is not there; she's much more fearful—though she tries not to show it—of the men who question her. Her presumed Yoruba ancestors from across the sea, unknown to her, had no fear of demons either, because their forebears had been created out of clay by Oduduwa and therefore they too were made of clay and clay—the good moist fertile pasty earth to plow, sow, grasp and squeeze in your hand, letting it ooze between your fingers—doesn't fear nothingness. No, there are no black masses nor witches' Sabbaths in the forest and Luisa has nothing or very little to say.

Far more incisive was the story of her escape, her return home—to one of her two homes. The five pirogues with her on board one of them head for the mouth of the Abey River, in Salinas, "to plunder some hacienda or some herd," the Kalinagos leap onto shore, leaving the women to watch over her so she won't run away—thus, by portraying herself as a captive, Luisa erases any doubts about her possible complicity in the raids. Then the women also jump out of the dugouts, dragging them along behind them they get bogged down in a swamp where they look for crabs, which in that area are particularly succulent, leaving Luisa behind; hiding in a thicket of mangroves, she stays there, among the foliage and canes, a whole day, half in the water, "commending herself to God and Our Lady Santa Maria," until she starts walking and comes to a pen for cows and sheep. The first sign of civilization; not a puma or caiman lying in wait to pounce but the well-established alliance between man and animals unbroken by millennial slaughtering, the bovine warmth of the manger that for her is a humane warmth, breath that warms her as it warmed the baby Jesus.

From there she reaches *"esta capital."* Of course, to enter she must pass through the Caudine Forks of the Inquisition, a narrow door that she manages to widen just enough. She returns from a darkness and an unknown that shrouded her during those four years of her life and that remain a dark unknown, despite the valuable information that goes around the capital and has people talking about her; for a short time almost a leading lady, praised by Attorney General Pablo Bermúdez de Quiros for the useful reports she provided, vaguely feared for her frightening tales yet also admired for having faced those frightening things.

Not a word about the children left behind in the forest with the *amo*, their father, and their family tribe. The reintegration of the black woman in the white world demands that the bond with the red children be broken, perhaps all thought or memory of them as well. Law of the forest? The female animal protects her offspring at all costs, but when they grow up she abandons them or they leave, and if they meet again, drinking water from the river or lying in wait for prey, they don't recognize each other. Of course, when she leaves her children in the forest, they are still possible prey, young and defenseless. With her red mestizo children Luisa behaves the way white masters do with their black mestizo children.

With her return, her story ends. How would her husband, her children, have received her? The unknowing progenitor of an imaginary, literary genealogy—the captive queen of the Caribbeans, an abducted woman and goddess worshiped by her abductors who were also her jailers, the stuff of novels and Technicolor films in centuries to come—sinks back into the domestic shadows, into the obscurity of the feminine condition, less fearful, but more opaque than the obscurity of the forest. She's only twenty-three years old and is likely to live many more years, years that have been erased. "*Doch man sieht nur die im Lichte,*" "we only see those in the light"—no, Luisa thought, humming the Ballad of Mack the Knife, he certainly would not have loved either Brecht or Kurt Weill, it wouldn't have occurred to him to get to know them, but in his Museum she would have them boom out at the end of Luisa's story—"*Die im Dunkeln sieht man nicht,*" "we don't see those in the dark . . ."

A fleeting, small candle that for a moment streaks the black sky, like a scream shattering the silence. The cry of the maroon, the runaway slave—the immutable order of slavery is slashed like a torn curtain, on the *morne* where the maroon runs faster than the dogs that chase him, the grass parts beneath his feet like the sea sliced by the bow of a ship but closes behind him, grass as tall as walls. One maroon, many maroons, fish no longer only caught, but attacking their fishermen with big, sharp teeth, the blood reddening the waters is no longer just black. Luisa progenitor of maroons as well, the Eve of female marronage, as some have said? No, not yet, too soon. Her fate is the shadow that swallows those who arrive—in the world, in history? Too premature, a guest who gets the time of the invitation wrong, dinner isn't ready yet.

But when is it time for female marronage? It is always too soon, like with Catalina, the first maroon of the New World, the Indian woman who escaped from Columbus's ship anchored in the waters of Hispaniola, jumping into those waters that do not rage against the arrogant ship that has come in the name of the king and of God. For that matter, the male maroon will remain a mere phantom for a long time, the black man who gets drunk on rum and kills children, "close your eyes, little baby"—the Antilles lullaby goes—"close your eyes, little brother / baby don't cry / or the black dog / will howl and bark / until the even blacker man / the maroon / eats you up . . ."

40.

Room no. 12 — A large panel under glass, mounted vertically on the wall. In the center, a reproduction of a banknote with the highest denomination in the world. A Hungarian banknote from 1946, in pengö. Around it, bills in other currencies. 220 million marks indicates the price of half a kilo of bread in Germany in 1923; dollars, liras, florins, crowns, dinars, yen, yuan, dirhams, levas, leus, rubles, assignats issued during the French Revolution, huge sacks of paper spill into relevant trash bins, which quickly fill, the bills overflow, strewn about on the floor like garbage, the wind scatters them here and there.

The most powerful weapons in the world, one of his notes reads. V2s or napalm make me laugh. Indeed Bernardino de Mendoza wrote that victory goes to those who possess the last escudo. The zeros multiply, the ranks of people dwindle; that paper depopulates cities, drives multitudes out of their homes, biblical migrations of displaced evicted exiles. Unrestricted warfare, write Qiao Liang and Wang Xiangsui, two brilliant Chinese strategists worthy of Sun Tzu. The banker Soros moves a lot of zeros and brings about the collapse of an entire Asian country, more destruction than a thousand bombers would cause. From the ruined cities, from the devastated countryside, from the ravaged, churning seas, a huge mushroom cloud of paper rises; the paper flutters, scatters, billows slightly in the toxic wind.

41.

Room no. 18—*A video continuously transmits a program recorded on the tenth anniversary of his death, entitled: "Witness, historian, collector or maniac? The mystery of a death and of a life."*

A rather obese man, sitting at a table, in front of a nameplate with his name, Carlo Fozzi. A journalist from RAI. As he talks, he slides a finger between his shirt collar and his neck, trying to smooth a roll of fat under his chin that bulges over his tie.

"A great scholar, a fraud, an impostor, a great hallucinator? Perhaps simply one of the greats, as has been said. And perhaps only a city of lunatics like Trieste could have produced a personality like his, bizarre, eccentric as they come, so difficult to understand, but great. Of course, I do not think we should be fooled by his tricks, by his fictions. He was very good at pretending to be an oddball, he knew that it could be convenient, it facilitates things, it sanctions any flaunting of grandeur and excuses any blunders, genius and immoderation so as not to pay the piper . . . but genius, intuition of great things, an amazing ability to live and to sacrifice himself for a higher ideal . . ."

Beside him, a thin young man with glasses. His movements are nervous and aggressive, his words caustic. Dr. Giovanni Cante, researcher at the Institute for the History of the Liberation Movement. In front of him are several volumes on the Risiera, as can be seen, though vaguely, from the titles.

"With all due respect for his tragic end, we are not interested in the idiosyncrasies of an eccentric or the manias of an obsessive collector. Nor in his collections. What good are rusty guns, wrecked fuselages or old bayonets to us? There is only one thing that can be of interest to us. That could be of interest to us, in view of the fact that it has disappeared, it's gone. I am referring to the documentation of the writings they say he copied, at least in part, from the walls of the Risiera of San Sabba.

"Once again, the bourgeois, fascistoid Trieste, collaborationist by calling even when it isn't able to collaborate, having washed its face and reapplied its makeup. Everyone respectable; only in a few other cities in Italy did industrialists, financiers, ship owners and bankers align themselves so explicitly, I would say instinctively—certainly also prudently—with the Fascists and, when necessary, the Nazis as well. Even while conceding something, and more than something, to the Resistance, you never know.

"Haven't you read the testimony, so deeply felt, of the young man, poor innocent, who had been rounded up by the Nazis in the street after the attack on the Deutsches Soldatenheim canteen, and taken to Gestapo headquarters? He too would probably have ended up being hanged on Via Ghega with the other fifty-one, if just then, luckily for him, old Baron Wenck hadn't showed up, the counselor for the Silba shipping company having come to see his buddy Stulz, formerly his classmate in Monaco and now captain of the Gestapo. As the handcuffed young man was being shoved into a cubbyhole, the baron, passing by, recognized him—since he had worked as a gardener at his villa some time ago—and was moved by him; he promised to help him and in fact, after the baron spoke to Stulz, the poor devil was released. He remained grateful to Wenck for life, of course, but don't you find it disturbing that one of the shipping bosses of Trieste was on such close terms with the Gestapo and actually had the power to bring about the release of an unfortunate wretch who was likely headed for torture and the gallows?

"The baron lived many more years, influential respected and at ease in the Free Territory just as in the Italian Republic and the Habsburg Empire in its time, and with him his cronies, the Trieste that counts and that has rinsed her underwear in the channel. They even managed to make the Risiera disappear—for years no one ever talked about it, not even the anti-Fascists, no one knew anything about it, yet it was the only crematorium existing in Italy, and no one actually knew a thing, that's the tragedy of it, they had managed to erase that truth, that reality... Not even on April 25, at the official celebrations, was it talked about. Anniversary celebrations, commemorations occurred, but later. Now of course there are ceremonies and conferences, they're obligatory, but we had to wait for the trial to know, to be aware of knowing those horrible things, in our own backyard, right under our noses, our own involvement... And in this case the professor was neither maniacal nor eccentric nor wacky, when he discovered those graffiti, those denunciations by those about to die that probably revealed the names and surnames of the killers' accomplices or at least their good friends and acquaintances, and copied them down. He wrote our city's greatest history book, crucial though nonexistent—that's right, the wall writings were erased, covered with lime, and his notebooks, the ones it seems they were recorded in, at least in part, vanished as well...

"It's strange, isn't it, that those particular notebooks vanished, or are in any case inaccessible—not even that is known with certainty, whether they exist somewhere or whether they don't exist at all—the only important, fundamental notebooks, the book of truth and accusation, of the *Dies Irae, Liber scriptus proferetur in quo totum continetur,* but the book doesn't exist, it's vanished, all that remains are pages where he copied innocent obscene inscriptions, pornographic drawings in the latrines, especially during his stay in Rome, after the war... deplorable smut that we don't know what to do with. The respectable bourgeoisie is priggish but also benevolent and tolerant, it closes its eyes to obscenity but God help us if a tip-off that sent a Jew to Auschwitz turns up, or even just silence about those crowds on their way to Auschwitz, that's bad manners and it is unacceptable to talk about it..."

Riccardo Wulz, psychologist and psychiatrist. He starts off speaking with detachment, almost disdainfully, then he gets worked up, he gets excited, at times he's pleased with his images that are meant for effect; you can tell he likes to seduce his listeners, like certain teachers at school.

"What's strange, and therefore interesting, is that he began quite late after all, and rather suddenly, to take an interest in those writings at the Risiera and its environs. I'm not talking about copying them, because he started doing that fairly soon, adding the notes to all the others. But it was as if he hadn't realized what they meant, the tremors that they could trigger. For years those writings—the names that everyone now wants to know or close their eyes to, that worry authorities and everyone else, a true collective trauma in the city—are no different, for him, than punched tram tickets, bottle stoppers, scurrilous scrawling on the walls, which he copies and collects indifferently, without distinction, not placing more importance on one rather than another. For him finding the original copy of the *Divine Comedy* or a shabby old umbrella in a trash bin would be the same thing, like a child rooting around in his own poop."

He also collected rags, broken pottery, old scraps of iron; in Rome, where he had gone hoping to get a little money from the ministry for his Museum, he even picked up discarded paper from the ground or the dumpsters, as long as it was scribbled on . . . Slips of paper with obscene sketches, figures drawn with just a few simple lines from which gigantic phalluses swell, fleshy, moist erections, tongues pushing into crude mouths. There were some, which RAI had censored when recording the video, that were even worse, especially graffiti copied from walls, detailing addresses and phone numbers with indecent promises and invitations. The crescendo of his mania is stunning, the increasingly feverish, undiscriminating accrual of masticated American chewing gum, empty cigarette boxes, torn newspapers. The kind of death inherent in all collecting was inflating like a snake that swallows everything and balloons into a slimy, monstrous ball. There was also a note of his, at the bottom of a paper bag, next to a number, apparently the price of what was in the bag: "What if bacteria, as a result of a genetic mutation, were to become as large as elephants or whales, new masters of the earth. Never mind the triumphant bedbugs in Querétaro; insects, compared to bacteria, are poor devils, like men. Who knows whether, after dropping all those atom bombs, perhaps in a few centuries . . . men destroyed, like red corpuscles by anemia."

He was obsessed, Luisa thought, playing the recording back and forth and wondering if she should put it in the Museum or not. If God created life, he had once told her, you could defeat his grandiose strategic plans by universally putting an end to life, that is, by refusing to reproduce it, letting the gonads protest, ever more weakly until they die along with the poor wretch they're protesting against and it's all over. He, Luisa had noticed from the beginning, always declined in the masculine gender. In his grammar, the feminine gender barely existed, only when it was really inevitable. Millions of years to create man in His image and likeness, he pontificated, so that he might sin and redeem himself or be redeemed *ad majorem suam gloriam*, and a single generation checkmates Him, simply by silencing testosterone's bright ideas.

That's his problem, which might have been of interest to the golden age of psychoanalysis, but that certainly no longer interested anyone—least of all her, convinced that every mouth kissed and loved was a fiat for creation and that the Song of Solomon knew far more about it than the sexologists. But he couldn't understand that, didn't get it; perhaps he couldn't even see the contradiction between his denial of death by way of his theory of the inverter and the fever of death that at times seemed to possess him. He was incapable of logic and therefore of love as well, which goes wrong and breaks down when there is confusion. *Logos* is the love of God and therefore of men. Without *logos*, there is no love; grammar and syntax should be studied, they help to distinguish between good and evil. No, he was not brilliant; at most an intellectualoid. An ugly suffix, that "-oid," deforming any quality, the most prodigious pejorative of low blows.

But suddenly, all that had changed and even his deliriums had flown away like birds from a wind-tossed tree.

"Up until the time in Rome," the psychologist in the video went on, "he was merely, and increasingly, an all-absorbing caricature of the anal temperament, assuming that these convenient outdated formulas can still tell us something. In any case, he seemed like a text-book case, were it not for certain Oedipal fantasies, undoubtedly embarrassing, compulsive, but pervaded by a sense of sorrow, a wound causing him to suffer somewhat nobly, despite the pedestrian mania of the images. There is a phrase, no, just three words, a word repeated with anguished fury, jotted in a notebook without any connection to the rest of the page: 'Shit shit shit.' I know that a psychologist should not talk like that, vulgarity or obscenity must not be part of his vocabulary. But no man, with all due respect to my many distinguished colleagues, is only or mainly a case report, a patient on the table. To return to our subject, since childhood, though also as an adult, he is particularly attracted to what is obscene — to imagining, saying, doing and especially writing profanities. A relish for defiling himself and those he loves most, which conflicts with his stiff Austro-Hungarian dignity, with his eulogy of discipline and authoritarian and military principles, beginning with his extolling of strictness in school, even though he himself was a victim of it in high school — maybe actually because of that — with all the relative consequences of punishment at home. Nothing out of the ordinary, in fact a seemingly typical mundane case. Nonetheless in that disturbed subject — there, that would be the professionally correct language — one senses a tension, a moral passion, a hallucinatory, but right-minded feeling, for which he lived and died.

"And abruptly, all of a sudden, Saul is thrown by his horse, a flame is lit in him and for him, his obsessions disappear. Forgetting about the garbage, he hastily returns to Trieste and for a long time can regularly be seen at the Risiera and in the vicinity of the Risiera. He copies and collects, in particular he makes notes, as usual. But he copies and collects other things! Listen to what he wrote on this page, likely an inscription read on a wall: 'Tomorrow, it seems they're taking us to Germany. I'd been exempted — apparently I'd managed to make them think that I'd been hauled in off the street by accident, just because I happened to be passing by during a roundup — when Captain Otter came in with a sheet of paper in his hand and showed it to the sergeant; the two whispered together, then the sergeant shouted my name as a member of Justice and Freedom. It must have been . . . who reported me.' The name is missing, evidently it had already been erased from the wall. He picked up wads of paper, scoured the walls, looking for names, names of those about to die, of those who'd died, of executioners—he no longer collected, he was searching for the truth, the sorrow, the infamy . . . 'We the living—good-bye Kira.' There is a grandeur in this man, at least at the twilight of his life . . ."

In fact, a couple of photographs from that period, which Luisa thought of mounting under the video, show a different face: alert, sad, relentless. There is no sweat on that face anymore, she'd thought as she'd looked at the photos, selecting them and considering their placement, the sweat whose acrid, sour odor she seemed to smell; the face is tense but composed, the eyes no longer fanatical or feverish but melancholy and yet unwavering, the eyes of a dog that isn't sniffing at excrement anymore, but searching for someone, something, an owner carried off by assailants, a friend who has vanished. A big hunting dog that isn't after game but the vile poachers who set horrific leghold traps and took everything away from him; he keeps on looking, maybe even finding something . . . A noble bloodhound, a true friend of man . . .

Yes, the psychologist was right; all of a sudden his life, his passion had changed. But where had it come from, that transformation which had turned a poor, sometimes embarrassing maniac into an archangel of justice and revenge . . . ? That was his mystery, not his death in the fire nor his stupid arsenal, which she was sick and tired of, though she had to hurry up and complete the plan to house it, that's what they paid her for. Still, what interested her was his metamorphosis, his conversion, a true resurrection . . . Perhaps, in his own way, he had actually defeated death, that of his heart; he had actually found an inverter that had taken him back, from death to rebirth, a truly unexpected rebirth after the pathological delirium of the days in Rome.

Luisa was sorry to have met him so few times after that transformation. Almost a metanoia, to use a word of the Gospel that she loved; the possibility of really changing one's life, of spiritually turning inside out like a glove, giving the finger to the Old Adam who dies in the heart and to the pomposity of things, all the bonds and resolves that thought they had tied him up for good, to his story that no one believed could change and become something else. For a long time that man had struck her as tedious and dreary, with his repetitive obsessions—yes, she'd felt respect for him and even sympathy, compassion, as one feels toward those who are crazy or sick, though this did not mean she found his obsessions any less tiresome, repetitious and at times disgustingly evil.

She was sorry to have known only the first man, compulsive and banal in his mania for the Museum, and to have exchanged only a few words with the new one, the risen man, no longer oppressively boring, but distant and enigmatic, driven by something that was more than the mania of an obsessed collector. The turning point had taken place in Rome, as noted in a page that disturbed and disconcerted her because she didn't know whether she had the right, indeed the duty, to make it known, or if doing so would mean profaning it.

42.

He had begun going to Rome frequently after the end of the war—the end, so to speak, especially in Trieste, though not only in Trieste—which for him had at first primarily resulted in a priceless haul of weapons. Tanks, cannons, two helicopters, machine guns and rifles, a jeep, buckles, belts, abandoned or sometimes even handed over to him personally by retreating Germans or arriving Americans. But he had encountered the problem of finding space to store them and the scorn of authorities who, due to a lack of understanding, rather than give priority to his Museum, were concerned about where to house refugees from Istria, albeit only temporarily, or with reorganizing schools and hospitals. More and more skeptical about the possibility of obtaining funding in Trieste, he had managed to establish some contacts, very soon after the war, with the Defense Ministry and the Ministry of Public Education, which he expounded with arrogance and pompous assurance—*el fazeva maravèe*, exaggerating as always—and often went to Rome, to have whispered discussions and lose himself in the muffled corridors of scarred Roman buildings. Apparently he also took advantage of those trips to try to get his hands on a catapult from Augustus's time, which he had read about in the papers, found in the Sabine mountains. It's likely that the futility of his attempts had exacerbated his mania, his lust to collect and classify everything—the final, sordid blaze of his obsession, before falling from his horse on the road to Damascus.

Use them or destroy them, those extreme, excited, frenzied notes of his final days in Rome, at times left incomplete? Obey the law of professional integrity and historical rigor, which requires that each document be published without moral or other censure, or the law of respect for the impenetrable secret of every soul, for the opacity which everyone has a right to before judges, scholars, investigating reporters, those who write books and those who organize exhibitions and need to steal private pictures? Is it right to actually enter a heart, even if you've spent so much time at its door, peeking at what's inside, gathering information and gossip from neighbors who pass by that door, in short, searching, so to speak, for its truth?

But when you've finally found it or think you've found it, you feel like doing what detectives in films do, once they've discovered the identity of the man they're looking for and have maybe caught him or are about to catch him: they turn around and take a little walk until the wanted man has cleared out, once again nowhere to be found, because they don't like putting him away either. And maybe it's the right thing to do when the man you get your hands on is also pure of heart. It's the purity hidden in the filth that you shouldn't violate, like a child's sense of wonder. With obscenities and secret vices, Luisa thought, you could be less conscientious; after all, those are all everyone talks about, discovering them everywhere and continually shouting them from the rooftops, so that no one even pays attention anymore or remembers who it was who did or said one impropriety or another.

But if someone or something is truly good, pure, though perhaps mingled with all that scum, spying on him through the keyhole and blabbing about him could be a sin, a *hýbris* worthy of the gods' punishment. The problem would not arise, however, since the family would hardly have authorized the publication of the Roman notes, as well as those regarding the festive gathering in Miramare in honor of Hitler's birthday, where he had evidently managed to slip in — provided he had not reconstructed them in part from newspaper accounts and in part from his own imagination, as authors of historical novels do. Meanwhile she alone was reading them, then we'll see. Indeed reading those journals of the final days in Rome was different . . .

43

"That close, muggy afternoon in Rome, through the narrow streets of Trastevere. My face shiny, oily more than sweaty, sour like the taste in my mouth. I had left Elsa at the pensione on Via del Governo Vecchio. My satchel was crammed full of papers, loose sheets, notebooks. I transcribed and collected what I saw here and there, graffiti on walls, tattered posters, scraps of paper scribbled on and tossed away. I made a quick copy of a sketch depicting fellatio drawn on a low wall, a scrawled 'Viva Rome,' a telephone number and another scribble 'if you like ass; a huge cock' penned in broad ink strokes on the tiles of a urinal in a lavatory, where I was careful not to soil the sheets on which I had copied the inscriptions and doodles that no longer fit in the crammed briefcase. I looked at my hands, foreign to me, two flat creatures that I had seen at the aquarium, crawling on the bottom, opening and closing their tentacles. I took note of the license plate of a car, the number is almost the reverse of that of my ID card.

I collected a lot of stuff, cigarette butts, a penknife, bottle tops, a fountain pen cap. I collected everything. The world. The universal garbage dump. Anything can be a clue. Don't forget the piece of ladder that led to finding the Lindbergh baby's killer; anything can be, is a weapon. They get rid of the evidence in landfills and then cover over the dumps, but I find them, dig through them, an immense amount of material for the prosecution. I read about that association in England which asserts that the earth is flat; maybe they're right and the great seas rush headlong off the world at its edges, plunging into a dark, empty universe, dragging all the evidence behind. Place a sieve, an enormous net that will retain every residue, every clot, every drop of dried blood so that it can go on crying out for revenge. I will make sure to collect everything on that extreme edge, as in Grado when I flushed crabs out of the sand that was left by the surf's backwash.

Even this cigarette is a weapon, a blowtorch that opens the way to my heart, to expose it and find out what's inside. The light westerly wind had languished that evening, a pale yellowish yolk lay squashed on the Janiculum, a resinous effluent of light dripped from the pines. As I smoked, I saw my face pasted on the window of a shoe store, pale, feverish. My eyes stared at me, the world around me disappeared, wiped away by that yellowish rag of light. It was just the two of us, myself and I. The rag passed over our faces but did not erase us, whereas it made everything else vanish. There were only two faces, like at a target shooting range. I could hear the abrupt, hollow detonations of air rifles in a booth behind me, muffled, because I had started walking quickly.

The hotel was now close by. Elsa . . . how could she have thought that the two of us, we two of all people, hot, sweaty . . . she held me tight. I didn't remember her smell, maybe I had never known it, maybe she had lost it at one time; the one she had wasn't hers, it was the stale smell, the same everywhere, of Rome's sultry streets. I stroked her mechanically, she wanted to kiss me, our tongues were dry, no saliva, I felt drained. How had Leopold managed to be born, I wondered. For a moment I thought that perhaps he wasn't mine, that Elsa, after those nights of abrupt fever on the Karst, had maybe . . . But I hadn't experienced jealousy or anger at the idea, nor pleasure either, like when I looked at those newspapers, those photographs, those mouths, those feet, those impudent eyes, those breasts that God knows who put their hands on. Even in the underground Red Room in the Old Town I used to enjoy thinking about who had possessed the womb of which only the pelvic bone remained.

If only you could sleep alone, without having to feel ashamed about the sweat-drenched sheets . . . but they all want to make love. Then too, women . . . life would be so peaceful without love, without the battles and defeats. No, the defeats are fine. That's why I always liked weapons, spears, wars, because wars are lost, spears run you through and there you are, bleeding and wounded, no longer obliged to fight, to hurl spears at others. War is someone else's triumph, as he parades proudly before the cheering crowd, dragging behind him the trophies he won, the guns and tanks he captured, the prisoners in chains, you as well, dragging along in chains. I am so happy in my Museum; alone, defeated, winded from keeping up with those trophies borne in triumph, the victorious crowd's cries of derision distant, muffled, held outside the Museum's iron gate. There too everything is full of *eros*, but *eros* in armor, without flesh, harmless. The weapons, the Museum were for me a real fallout shelter, keeping out the devastating power of love. I remember that at one time I would have liked to be given the Hiroshima contraption, write the word 'Love' on it and leave it outside to stand watch in front of the Museum's gate. Instead a few days later, having returned to Trieste . . ."

44·

"Yes, the bomb exploded. *De profundis clamavi ad te, Domine.* Do I have the right to write, even to think these words, after so much depravity? Or should I be ashamed to pray, after having forgotten my prayers for so many years, and earlier, as a child, having only repeated them mechanically when they made me recite them, annoyed and almost disrespectful?

I felt nothing for that God I invoked as I was ordered to. I imagined a big man, tall, massive, seen from the back, in dark waiter's livery, black, very black, a curved black arm holding a kind of tray, as I had seen in a giant advertisement for liquors and coffee that filled an entire shop window. All you could see was the black and when we passed by I was scared, I tugged my mother's hand so she would walk faster. You couldn't see his face, turned away, only the huge black back that stood there, massive and indifferent. What does that back have to do with me? I thought as I repeated the Lord's Prayer. That reassured me a little. That black tailcoat had nothing to do with anything or anyone. It had nothing to do with Poldo, for example, the dog that licked my face and ears anytime he could—which was often, because whenever possible I would lie down next to him, that hot tongue on my ears and neck and those questioning eyes, anxious and obliging, were my joy; I, too, had been happy, stretched out with Poldo on the frayed carpet. And joy, even experienced only once, should be enough. Poldo ended up under a car and then in the trash, but it hadn't been because of that black back, which had nothing to do with those licks or with the wheels of that car or with me in general.

But who did have anything to do with me, then? No one, ever.

Let alone the black back turned away, worse than mannequins in clothing stores, because at least those have eyes, even if they're blank, just an empty cavity, but sooner or later you could put something in there, a glass eye or a button. That figure, however, has only a back, he's just a back, like all the others you've seen, for that matter, since all you've ever seen are backs, everyone has always turned his back on you. How could I have prayed to that back? Immense and black as night, a vast empty night. Now, however, it seems natural to call to you, invoke you, tell you to turn to me, as you must already have done, because otherwise I would never have imagined that on the other side of the window, in a corner of the shop hidden by the poster pasted on the glass, at the end of that bar there might suddenly . . ."

45.

"I had set out, without really knowing why, to San Sabba. I had recently returned to Trieste from Rome, with a suitcase full of worthless paper that I'll throw away now. Elsa came home in the evening, just in time to heat the soup she makes every two or three days, it's already asking a lot considering all the hours she spends cleaning at that house and keeping after that senile old man. If she didn't make it, there wouldn't even be the reheated soup, I know that. Have supper, avoid each other, go to the toilet, go to sleep. When I can. But she falls asleep right away. During the day I roamed around Trieste as usual, always finding something to pick up and bring to the large warehouse, waiting for them to throw me and my stuff out of there too, since I hadn't paid the rent for months. And how could I have.

At San Sabba, down Via Valmaura toward the sea, there's a bar. Rossoalabardato, it's called, the red halberdier. Bar Rossoalabardato. I went in to have a Pelinkovec. Wormwood disgusts me, but when I have that bad taste in my mouth it seems to taste like wormwood and I feel like having wormwood even though I feel even more nauseous afterward. She was there, sitting at a table, smoking. The slack gaping mouth gave her face an expression of lazy insolence, the same as always, like when we used to play in the courtyard behind the house — a few, very few eternal times, the futile irresistible call of destiny, a rope tossed into the slimy waters of my life that I had not grasped, a moist, promiscuous, welcoming ark that I had not had the courage to enter and that for my damnation I saw disappear in the flood in which I was left to rot, eaten away by water and by ferocious fish for far longer than forty days and forty nights.

Unrecognizable, I recognized her, fatter, indolent, imperious as ever. The way she snapped her head up made her look agile, light; the ungainly capercaillie shook her feathers and was once again a sparrowhawk soaring high in the air, the queen bee flying circling and seizing the dazed worn-out drone between her hairy legs as he's about to drop, she puts him in her mouth, sucks him, her mouth tastes of honey, I looked at her, I felt sucked into that fleshy voracious mouth, content to feel myself the slave of that tyrannical nose again. Now it was somewhat distended, sunk in fat, but my eye made its way between the folds and rolls of fat like a scalpel, extracting that capricious tender cruel nose—somewhere I'd read that in every rock, in every shapeless boulder, in every gnarled and twisted tree trunk a figure is imprisoned and the sculptor liberates it, lets it out of its cage. My desire of years, of decades, of forever, liberated the princess from the oppressive prison of time; beneath the soft slushy snow, just about to melt, I rediscovered the slender shoot, released from the heavy snowfall.

She came forward in the small bar, passing between the tables holding an ashtray full of cigarette butts and a cup of espresso encrusted with whitish sugar; from heavily made-up eyes, cat-pupils impaled the gazes they met, dropping them like birds shot down in flight by a hunter. Regal shoulders arching above her breasts, pomegranates ready to squirt their seeds in the meadows of asphodel, a deep inlet, a foamy ravine where the sirocco tide of years ebbed, the fake emerald of glass shards, imitation pearls on the dazzling white of those two stacks. The pudgy hands, with their black-rimmed nails, and the feet as well were as white as the pebbles on Istria's beaches, those white agile feet lightly advancing, though now they'd become fleshy fruit languidly imperiously slid out of their shoes as soon as she sat down. Those feet that I had dreamed of kissing, white cats ready to play, to tear the unwary prey to pieces with their claws, as she had done to me unknowingly for a lifetime; mine, at least.

The only flesh I had dreamed of—merely dreamed, because after those few games, still childish, indecent and innocent, I hadn't seen her again. She had disappeared shortly after she became a woman, though already an expert at capturing the world in her net with that languid, overwhelming come-hither look—eyes painted like those of an erstwhile courtesan, my father used to say, why don't you put the moves on her, why let the neighborhood guys steal her away from you? She had disappeared from the balcony across the way, where she would lean her generous breasts when we chatted from house to house, headed for a fate that was talked about and that envious curiosity embroidered upon, failed marriages (who is it who fails, in this case?), shameless affairs, a murmured opulence of life. Why don't you make a move on her? Yes, always on her, I would get aroused; submissive humiliated rewarded slave, I was thrilled; I had dreamed of only her, desired only her, alone or making love with whoever came along—love? Maybe it was, but only for her image that was always before me as I came, no matter in whose cunt, strong and virile thinking of her, otherwise limp and timid between other women's legs. Only her had I desired in all—the few, very few—other women; only her image blazed and when it blurred I went back to being the miserable lover sweating from embarrassment and fear.

Corrupted and scarred by time, her spell unchanged. I sat down casually at her table and she put a lit cigarette in my mouth, as if we had left each other moments before, at home, getting up from bed, our bed. I could feel my face burning, but bold, not sweating. Maybe even good-looking, attractive; I read it in her mocking but tender gaze in the dark depths of the lake. I remember the room she took me to, the big pink bed, tacky and smelling of cheap talc. Vulgar and generous, like the way she took off her shoes and lightly kicked my face as it followed that white foot under the covers like a fish going under. Unrecognizable, but as I held her and touched her and kissed her, the alluring and slender figure of one time emerged from her shapeless body and from the clothes that I had removed for her. A mask dissolved and let me glimpse the slim nose and delicate lips of one time, the eyes, slightly bulging due to a hint of Basedow, drew back within the banks of the lake, green as the sea in which I was sinking, dying, being reborn.

She rolled over, mounted me, suffocating me milking me freeing me; high above me, a figurehead leaning into the sea in which I was foundering, redeemed drained born-again. Glorious resurrection of the flesh—mine, because hers had never died—of my arid miserly flesh. In that ravaged body that bloomed again, young, regal, perhaps for the first time I loved myself as well, not with wary miserliness but the way you love a gift that you are happy to offer. I pitied the vainglorious foolishness of time that claims it can fade a face and wither a smile, both indestructible and ready to be reborn in every kiss, a rosebud preserved within the most overblown rose, an undersea grotto moist with algae and the sea that flows in it and from it flows. Yes, everything was different now. *De profundis clamavi ad te, Domine,* and you heard me, you came to me through that sagging glorious flesh to make me see the wretchedness of my miserable existence. I left that house and walked back up Via Valmaura. The Risiera was in front of me, red, squat, black, deadly. Through there had passed countless faces of God, tortured, slaughtered. Debased bones. I set out for the bleak building and since that day, every day . . . The debased bones shall rejoice. Mine as well?"

46.

From that time on the obscene drawings copied mechanically from the walls, the odds and ends of all kinds, even the lists of weapons disappear. He goes in search of names only, names that have been erased and made to vanish, including those he'd unthinkingly noted long before, not attaching any particular importance to them, which he now tries to probe, to find out who they may have been, who they might be, those names that have been whitewashed, scraped off and later made to disappear along with the notebooks in which he had transcribed them. Maybe he had hidden them at his home—his, so to speak; his home was the coffin in the warehouse that later went up in flames, but it's possible he left them in the old house where his family lived and where he only kept his papers, because he thought they were safer there. Since he'd been on a hunt, he too felt hounded, like a dog and an animal whose tracks chase and cross each other, so that it's not easy to immediately see who is the pursued and who the pursuer. In his megalomania, he thought that everyone was after him, especially after he had copied those writings, whereas no one was interested in or worried about his family.

The family, in turn, had later been vague and confused about those notebooks. One man had spoken about a police search after his death, but said he didn't know whether or not anything had been seized; later it was said that, by mutual agreement, they had handed over all the notebooks to the agents, or rather to a commissioner—no, they'd corrected, only some of them, since, as the commissioner had said, some might not contain anything serious, of course not, but personal things that it was best to keep private, whereas it was appropriate, even a duty, to make all the rest, everything documenting their relation's tireless efforts, accessible to the public.

At the trial, a lawyer for the plaintiff had asked that the missing papers be produced in court, without however being able to say who should and could produce them, and it was then that their disappearance had appeared, as it were, which earlier had been covered up, skirted, suppressed. Disappearance, that which is not there, must also be noticed, and it's not easy. Indeed, the act of disappearing and especially of causing something to disappear is the number one objective of concealment and oblivion. Of repression, Dr. Wulz said at the trial. Obliterate the absence, expunge who and what no longer exists; eclipse not only the memory of those who are gone, but also the mindfulness that he, she, someone is gone. Those who are no longer with us are troublesome, an unsettled account, a hole in the wall; so you do everything you can not to know that they are gone, that they never were, to obscure and cover up the hole.

It's not easy, because a vacuum is tenacious, it doesn't let you wipe it clean like a stain. But it can be done, yes, absolutely. All of human history is a wiping away of consciousness, above all the consciousness of what disappears, of what has disappeared. If someone or something is missing, it hurts, and so, after getting rid of it—in some cases wasting no time, like at the Risiera—you get rid of the consciousness and the recollection of having done so as well. History, society, societies are masters of neurosurgery and are making rapid progress. Our city as well, which remembers every anecdote about Franz Joseph and every detail of the arrival of the Bersaglieri but little about the Risiera, about those who evaporated in the fetid smoke of its crematorium, about my grandmother, Luisa thought, who vanished in that smoke and about the fact that anyone vanished in that smoke—about five thousand people, it seems, according to less inflated estimates; it's difficult to ascertain how many were gassed and how many were killed beforehand by a firing squad or bludgeoned to death. The latter method—who thinks about it anymore?—was the specialty of a giant, blue-eyed Polizeimeister, a certain Otto Stadie perhaps; it wasn't just his specialty however, let's say he shone among other zealous enforcers. The crematorium offers excellent surgery to produce oblivion.

My mother, Luisa imagined, realized it right away, on the terrace of the Prestons' villa. Smoke that quickly dissolves doesn't exist, you don't see that it doesn't exist. You don't miss the man who became smoke. You can see a chasm on land left by an earthquake, the gouge of a bomb on a wall, they're there; death does not conceal its absent face, it's there, a conspicuous empty frame. But who notices smoke that disperses, invisible, drifting off somewhere, the absent stench of burning flesh? Yes, he had understood. Late, but he'd understood. "The Germans," he writes, "when it all folded, destroyed everything: the chimney, the garage, the crematorium, the documents, ledgers, tons of paper; it was Joseph Gaspar Oberhauser, an SS lieutenant who ended up as a contented brewpub keeper in Monaco—he'd loved the slaughtering as much as he did the women he took to bed before having them slaughtered—who had all that stuff blown up and burned, at two or three o'clock on the morning of April 30, along with the stationary gas chamber and the portable ones constructed by Kriminalkommissar Christian Wirth, a leading expert on euthanasia—the common abbreviation for the Euthanasia Section of the Führer's Chancellery, based in Tiergartenstrasse 4, Berlin, was T4."

On the night between April 29 and 30, a different smoke rose at the Risiera, driving out the earlier one, before it too disappeared and with that smoke, which a little bora sweeps away and makes you forget, the disappearance of many disappeared—prisoners who were tortured, butchered, gassed, deported, burned. "It's that smoke that I'm in search of, those names turned to ashes. I'm not fighting against oblivion, but against oblivion of oblivion, against the culpable unawareness of having forgotten, of having wanted to forget, of not wanting and not being able to know that there is an atrocity that one wanted—had to?—forget. In Trieste, on every street, I see the smoke that no one wanted to see."

He was right. Neurosurgery has made astonishing progress. In Trieste it was on the cutting edge. A huge brain, the city; brilliant, troubled, torpid, resilient. They managed to remove a nice piece of this brain's hippocampus, the part that contained the Risiera. Excellent scalpel job, meticulous work, which did not cause any harm or negative consequences. The seahorse extracted with such skill is sitting in a glass case at the Museum of Natural History. The memory of the atrocities is well-guarded and isolated inside the armor of osseous cutaneous shields, no one dreams of going to see what's behind the integument; if anything it's fun to see that solemn horse head and the long tail that curves impishly like a wave at the base of the cerebral fissure. Now it's all dried up, but in the mating season the seahorse is very lively; like the city, for that matter, a little withered but libertine and somewhat depraved.

The gray cord was cut well. A beautiful city, overlooking the sea, a beautiful house, a couple of cellars and attics emptied, but still airy, open; it's a pleasure to sit on the terrace and breathe the salt sea tang with no memory. In the head—in the heart?—a piece of that seahorse, a chunk of neurons, is missing, but the face is nice and vigorous. At times courteous, as befits those who have been brought up with a good *Kinderstube*; sometimes a bit coarse, in the Longera or Rena Vecia districts, but even the faces of those *negroni*, lowlifes, as they say in dialect—right, it's funny that I say it too—are wholesome and likeable, like those well-cared-for faces at the Nautical Club, for that matter; faces tanned at a solarium or under a quartz sun lamp, depending on the season. The mouths of elegant, athletic ladies a little hard and snobbish, more Diana the Huntress than Madonna Lactans. The piece of hippocampus is something missing, just as love and life's warmth may perhaps be missing to those clamped mouths, those lovely hard lips. The memory of what happened doesn't exist, it never existed, you don't know that it existed and that it was excised, because it took away with it everything that had happened and that therefore never happened. The smoke from the Risiera's chimney drifts out, recycled and blameless, from the lips of beautiful women smoking. I myself was advised to design the Museum as a theater, albeit one of war, that might be a fitting part of the lives of respectable people. A theater pleasant to visit, which helps make us forget the unspeakable reality that lies hidden behind war. A beautiful opera house, where you can listen to good music without thinking about anything else.

That bleak blackish and reddish structure, the Risiera, is the site of the Prima Pilatura Triestina di Riso, the former rice-husking plant, and that's all you need to know. At most the fact that the building was completed in 1913 and that year the company's budget had a deficit of 399,698 crowns. It's good to think about these things, to remember the Great War and the Belle Époque that preceded it, Irredentists against *leccapiattini* or pro-Austrians, but all in all, a civilized world. When, at the outbreak of war, Baron von Fries-Skene, Habsburg governor of the most loyal city, is required to subject Silvio Benco, a great man of letters and Italian patriot, to a daily check by the police, he offers him an apology for the distasteful imposition to which his office obliges him.

There is nothing about that felicitous era to conceal and to forget, not even the dreadful massacre with which it comes to an end in the Karst, as in Galicia and, on the other side, on the western front of the madness, in Verdun. Useless slaughter, Europe's suicide, mass butchery, gray-green or yellow-black companies decimated or wiped out for fifty meters of rocks gained and then lost the following day at the same cost, but few things that must be forgotten to survive; when it was over the survivors at the hecatomb of the Isonza shake hands and respect one another, the memory of Podgora or Leopoli, graveyards of men, is terrible and painful, but it is not fetid, it crushes but does not defile the soul, there is no need to excise the seahorse.

But after the Risiera things are different. Life has been shattered, ripped apart. And most importantly freed from the memory of its wounds, its lacerations. The net has no more holes, the slashes were stitched up, the tears are gone. The absence, the absent never existed.

Just as those pages, those notebooks, did not disappear, they never existed. Or maybe they did, only for him. He would search and note traces of atrocity and infamy; farewells, cries for help, desperate messages of those dying or worse than dying, testimonies about denunciations, about torture and torturers, remnants of bloodstains.

Who knows where that of the dark, curly haired child, a Jew or a Balkan or both, had splattered, the one whose head the SS had kicked open with his boot because the boy had tripped as he was being led to a cell; the heel struck him and the blood spurted out on the floor and on the wall. He wanted to know the exact spot where the little head had been crushed by the SS's boot; it's important, you have to be exact, precise, when gathering evidence for the prosecution for an eternal death penalty. "I want to know where I'm putting my foot. Just as I don't step on a grave at the cemetery, I don't want to step on the sacred, cursed spot where that child died."

He was seen caressing the walls of the cells with his fingers, the seventeen torture cells and the anterooms for the crude gas chamber and crematorium. He stroked the walls with his fingertips, scraped at them, studied the peeling squiggles traced by dampness as if they were messages in an unfamiliar alphabet. Sometimes, after running a finger over the wall, he sniffed it, to see if any vestige of the stench of burned human flesh remained, which the fetid sirocco was said to carry everywhere, the odor of Zyklon B. "It must still be there, somewhere, that smell; it must have crept into some crack like a lizard, to escape the universal disinfestation that makes everything clean again, the deodorizers liberally poured over the miasmas of extermination. I'll find it, that smell. I'll seal it up in a phial. Evidence for Judgment Day."

He must have found some evidence, traces, names, if he had filled so many pages, subsequently torn out and now missing. "I have carefully examined the wall writings (graffiti) made by Jewish and non-Jewish prisoners in the Risiera of San Sabba, where many were killed and from which others were sent to Auschwitz for annihilation. In the absence of a camera and necessary lighting, I made faithful copies of the inscriptions and writings, accurately rendering them with their characteristics in my historical journal no. 65 . . ." Ancona Margherita, Givré Raffaele taken from the asylum in San Servolo, Iesorum Marisa, Levi Grünwald Margherita . . . Those names were not obliterated nor did anyone tear out the pages that recorded them.

In fact they are not dangerous, as they had not been when they were arrested or killed. They are not a concealed secret; the families that lost them know them, as do the judges who demanded an explanation for their fate, though known to all. They are a formidable indictment, but against Nazism, Fascism, racism and abstract entities—though vigorous—around whose neck you cannot put a noose. And everyone, outraged, is ready and willing to speak out against Nazism, Fascism, racism.

There is a page from those notebooks that is not completely torn out, where part of a drawing remains, copied—the note says—from the wall opposite cell no. 8. It's half a face: a plump cheek, a somewhat slack mouth composed in a polite smile, an elegant, aquiline nose, a respectful gaze, good for any situation; neither beard nor mustache, slightly balding. As an Identi-Kit it's not much; leaving aside the tear, the drawing is hesitant; the hand of the artist, the prisoner—convicted? tortured?—is a bit awkward. Who knows, maybe if you could see the part that's been torn away, perhaps . . .

47.

Room no. 31—On the upper part of the large white wall facing those who enter, an enlarged projection of the torn page with the half-face. At the bottom, on the left, a computer screen that attempts to reconstruct the entire face, constantly correcting it.

How many times had he kept on trying to complete that drawing copied from the wall, which had been whitewashed in the meantime. Half a face should look like the other half; if one cheek is plump the other will be too, with that hint of a dimple as well. With the lips it's more certain; it is unlikely that, above and below the molars on the other side, the well-kept slackness will all of a sudden become an assured, decisive half-mouth. There must be a golden mean in a face, a mathematical ratio between nose and cheekbones, and the proportions of the features, including that between an avid, evasive look and the twist of a mouth. And between composure and insinuated cruelty. A grid of boxes, like those in crossword puzzle magazines; the pencil discovers and fills in the right ones and that's it, a profile appears in the blank, white squares.

He must have started hunting for that face, the face of a murderer or, who knows, one of his minions, an accomplice, an informant; maybe just an acquaintance who did not actually do anything but knows everything, and isn't uncomfortable when cordially shaking his hand. Evil is a chain of hands that politely shake one another; all you have to do is clasp the last one, cleansed of all traces of blood, to get back to the first one, which still has blood under its fingernails—just as all it takes is an old sock for a trained dog to pick up the scent.

Certainly it must not have been easy, given that unremarkable face, urbane and generic, the face of a social class rather than an individual. With the real butchers, the hunt was simpler. For Globočnik just a detail would have been enough to reconstruct his face, for example, the flabby little double chin, obscenely infantile. Also the belly, the rear end, those calves in their martial boots. *Come te sta, mona de Marieto?* How are you, you old fool, he had greeted his childhood friend, the attorney Mario Losich, when he returned to Trieste after so many years, to do his butchering not only in Treblinka — it wouldn't have been fair — but in his hometown as well. But for Globus there was no need to reconstruct an Identi-Kit; there were numerous photographs of him in uniform, rigged out in his finery, saluting the troops, or all smiles at the Dreher Brewery with a *Stiefel* in his hand, or the last one, in Paterniano, in the Drava Valley, lying belly-up on the floor beside the courtyard wall of the fortress where he'd been locked up. No Zyklon B for him, a prussic acid capsule instead, his face above the dark jacket covered with a filthy white cloth, a sheet or a raincoat. The face is also grayish-white, spongy, a lump of rancid fat. But who and why had drawn that other unexceptional face on the wall of the Risiera?

He had returned to the Risiera a number of times, but there was nothing more to see beneath the lime with which the wall had been whitewashed. He'd returned to the Risiera with a good magnifying glass, but too late. Still, that face . . . make it known, put up posters everywhere in the streets, *Wanted*, like in the westerns. He couldn't prove anything, but he was convinced: a prisoner, who likely died soon afterward, had tried to draw — probably not his murderer, no, you knew who they were. Maybe a spy, an informer who had denounced him, or one of the distinguished visitors who occasionally came to salute the chief butchers, to schedule an appointment or invite them for dinner. If he was still alive, he would find him.

48.

"This meticulous list, which I keep in the right-hand pocket of my jacket, is a list of guests, a kind of mailing list. Occasionally I finger it, not just because I'm afraid of losing it before it's been copied and filed as it should be. That's the first thing I'll do, you have to have order.

"I didn't hope for as much when I went looking for that Dr. Ruzzier, the secretary or whatever he is, a minion of Zanchi at any rate, the president who however passed on to a better life. The good thing about this hunt for just one man, which at first seemed so daunting and impossible, is that the paths radiate out, like a starburst, every trail you find is a junction that branches out in many directions; it's tiring to follow all of them, many traces are lost in the grass and you have to turn back, but among the many clues that come to nothing, there are quite a few that lead to the lion's den. Too many clues even; they make your head spin and you want to give up or comb the whole city with a butterfly net.

"'That's right,' Ruzzier told me, 'they often came to the villa, the president's villa, for dinner in the evening. The top leaders, of course, all or almost all of them; they arrived by car, always with guards who then ate in the kitchen. Who would have thought that not long afterward I would see some of those faces in the newspapers like that, General Globočnik's, for instance, lying on the ground, that puffy white face . . . They dined together; yes, me too, for years I'd been President Zanchi's secretary, he was very kind and I think he valued me, he even assigned me missions that were highly confidential, delicate . . . A couple of times the high commissioner came as well. The president's father had many acquaintances in Carinthia; during the war—the first one, the Great War—he'd had a contract to furnish rod bearings to the Imperial Navy and so he knew a lot of people, respectable people, in those parts. I think the president and the high commissioner also knew each other before then, they'd met somewhere in Austria. So they saw each other in Trieste as well. Lovely, peaceful evenings; all people who more or less knew one another, through the president.

"'Sometimes they also talked business, at dinner or after dinner, but rarely. Not that I like these kinds of dinners; boring, always the same conversations. But still, to be able to dine well like that, while there's a war . . . Anyway, here's the guest list . . . No, I never went to the Risiera. Sometimes, though seldom, the president would go there, to pick up Rainer or Oberhauser with his adjutant, however they always had a couple of soldiers accompany them in the car. Did I hear anything during those dinners? No, they never spoke about *Fachinteressen*, as they say in German; it's bad manners to talk about business affairs at the dinner table. Only once did General Globočnik ask a guest, Cavalier Tomasi, the one from the transport company, if he could supply him with a couple of trucks to transfer some people to Germany, or rather to Poland, because the army was short of vehicles. I don't know what happened to the request after that.

"'Why didn't I ever tell you these things before? Yes, of course, partly because they seemed trivial, of no importance. But also . . . I mean, it hadn't occurred to me that those lunches, those dinners, those trucks . . . I don't know, there was a war, everyone knows that all kinds of things happen in war and that the worst things don't happen on the battlefields, but you carry on. You hear so many things, who knows if they're true or false, or at any rate exaggerated. One has the good fortune of not having to hold a gun, to have a good job, pleasant occasions, dinners, lunches, boring people but none you need to fear, because they have nothing against you . . . Yes, it had shocked me on the last, the very last days of the war to hear Oberhauser tell the president—I overheard them by accident, I didn't know they were behind the curtain and I withdrew before they could realize that I had heard them—"Agreed, only for a few days, it will be more than enough time, they surely will not come looking for me here, and besides I already have a plan . . . But if something goes wrong, I'll come clean . . ."'

"I wasn't quite sure whether Ruzzier had spoken those exact words, since as I was transcribing his account, the recorder had jammed. Someone says a word, and someone else hears a different one. You talk the way you talk, I write the way I write. But the dinners and Oberhauser's requests for vehicles, all true, corresponding to what Ruzzier had said. And the list, the names—first names, surnames and ranks—I'll try comparing them with those copied from the Risiera's walls, maybe some of them coincide. Let everyone know which sewer rats they were thick as thieves with, in those cesspool villas of theirs, never mind the brothels that every now and then their wives found out about. I'll make a copy of the list. I'll copy it precisely, names on the left, ranks on the right, meeting dates and locations in the center. It will be an elegant thing graphically as well, a kind of musical score. Maybe none of them did anything but for sure one or the other knows something about some atrocity, those vehicles to Poland, that is Auschwitz, for example . . . I'll make them talk, I'll make them dance, I'll snap the whip, make each name jump.

"'Oh!' Ruzzier blurted out at a certain point, 'how come I'm now telling you what I've never told anyone, not even myself? In fact, I knew nothing about it . . . What do they say? That I didn't want to know anything? Maybe, I'm not sure, but . . . Why now though? Well . . . I have a nephew, my sister's son . . . Wait, it's relevant, you'll see . . . One day, not long ago, he brought a girl to my house, his girlfriend. You know, I'm alone, my wife has been dead for several years, we didn't have any children . . . You become attached to the girlfriends of your children and nephews and I felt she was a bit like a daughter . . . They came to see me every now and then; we talked about this and that, nothing in particular, but with that mischievous and imperious air she put on when she dealt with me, well, I felt a little like I was still with my wife, relaxed . . . Until, one day, it came out—thoughtlessly, stupidly, I never thought it could offend anyone, the subject had come up by accident—I simply said that I had met the high commissioner one evening, at dinner, and Lucia—that was the girl's name—got up abruptly from the couch where she'd been sitting, along with him, across from me. There was a fear, a fierce, bewildered stupor on that face which was usually so sweet, so tender, especially with me; icy tears in those blue eyes that were suddenly hard, incredulous, merciless . . . No, what she said isn't important. Or rather, yes, it is important, it's the thing that matters most to me, eternal and irreparable, but it doesn't concern you.

"'She left, my nephew awkwardly behind her, mumbling that he would explain. Lucia's father, vaguely connected with Justice and Freedom, had been rounded up—apparently as a result of a tip-off—and taken to the Risiera, where he had ended up clubbed to death. Maybe on the same evening of one of those dinners in the president's villa, I wondered, with me amiably filling the glass in the hand of the one who raised the club? Yes, it's unlikely, they were tasks for subordinates, but sometimes even high-ranking officials took pleasure in practicing, I later found out . . . '

"Those evenings, those dinners, a nice photograph or two; the guests laugh, smiling faces flushed and perspiring from the wine and flashbulbs, photos taken with a red filter, foolish grinning devils, he, Ruzzier, there among them, smiles, the ruby-colored wine in the glass in front of him reflects on his mouth, open in an idiotic smile, teeth the color of blood, fatuous fires of hell, candle flames flicker and disappear in the guests' mouths, fire eaters at a circus, and meanwhile Lucia's father . . .

"'That's why I now spoke out and wrote that list of dinner guests. Of course, put my name on the guest list as well; I already did so myself, my place is in the dock along with the others. I am, I should be considered one of the accused. One who collaborates, though not to gain a commuted sentence. There can be no commutation, because there is no sentence. This is hell; general amnesty, absolution before trial, the decision not to prosecute. Ignorance is not a mitigating factor, but an aggravating one. He who ignorantly sins, like me, is ignorantly damned. Or rather should be damned, if there was a hell. The Risiera was a dress rehearsal for hell, the cast of executioners got their golden handshake and that's all. I at least have my sentence and I carry it with me, Lucia's indelible face. In any case, here is the list. It might always be useful.'"

49.

"Yes, he'd asked me if I had photographs of the festive gathering on April 20, 1945, at Miramare Castle. Photographs, negatives, anything from that night, he said. I didn't even know what he was talking about, how would I know, I was a child at the time . . . but he kept insisting so, in order to get rid of him, more than anything else, I went to look in the files. I had a hard time making sense of anything; since I'd taken over the shop after the death of Mr. Deveglia who had hired me originally, I had never searched through those boxes. They didn't interest me; I'd left them there out of laziness, I promised myself I'd throw them out one of these days, after checking to see if there was anything interesting, who knows, maybe a photo of some famous person, you never know . . . Rummaging around, I found a folder, April 20, 1945, Hitler's birthday, written in pencil on the cover. But in it, only a single piece of paper: 'material delivered March 28, 1947, to deputy inspector Giuseppe Bartol of the civilian police, and a British officer who was with him, whose name he did not tell me, by order of the AMG.' He copied that note.

"Then he saw another folder, 'Inauguration of the Goethe-Institut, 1958.' He opened it, then immediately closed it again and left in a hurry."—statement of Giordano Mazzi, proprietor of Universo Foto Shop, Via Mazzini 15, Trieste.

50.

Miss Erika Hauser, former secretary of the Goethe-Institut, had been very kind when Luisa, after meeting with the photographer, had asked her if there was any documentation relating to that period or to the years immediately following. "Yes, he asked to see the photos taken during the inauguration of the Goethe-Institut, but they weren't the ones that interested him. He wanted to know if we had the photographic archive, or part of it, of the Italo-Germanic Association. Unfortunately we had nothing; when the Trieste branch of the Goethe-Institut was founded and opened in 1958, we started from scratch. Indeed, by specific direction from Munich headquarters we had been told not to represent ourselves in any way as heirs or successors of prior German cultural institutions. The Goethe-Institut has nothing to do with either Schillerverein or the Italo-Germanic Association; Secretary General Ropp explicitly emphasized that during the inauguration, having come expressly from Munich. You should talk to some of our early members, the older ones who may know something about it. Yes, I vaguely recall that he showed me a page with a sketch, a kind of incomplete portrait, asking me if I knew the man, if he reminded me of anyone. No, I told him, I truly can't think of anyone, I really wouldn't know. Try Dr. Bohrer, I said, he's one of our oldest members, perhaps he'll think of someone. I, honestly . . ."

51

"I'm at peace, mission nearly accomplished. Sixty-eight pages, with names, surnames and dates. Spies, informers—not many, rather a small number in fact. Anyway . . . Occasional visitors, courtesy calls, practically family friends. All written down, copied, recorded. Now you no longer see anything on those walls—correction, you can see and read a lot of things, but only those that can't harm anyone. Sorrow for the victims, outrage at the slaughterer's atrocities. All agreed, there's no risk in saying that Globočnik was a murderer. There's no need, in this case, for a coat of whitewash. You can talk about the dead. But not about the living, not about certain of the living. In those cases it's definitely necessary to cover everything up with lime, as they did. The painter started a trend. But I was faster than the painters.

"Here they are, the names of those who came to visit, maybe some who were spies. Not many, of course. Still, it's fortunate enough that prisoners were able to leave us those graffiti, those sketches, those names. The Book of Judgment was written by them, with their fingernails and their teeth. I am merely the copyist, the registrar of Judgment Day. What's missing as yet are some references relating to seized property; the names of those who took things from the homes they looted or from the fingers and mouths of the corpses, those who delivered them, those who distributed them. I know that Giuseppe Montrone, barber to the German commanders and then to the British and Americans, was in contact with the relatives of those arrested; he brought them requests for money but I don't know if he also collected it to deliver it to those concerned, maybe after deducting a small personal commission.

"I've managed to track him down and I think I'll be able to meet with him, one way or another. I'm especially interested in knowing who the big shot from the police was who protected all those operations, whether he did it on his own initiative or was following instructions from higher up, which officials of the AMG (British? American?) he was in contact with, and above all from whom he received any orders. But I'm even more interested in knowing which law office dealt with the business of property confiscated from the Jews, without leaving any traces. It's not just attorney Schellander, the official, recognized adjuster; the skein is bigger and more tangled. I also tracked down Karpenko, as he's now called, one of the most sadistic torturers. How he managed to get away with it, to settle down in the city and find a job in the porter's lodge on Via Combi, is a mystery. It seems he was one of those Ukrainian SS who managed to flee — some even to America, like that Ivan Demjanjuk, the most vicious of all, who'd gone to the Risiera from the lager in Lublino and then fled to America, complete with a visa obtained without too much difficulty. And that Karpenko — if it's really him — also got away scot-free.

"That's right, by marrying a Triestine porter. Marriages avert so many things. It's no accident that names change, at least — up till now — those of women. Marriage, an institution for changing and falsifying identity. Indeed the bed alone solves many things, forcing you to close your eyes. If it's then legalized with a license, everything is just fine. You don't invite a whore to dinner, but if she's the wife of the managing director it's a different story. It's even the proper thing to do, a first step toward gender equality. A pimp has never had trouble getting invited to dinner. Maybe his spouse, before becoming such, had some trouble, but since she became his wife she no longer has a problem. Just as well. That Karpenko's fate is another example of the emancipation and status of women. It's thanks to her, his porter-consort, that he's been able to become a porter, that is, a respectable man. Maybe he knows something about those dealings between the

Risiera and the police, a widespread enterprise that seems to have recycled valuables and money, and later on maybe someone from the Allied Military Government . . . Well, if I knew those names, that law office . . . they would complete my list creditably and would resolve a lot of other things . . ."

52.

His final note, at least the last available one. "Porter's lodge on Via Combi—broad face, pressed against the booth's peephole. And what if he were one of those who, in the room next to the chimney, had hidden behind the door and when the detainee was shoved inside, bashed his head in with a club and then burned him with a little wood and naphtha? 'The Risiera, what Risiera? The Germans, me with the Germans? But I was their captive, taken prisoner in Russia and then brought to Germany and liberated by the Americans! I arrived in Trieste in '46, I even have a document from the police. I was a laborer on Via Madonnina, then the British even took me into the civilian police force. No, she's the porter, she's my wife, I'm retired. Yes, earlier I was also Commendator Zanchi's driver. A fine gentleman, that man, he paid well and gave me generous tips, besides room and board . . . Did I know him before? When, before, since I came here in '46? A gas smell? No, sir, don't worry, you're not used to the sour smell of borscht, I'm the one who taught my wife to make our Ukrainian borscht, now she can make it quite well, better than your typical *jota* . . .'"

Why did things often seem to prove his phobias right, those which in the end he too seemed somewhat ashamed of, since he hardly ever talked about them anymore . . . Sometimes, thinking about her father and mother—and, with a small pang, about herself—Luisa imagined how Adam and Eve and their descendants must have felt when they were driven out of Eden, setting out painfully to blunder, to desire and shun one another, to love and wound one another. Perhaps that was the original sin—but committed by whom, since the progenitors had loved each other even when they had transgressed together, as the Midrash recounts? Who and what had condemned men and women, nearly all of them, to not experience that Eden of love, that shared existence, to wander alone so often even when they walked together? Lovers, you see—she repeated that fatal verse of Rilke to herself—don't know that a kiss destroys the enchantment, that it's then that deception begins. Yet each time that kiss was also the enchantment—that's how it had been for her a few times, various relationships that eventually faded into one another like summers into years.

The kiss, bodies blissful and for a moment indistinguishable; sometimes falling asleep together while still coupled and filled with one another, it was heavenly to doze off immediately afterward feeling him still inside her quiver and gradually contract though not completely, at least not before they both fell into a short contented sleep where love lingered sweet and tender after the sweet and tender violence, continued almost on its own, with them oblivious in their surrender to sleep. That kiss, that tangled plunge into a dark, fiery sea were, again and again, the end and the beginning of time, a drawn-out summertime when awakening and becoming aware a moment later seemed like being born. No, that kiss in the darkened room or, as at one time, in the shadows of a terrace on a dark night that no eyes could penetrate, was not deception, not the end of enchantment; it was its blossoming, a new creation.

But even the creation, though it seemed good to its creator when it first came from his hand, had soon, very soon, begun to grow wild and wither and, as it was written, to moan and suffer as if the birth had not yet really taken place but were struggling to make its way through the pain, closer to suffocating than to seeing the light. And each time an awkward mix of estrangement and intimacy had soon arisen between her and the other, the others, who practically became one single figure, the tongue-tied discomfiture of those who have so much to say but find it difficult to say and would, should, must hide those difficulties that can nonetheless be read in the face and gestures of the other, in the effort to disguise them that makes him even more of a stranger. Yes, every creation is again the last of the thirty-six imperfect ones, which the Talmud spoke of, and the need to conceal it, first of all to ourselves, was the deception created by that first blissful kiss that so often brought with it defeat, disillusionment and pain.

How much freer and more spontaneous, virgin in its ironic awareness of game over, is the relationship between exes, who still love each other but in a different way, a way that doesn't hurt, because they know they can't really love, that they are two rivers that don't flow into each other, nor into the same sea, but diverge, without pretending to merge their waters and their course, but with a deep, genuine closeness that doesn't need to pretend to be something else. Love that grows apart, that has already grown apart, is real love, because it is limited — and knows it is limited — it cannot cross the line of reciprocal distance and solitude, yet it conserves for all time the memory of that kiss that is no longer possible and that is an indelible part of each of them.

Yes, it's at that moment, with that first kiss that deception begins, or at least it had been that way for her. Not for her father and mother.

She didn't even want to think that there had simply been no time for them to grow apart, that the wind shear on the runway at Aviano had come sooner than estrangement, not just because their love seemed to be constitutionally immune to disaffection, a body that due to some rare chemical combination is impervious to that bacillus and that contagion. She could not imagine her father and mother as exes. The very idea made her laugh; they would have been ridiculous in a role that wasn't meant for them, and she enjoyed picturing them as awkward and out of place in it. For them, shared love — passion, tenderness, complicity — was like an animal's habitat, the only space in which to live. The bird *malfini*, on that island of flowers and light, soars through the air like the note of a song rising from the woods, when he hops on the ground he's an ungainly clown.

I, on the other hand, seem born for the part. Loving and leaving — not necessarily loving each other any less than her parents had loved each other, but loving in a different way. A different arrangement of the great score of love, Mozart played on the concertina or on the drums in a jazz bar, different and the same, a pang that hurts and goes away. But why had it been necessary for her, often enough at least, to leave in order to save love from deception? She was almost home, Carlo was waiting for her — it was the only thing he could still do, wait — in the bed that was his whole world, since multiple sclerosis had broken through his body's trenches. The bed, a large white raft that held him afloat above the muddy flow of time and from which he would never disembark, or only when he would no longer notice that he had reached the shore. Our bed? Soon, Luisa thought as she went up the stairs, she too would climb onto that raft, to sleep beside him, close by yet far away, after helping him eat, wash, change. What was she doing there, what exactly was she lying next to him? No longer his woman, not yet his ex; always and forever his woman but in a different way, and not because soon it would no longer be possible to sleep beside him — nearby, yes, in another bed moved alongside, which was not, however, would not be his raft. The death that was slowly taking possession of him had come too late and too soon — by now Luisa was no longer shocked by this wicked thought. Too late, meaning when it was almost over between them though it wasn't over yet and everything was drifting in illusory uncertainty, because they both knew and didn't yet want to know that the end was quite certain and that only the ending itself was dragging its feet, pausing, starting up again to no avail.

If Carlo had gotten sick before, when they were one flesh, everything would have been different—misery pain fear, true, but they would have been powerless against their bond and she would have lain beside him as always, like a wife, the body that was wasting away beside her would have been like her own, one's own body that is never repulsive. But the blow had come when something had died or at least dimmed—Luisa didn't know why, there is no why in these things and it's senseless to wonder; Carlo's body was still his, but she was breaking away from it even though she still hadn't broken away and didn't want to think about it. The illness had fallen between them when they were no longer one thing but not yet separated, and their living together was a tacit postponement of what would have happened if the illness had not come, because it had never occurred to Luisa to abandon the man beside her whose fibers were giving way, although he wanted her to and insisted forcefully. And so they were together, but only because they hadn't left each other after realizing that they were irrevocably foreordained to leave each other, though the decree was now invalidated by the illness.

But the blow had also come too soon, it had come before they left each other as was inevitable and now no longer possible. If it had come when they were already distant, Luisa would have rushed to support him, to be with him in every way up until the last, with all the love that remains after a true love ends, which is still love, no less intense though different, brief like all things but indestructible until death takes both parties. It would have been different, holding each other without equivocation or wavering; not an embrace in the fullness of love, which is not subject to fading and shifting, nor the uncertain embrace indulged in to put off the end, but the embrace of two people who have loved each other and therefore will always love each other though in a different way, no less genuine where the heart is concerned.

Now however Luisa was sleeping next to a man who was no longer her lover—though certainly not because of the illness that prevented it, that wasn't it—and who was not yet, and now could no longer become, the friend in whom the lover is transformed—at least that had been her experience with the three or four other men in her life. There was something indecent and promiscuous in the physical intimacy with Carlo, which continued because there had not been time to end it, the awkwardness tainting gestures, feelings and thoughts; it wasn't Carlo's illness that came between them, but an uneasiness, unspoken even to themselves though to no avail, a sweat that comes not from fatigue or heat, but from discomfiture.

How is it she had gradually snuffed out that flame, sacred or cursed, within her instead of conveying it like an ancient temple's torch, like the red glow that evening passes on to morning? She had let the years slip by in a kind of suspension, a cloud drifting along, never scattering in sun or rain. She felt doubly unfaithful, to both of her progenitors, who had been promised and enjoined to be as numerous as grains of sand in the sea and stars in the sky, and only by obeying that order had survived the holds of slave ships and the Risiera. Can he be winning his senseless battle, otherwise forever lost, with me, with me alone? Or will everything always begin anew? *Quando noi trascoreremo / cominceremo a far l'amor*, when we pass on / we'll start making love again; funny that old song comes to mind, she thinks as she sinks into sleep, not far from but not close to the body beside her.

53

The end . . . a Museum was a good figurative representation for his inverter. When you come to the last gallery, you turn back to exit, you retrace the route you followed earlier, rediscovering everything you thought you had left behind, and you leave through the same door from which you entered. The final room, at least before going back. The fire. Afterward, except for the journals or the calendar hanging in the kitchen, for him there had been nothing more. Luisa clearly remembered having been among the first to arrive that morning, as soon as she'd heard about the blaze, about as useless as the firefighters who, rather than smothering the remaining embers that had not been extinguished by the night's rain, were rummaging through the smoking ruins.

A person's death, incomprehensible and inexpressible, even more so than his life. His flesh burning in the flames, irreducible to words. But his stage exit had to be a part of his Museum, even though he, the only witness, could not describe it. The final war — lost, like all wars. But who — had it been he who said it over and over — who recounts wars? Master Sun said . . . Sun Tzu, maybe Sun Wu, or someone else, maybe no one or God knows who. Dr. Brooks, when you write about me, please write "I" or "he," it makes no difference, write what you want, however you want, even when copying my words, because the hand that writes is the real author. Master Sun said . . . No one dares ask how he knows what he says.

Describe his end, a word he did not accept? Perhaps only those who die can recount their own death, as Moses does when he writes the Pentateuch, something he never tired of reminding everyone, a true fixation. When you write about me, write what you want, however you want . . . well then, maybe just to keep my word to him . . . The warehouse at 7 A.M.: charred—here and there, where the fire had blazed more intensely—like the flesh that rose from the chimney of the Risiera. A few hours earlier, intact; full of things, of objects, of fire-resistant swords, indestructible like the soul of the man about to doze off in his bizarre bed.

The coffin-bed is at the foot of an armored car, between a dented mortar and a panoply affixed to the wall, from which hangs a Japanese *katana* and a *naginata* from the Kamakura period, with a very curved blade that widens toward the tip. As he does every night before going to sleep, he rubs his thumb lightly over the edge of the blade after removing the wooden sheath of lacquered magnolia and the silk case covering it. He repeats the gesture a few times pressing harder with his thumb, never too hard, he wants to see how far he can go without causing a single drop of blood to appear. Whose blood? Tonight there's no one there. Strange, to move about without casting a shadow, not even passing in front of that pair of lamps. So no one is moving, in fact there's no trace of blood on his hand. However a samurai should also be able to graze an opponent's cheek with a swift, light slash that just for a moment leaves a thin, pale pink streak, like Saladin who with a single stroke slices the odalisque's veil into seven pieces that then drift down through the air, or Zorro who in the old movie severs a lit candle in two with his sword, without toppling it or snuffing out the wick.

He, in truth, is not cut out for capers like that; clumsy and awkward as he is, he can't even hammer in a nail without banging his finger, or have a drink at the table without spilling it on himself. At most he's able to hang that *katana*, certainly not wield it. Even now, bumping the coffin to settle in more comfortably, he unintentionally overturns the small console table where, when he gets up in the morning, he places the Samurai mask—a *hoate* type of mask—that he wears over his face at night. It's part of a *koshozan*, the handwritten tag says—or rather would say, if anyone could decipher his pointy, spastic writing, a real electroencephalogram of Trieste—a bowl-type helmet used in Japan from the sixteenth to the nineteenth century, but he managed to detach the mask from the helmet, because, when he lies down, he prefers to wear a Prussian spiked helmet on his head. He always had a passion for everything German, the Museum is crammed full of German stuff.

He restores the table to an upright position and smothers some papers that the cigarette had set fire to, a feeble spark already extinguished before he stamped it out. He undresses and sits in the coffin, settling back against a concave leather saddle from a regiment of *uhlans*, its hollow quite comfortable on the back; he sets up the small battery-operated projector, illuminating a blank screen stretched between two antiaircraft gun mounts several meters in front of him. He inserts, removes, reinserts photographs, transparencies, slides into the projector. Slowly, then more quickly, faster and faster, he reinserts those he's already seen, removes them, replaces them, a face appears for a moment then disappears, it must have fallen on the floor, he can't find it, that half a face torn from his notebook is now broader, snub-nosed, what was the name of that old movie, oh, right, *The Mask of Fu Manchu*, torturers with vaguely Asiatic faces and somewhat slanted eyes. Slavs too have those broad faces and Mongolian eyes, the Slovenians and Croatians clubbed to death at the Risiera and the Ukrainians whom Globus and Oberhauser brought to Trieste from Lublino in '43 and clubbed to death looked alike, just as German Jews look more German than the Germans. The face of that Karpenko in the porter's booth, that sour smell, of course, borscht . . .

A damp night, an air of misery about him. The small electric heater, plugged into the only outlet in the big room that still works, is on. The smoke of countless cigarettes slowly dissipates, drifts in front of the projector and the screen like a cloud. "Dear professor, in response to your letter, I must inform you that it is impossible to consult those files which you have asked to see, because they are material that at the time was classified by the Allied Military Government and shipped to London in October 1954, along with the entire archive of said AMG, shortly before it handed over the reins to the incoming Italian authorities . . ." All documents, even those of the

Passport Office. Like the one issued for the United States in 1952, complete with a visa from the U.S. consulate, to Ivan Demjanjuk, a murderer in Lublino and at the Risiera, a visa that the U.S. consulate, in Rome, denied however to the originators of neorealist films, suspected of being communists . . .

The droning of the dilapidated projector, the screeching of unseen insects in nocturnal frenzy. Fortunately there is notebook no. 65, the journal in which he copied the wall writings and drawings by the Risiera's inmates, markings that were later whitewashed. "Arrested September 24, 1944 husband Aldo Sereni born Dec. 19, 1896. Left October 12. Jolanda Moriz Abbazia leaves 1/11/45. For?—4/IV 944 Kabiljo Albert Levi Ida Manzato Evarisio arrived here Marcherita Levi Grünwald arrives here 11/30/44, leaves for X 1/11/45." But that's not what matters. The dead, the prisoners, even those tortured, shouldn't be concealed, or whitewashed, everyone quick to deplore, to condemn, contrite; the dead pass on, the living make merry. Speaking of the living . . . "Dr. Zanchi from the Industrial Union came with a German from Adria-Gesellschaft, a certain Beckmann, I think, they spoke to Allers—the one with the scar." In pencil, at the bottom: "*El ghe ga dito se el podeva invitarlo a zena, da l'avocato Tittoni Sluga, che ghe saria stadi anche quei de l'Adria-Gesellschaft e anca de l'Associazione italo-germanica*," "He asked him if he could invite him to dinner, at attorney Tittoni Sluga's home, that those from the Adria-Gesellschaft and the Italo-Germanic Association would also be there . . ."—Ida Levi, Evarisio Manzato, respects to the victims of the war tragedy; Dr. Zanchi, engineer Beckmann, never existed, at least they never passed through those doors. Dinner at the home of attorney Tittoni Sluga, never happened. A coat of whitewash and there you are. The murderers' fingerprints remain on the walls, a bloodstained thumbprint on an ID card.

The prints of those murdered as well, but identifying the thumb is more difficult, because it was smashed to a pulp with a sledgehammer—Otto Stadie loved crushing the prisoners' fingers, it was a habit of his. But never mind, pay respects to the victims, the city wants law and order, *Ordnung und Legalität*, if there's a New Order Party from Berlin, never mind, we'll adapt, the fingers of Giacomo Pertici, formerly Perticich, director of the Industrial Union, will not end up under that hammer; if he wins his freedom all the better, the Fascist mayor is the first to rejoice, after all, some of his Home Guard died on April 30 under German fire, as did others in that of the Yugoslavs. It's no use being pedantic and bringing up the fact that some in the Home Guard helped the Nazis. The Resistance is a complex business and those who resisted multiply all the more as the years go by; even those who died at that time, the dead on all sides, multiply and reproduce. Underground or in the ashes they must fuck like crazy, their number is growing and everyone is pleased about it because they can accuse their enemies of greater butchery than the one they themselves are responsible for. Victims of the world be fruitful and multiply, that way every executioner may denounce one whose work was even more wholesale. Yes, I killed your father, but you, thank God, killed my father and my mother and it's a great satisfaction that the skeletons in your closet are more numerous than those in mine.

In any case, the important thing is order and peace. And freedom, of course, we're all anti-Nazi; at least after '45, even the last Fascist mayor hoped that his status as a Resistance fighter would be recognized. Respects to the victims and disgrace to the murdering hands, but never mind those that only cordially shook them or maybe even drank a toast together at dinner or kept their papers in order. It's one thing to dig around among the bodies and ashes to retrieve a gold filling and . . . Enough cigarettes, for tonight, there's already too much smoke, it's hovering and swirling lazily in front of the mouth of that old cannon. Smoke and darkness; that cuirass on which a large helmet rests is also shrouded in fog, it's strange that all it takes is a few cigarettes, quite a few, all right, to obscure the Museum, the world. Whorls of smoke spread out in the shadows, snakes coil around the cuirass, the warrior remains impassive, under the helmet fiery eyes glint, lit by the lamp's reflective glare. Vacuous, vague shadows, plumes of smoke, a rank smell rising from the butts in the ashtray— true, okay, from the floor, there is no ashtray, I toss the butts on the ground or in the mouth of that howitzer, sometime or other I'll empty it. Now the smoke is more dense, it's enveloping that tank, maybe it's not a tank but a big buffalo in the jungle ready to charge, no one in here is afraid of it, fear doesn't exist in the Museum because death doesn't exist, that hideous masquerade has lost its tricks and before long will no longer scare anyone, because they will finally realize that it's only a broom covered with a black sheet.

Yes, I should open the windows, I'll open them, but I like this increasingly thick cloud. You have to pass through the smoke to come out in the open; burn the theater in which, as a result of playing the role of those imprisoned deported enslaved tortured in the script that you've been handed, you end up really believing it, dealing out real blows on the stage, the actor who plays Hamlet stabs the one playing Polonius in the belly and the latter really feels the pain and sees his own blood spill out. The wall with the collection of hand grenades is no longer visible, and neither is the big antiaircraft gun mount. Everything is so confused, the boxes of war posters glow reddish in the ever-violent light, blowtorches red to bursting, posters calling to the flames, in this smoke they seem to ignite; yes, it's impossible, but faces twist and curl up, it's not fire, it seems like gold, gold immune to the flames, to the ashes . . .

Hands grope among the burned bodies if they haven't first opened those rancid, bloody mouths, still breathing, to snatch a few gold teeth; who cares whether they pull them out of a mouth that's still breathing, or in any case dying, or from a nearly charred skull. Treasures looted and hidden, ships attacked by pirates and shipwrecked, gold, silver, pearls buried in the sand or stashed behind a waterfall, the sun's rays make the cascading water sparkle, fiery rainbows of crystals and gems. The scourge of pirates assails its prey, from mouths split, scorched, pried open by the picklocks of rapacious fingers, gold coins emerge, hidden treasure.

There's no point in leaving it to rot under the bed, if money doesn't yield it does no good to anyone, neither the living nor the dead; the average earnings obtainable from an inmate at the Risiera (dental gold, clothing, currency, daily fee if he's rented out for some project, use of the bones and ashes), I clearly remember, is about

1,400 marks, and it's logical that bankers, lawyers and insurers would be much better at dealing with it—that's why they came to visit at the Risiera and maybe later talked about it further at dinner—than the local Economic and Administrative Office of the SS, what's that guy's name, the director . . . oh, yes, Oswald Pohl—those soldiers and paramilitaries are always fighting with each other, like Pohl and Globočnik, some may even steal, and then the Reichsbank, to which the profits are sent, ends up losing its patience and causing a fuss.

Better to rely on competent professional Triestines. Attorney Erminia Schellander, for example, an adjuster of assets seized from the Jews, earns 5 percent on the first 500,000 liras and sees nothing wrong with it, because she certainly was not the one who went to confiscate the paintings and jewelry in the looted apartments, it's just that, for the sake of good business, good for everyone, it's not enough to break down doors and clean out precious things, you must then know what to do with them, and for this there are any number of skilled professionals.

Why should a company, active in the area of the port and affiliated with a fictitious company in Switzerland, be reproached if it transfers a little of that bounty directly to Switzerland? It's not even German and certainly not Nazi. After all, the money taken from the Millennial Reich can be considered a form of sabotage, an act of meritorious resistance, which, by depriving them of that money, prevents the Nazis from manufacturing a Stuka or a Panzer, more and more of which they need, and it's right to honor the company, all in all it's a little like the Norwegians who blew up the heavy-water plant and prevented the Germans from building the atomic bomb. It would only be right to invite the executives of that company to the April 25 festivities. Those other ones as well, the companies that were commissioned by the Germans to construct bunkers and later, by the AMG, to demolish them. Where there's work, there's hope. *Arbeit macht frei*; with some money in your pocket, earned by the sweat of your brow, you are in fact freer. Sure, everyone is happier to demolish those bunkers than to build them, because it means they're no longer needed and that we'll be at peace. No one likes living in danger of being killed; with peace good manners and correct social dealings are restored.

People shake hands, exchange greetings and, when the calendar calls for it, offer best wishes — Happy New Year, Merry Christmas, maybe Happy Birthday after a while when they know each other better. What's that? Congratulations on the victory? Not on your life! Who thinks about that anymore, water under the bridge, we're all friends now, together again, allies. Not even Colonel Ernst Lerch — the man assigned to send the Risiera's prisoners to the small onsite gas chamber or to Germany, depending on the case and on reports drafted by the Collotti Band at Villa Triste following the torture, or by the various German police, *Sicherheitsdienst, Sonderkommando, Einsatzkommando*—not even the colonel is all that sorry that the Führer lost the war. Nor does he regret his career at the Risiera, because even in his Klagenfurt, where the Café Lerch is booming, he's managed to move up and is president of the city's Tradesmen's Association. Much better to be president of the tradesmen than colonel; a little less excitement, but a lot fewer risks. Count von Czernin, Globočnik's adjutant, isn't too sad about the Reich's defeat either. He too is Austrian, the son of a country that was a victim of Nazism.

Life in Trieste is hard in wartime, for those killed as well as for those who kill, it's not an easy job, but in postwar Trieste life in peacetime, so to speak, is sweet and Lerch gladly returns. Three fine years between 1947 and 1950 in a beautiful villa on the Karst and evenings with Anglo-American officials and bureaucrats, even Colonel Bowman, chief commander of the Allied Military Government in Trieste, a man of the world, seems to have a Slavic mistress and doesn't care too much for the Italians, especially when they demonstrate in the streets and piazzas for Italian Trieste, it's understandable, all Fascists, those Italians, and now they're of little use even against the communists.

Lerch doesn't like the Italians either, neither those who betrayed the Führer nor those who died for the Führer and who in Trieste stirred up a bit of trouble against the Adriatisches Küstenland and claimed they were recruiting soldiers for the Republic of Salò and

Mussolini. Count von Czernin smiles and Baron Wolsegger, with his white hair and his fine goatee—formerly the impartial Regierungspräsident during the period of the Adriatisches Küstenland and particularly skilled in Habsburgian sagacity—also smiles. The men demonstrating in the streets make them laugh, ignorant little hooligans who mistake the most loyal city of the empire for an extremely Italian city invented by some shrewd Jews.

In Lerch's beautiful villa they all meet again; the prefect, the mayor and the two deputy mayors, whom the baron had appointed with Habsburgian administrative acumen, though no longer prefect mayor and deputy mayors are nevertheless director or deputy director of something. Neither Lerch nor Czernin nor Wolsegger nor anyone is scandalized by the fact that a decent man might generously subsidize not only the coffers of the government of the Küstenland but the partisans as well, you never know. But who gives a damn about Trieste and its tribulations. Better to talk about Vienna, that's more agreeable for everyone. Hands shake, the dried blood under the fingernails is long gone; History, though brief, is a good manicure.

Get up, open a window, so thirsty. A beer, cough, gasp; time to move but he's still there, on that coffin-bed, maybe sitting up, or fallen to the floor. A beer, to be able to drink a beer, throat parched and sour, a beer, Herr Oberhauser, please, you've been sentenced to life imprisonment but what do you care about Articles 483, 488 and 489 of the Code of Criminal Procedure, much less Articles 36 and 72 of the Penal Code, after all, you're still chief commander, earlier at the Risiera, now in your brew pub, there you're even more comfortable than in your room at the Risiera, the eiderdown quilts in Munich are better than the woolen mattresses in Trieste, and if that poor Magda isn't in your bed, and the Jewish prisoner isn't either, the Bavarian barmaids are even better and maybe they have a good time, because, unlike Magda and that Jew and all those other women, they know you can't send them to your gas chamber, so they show you a good time too. For a beer you can even turn a blind eye—refreshing cold beer, sliding down your throat, it's like you're swimming in beer, waves of foam undines in the Danube, yellow like the beer, afterward it's so pleasurable to piss, it's the same foamy frothy yellow wave, the river is tinged with yellowish glints and flames—Get up, put out those flames . . . A pitcher, a *Stiefel*, a keg of beer to put out the blaze, pissing won't do it, the flames are too high, the beer burns like gasoline in the sea, when Oberhauser, in the valley of Muggia, where the Patòc ends, burned and threw documents, ledgers, lists, clothing into the water . . .

What time is it? The blood is pounding in his ears, there's a roar of thunder in his head, the chimney explodes, the cabinets with the lists crash to the ground, a beam falls from the ceiling, the warehouse explodes, the crematorium explodes, the Museum explodes, it's the final night, I'll die but tomorrow I'll be alive, I've entered the inverter and tomorrow there will be an insurrection, the Germans will surrender to me, General Linkenbach will hand over his jacket to me, in fact, I'll put it on now, but why is it such an effort to get up, there it is, neatly pressed, draped over the hanger dangling from the row of spears, at least I think so, I can hardly see a thing. How foggy it must be out there if the fog seeped in here, thick, acrid, the jacket sways in a halo of flame, behind him they're still shooting, something is burning in the command office from which the general comes out coughing, I take charge of him, with me he's safe, nothing can happen to him, nothing can happen to anybody.

If only I could get up, open a window; the smoke is clinging to my face, to my beard, slick with sweat, I need a shave—no, not you, what is that barber doing, who let him in, with that razor in his hand—I know you, I already captured you, recorded you in my notebooks, a piece of my Museum—Giuseppe Montrone, the Figaro of Puglia, even if they take me away or burn my notebooks, it doesn't matter, I have it all in my head. The favorite Figaro of the *Einsatzkommando* leaders and later of the Allied Military Government, one hand washes the other and a razor scrapes even cleaner, shaves it all away. Between a quick lathering and a snip of the nose hairs with his scissors, he was good at putting the executioners and the victims' relatives in contact; Maria Del Monte pays Otto Stadie 380,000 liras, roughly the price of a villa outside the city, and it's only fair that the barber, after he removes the towel, gives a final brushstroke and says "there you are," should receive a tip. The razor passes over my cheek, he must have lost his touch, it hurts, just look at the scar—it's horrible, no, the mirror is lying, actually it's a shield that I propped against that torpedo, usually it reflects better than glass but now it's clouded, a mirror of soot, that can't be my face. It must be Allers, attorney Ernst Dietrich August Allers, inspector and supervisor at the San Sabba camp—it's his famous scar, who put it on my face; it's not me—I'm not a criminal—yes, I know that evil, criminality is a virus that infects everyone, no one is innocent. At San Pietro del Carso in Kočevje I did not denounce anyone, on the contrary—such coughing, so nauseous—but that's not enough, no, not enough. Those who are not innocent are guilty, the gray area is a convenient invention—all gray and impervious, raincoats swinging from hangers in the antechamber, while inside, in the room, someone with that scar on his face sends the postulant to get a lungful of gas or have his head crushed by the blue-eyed Polizeimeister's club . . . *Im Sinne der Anklage, unschuldig*, innocent for the purposes of the prosecution.

The raincoat flutters and sways against the wall every time the door opens and a draft enters, where's the harm? Even though I introduced Professor Wagenmann to the Italo-Germanic Association, when he gave his lecture on "Issues Concerning the Great European Economic Scope," I didn't harm anyone, and the numbers that Professor Wagenmann brought out didn't harm anyone either. Besides, there were some genuinely honorable men among the association's German teachers, all they did was give German lessons.

There are those who speak and those who listen . . . Is listening innocent? "Trieste must and will be up to the tasks that victory brings to it," inaugural speech given in Sala Littorio on January 19, 1942-XX, the twentieth year of the Fascist era, by esteemed counselor attorney Cesare Pagnini, illustrious Winckelmann scholar and Fascist mayor who in the days of the final battle would lend a hand to the Resistance. "From this war, oh comrades, the war of blood versus gold, the new Europe will rise . . ." Is it wrong to speak, wrong to listen, applaud at the end of a dinner if only out of courtesy, good manners? How had

Rainer put it at Miramare? ". . . The rise of a new European idea that will assure its young people, in complete unrestricted collaboration, of their national existence and their cultural freedom. We therefore proclaim our confidence in the Führer who at a time of maximum danger has remained loyal to the destinies of Europe, its freedom, its unity in which all peoples are assured of a place." Triple salute to the Führer.

Fine words, which those present may even listen to without being ashamed. April 20, 1945, the Führer's birthday, Miramare Castle. But where is that notebook with half the pages ripped out, what happened to it, don't tell me it burned, after all my efforts . . . There, that's the last photo of High Commissioner Rainer in uniform, a few days later he cleared out, and fled to meet his death, for the moment only deferred. Put off till later, a year later, still, better than nothing. But the photo, that other photo, with all of them together, where did it . . . you have to see them, recognize those faces, the ones who were there, who drank toasts, freedom to the people, triple salute to the Führer, the smell of sulfur, unveil yourself, *schreckliches Gesicht*, this infernal smoke suits you, two-bit theater of evil, show yourself, show yourselves, your faces, the faces at that birthday celebration, at those dinners, those visits, the photos, someone stole them, they're gone. I'll get up, I must get up, all these papers, these cigarette butts . . .

An elegant but abstemious seafood buffet, as the menu saved in the archive of Miramare Castle reads. The Führer is abstemious, strange that he isn't vegetarian; he doesn't like them to butcher animals for his gullet. He strokes his wolfhound, he's appalled that in China they eat dogs. Fish is permissible. Perhaps they don't even suffer, stupid and cold as they are. Not everyone suffers equally, not everyone has the same sensibility. The Aktion T4 program for euthanasia is very humane; it eliminates the disabled, the handicapped, people who don't have the proper credentials to suffer like others. It's the superior races that know pain, the pain of creating and destroying, of destroying to create. Blacks, for instance, suffer less than whites. Jews, less than the Germans. That's why they often seem so brave, when they enter the gas chamber. Sensitive people would suffer more. It's not about fear, we have more courage than anyone, but sensitivity. Even to dirt, for example. The Germans are clean, they would not be able to stand the stench and filth of the camps like the Jews. Even in here there's a rank odor . . .

So then, fish is okay; General Esposito, after praising the bonds of comradeship between the armed forces of the Social Republic and those of the Reich, eats one sardine canapé after another, as does the party secretary, Sambo, for that matter, who deserves them after his speech in German in which he fervently saluted the Blackshirts. Not only sardines and mackerel, but also fillets of giltheads and croaker. Caught in Muggia Gorge, where the Patòc flows out, the Rio Primario that runs down from Valmaura and the Risiera. But everything done as it should be, properly checked; with so many disguised enemies around you never know, somebody might toss in some poison. No danger of finding a human tibia or patella in the fish, as happened a couple of times after the SS had dumped waste into the sea, waste from the Risiera. Filthy remains of Jews, maybe even Slavs. The prefect extends our province's best wishes and greetings to the high commissioner.

The prefect, the general, the party secretary? The photo fades, crumples up in the fire, smoke and dankness erase the faces; nothing but blank spaces, holes. No one, no birthday party, no trace. General Esposito sentenced to thirty years is released from prison after serving two, and after eight more years is reinstated to his rank; Deputy Commissioner Gaetano Collotti, a torturer at Villa Triste, doesn't save his skin but later receives a bronze medal in memoriam. But this time those pages will finally show everyone that—damn, where the hell did they . . .

Oh, there they are, they fell off the shelf. The blaze reaches them, the pages scatter ignite unfold, the names are magnified—the names that no one wants to know about, huge, written in fiery letters on the walls, they quiver in the flickering flames. A great hand of fire inscribes them forever on the walls but the walls crackle, some of the names begin to curl up, one letter after another, dissolve into ash.

Open a window, I can't. Someone or something must have

blocked the casings. These hot embers, how did they get all over me
. . . The door won't open either, where did the key go, who is it who . . .
A set of shelves collapses, the papers are already a fierce blaze. In the
Risiera's crematorium tons of documents and ledgers burn, but in a
more orderly way. Oberhauser calmly directs the destruction, everything burns, everything explodes, chimney garage crematorium, but
it doesn't matter if the traces disappear, the names of the victims and
the executioners don't interest me, I know who they are, we already
know who they are. It's those other names I want; not the hands with
blood on them, but the ones that shook them, the clean hands of
the true masters of the world—never mind if Oberhauser continues
to thrive in his brew pub, he's not the one I want, but the one who
placidly drinks his beer paying no attention to the bloody cardboard
coaster on which the tankard rests.

My head is spinning, can't breathe, shelves collapsing, reduced
to ashes. I hurled a helmet against the window and managed to break
the glass, air is coming in but too late too little—gusts scatter the
ashes, the air is a dark blizzard, *lapilli*, lava, tongues of flame. The
Risiera's chimney explodes, its red and black bricks flung in all directions. The garage blows up the gas pipe bursts a thud a huge belch a
wind flatus from Hades. How many people died with that tube shov-
ing the stench of the world into their mouths, their hearts? The world
is nothing but a foul stink, a fart Hitler expelled. The crematorium
explodes as well, fire destroys fire, destruction destroys the traces of
the destruction and the destroyers.

Pages flutter to the ground, covered in soot, what's that big calendar—fiery letters on the wall—a date, it can't be, it's a mistake, but
what does it mean, only blank numbers of days and years, everything
courses by and returns. Well, maybe the fire is dying out, my temples
aren't pounding as hard, it must be 10:30, maybe 11, the hour when
the executions take place, but Oberhauser opens the door, now he'll
open mine too, he lets us out—free, in the night, where we move
along, I too skirting the stadium, everything is dark, what's that noise,
gunfire in the distance, the night is cool a gust lifts some pages from
the flames and sends them flying toward the sea, I chase them, they're

mine, they circle high above a German truck plunge into darkness over a lorry with a big red star.

I set out toward the sea, like the others. The night is clear. No one speaks. No one seems to cast a shadow, but it can't be, it's just that I'm so tired . . . Maybe we're already at sea, there must be a full moon tonight, festive, fireworks ignite in the water I can't tell if it's cold or warm—before it was fiery, burning, now it's the color of fire but that too dies out, it isn't burning, I must have entered the submarine that I had the Navy give me. Yes, I'm going under; through the porthole I can see the white pages with those numbers and names sinking to the bottom. They dumped the waste into the sea, into the gorge, they dumped us here, between the Patòc and the sea, the water can't be very deep, but we're going down, down, throwing garbage into the sea is a crime and so is throwing men in, but the judge declares there is no cause to indict.

Writers, the Greeks had proclaimed early on, tell many lies, which is to say they invent. But the etymology suggests that invention, *inventio, invenire,* to come upon, is closely related to finding something real—a story, a character, a detail—something factual. Every invention, substantial or modest, is inspired by things that really happened and people who really existed, which life—always terribly original, Svevo wrote—unexpectedly comes up with. Invention, fiction, is inevitably inspired, to a greater or lesser degree, by truth, which Mark Twain described as more bizarre, more fanciful than any fiction. Moreover invention, the "lie," is perhaps one of the things that is most ours, ours alone, for better or more often for worse; the truth is out there, objective, though almost never fully accessible. It stands on its own, regardless of our thoughts and feelings.

Invention nurtured by reality characterizes many great writers— Turgenev declared that he owes Bazarov's essential traits to a young physician he met in the provinces; Thomas Mann claimed the right to borrow required elements from wherever and whomever he wanted for his invention, wherein those elements may no longer have anything to do with the situation or individuals from which they were taken—even though, as Mann was well aware, it might sometimes, in spite of everything, turn out to be problematic or troublesome.

As with any right—for example, the right to vote—this one similarly applies both to gifted writers and to anyone who takes pen in hand to tell a story. For the unnamed protagonist of this book I too was liberally inspired by an individual of considerable prominence who actually existed, Professor Diego de Henriquez, a brilliant, uncompromising Triestine of vast culture and fierce passion, who dedicated his entire life (1909–1974) to collecting weapons and military materiel of all types to build an original, overflowing War Museum that might, by displaying those instruments of death, lead to peace. He devoted his life to this obsessive dream and to this project—which has now been realized in Trieste—facing difficulties and sacrifices of all kinds in an era particularly ravaged by conflicts and carnage, even meeting his death in a fire at the warehouse where he slept among the objects of his Museum, a mysterious blaze that initiated an investigation and proceedings that did not result in any action.

Without this man and his all-consuming passion this book would not have been written. But, as with every literary invention that elaborates on what reality has found and put in front of it, the story and portrayal of the protagonist of this book are complete fiction; no incident or detail has anything to do with the actual experiences or the real persona of the tragic collector from Trieste, who is not in any way portrayed in the book but is invented, as is the character of the woman who, in the novel, is assigned to plan the Museum. Any resemblance, as the ritual disclaimer says, is therefore purely coincidental. I would like to recall instead, in memory of Diego de Henriquez, something he actually did say, inviting the unknown person passing by his grave to hand over his sword to him, so that the sword might never strike again.

C.M.

TRANSLATOR'S GLOSSARY

Adriatisches Küstenland A Nazi German district on the northern Adriatic Coast created during World War II, the Adriatisches Küstenland, also known as the Adriatic Littoral, was created from territories that were under Fascist Italy control prior to the German invasion. It included parts of present-day Italy, Slovenia and Croatia, and its capital was Trieste.

AMG Allied Military Government.

anathema sit A formal ecclesiastical curse involving excommunication for those holding heretical or blasphemous views.

Anschluss Meaning annexation, it was the Nazi propaganda term for the invasion and forced incorporation of Austria by Nazi Germany in March 1938.

augellin belverde *L'augellin belverde* ("The Pretty Little Green Bird") is a play by Venetian dramatist Carlo Gozzi.

balilla A male member (aged 8 to 14) of the Fascist Youth Movement.

béké A Creole term to describe slave masters on plantations in the French Antilles, usually of French origin.

bonze A Buddhist monk.

burčák A fermented Moravian wine.

cacique A chieftain or tribal leader.

Cactus marcescens Hitler *Serratia marcescens* is a species of bacteria; German agents had allegedly tested dispersion of it.

Casa del Popolo A meeting place for Communist Party members.

Caudine Forks A figurative expression to denote bitter humiliation. Its origin lies in the defeat of the Roman military in 321 BC, when the army found itself trapped between two mountain passes at a place known as the Caudine Forks, between Capua and Beneventum.

chabin Blond, in Creole.

cheder A traditional Jewish elementary school for teaching the fundamentals of Judaism and the Hebrew language.

chifeleti Fried potatoes.

Cïfï The name of the mythical progenitor of the Chamacoco tribe.

CLN The National Liberation Committee (Comitato di Liberazione Nazionale), the democratic organization of the Resistance.

CMT-KMT *See* KMT.

cornac A person who rides an elephant; also called a *mahout*.

Créolité A late-twentieth-century literary movement developed by Martinican writers Patrick Chamoiseau, Jean Bernabé and Raphaël Confiant, whose *Eloge de la créolité* (In Praise of Creoleness) focused on the linguistic and cultural heterogeneity of the peoples of the Antilles, specifically of the French Caribbean.

CVL Volunteer Freedom Corps (Corpo Volontari della Libertà).

Deí-ć The Chamacoco god signifying the Sun.

di'oŕa The twisted, crooked ankles of the Chamacoco and other tribes, caused by walking through the forest with feet pointed inward to avoid thorns and poisonous insects.

diamond of the sea An allusion to Diamond Rock, a large rock island, as bright as a diamond, off the coast of Martinique, opposite the town of Diamant.

doline A shallow depression in the ground formed in limestone regions; also known as a karst pit or sinkhole. Anti-Fascists and civilians executed by the Nazi Collotti Band in Trieste were thrown into such pits (*foibe*).

Domobranci Members of the anticommunist Slovene Home Guard, which collaborated with the Nazis.

druže A Slavic Partisan in Tito's communist units.

Dudel-Dudel A German expression indicating a sentimental, catchy tune, such as a waltz, mazurka or polka.

El Coroneo The Coroneo is the name of a prison still in existence today; formerly a Jesuit college. In Trieste, the Germans at first concentrated Jews of the Adriatic Littoral in the Coroneo Prison, subsequently in the Risiera of San Sabba.

el fazeva maravèe An expression in Triestine dialect that literally means "he worked wonders"; by extension it applies to someone who inflates things, pompously putting on airs.

Feldataman The highest rank in the Cossack hierarchy, traditionally re-
    served for the tsar.

Feldgendarmerie Uniformed military police units.

fou-fou An Antillean-crested hummingbird.

fury of disappearance A Hegelian concept (in German, *Furie des versch-
    windens*) taken from a collection of poems by Hans Magnus Enzens-
    berger.

Galuth The Hebrew term for the forced exile of Jews to escape persecution
    in countries where they were oppressed.

Gauleiter The party leader of a regional branch of the Nazi Party.

golem In Jewish folklore, a golem is a figure made in the form of a human
    being, created from amorphous, inanimate matter, usually stone and
    clay, and endowed with life. The word "golem" occurs once in the
    Bible (in Psalm 139:16) to connote the unfinished human being be-
    fore God's eyes. In some tales, a golem was inscribed with the Hebrew
    word *emet* ("truth") written on its forehead to make it come alive. The
    golem could be killed by removing the aleph in *emet*, leaving mem
    and tav, which is *met* (meaning "dead"), thus changing the inscription
    from "truth" to "death."

Gothic Line The last major line of defense as German forces in Italy re-
    treated during the final stages of World War II, continuing to fight
    against Allied troops as they did so.

guaimipirés A thorny shrub in the semi-arid Paraguayan Chaco region.

guayacán A tree, guaiacum, or the resin obtained from it.

Gulaschkanone A mobile field kitchen; literally Goulash Cannon, called
    that because when disassembled for towing, the stove's chimney re-
    sembled a weapon.

Hitlerjugend Hitler Youth, the youth organization of the Nazi Party in
    Germany.

hoate A *hoate* ("cheek protector") mask covers the cheeks and chin, unlike
    the *mempo* ("face cheek") mask, which covers the whole face.

Höherer SS und Polizeiführer A senior Nazi official who commanded
    large units of the SS, the Gestapo and the regular German police.

hoplite A heavily armed foot-soldier of ancient Greece.

Hupp Cossack! A phrase typically found in Yiddish improvisational the-
    ater, from a triumphant tune associated with a Chassidic Rebbe's self-
    sacrifice in saving the life of a fellow Jew.

Irredentist An advocate promoting the restoration to Italy of any territory
formerly belonging to it and having a primarily Italian population
(*Italia irredenta*).

Italietta A term denoting a weak, ineffectual, frivolous, shallow Italy, in
contrast to *Italiona*, the big muscular Italy associated with Fascism.
Italietta suggested a comfortable, bourgeois life, whose leading critics
were Benito Mussolini and Gabriele D'Annunzio.

Jadransko More Like *Mare Nostrum*, a nationalistic cry to call attention to
the Italian or Slavic character of the Adriatic.

jota A Triestine soup, typical of the Karst, made with cabbage.

Kaddish The Jewish prayer of mourning for the deceased.

Karst A limestone plateau north of Trieste, its terrain characterized by
sinkholes, dolines and underground streams.

katana A long, single-edged sword used by Japanese samurai.

kepi A military cap.

Kinderstube Upbringing, breeding; childhood; the past.

Klipo Kripo and Krupo Anagrams indicating various special units of the
German Army and police, for example, Kriminalpolizei.

KMT The Kommando Mesta Trst, the Command of the City of Trieste
instituted by Yugoslavia.

knout A whip of raw leather, used to flog criminals.

kolo A Slavic dance performed in a circle.

koshozan A bowl-type helmet used in Japan from the sixteenth to the
nineteenth century.

Kronländer Crown Lands; the hereditary countries of the House of Habsburg and, after 1867, of all kingdoms and countries represented in the
Reichsrat.

kuguluf Bundt cake.

Laline In the mythology of the Antilles, Laline is the mother of the god
Yali, who lay with her brother. Laline is also the name for the moon.

lapilli Small stony particles ejected from a volcano.

leccapiattini Supporters of the Austrian monarchy earned the epithet
leccapiattini, or plate lickers, based on a pro-Austrian demonstration
in the Cologna district of Trieste, where demonstrators drove patrons
out of a café and ate the leftover ice cream without spoons, straight
from the dishes.

libro tavolare An official land register, or *cadastre*, used as a basis of property taxation. The cadastral system (in German, *Grundbuch*) was used in Habsburgian Austria.

Libussa The mythical founder of Prague and the Czech people as a whole. According to legend, she married a plowman, Přemysl, with whom she founded the Přemyslid dynasty and the city of Prague in the eighth century.

Lidice A village northwest of Prague that was part of the Nazi Protectorate of Bohemia and Moravia. In 1942, in reprisal for the assassination of Reich Protector Reinhard Heydrich, it was destroyed by the Germans on orders from Adolf Hitler and Reichsführer-SS Heinrich Himmler.

Liston The main avenue, boulevard or *corso* of a city.

Luisa de Navarrete Called the Black Pearl of the Caribbean, she is considered a representative of three cultures — African, European and indigenous — and a symbol of emancipation.

macuahuitl A Nahuatlis word for a sword made of wood, having obsidian blades.

Malá Strana A historic district of Prague.

malfini A broad-winged hawk, featured in *The Neuf consciences du malfini* by Martinican writer Patrick Chamoiseau. In the book, which takes the form of a fable in which birds are used as metaphors, the *malfini*, a bird of prey, learns a lesson or two when he comes to know two small, vulnerable birds, the *coulibri* (the blue-crested hummingbird) and the *fou-fou* (the Antillean-crested hummingbird).

Malleus Maleficarum A treatise on the prosecution of witches, written by Heinrich Kramer, a German Catholic clergyman, and first published in Germany in 1487 (English title: *Hammer of Witches*).

Mare Nostrum Like *Jadransko More*, a nationalistic cry to call attention to the Italian or Slavic character of the Adriatic.

maroon/marron A term used in reference to fugitive slaves or those born from runaway stock. Le Morne Brabant Peninsula was notorious in the early nineteenth century as a refuge for runaway slaves.

melius abundare quam deficere Better too many than too few; better too much than not enough.

metanoia A profound, usually spiritual, transformation; a conversion.

Millennial Reich In Hitler's vision, the Third Reich would last for a thousand years; ultimately the Tausendjähriges Reich lasted only twelve years, from 1933 to 1945.

moles, not eagles A reference to Karl Marx, who said that revolution was not an eagle but a mole that gnaws at power from below until it causes the state to collapse.

most loyal city The title "most loyal city" (*la fedlissima città*) was attributed to Trieste because during the course of Italian reunification the city remained faithful to Austria.

naginata A type of traditional Japanese blade in the form of a pole weapon, originally used by the samurai in feudal Japan, as well as by warrior monks.

National Socialist A member of the National Socialist German Workers' Party, namely, the Nazi Party; its predecessor was the German Workers' Party (DAP).

nematode A parasitic intestinal worm commonly known as the Old World hookworm.

Nemur The most powerful of the demon-gods, he is said to have called upon the help of the North Wind to escape from the human Syr. He then caused a river to spring forth to separate him from the man; the river is today known as the Paraguay River (*The Curse of Nemur: In Search of the Art, Myth, and Ritual of the Ishir,* by Ticio Escobar).

nopal nocheztil The Aztecs referred to the nopal plant as *nopal nocheztil,* "the cactus that produces the blood fruit." The Indian fig (*Opuntia ficus-indica*) is known as the "prickly pear"; the fruit is called *tuna,* the paddle *nopal.*

Nor Yo Rī A monster said to paralyze solely with its gaze; the Chamacoco say it looks like a caiman and lives in the swamp of death and the unknown.

Osvobodilna Fronta The Slovene Liberation Front, active during World War II, was the chief resistance organization in the Slovene Nation's anti-Fascist and anti-Nazi struggle.

patoco The so-called true Triestine dialect.

Pelinkovec A wormwood-based bitter liqueur referred to as "Croatian Absinthe"; the name of the herbal brew comes from the Serbo-Croatian word *pelin,* meaning wormwood.

pengö An old Hungarian currency.

phacoemulsifier An instrument that breaks a cataract into tiny pieces so that it can be aspirated from the eye.

piccola italiana A female member (aged 8 to 14) of the Fascist Youth Movement.

Pitínno The anteater bear.

Polacken A term applied to Jewish Poles.

porzina Dialect for *porcina*, pork; boiled and served with mustard.

pre-March Fascist Someone who joined the Italian Fascist Party prior to the March on Rome, which occurred on October 28, 1922.

Protocols of the Elders of Zion An anti-Semitic text purporting to be a plan for Jewish domination of the world; a hoax, it was first published in Russia in 1903.

Purge Commission The commission that, after the war and the fall of Fascism, examined the accountability of those holding important posts, to determine whether or not to purge them, i.e., drive them out of those positions, as supporters of Fascism.

Red Vienna The capital of Austria was referred to as *Rotes Wien* during the period (1918–1934) when the Social Democrats were in power.

Refosco The name of the grape from which the wine Terrano or Teran is made; it is typically served with *porcina* and sauerkraut in Trieste.

Regierungspräsident Chief administrative officer; chief executive of an administrative district.

repubblichini Supporters of the RSI, the Italian Social Republic (also known as the Republic of Salò).

Rive, Le Waterfront promenades in Trieste; literally banks or seashores.

Roaring Forties High winds and rough seas.

RSI The Fascist Italian Social Republic (Repubblica Sociale Italiana), formed as a puppet state in northern Italy with Mussolini as its leader.

s'ciaveto An ancient rite of the Mass, later banned by the church, in the Glagolitic liturgy, which existed only in Croatia and Dalmatia. There is also a local wine, *vin s'ciaveto*.

Śakuruku The Chamacoco name for the moon goddess.

salmiak Salty licorice, also known as *salmiakki*.

Saujude A *Saujude*, or *Judensau*, literally "Jewish sow," refers to an obscene image, popular for centuries, of Jews copulating with a large sow, considered an unclean animal in Judaism. In Nazi Germany, the *Judensau* could be seen in German churches. The term exists as a neo-Nazi slur.

Schlimazel Someone prone to having extremely bad luck. From the Yiddish, *shlim* (bad, wrong) and *mazl* (luck).

Servant of God The first of four stages of canonization in the Catholic Church, followed by Venerable, Blessed and Saint.

sgnanfo Someone who speaks with a nasal twang (in the book it's the name of a tavern).

Shir Hashirim The Hebrew name for the Song of Songs.

Służba Bezpieczeństwa Security and Information Service; Polish secret police.

smafari Good-for-nothings, con men, crooks, swindlers, cheats, frauds, rascals, scoundrels, villains, rogues.

Stiefel A beer glass in the shape of a boot, which traditionally held two liters of beer.

strucolo Strudel.

stur Stolid, impassive.

T4 The Nazi euthanasia program to eliminate "life unworthy of life," code named "Aktion T4," was begun by Hitler in October 1939. Ostensibly billed as "mercy killing" of the sick and disabled, "euthanasia" was actually a euphemism for a clandestine program of systematic elimination. The code name of the secret enterprise came from the street address of the office in Berlin: Tiergartenstrasse 4.

tapetum lucidum A layer of tissue in the eye of many vertebrates (Latin: "bright tapestry").

"Tapim tapim tapum" One of the best known songs sung in the trenches during the First World War; the refrain is inspired by the sound of Austro-Hungarian gunfire.

tepoztopilli A wooden weapon, like the *macuahuitl*, traditionally made from two pieces, the shaft and the head; the *tepoztopilli* head was similar to the *macuahuitl's*, with obsidian blades inserted.

Ti-Jean A figure in French Antillean legends; the beast with the seven heads represents oppression and tyranny.

TLT Territorio Libero di Trieste (Free Territory of Trieste), formed at the end of World War II, when Trieste was contested between Italy and Yugoslavia. The provisional division established two districts: zone A, which included the city and surrounding region, administered by the Anglo-American Allied Military Government, and zone B, governed by the Yugoslavs.

trapolèr A Venetian word meaning a schemer, a finagler, a shady dealer, a wheeler and dealer, a swindler, a cheater.

tre tre fala denari A term used in card games, having to do with discarding useless cards during one's turn at play (in the book it's the name of a tavern).

Trst je naš Trieste is ours.

uérzis disfritis Savoy cabbage.

uhlan A member of a group of lancers in a light-cavalry unit.

Uo-De A Slovenian-Italian partisan formation, in April and May 1945, controlled by Tito's communists. Literally the Unione Operaia-Delavska Enotnost, which means Workers Union in each language.

Uskoks The Uskoks (in Croatian, Uskoci) were pirates who plundered and looted along the eastern Adriatic coast in Habsburg Croatia.

V2 The Vergeltungswaffe 2, a German flying bomb used during World War II.

Velebit A mountain chain on the Croatian Coast of the Adriatic Sea. The Velebit is also a national park in Croatia.

Villa Triste Meaning "Sad Villa," the name refers to the headquarters of a Special Inspectorate whose task was to repress partisan operations and control workers in large factories. The inspectorate collaborated with the Germans in operations against anti-Fascists and in rounding up Jews; its operational arm, which engaged in torture, was notoriously known as the "Collotti Band" (after its head, Commissioner Gaetano Collotti).

Waffen-SS A paramilitary organization within the SS.

Well of Souls A chamber or cave found in the tunnels of underground Trieste, beneath the Old Town. There is also a Well of Souls, partially natural, partially manmade, located under the Dome of the Rock in Jerusalem; medieval Islamic legend has it that the spirits of the dead can be heard awaiting Judgment Day there.

yakaveré A type of bird.

yataghans Turkish sabers.

yetit carhï The sky before the stars and other things emerged from the good darkness and nothingness.

Yoruba The African tribe from which it is thought that Luisa de Navarrete or her ancestors may have descended.

Zeitrafferphenomen The Zeitraffer phenomenon is the altered perception of the speed of moving objects, *Zeitraffer* meaning time accelerator.

Zyklon B A cyanide-based pesticide employed by the Nazis during the Holocaust; also known as prussic acid, it was used in gas chambers in Auschwitz and other extermination camps.

CLAUDIO MAGRIS is the author of the best-selling novels *Danube* and *Microcosms*, which have been translated into over twenty languages. He was awarded the Erasmus Prize in 2001, the Prince of Asturias Prize in 2004, the Premio Viareggio Tobino (writer of the year) in 2007, the 2009 Friedenspreis, the FIL Prize in Hispanic Literature in 2014 and is a perennial contender for the Nobel Prize in Literature. Magris is also professor emeritus of Germanic studies at the University of Trieste and currently writer in residence at the University of Utrecht. In addition to being an author and a scholar, he has translated into Italian authors such as Henrik Ibsen, Heinrich von Kleist, Arthur Schnitzler, Georg Büchner and Franz Grillparzer.

ANNE MILANO APPEL was awarded the Italian Prose in Translation Award (2015), the John Florio Prize for Italian Translation (2013) and the Northern California Book Awards for Translation-Fiction (2014, 2013). She has translated works by Claudio Magris, Primo Levi, Giovanni Arpino, Paolo Giordano, Roberto Saviano, Giuseppe Catozzella and numerous others. Translating professionally since 1996, she is a former library director and language teacher, with a B.A. in art and English literature (UCLA), an MLS in library services (Rutgers), and an M.A. and Ph.D. in Romance languages (Rutgers). Her website is www.annemilanoappel.com.